LILITH LIVES

in Elise, the loving wife who tries to escape her horrifying heritage

LILITH LIVES

in Talia, the ravenous career woman who uses her satanic sensuality to make men of power her slaves

LILITH LIVES

in Bree, the dedicated physician who hopes to use the fearful force within her for modern good instead of ancient evil

LILITH LIVES

in Michael, determined to prove that he as a man is more worthy than any woman to mount the throne of darkness

LILITH LIVES

and so many are fated to die. . . .

THE LILITH FACTOR

Jean Paiva

THE LILITH FACTOR

We are not all children

of Eve . . .

AN ONYX BOOK

NEW AMERICAN LIBRARY

PUBLISHER'S NOTE

This book is a work of fiction. Names, characters, places, and incidents either are the product of the author's imagination or are used fictitiously, and any resemblance to actual persons, living or dead, events, or locales is entirely coincidental.

Ⓑ Onyx is a trademark of New American Library

SIGNET, SIGNET CLASSIC, MENTOR, ONYX, PLUME, MERIDIAN and NAL BOOKS are published by NAL PENGUIN INC., 1633 Broadway, New York, New York 10019

First Printing, February, 1989

1 2 3 4 5 6 7 8 9

PRINTED IN THE UNITED STATES OF AMERICA

to
SMB,
with love

I would like to thank and acknowledge the following people for their help, technical or supportive, direct or indirect.

To Warren Murphy for planting the seed and to Marvin Kaye for nurturing the growth.

To John Cryan for his review of the science and for and to Brian and Margie Duncan for their time and the tour of Princeton's Molecular Biology facility, and to Robin Falkov for her research assistance.

To Ellen de Bard for her nursing—both factual for the book and practical for my mental health— and to Brent Felgner for his valuable insights into a political campaign.

To Laurie Babson and Donald Maass for their constructive comments on an earlier draft and to Irv Babson for the extra day each week to write.

And to John Silbersack, for having faith.

The man named his wife Eve, because she was the mother of all the living.

Genesis: 3:20

Adam, having parted from his wife, after it had been ordained that they should die, begat with Lilith.

Midrashic legend,
Encyclopaedia Judaica

**We are not all
children of Eve . . .**

Prologue

On most mornings mist rose in smoky tendrils as if from fires scattered throughout the hills. On these mornings the girls played with magic wands made by their mother from hickory branches, each wand carefully carved with their own name running the length of the stick. Some days they were the fairy queens who could change toads to princes. Other times they would change princes to toads. They played that their wands would start the imaginary fires that made the morning mist. Somehow the flames that burst into being far away from the girls—yet in the direction they pointed their wands—went, for the most part, unnoticed.

This morning was like most. Misty white smoke rose in lazy spirals from the soft blanket of fog covering the earth as the Kentucky mountains fenced in the quiet valley, enclosing and protecting. A rough-hewn cabin stood above the holler, wood smoke puffing lazily from the single stone chimney, drifting and melting with the gentle valley fog. The cabin's single large room was bracketed by a pair of sleeping lofts, raised to near ceiling height. A woodburning stove, the flames in its belly licking at the fresh offering of ash wood, burned year 'round in apparent tribute to cooking, washing, and heating. In reality, it was the gentle smoke that was the true worth of the fire.

Behind the stove stood a tall woman, her stern face and gray hair belying her age of almost twenty-five years by a score of years. A supply of ash splits mixed with hickory branches lay in a bin almost as large as the cast-iron stove itself. Picking another length of ash from the bin, the woman paused, remembering her grandmother's warning to always use ash wood; that hickory was all right in a pinch but never, never use anything else.

There was only one time she disobeyed. An old elm had crashed down after a summer storm, split by lightning into easily hauled sections. By the third day of the elm fires there was a strangeness over the house, and it showed, most of all, in her twin daughters.

One, always golden from the sun, who could talk the feathers off a chicken, became withdrawn, pale, and listless. She just sat at the window, dazed. The other, whose quiet, darker looks were set off by her pale, ivory skin, left the treasure chest of books she prized above all else and tore weeds from the kitchen garden with a fervor that resulted in troubled dreams and a ruined crop. Almost by accident, a stick of ash had been tossed into the stove, and with the smoothing smoke, life returned to her golden girl and peace came to her other. Ever since, she'd kept the wood bin filled with ash and hickory.

The girls, now hungry from their early-morning wanderings, headed home. A quick stop at the pump removed most of the morning's red dirt from their hands and a splash of ice water left their faces somewhat cleaner for the effort.

"Childs, it's to the table and you'd better be clean. I haven't time to turn the grits before you can dirty up all over," the mother's clear voice twanged from the open window.

Turning her back to the stove, the mother watched the two near identical heads, with two sets of her own slanted hazel eyes, move toward the house. "Alike as they may be," she spoke softly to herself, "you can tell them apart at a distance. One wears the sun she plays in on her face and in her hair, her eyes turned to near gold in the warmth. My other seems touched only by the moon and the night, and those green flecks in her eyes shine over all else, and win."

Memories flushed the mother's face. "I do love them," she murmured. "I know I do, but I can't feel it.'' She remembered the surge of emotion, of love, she'd felt when they were placed in her arms, both babes wet with birthing, wrinkled as prunes, greedy-hungry mouths searching for milk. Then, the room tidied of the birth, herself comfortably under the Windmill quilt she'd stitched for her marriage bed, the midwife called in her husband.

She could still see his face contort and darken when he saw the girls. ''They're not mine,'' he stormed, a bitter and undeserved accusation in his voice. Without a backward glance, without more than the shirt on his back, he left. What he thought, what he saw in the newborn faces, was a secret he took with him. As had her own father.

She'd heard he started a new family somewhere west of the ridge, but news was hard to come by. Other than what she picked up from the church elders, the outside world didn't get very close. A war in Vietnam and men walking on the moon were unbelievable events that did not reach her.

Bursting into the room, the girls' energy carried them just short of the table, where they stopped, waiting for the nod that meant they could sit and start talking again. The nod came and they slid as one onto the slat benches, waiting for the plates in front of them to be filled. They not only moved as one, she noticed for the hundredth or thousandth time, they lived as one. As soon as they could crawl, they stayed within their baby arms' reach of each other, as soon as they could talk they'd spoken to almost no one else. Sometimes there wasn't room in their lives for her, their own mother.

Still deep in her thoughts her daughters' chatter went unheard, but their plates were duly filled.

''I can't seem to reach them but Grandmom always said I was lacking,'' the mother whispered to herself, remembering her own girlhood and her grandmother's words, words uttered countless scores of times: ''It passed the child by.''

Her mother had told her what her grandmom told

her: there's something special in the family women-
folk, always had been. Even she, though it "passed
her by," knew the earth, could grow and heal. But
these girls have something else, something more. That
much she did know. She looked at her plate, her own
food untouched, the girls almost finished with their
meal.

"Can we go down to Sil's holler after," the voice
of one of the girls broke through the reverie. Not sure
which girl asked, the answer was automatic.

"No, you know Sil don't want you around."

"But, Ma"—this time she knew it was Elise asking
and looked up to watch the girl catch the sunlight she
seemed born to live in—"we won't go near his house.
It's just the cave on the back of his planting ground
we want to go to."

"A cave?" The mother looked at her daughters,
concern shadowing her creased face. "I don't want
you two playing in any open caves. The next thing I
know you'll be swallowed up by the earth and I'll
never see you again."

"It's not really a cave, Ma. It doesn't lead anywhere. It's only an overhang, just big enough for us to
sit under. We take our families."

The mother smiled. Their families were twig figures
that they learned to make from Parson Caffrey. The
parson thought it best for the girls not to have outsid-
ers around. The girls, he said, needed only each other,
and she should know that best of all; if she didn't
know it now, he added, someday she would understand. She wasn't at all sure what the parson meant,
but she trusted him implicitly.

When her own mother died birthing her, he raised
her as his own, even though he'd no wife to share the
burden of bringing up a headstrong young girl. Her
grandmother, a shriveled old woman even then, had
offered little help other than demanding weekly visits
from her as a young girl and tediously lecturing during
each session: how to grow herbs and feed fires with

ash and sometimes hickory; how to stitch clothes and watch the moon. The lessons were joyless and endless.

It wasn't until she'd grown and married and brought the twins to their great-grandmother's bedside, the woman so close to the end of life her grave was already dug, that she'd seen the first spark of real interest ignite in the bedridden woman. The old woman's milky, clouded eyes flew open and cleared at the sight of the twin girls; her liver-spotted clawlike hands reached out for their plump bodies. The effort was monumental and the gaunt, aged woman fell back, gasping her last words.

"Never thought I'd see the day," she'd barely whispered, a coughing spell racking her frail body. "Remember what I taught you. Keep the ash fires burning," she hissed what was clearly a command, and closed her eyes for the last time.

The parson had been there and had seen the life burst back into the frail, dying old woman. He heard those last words. He'd turned to her, alone again with a husband already far gone, and held her close, hugging her twin daughters between them. He'd always take care of her, he promised . . . and he had.

Last year, when the girls were old enough to start wandering on their own, he'd posted his church elders at the foot of their path to watch they didn't travel too far and, not incidentally, to turn away the occasional visitor. They alone brought her the few store goods they needed, mostly flour and salt for bread. That, plus the land, provided.

Elise continued the plea. "Please, Ma, I'll watch out for us."

This promise made all the difference.

"You can go, but not into a cave and not near Sil's house. He still says his cows' milk soured after you were near."

Elise's smile lit up her face and Talia's eyes sparkled even brighter. With their plates brought dutifully to the chipped sink, they scampered from the room, grabbing the wicker carry basket on their way through the door.

The path they took continued around the hill and was far more overgrown than the one they'd played on before breakfast, testimony to the forbidden area it led to.

Winding their way along, the girls stayed silent. They listened to the caressing sounds the woods made: small animals chattering, birds talking in whistles and hoots, dew trickling to the leaved floor, and the constant whisper of mountain breezes in the treetops.

"If we walk straight down, we'll get to the cave faster," Talia directed her sister.

"But we can't. That'll lead us near Sil's barn and we promised not to," Elise reluctantly responded.

"You promised. I didn't," was Talia's guileful answer.

"Please, Talia, don't make trouble. Old Sil Cody will have a near fit if he catches us and he'll tell Ma and she'll tell Parson Caffrey and we'll end up back in that room with the doors locked, and it felt like days last time."

Talia stopped short on the memory. "All right. We'll go the long way. But only because listening to you is worse than the extra walk."

Leaving the marked path, the girls quickly made their way out of the dense woods, through thinning trees, and walked even faster when the small hill came into view. The overhang sat halfway up the hill, but still took another half-hour to reach. Once there, the girls scrambled into the wide opening and quickly settled down Indian-fashion on a piece of smuggled blanket.

Calm surrounded them. The extravagant birdcalls did not encroach upon them as they sat hidden in the hill, arranging the slender dolls dressed in colorful bits of ribbon and cloth. This was their family and their friends; as all young girls do, they created a past and a future for each member of their doll family. The collection had begun modestly enough, with a mother

and two girls. It grew to five figures, then ten. Sometimes, not often and never noticed by their mother,
the family would be smaller, marked only by a small
grave of broken twigs. Then, a new doll would be built
to take the place of the offender—the lives and living,
deaths and dying known only to the girls.

Immersed in the weaving of tales, Elise and Talia
failed to notice the soft padding sound nearing them.
Nor did they hear the tentative scratching of small
claws on the earth outside their shelter.

Talia, the quicker of the two, sensed the intruder
and turned to the opening, her eyes focusing quickly
from shadows to sun. "Something's here," she said,
a sharp edge to her voice, as she scrambled up from
her cross-legged position. Standing, she carefully
scanned the brush area. "Nothing's come here," she
said, "not since the time we found the coon."

Elise, still seated, lifted her head at the mention of
the raccoon family; a long shudder shook her small
frame as she remembered the coon's fate.

Striding out into the sunlight, her small hand shading her eyes, Talia carefully searched for the source of
the offending noise. "There's something out here, and
I won't let anything, ever, ever come here. It's my,
our, place."

In the bushes the offending creature's tail moved a
branch. "There it is!" She pointed.

Rising to join her sister, Elise moved into the puddle
of sunlight, her eyes sighting along Talia's pointed finger to a spot where, almost hidden, a runty dog
crouched. "That's one of the litter from Sil's bitch.
It's been coming near our house and I've been feeding
it scraps. Ma said not to, but I've been doing it near
the wood and keeping it away from the house."

"You fool," her sister spat. "Now the mutt has followed us here. You know we can't let nothing or no
one near our secret place."

"Why not? It's just you who said nothing could
come here. Just us you said. Well, now I've a dog and
he's mine 'cause he followed me. And if he's my dog,

he can come here too.'' She tried to remain firm but
her eyes misted and her stern look slowly dissolved.
''I want to keep the dog. Please.''

As if it knew it were the center of attention, the
black-and-white hound moved out of the bush and
playfully began to lumber toward the two girls, bearing a straight line to the one he knew was his. The
other human went unnoticed in his joy.

As Elise reached down to embrace her dog, her sister's arm stopped her short.

''We can't have the dog,'' Talia insisted.

''But it's mine.''

''No, you can't have anything I can't have. That's
the way it is.''

Talia's arms shot out, her small hands tightly grasped
the puppy's head; her hazel eyes, green flecks shining,
locked with its baleful brown. The whimper grew into
an anguished howl as the dog met her stare. The terror-
filled howl held for an indeterminate time as Elise
watched, unable to move to her sister or the suffering
puppy. Elise finally forced herself to take a short step and
Talia's eyes snapped away from the yowling creature to
meet her own. The warning in Talia's hateful glare was
implicit and stopped Elise in her tracks.

The animal's pitiful cry finally broke and changed into
a gurgle as the dog's eyes clouded over, as if steam were
filling the small creature from within. Soon, heat radiated
from the animal's short fur, the odor of burnt flesh rushed
from its mouth, and its trembling legs crumpled. The last
sound it was to make started in its throat but drowned in
the gush of dark, boiled blood that shot from its jaws. One
final spasm shook the dog before it lay still.

Elise closed her eyes and swayed backward, catching
herself before she fell. Her own anger revived her and she
screamed at her sister, ''You've done it again. Every time
I have something you don't, you get rid of it. I can't have
anything—you want it all.''

''I want it all for us.'' Talia spoke softly to her twin,
her breath carrying the scent of dying flowers. ''For us.

Not for you. Not for me. For us. Together we can do anything, have anything, be anything we want.''

Talia turned and quickly gathered the twig dolls into the wicker basket. ''We're to be home midday, and it's almost that now. Come on.'' Without looking back she started into the woods leading home.

Elise took a small step forward, then looked down at the dog's body, still smoking at her feet. Bending forward, she reached out with both hands to the warm fur. She closed her eyes and thought of the puppy as it was when it was still full of life. A tear fell from her eye but she ignored the delicate path it took from her cheek to her chin, and kept her hands on the animal's back. The fur and flesh began to cool under her fingers.

She stayed, unwilling to move from this creature that had loved her, and only her. Talia called back, the woods muffling her brittle voice, demanding that she leave their place, that she was not to stay there alone. But she stayed just a while longer. Until the breathing started again.

BOOK ONE

1

JOLTING THE THREE MEN FACING HIM BY SLAPPING down the slim file, Frank Jordan pushed his heavy chair away from the table. The harsh scraping sound on the parquet floor echoed off half-paneled wood walls. Standing, Jordan glared at the three men facing him, each of their faces equally grim, and began to pace the length of the table. When he reached the end chair, Jordan nodded to the fifth man seated there, then turned back to pace the length again, and again, letting the silence build. When he sensed that their attention was total, that the three sets of eyes were focused entirely on him and the outbreak shared by all three had abated—that instead of the earlier solidarity there was now individual anticipation—he stopped and faced them.

The long, solid walnut table was surrounded by fourteen chairs with five files, each significantly closed, resting on the polished wood. This was not a meeting to compare work notes. Small brass lamps, one in front of each place, were invisibly wired to turn on or off by a touch to the base. Tonight, four of the brass lamps were lit as Frank Jordan, project administrator, continued to face down the three scientists sitting across from him.

Frank Jordan repeated the phrase that had almost ended the meeting.

"There's no way we can credit this to Spiral. It was understood from the beginning that any developments of any consequence, anything outside our objective,

would be channeled through whichever publicly known
project was appropriate.''

"But, Frank,'' one of the three men in white jackets
spoke up, further irritating the administrator by using
his first name, "this is a major breakthrough. It's the
find of a lifetime. Nobel material.''

Judd Thacker, his brief outburst succinctly defining
the topic at hand, sat back. Spokesman for the group,
he wore a deeply lined face that did not reflect his true
age; he'd just passed forty. The deep vertical creases
in his forehead were a trademark of the curious research associate, as were his heavily crow's-footed
eyes, the by-product of constantly peering into one of
the many high-resolution electron microscopes. As elder of the three scientists, he'd easily won the role of
group spokesman after one of his all too frequent
pompous summations. It had been suggested by his
associates, though not within his hearing, that these
extensive dissertations were not limited to his having
an audience, but no one had yet successfully caught
Dr. Thacker orating to the mirror in the men's room.
Though they tried. And once came close.

Indirect lighting fanned out from wall sconces
placed at regular intervals around the large private
conference room and cast overlapping pools of light
and shadow. This was a room rarely seen and never
before used by the research staff. They were invariably
assigned to the smaller and more austere meeting
spaces, that is, when they remembered to actually call
a meeting. More frequently they would meet, whoever
was present, in the cafeteria or lounge. That the small
group had been summoned to this room, a room tra-
ditionally locked but rumored to boast state-of-the-art
security equipment, had unnerved all but Bill Blaiser,
the youngest of the three scientists—or, as they were
officially designated, research associates.

Judd Thacker had, upon entering the room, held the
file he carried—a duplicate of the files that sat before
Jordan and the others—close to his chest as if the slim
folder would be snatched from his hands and taken

from him forever, a physical act mimicking the meta-physical outcome he and the others most feared.

In the chair at the head of the table, an unlit lamp before him, the fifth man sat back in the shadow. A tall, rugged man, his chair pushed back, his legs akimbo, he kept one hand to his forehead as if shielding his eyes from the dim lighting. The chairman of the advisory board rarely visited during prime lab hours; he, and his late-night visits, were legendary at the facility.

Frank Jordan, himself tall though more wiry than muscular, sensed rather than saw the nod directed to him by the chairman. Jordan, impeccably dressed in an Armani gray silk suit—a color unerringly chosen to match the cold gray of his steely eyes—continued to address the three men facing him across the table.

"I don't blame you for making a proposal to take your findings public. You *have* made a breakthrough. First, discovering this genetic factor, then splicing it into a replicable chain and developing a synthesizable vaccine for the probable—and I say probable, not possible—prevention of a single-gene defect disease is more than enough to give the world, not just the scientific community, cause to beat the proverbial path to our door. Connecting this obscure genetic factor to acquired immune deficiencies—caused by the HIV strains feared by every human—is an even more powerful and promising breakthrough. The treatment . . . no, the cure of the most deadly virus now known to man is not only Nobel material, it would promise sainthood."

Judd Thacker, somewhat mollified by the apparent agreement and unexpected support from the man he considered his main adversary, again spoke for himself and his two associates. "So, we do publish."

"No." Frank Jordan firmly voiced the single word. Placing his hands on the table to balance himself, he leaned across to look each man, in turn, straight in the eye.

The three researchers were stunned. Ed Hawthorn

and Bill Blaiser looked to Thacker for support. Equals
in the lab, the three sparked an unusually productive
symbiotic team. Judd Thacker was deep in thought.

"Those releases we signed. What were they really
designed for?" Judd Thacker asked, now directing his
question to the fifth man, in shadow, at the head of the
table. "They weren't just the usual relinquishments of
personal claims on discoveries made during employment, were they?"

"Thank you, Dr. Thacker," Frank Jordan answered, cutting in between Thacker and the chairman,
"for taking the time to finally read your copy." He
bowed his head to the three research scientists, an
irony not lost on Bill Blaiser, whose growing anger
could be measured by the degree of flush in his face.

"You're right. They weren't just the standard release forms where you get personal discovery credit
but any patents and all processing and financial ben-
fits accrue to the company. You not only signed away
ny and all individual credits, including all publishing
ights, but in fact, the right to any recognition or con-
ection whatsoever with the project."

Ed Hawthorn, a slight man with thinning blond hair
and often the butt of playful jokes for his stereotypical
absentmindedness, was not known for any tempera-
ment, and the anguish in his raised voice was completely out of character. "You can't do that. It's
unethical to take the credit for our discovery. I won't
let you present our findings as your own."

"You don't understand, Dr. Hawthorn," the chairman, still in shadow, spoke softly but with a force that
nonetheless commanded complete attention. "We're
not going to take credit for this. No one here, in this
room, at this laboratory, or anyone in anyway associated with Spiral, will get credit. We're going to turn
the findings, your findings, your documented work and
your project over to another research facility. They'll
get the credit."

Leaning forward, an abashed Judd Thacker spoke

equally softly, but his words were crystal-clear. "This is unheard-of."

"No, it's not," the chairman continued. "It happens often, not that you'd know, but not usually with a finding of this magnitude."

"Why?" Thacker asked. "This discovery must be more important than anything you could hope we'd turn out on the Spiral project."

Frank Jordan sensed the weakening resolve of the three scientists. He walked around the table and, from behind, removed the folders from in front of each.

"The problem is you haven't really been included in the full scope of Spiral," Jordan said, his voice soothing. "It's easy to imagine why you think that this finding, as important as it is, should take precedence. You stumbled on this at our direction, working in the areas we asked you to, and paid you to, focus on.

"Most genetic research concentrates on the cell's nucleus. You were directed to work only on the cytoplasm and you zeroed in on the small organelles known as mitochondria. In working with this unique mitochondria DNA, you substantiated that the MtDNA codes are almost always different from the DNA codes of the cell nucleus—even from those found in the same cell. But your particular finding, as monumental as it may very well prove to be, was not, *is not,* our goal. And our research must go on in the direction it was designed for and, more importantly, is funded for."

Bill Blaiser, silent until now but slowly reaching a boiling point, let loose. "We don't even know what the . . . what *your* fucking goal is. Excuse us for coming up with a major breakthrough!"

Frank Jordan paused on the way back to his chair. His sitting across from the three scientists was a tactical move; by facing them he became not just their adversary but a figurehead with untold resources behind him—including the project chairman.

At the head of the table, the chairman's conservative three-piece suit and crisp white-on-white shirt was set off, as usual, by the familiar school tie he was known for; bets had been taken as to the number of ''rep'' ties—all with the same striped pattern and colors—he owned, but no count could ever be made and no winner ever called. He was known to all as the driving force behind the original funding, but his sporadic attendance at the facility, leaving Jordan in charge, and his seeming disinterest in all but one facet of the research, confused the research staff and often left them feeling undirected.

The chairman, slumped in his chair, used both hands to cover his face. He seemed not so much tired as weary of the debate, which had taken the better part of an hour. The lines etched around his eyes pinched his face into a pained expression.

''They're right, you know,'' he said to Frank Jordan. ''They should know more than just our general direction. If they can produce these kinds of results just by winging it in researching the cytoplasm DNA, the potential for them hitting the nail on the head is greater than I hoped.''

''I've never been given the authority to tell them,'' Jordan responded. ''Spiral is set up on the need-to-know basis. Even I don't even know everything.''

''What do you know?'' Dr. Blaiser, now reasonably calm, asked.

Frank Jordan looked to the head of the table and, getting an affirmative nod, turned to the three men in front of him.

''It might surprise you,'' Jordan answered, obviously not happy with the admission, ''but Spiral began as a privately funded project.'' He nodded credit to the man at the head of the table. ''A grant was used to develop a small research team who were then given a very specific direction—a goal, coincidentally, very close to the one you just reached: breaking into a single-gene defect. After a few years the original funding allocation was nearly exhausted and the research team was no closer to achieving the goal than they had been at the start.''

Jordan paused to take a sip of water and, seeing he had the scientists' complete attention, continued.

"The researchers were brought tissue and blood samples to study. The subjects were unknown to them and chosen by the founder of the project. One day, close to the scheduled shutdown of the project—about five years ago, before any of you came on—a blood sample was brought for the usual array of testings. An analysis was run, complete with autoradiographs on both the nuclear and mitochondrial DNA, and a surprising find was made. Not only was the MtDNA unique, but the mitochondria themselves, which can number thousands per cell, were incalculable. With the original funding drying up, yet with a brand-new direction to study suddenly materializing, I was brought in to find additional financial resources. As you may know, I'd just retired from, well, a government position. Now, Spiral is funded by the military—"

"Oh, shit," Bill Blaiser loudly interrupted, "the one fucking thing I promised myself I'd never get involved with." Quickly pushing his chair back from the table, he moved to get up.

"One moment, Dr. Blaiser, perhaps you should hear more," the man at the end of the table said, his words soft but with a distinct edge.

"Thanks but no thanks. I didn't risk a jail sentence staying out of the war to end up developing new ways to kill people. You've got the wrong man."

Belatedly realizing his folder had been taken by Jordan, Bill Blaiser turned and walked purposefully to the door. His two associates looked at him and then each other, undecided whether to follow or to hear the project administrator out. Blaiser paused at the door, looking back at his associates, challenging them to join him in his righteous stance.

Looking at him, then at each other, Judd Thacker, who had somehow barely noticed there had been a war or anything else going on outside of his immediate studies, and Ed Hawthorn, who had been found physically ineligible for military service, made no move to join him, their scientific curiosity clearly winning out over their far less devout pacifism. Blaiser, realizing he was alone in his stand, reached for the door handle and resigned himself to abandoning the first project he had found vitally interesting and potentially productive. A metallic snap sounded clearly in the otherwise silent room; the door, he found, was now securely locked.

"I ask only that you listen. Dr. Blaiser," said the chairman. "And that you and Doctors Thacker and Hawthorn take some time—a full day if you will—to talk among yourselves about what else we have to tell you. You've earned the right to know, in more ways than you can imagine. You see, by chance you crossed back to the original purpose of this project, and the breakthrough we achieved in familia hypercholesterolemia—the single-gene defect resulting in mutant cholesterol levels—was a by-product of *your* work and was the founding reason for this research facility. My wife died from the disease and it was her family's money that started the project now known as Spiral. Even though the original direction is no longer our goal, you not only achieved that purpose but tied the concept of single-gene deficiency to HIV. And for this I am grateful."

Frank Jordan, surprised at this unexpected disclosure, sat quietly while Bill Blaiser, somewhat mollified but still flushed with anger, returned to his chair. The noise Blaiser made as he pulled the chair back to the table would normally account for a roomful of men.

Jordan waited until the room was once again still.

"You all ready know the mitochondria are considered the powerhouses of the cell and, as such, are the source of energy in the body. We were primarily interested because they transport during all energy-transducing activities—mitochondria are the major source of metabolic activity and, as a result, are particularly numerous in those cells that have a high demand for energy, like muscles. Now, imagine the most intense concentration you can, then increase it tenfold. The sample we saw had a mitochondrial count that far surpassed any prior recorded accounting. In fact, such an extraordinary quantity was present that we began to project what this increased mitochondrial factor could mean.''

Frank Jordan paused to let the men begin their own extrapolations. ''Gentlemen, we're sure it means a more powerful human being. Potentially, a person with enormous but unknown resources at his or her disposal. What the renewed funding, the government funding, is designed to produce are the answers to how much more powerful, in what ways, and why. Once we have these answers, we'll decide whether or not to launch the second stage of this project.

''To duplicate the factor and thus the abnormality.''

2

THE BROWNSTONE BUILDING STOOD, LIKE THE
dozen others lining either side of the street, in quiet
disrepair. Red concrete steps were weathered and
scrubbed, ready for the footsteps the doctors Elise
Crawford and Jeff Vaughan, very much married to each
other, were depending on to provide a steady flow of
patients to their waiting room. Mercifully, the tan paint
once applied in a vain attempt to modernize the time-
less beauty of aging brick had almost all flaked away,
leaving large expanses of the natural red facade showing through, gasping for breath.

This must be fate, thought Elise, struggling to remove the tattered wallpaper. If it were opportunity, it
would have knocked once and then gone away. But this
has taken years. Finding a building within their budget
while still in residency had been, it seemed at the time,
pure luck. That is, if you didn't count the months of
days walking streets together, making the luxury of
their scant time together count toward a common goal
and, finally, a year and a half ago, finding a FOR SALE
sign on one they could conceivably afford.

Here, on West 122nd street, they had finally found
their home-cum-castle, spotted the one and probably
only day they weren't actively looking. An associate
intern who was also a weaver—where she found the
time was a mystery—was having her first showing at
the Columbia University Crafts Fair. Elise promised
to attend and arrived with Jeff in tow. After the show
they'd wandered through the crisp fall weather, enjoying the spaciousness of the streets, pausing at St. John's

Cathedral to bask in its splendor, and found themselves on Morningside Drive overlooking the hillside park. Descending the steep stairway at 116th street, they surveyed the densely tree-filled area, lush with a blanket of red and gold leaves.

Crossing back and forth between the stone steps and the wooded areas, they continued on to the other side of the park until they found themselves in front of a statue at the 114th street entrance; the god Pan, his pipes beside him, crouching and hiding from an almost life-size bear. Energized from their discovery—another mythical statue for their private list—they turned to walk up Morningside Avenue, Morningside Drive far above and across the park. Once outside the park they noticed the squalid buildings lining the east side of the street and at 116th street, suddenly aware of the chill, spotted a neighborhood grocery, the bodega sign visible a block away. They decided containers of hot coffee were in order.

Sipping from their paper containers, plastic lids torn back in small triangles, the fashion of veteran takeout habitués, they stood by the floor-to-ceiling glass windows, perfectly content in each other's company. An old but energetic man blustered in for bread and bananas; they exchanged amused looks at the man's shopping list, not dreaming that this craving for fried plantains would be their salvation.

Señor Pérez, as the old gentleman was respectfully addressed by the clerk, was fed up with the endless repairs and chores of being homeowner-landlord-handyman and had opted to spend the rest of his life in comfort: let someone else repair the leaking hot-water heater, the electrical wiring, the intercom system, the chipped plaster, on ad infinitum—he raved—if only he could sell the building. It was too small for anyone outside the neighborhood, they wanted what they called "real" brownstones, not a tiny row house all the way up on West 122nd Street, and the wrong side of Morningside Park to boot; the New York City taxes were too high for anyone who already lived in the neighborhood, and besides, locals couldn't afford the down payment. Elise and Jeff listened to his heavily accented complaints, a palpable excitement growing between them.

As his simple purchases were sacked, he looked the grocer in the eye and completed his agonized monologue with a short but potent statement: "If anyone made me a decent offer for the house, I'd be out of here before you could close for the night."

So they did.

They almost pounced on the startled man as he turned to leave the overheated store, jointly exclaiming a desire to see his house. A short walk away, between Morningside and Manhattan Avenues, 122nd Street was an oasis in the near war-torn area. Lined on both sides by small brownstones—more accurately row houses, as Sr. Pérez had accurately noted—not one building stood above three stories—four if you counted the floor below street level—nor was any wider than two windows. Passing two boarded-up row houses, they turned and walked up the cement steps to a landing fronted by a double glass door. An ornately carved wooden door behind the glass literally took their breath away; the carvings were nymphs and elves frolicking in an elaborate garden.

Exchanging looks, they knew it almost didn't matter what the inside of the building looked like.

While it took a few weeks to complete the negotiations and necessary paperwork, Sr. Pérez was true to his word and moved out, taking his two remaining tenants with him, the day after the closing. For the last eighteen months they had repaired, renovated, and otherwise scraped, pried, hammered, torn down, and built up with their own four hands, hands once destined only for the scalpel. Walls fell as the maze of small rooms fronting the street on both the first and second floor were turned into one large room per floor; the first floor ideal for their reception and waiting area and the second floor for their master bedroom. The stairway was exposed between the two floors, broken bathroom tiles pried loose and replaced, plumbing needs carefully fit to existing pipe layouts, and the rear ground-floor area opened to house a large eat-in kitchen and pantry.

Their patients at the hospital hadn't complained when the hand holding the stethoscope had been more callused than expected, and in fact, more than one laborer had smiled when he recognized his doctor's hands as belonging to someone who knew how to work with them outside of medicine.

Two floors for themselves, immediately, and the promise of the third floor if—no, when, they needed it. The below-ground level was well-suited as a garden apartment and once the plumbing was completed, the heat and hot water running, they would spruce it up with a final coat of paint and possibly rent—the extra income could be welcome over the next few years—if its planned use didn't materialize.

The first floor would be their office space: a reception area, two small offices with adjoining examination rooms, a minuscule laboratory, and the kitchen-pantry. They would complete the second floor later; for now their bedroom and master bath was more than adequate for comfortable sleep and morning ablutions. Any more, on their budget, would be an indulgence and, with their lives just starting and their dreams almost enough food to sustain them, the second-floor living room and study could wait.

The next to the last panel of wall paper peeled away in even lengths. Plaster dust shook loose from aging walls and fell gently on smooth skin the color of lightly toasted almonds, powdering Elise's taut cheekbones, whitening her golden-brown hair.

Sitting back on her heels, Elise surveyed the large ground-floor room facing the street. Only one more panel of faded paper needed to be stripped from what had been the corner wall of one of the small first-floor front rooms. Very little real work and not all that much, considering what had already been done. Some plaster and sanding and the walls would be ready to paint. She imagined the room when the paper had been hung, the first owner looking with pride at the even and balanced pattern. Smiling at her own flight of fancy, she brought herself back to reality by scrutinizing the walls for any damage, but the plaster base seemed surprisingly firm for an old building. Very few chunks of wall had come off with the paper and the spackling job to follow would be, after the tedious paper removal, a relatively easy task.

The room itself held even more promise. A small fireplace stood centered against the west wall and, much to their surprise, was operable. That is, once the chimney had been swept of decades of soot and grime. The rationale for the restorative expense was simple; getting this fireplace working meant the one in their bedroom above would also operate and would help keep heating costs low. Twin windows, each almost the height of the room, faced south and flanked the entrance, a space hardly large enough to call a foyer. The resultant area, created from two rooms and a hallway, was large enough to comfortably sit a handful of patients as well as house the reception desk and file cabinets.

Lost in thoughts of drawn curtains and baskets of Boston ferns, Elise—no, Dr. Elise Crawford she corrected herself—sat among moving boxes packed with reference texts. Worn denim jeans and dusty sweatshirt completed a schoolgirl's outfit, yet she fully realized, and spoke out loud to emphasize, her status, "I'm a doctor and have been for almost five years. Now I'll have my own practice. Enough residency tours-of-duty. Enough catching whatever sleep I can in the lounge. Enough . . ." And with a fit of giggles she scooped up handfuls of torn wallpaper and tossed the shreds into the air, falling back to let them flutter about her slim figure.

"I've been watching you, Dr. Crawford, and my immediate diagnosis is definitely complete regression and total madness. On the other hand, it could be hunger, and I'm willing to rectify that situation."

Jeff Vaughan stood in the wide doorway. Smiling up at him from beneath the bits of paper, Elise knew that no matter how happy she thought she was with the house and the planned private practice, she would never be happier than she was with her husband.

"Madness is more like it. We must have been insane to marry during residency, but Jeff, oh, Jeff, right now it's worth every crazy moment we had. To go for days without even seeing each other, then to barely catch sight of you sleeping when I was too tired to keep my eyes open. A weekend every other week, if we were lucky. But now . . . Wait a minute!" Elise sat bolt upright, still clutching the wallpaper. "Just what do you mean by total regression?"

"I mean that you're the same wonderful girl I fell in love with in college. And don't ever change. Not even for lunch," Jeff comically moved his eyebrows and played an imaginary cigar. "Now for lunch, and the rest of my prescription." Bending to lift his wife, Jeff slipped his arms around her and gently pulled her to her feet. Elise moved her hands to the front of his work shirt and traced the neck opening down his broad chest.

"Lunch sounds like a good idea, for now."

Linked arm in arm, the couple walked as one to the renovated kitchen, the pungent smell of freshly oiled banisters and paneling sweet to their senses. Elise's slim figure was complemented by Jeff's, and as he leaned over to kiss her cheek, she again thought of how well they fit, in so many ways. At a hair over six feet, Jeff had only to dip his head to kiss her full on the lips; with high-heeled shoes she could meet his eyes straight on. His blond fairness matched her own golden coloring; in the summer her hair would be almost as light as his, but his deep-blue eyes were uniquely his and, focused on her, held a love she felt lucky to share.

The eat-in kitchen had been scrubbed to the bone and painted glossy ivory with delft-blue trim. A moderately new refrigerator-freezer combination fit snugly in a recess that could have been built for it. But the pride of the room was the six-burner professional stove, complete with two warming trays, an inside and outside broiler, and twin oven units.

Jeff's eyes crinkled at the corners with affection as he followed Elise's gaze to the massive stove. "I don't know why I let you talk me into that, that thing. It takes up twice the space a stove should and in this kitchen we could have used one half the size."

Elise smiled and ran her hands over the gleaming chrome surrounded by black, pitted cast iron. "Because it's terrific. It was a super buy—the restaurant almost paid us to take it away—and the warming ovens will be our salvation when we have late office hours. That's why."

Even if the oven was never used, it was worth the price because it made Elise happy. Avoiding any debate of a small microwave versus outsized warming ovens, Jeff turned and opened the cupboard to rummage for the coffeepot. "In that case"—he planted the pot firmly in her hands—"you can use the monster to make the coffee while I, as chief chef, whip together a minor miracle for lunch."

"Jeff, not that I don't have the greatest admiration for your culinary talents, but I'd be just as pleased if you'd whip up a couple of peanut-butter-and-jelly sandwiches. And use paper plates. Enough chores for the day."

"Sandwiches it shall be, my lady, but the makings are my choice." Jeff had the refrigerator doors open and shelves raided before Elise filled the coffeepot with water. He swiftly plucked leaves from a head of spinach; simultaneously he unwrapped a loaf of bread and with a sharpened utility knife made swift work of a ripe tomato, Bermuda onion, and cold roast beef.

Lunch swiftly appeared in the form of a pair of double-decker, toasted rye-bread sandwiches accompanied by chilled long-neck bottles of beer, a previously unknown and surprisingly good brand discovered at the neighborhood bodega, a store visited often and always with fond memories of Señor Pérez.

"Make a third one like those and I'll pay the first month's mortgage," a deep voice reverberated from the open archway.

"In here, Dad, and you can start with half of mine. I've never been able to finish one of Jeff's creations, and if I hope to keep my figure, I never will." Elise smiled back at her father-in-law, a large man conservatively dressed in a three-piece suit who almost filled the door frame. "You, on the other hand," she continued, "are likely to eat this half, another whole one, and still be hungry. My guess is that after you finish a surgery you go logrolling to keep in shape."

Blushing, a trait surprising in the older man, Hal Vaughan patted his flat stomach. "I was going to invite you two out to lunch, but I see I'm too late."

"Dad, you've taken care of everything else. We can handle lunch." Jeff spoke softly but his words held a trace of cold determination. Despite his father's generosity, Jeff was resolved to one day pay him back what he considered a loan. It was more than enough, Jeff reasoned, to be lucky enough to have a father who could take the place of the legendary friendly banker in setting up a mortgage and allowing start-up funds, but the end responsibility would be his and Elise's.

"Jeff, you've done all the work on this house, you and Elise," Hal Vaughan spoke gently, aware of his son's sensitivity, "not to mention getting through medical school, your internship, and your residency with flying colors. It's a father's privilege, his right, to help out once in a while—especially when he's inordinately proud of his son . . . and his son's wife."

The tension, beer, and sandwiches quickly disappeared. Fresh-brewed coffee was poured into large colorful ceramic mugs, lucky mugs bought at the craft fair the same day they'd found their home.

Jeff sipped the fragrant brew. "Right now I've still got my fingers crossed and toes curled that we make it through the legendary first year of practice with our skins—and souls—intact. Your help is much appreciated."

Absently stirring her creamed coffee, Elise smiled at the thought. "Just one more week. We already have a small schedule of patients starting seven days from today. Thanks in good part to you, Dad."

"No, it's not thanks to me. More than half those patients are yours from the hospital. And a good number of neighborhood people your nurse is bringing you. I've only added a few."

"Dad . . ." Elise looked at her father-in-law, love and respect clear on her face. "It's more than just sending us a few patients, though the caliber of those patients will help us get started." Holding her hand out to prevent Hal from interrupting, Elise continued. "It's *all* you've done for us. It would have taken us at least another five years to get started, like this, without you. Stop, I'm not finished." Elise continued to hold her father-in-law's objections at bay.

"You've been there for us whenever we needed you, for anything. Without you, Jeff and I probably wouldn't even have met or, if we had, had any reason to talk to each other. Thanks to your clinic, and the stipends you paid for volunteers which got me to come in, you put us in the right place at the right time. We wanted to wait to ask you, but this seems a good time. Dad, will you join us? Not only in the practice, but move in. Live with us here. There's a private garden apartment that could be a showplace. You've been alone long enough. Louise died eight years ago. Jeff and I have talked about this, and we do want you. Both of us want you."

Hal Vaughan was speechless, and his eyes threatened to fill with tears. The lump in his throat made it impossible to talk—all he could do was shake his head no. A deep sigh, followed by a long swallow, cleared his voice.

"Just your asking means more to me than anything. But I have my practice on Long Island. I'm content there. I have friends, and," Hal added with a grin, "who knows, I might meet a lady and want to set up housekeeping. But your offer is very precious. Not many flesh-and-blood daughters would make it. Besides, helping you out was the one way of making sure you stayed nearby. Half my friends at the club seem to have lost their kids to California. But thank you, very much, for the offer."

Jeff leaned over to kiss the top of Elise's head. "It was her idea, Dad. Actually, I thought it was a pretty good one." Jeff turned to his father and winked. "After all, where else could two inexperienced practitioners find a live-in consultant?"

"Stop it, I hurt too much to laugh," Elise said while accomplishing just what she claimed not to be able to do. "This spackling is the proverbial straw and my back is killing me. That reminds me," Elise shot up, her mug only half-empty. "Bree is coming later this afternoon, and I want her to see the front room bare of the last traces of old paper. I've only one more panel and can finish—if I start now."

Blowing a kiss to her husband and, because he was closer to the doorway, bestowing a real kiss on her father-in-law, Elise disappeared through the archway. Poking her head back in, she looked at Hal with tenderness. "I mean it, Dad. We mean it. The offer still stands, lady friend or not. I might even have a good influence on you and get you out of those three-piece suits and silly striped ties. I know it's your old school loyalty but you should be wearing paisleys or something with some zip." Elise smiled her sincerity, winked her way around the mild sartorial reproach, and disappeared through the door.

"She's very special," Hal noted when the sound of the scraper started. "Very special. I knew it when she first came into my campus clinic. And"—a shadow crossed his face—"it didn't take long to prove I was right."

Gathering the emptied dishes in a stack, Jeff paused on his way to the sink. His father's shift in mood went unnoticed as Jeff's preoccupation surfaced.

"There's something more to Elise than I've been able to get hold of—even though we've been together since the day we met. She still surprises me. She grew up almost on her own; the aunt who raised her was almost a recluse. She's strong and bright; her grades were as good as mine. Yet, sometimes, she's so much the little girl. She'll still cry over a lost balloon. And she has a lost look sometimes that I don't understand at all. At times, even when we're talking, she seems so far away.''

Turning to the sink, Jeff moved the single-spouted faucet and quickly dispatched the dishes under running water. Wiping his hands on his jeans, he looked long and hard at his father, deciding whether to continue the confidence. He did.

''Last night, for the first time, Elise mentioned having a sister.'' Jeff paused, his confusion obvious. ''How could we have been together all this time without her mentioning her sister before?''

Hal Vaughan met his son's gaze, trying not to show his own interest and surprise. ''Ask her why. But do it gently. Maybe there are some difficult memories.''

''We plan to go out to dinner tonight, the first time in months, and explore the neighborhood. Tonight we'll officially dedicate the house—we moved the bedroom furniture in today,'' Jeff added with a grin. ''I'll talk to her at dinner tonight.''

Nodding, Hal Vaughan sat back. ''With the different shifts the two of you kept, all the work you put in on this house, plus the commute to and from the hospital, I'm surprised you managed to remember each others' names.''

Knowing the irony was not all that farfetched, Jeff nodded in agreement. ''Maybe you're right, Dad. Maybe we just haven't had the time together to talk.''

''Don't rush her, Jeff. It could be a painful memory. Let her take the lead.''

''I will. She's told me so little of her family. I've met her aunt, but she never talked about Elise's mother. And neither of them ever mentioned a sister.''

The last dish dried and put away, Jeff sat facing his father. ''All I'm sure about is Elise is the most wonderful woman I've ever known. And I love her very much.''

''As long as you remember that, everything will be fine.''

''I'll never forget it, Dad, never.''

3

NEITHER HER COMING RITES OF PASSAGE NOR THE altered juxtaposition her life would take in relation to the woman she was learning to call her friend were on Bree Sobole's mind. These events were unknown to her. Instead, she merely watched as bits of paper drifted on the sidewalk almost of their own volition. They moved in a very specific direction as if, when reaching the corner of 116th street, they would wait for the light to change and then cross Morning-side Avenue to the park. The cluttered street was other-wise drab and lifeless. Only the heavily treed park promised—within the month the breeze softly whispered—to renew life and bring color back to the neighborhood.

Bree Sobole listened and noticed because it was what she did best. She was a watcher. She watched her patients in the intensive-care unit for any change during the long hours of her night shift. And she watched them well. So well that her frequent requests to work days had been ignored by her supervisors. Days, they told her, were easy to manage. The doctors were around, the nurses stayed alert. She was needed nights, when the floor would be almost deserted and the level of attention often demanded in ICU in-creased. The doctors were on call, of course, but they wanted her competence there, on the floor, not only to place that call but to deal with the emergency until the doctors arrived. Extra-shift pay notwithstanding, Bree longed for the daylight hours to work in, to have the evenings and night hours for herself.

Coming home in the cool freshness of early mornings was the only advantage to working nights, but not enough to make it worthwhile. She could still be out in the morning, beginning the day instead of ending it. And she would be doing just that, starting next week. The hospital tried, at first, to reject her resignation, but when the supervisor realized the objections were futile, she attempted to appeal to Bree's "better side," a phrase that still brought a grin to the nurse's mouth.

Standing firm in her starched white uniform, Bree had responded to the near accusation of desertion. "My better side is my nursing, my family, and the Craft. Right now all I have time for is the nursing. With the Vaughans, I'll have time for everything."

"The Vaughans are the biggest mistake you will ever make." The supervisor almost spat the words, her anger betraying the unwritten hospital code of protecting its doctors at all costs. "That Dr. Crawford is one strange lady. Never even mind she won't use her husband's name. There's something seriously wrong with her, and I don't think it's medical."

Bree jumped to the defense. "Dr. Crawford is an unusually sensitive woman. I can assure you that I would know if anything were wrong. Besides, using the name Crawford is easier than having two Doctor Vaughans paged."

Abruptly closing Bree's personnel file, the supervisor signaled an end to the exit interview. "You'll see, you have no idea what they're saying about her in the doctors' lounges. And as for what kind of craft you putter in, I'd no idea being an artisan was so important to you. But if you're determined to go ahead with this, be warned."

"Determined" was putting it mildly. With only two days left at the hospital, she felt the excitement of a new beginning. She would sleep through today and, later this afternoon, see how Elise and Jeff were progressing with the office space. Not only was the thought of finally working days exhilarating, but the offices were walking distance from her apartment.

Starting Wednesday she'd be able to pitch in, full-time, helping to ready the space for next Monday's first patient.

The soul-searching of taking a position in private practice instead of facing the demands of a hospital had been adequately resolved by Bree's carefully thought-out answers: entering patient records seated in an office rather than standing eight hours over hospital beds, counts; helping patients who are still walking and not comatose, counts; leading my own life counts most of all.

Crossing east onto the block she lived, Bree took a deep breath. Though very tired, always the case when wearing a white uniform, her nearing freedom tasted sweet. The white reflected back the energy, energy she couldn't absorb and transform into strength. At home she'd slip into the midnight-blue robe of her Craft, the darkness drawing the energy to her and reviving her own drained resources. White, while normally a color only worn at burials, was serendipitously appropriate for nursing, and Bree was the first to realize the unintended but definite benefit gained from reflecting back the patients energy; most of those she cared for needed all the help they could to heal.

A commotion coming from the alley ahead shattered Bree's peace. Alert, her instincts took over as she briefly paused to determine the direction of the clamor. She moved quickly toward the disruption. Finding herself at the entrance to a dead-end, trash-littered corridor, she peered down its length. No doors or windows opened onto the passage and the only entrance was from the street, or over the chain-link fence at the far end.

In front of the fence two youths, adolescent truants, stood over and taunted a third. Their jeering echoed loudly off the alley walls.

"You told, you asshole," the taller boy screamed at the fallen youth. "We're all in for it, but you know what's coming to you first."

The other youth kicked the sprawled boy hard in the

chest. "Talking is bad for your health, fink," he chanted in a high-pitched voice. "You're getting us busted, but you get busted first." The youth giggled at his own perverse wit and, swinging his leg back for momentum, connected his foot with the fallen boy's jaw. Blood trickled from the boy's mouth, silent tears rolled down his cheeks. He curled himself into a protective fetal position.

"Busted all up," the tormentor continued, drinking from a small bottle wrapped in a brown paper bag.

"Stop," Bree shouted, unable to control her anger at what she was witnessing. "Leave him alone, now, or . . ."

The taller youth spun on his heels, seeing only a lone woman at the end of the alley. "Or what lady?" he countered, the bravado of the street and fire of the liquor strong in his blood. "You and who else gonna stop us?"

The other youth, his shoe bloody from spittle, grinned with malice. The two boys looked at each other, then back at Bree—a woman alone, carrying a purse, a nurse maybe with drugs but certainly with money. Wordlessly, a plan bridged between them and they moved toward her, pausing only to throw the now empty bottle at the fallen boy.

"Stop," Bree repeated her earlier command, the warning clear to anyone listening. But the boys weren't. They continued to move toward her. "Stop now," she said again, raising her arm and holding out a hand.

They kept coming, the click of a knife opening was the only sound they made. Their intentions vibrated out in front of them, a perceptible wave of twisted anger directed against anyone and everyone.

Taking a deep breath, Bree caught their hate and held it with her own fear. A flash of her bitterness, not directed against them but at what they were doing, escaped and shielded her as their vile emanations coalesced into a solid mass of negative energy. A touch of humor lit Bree's eyes as she watched their malignant force build. Her distress became protective, trapping

the blind hate in an energized web. The mass grew
into a static globe, burning with a malicious white
heat. Bree's shield—now thinner than the most delicate
mesh—stretched, surely and strongly, until it filled the
mouth to the alley and hid her from the youths. A
thought of fleeing now, behind this cover, crossed
Bree's mind. Then she remembered the fallen boy,
blood leaking from his mouth, his nose, and his ears.
Her anger flared—erratically and out of control. She
reached out to the charged globe, crackling with a life
of its own, and threw it at the two youths.

They crumbled in front of her, their eyes rolling
upward, their faces pale and covered with a slick
sheen. Stepping over the two—they'd recover—Bree
continued on to the fallen youth; he was unconscious,
his face battered and bloody.

"I'm glad you didn't see," Bree whispered as she
skillfully examined his head and neck for any fracture.
Finding none, she turned him over and methodically
continued her scrutiny. Heavily bruised, the boy
groaned as she ran her hands over his chest and found
a broken rib—fourth on the right—that would mend
well. She leaned forward and breathed gently into his
mouth, watching his eyes flutter open.

"Can you walk?" Bree encouraged, knowing he
could. "You'd better go before your friends wake up."

With her arm around the slight boy—a child yet, not
even a youth—she walked him as far as her building
and watched while he made his halting way up the
block. He never looked back, but that was to be expected on this street. Bree sighed and turned into her
own doorway.

Bree reached the fourth-floor landing without being
consciously aware of unlocking the downstairs door or
climbing any steps. "Instincts run strong in my family," she murmured, "in more ways than one." Bree
unequivocally knew she could trust Dr. Crawford—
both the Vaughans, but especially Elise Crawford. In
fact, she was increasingly certain that there was something special about Elise Crawford though she couldn't

quite place what it was. Bree promised herself that one day, when she'd had enough sleep, she would try to unravel any mystery that Elise Crawford held.

Standing at the multi-locked door to her apartment, Bree wearily dug into the side pockets of the large tote she used for all portables from lunch to paperbacks, cosmetics to white support pantyhose. She reached the keys and began to unlock the first of the deadbolt locks securing her meager possessions.

Safe inside, all four locks rebolted and the chain drawn, Bree nudged the practical rubber-soled shoes off her feet and slid into the slippers standing ready. Water in the tea kettle waited only for the flame that she lit before slipping off her light wool coat. Herbal tea was a welcome comfort before sleep. Bree washed her face and belted her midnight-blue robe before the kettle whistled its readiness. Pouring hot water over spicy leaves and cinnamon raised a fragrance almost as soothing as the taste would be.

The signal from her new electronic phone reminded her to check for recorded messages left during the night. Four calls were recorded, but the active phone demanded an immediate response. Not answering her private clients would be the one thing she could never do. A healer is always on call. Picking up the phone before the third ring was completed, avoiding the automatic answering mechanism, Bree was relieved to hear a familiar voice.

"Don't you ever call in for your messages? I thought you got the new machine because it has a remote. I've called at least six times during the night and left a phone number for you to call each time."

"JoJo, don't you ever sleep? I work nights but you're up morning, noon, and night. There were three emergency situations at the hospital, back to back. I had my hands full. Besides, if you're the only one who called, you only called four times. What is it?"

"It's your mother."

The phone gripped tightly, her knuckles white, Bree sank back in the large easy chair stationed near the phone. She pulled her robe close, not asking, just waiting for the news.

"She's . . . she's taken a turn for the worse. They don't expect her to live through the day."

"I need to be with her." Bree's response was barely audible, but JoJo knew the struggle it took to utter even that simple phrase.

"You can't be with her," JoJo continued. "You know that. She can only be with those chosen by her first clan to succeed her. Her power must be drawn down to one of them at the time of her death. But her people wanted you to know she's thinking of you, even now. She calls your name."

A broken sob escaped from Bree, and with mumbled thanks for JoJo's calling, she was ready to slide the phone back into its cradle when another thought surfaced. "Wait, does Michael know?"

"Your brother knows," JoJo sighed deeply. "Though I wish he didn't. He's still convinced he's next."

"It isn't Michael, so much. It's his . . . well, I guess you can call them his loyal supporters. They're convinced that Michael is the one. Michael is being pushed into a role by those power-hungry seekers."

"You don't know Michael, or won't accept. It's the other way around. Anyway, you're the healer, and you could be a lot more if you just tried. It's a struggle to get you to attend esbat services much less take a stronger hand in clan issues. You'd be first among the chosen if you did."

"You know I work nights, JoJo. But that'll change next week. I will attend esbat more faithfully. But no matter what, I've never let anyone down who needed healing. You know that."

"Yes, I know that, Bree. And so does everyone else. You are our favorite, no matter what."

"Thank you. JoJo, I need to be alone. I'm very shaken right now—and tired. I'm going to leave the machine on. If you see anyone who's trying to reach me, let them know why I'm not answering."

"Everyone already knows not to call you for a while. They'll call Mama Alice until . . . well, until . . ."

Tears streaming down her cheeks, Bree did not need to wait for JoJo to finish what was obviously a difficult statement—for him to make and for her to hear.

Stunned, Bree sat immobilized. Time passed unnoticed. The phone was silent, a testimony to JoJo's swift information network. With only the accustomed street noises from below, Bree's thoughts drifted to her mother: tall and stately with long hair so dark it barely caught the light, Bree saw her mother every time she looked in a mirror. The gentleness Bree's mother emanated never waivered. "An old soul," her mother had taught, "knows only love." And Bree's mother had loved. Her children, her people, and for the short time he had been with them, her husband—Bree and Michael's father. Why she had married a drifter no one knew; everyone had been stunned yet kept silent, grateful that in choosing such a man she would remain free to be with her people. Sitting at home with a husband could never have been a part of her mother's life; visiting the ill or homebound, healing and holding esbat services two or three nights a week for one or another of the groups had taken up almost all of her time. The few remaining moments had been used to hold her children close, to hug them and love them and whisper to them the secrets they would, one day, need to know.

At first glance both Bree's and her mother's dark good looks spoke of recent foreign roots—Greek or southern Italian perhaps; looking further into their faces, one saw high Slavic cheekbones set off by wide eyes, a brown so dark the delineation of pupil to iris was all but lost. Yet their noses evoked the fields of Ireland with a pert Gaelic turn. Not surprisingly, Bree's heritage included all these nationalities—and more. What was surprising was that the mix first occurred on European soil and not in the great melting pot of America. Those of the Craft married only others of the clan, no matter what the heritage.

The name Sobole was from the ancestral great-grandfather who made his way from the fields of France. He brought his bride from Austria to the heart of Pennsylvania via, as for so many others, Ellis Island. Unnoticed in the throngs that passed through the island's immigration facilities were the dozens of men and women, all handsome and healthy, all young and childless, who stayed close together, who spoke only among themselves. These couples, of whom the Soboles were one, pooled their resources and acquired a sizable tract of fertile land, staking out for themselves a corner of Clarion County, Pennsylvania.

The land was their religion or, to be more precise, a major part of their lore. They were Wicca and revered nature; the balance of the universe was one with every tilling and seeding, every harvest, every birth and every death. They planted and prospered, their crops abundant and their vineyards hardy. A growing list of wine buyers waited each year for the new vintage to be ready. What the clan was not one with was the annexation of land by neighboring towns and the resultant taxation levied by jealous city planners whose own fields would not reap the rich crops theirs did. Neither were they one with the town marshals who insisted their children attend public schools, nor could they deal with the bruised and beaten youngsters who returned home later and later each day.

By the third generation, that of Bree's—and her brother's—mother, the love had been drained from their homes and the life from their remaining land. They dwindled to a fraction of their original number. These few sold what acres were left and moved to the city, where, hidden in the throngs of people, they could find security. A single, small farm remained of the original colony and was open to all clan descendants to visit, to use to renew and refresh drained and battered emotions brought by intense and cluttered living.

Exhausted, Bree was ready for a visit to the farm. The comfortable chair she was sitting in claimed her body and her eyes unfocused. The room blurred before her.

* * *

Michael stared blankly, his eyes riveted on dancing motes of dust in the air. His tension radiated pure static electricity, standing the hairs on his body on end. His unadorned vestment, its worn softness caressing his bare skin, was older than he or anyone else knew. The saffron velvet robe emitted a soft glow of its own, a radiance of cosmic absorption accrued over the many years and many rituals it had seen. At least that's what he paid for.

The large loft space, made ready more than a year ago in anticipation of the coming ceremony—in less than an hour's time—was bare of any normal furnishings other than two ornate, wooden chairs facing each other in front of a tall, multipaned window. Deep golden-yellow drapes covered the wall, though not the windows. An elaborate, marble-topped altar was placed, as rules dictate, in the center of a gold leafed circle painstakingly drawn on the floor.

Michael had planned the ritual down to the smallest movement of his hands, waiting for the call. It came, just hours ago. His mother was finally dying. Clenching his powerful hands so tightly that his onyx ring bit painfully into his palm, Michael surveyed the room. All was exactly in order and only retrieving the girl was delaying the start of the ceremony.

As called for—although an extraordinarily fortuitous coincidence that this day should exactly coincide with the moment of his mother's imminent death—the timing was perfect. It was nearing the tenth hour of the first day of the week, the best possible time. The scent of cinnamon, mace, cloves, and narcissus burned for the hours prescribed, the heavy odor thickly permeating the air.

A unique harmony of the Tattvic cosmic tides should also prove most advantageous, especially with the Vayu Tattva at its apex and in conjunction with the lunar cycle. The records promised this to accord successful results. *Nothing had been overlooked.*

The four cardinal points were carefully drawn on the

golden circle, Michael's own secret name of power was written in the old, unreadable to most, language along the circumference. The mere sight of the circle often frightened new seekers, but Michael's renegade coven feared little. The points themselves were specifically marked, each one carefully wrought with materials obtained at great effort.

North was marked for earth with stones from a crossroad at the longitude and latitude auspiced by the ruling forces—the stones transported across two continents for this occasion.

South was marked for fire with rare red jade from China, jade that had been used before and whose power was known to be true.

East, marked for water, held an earthen bowl of rainwater. The salt that had been added to the water, symbolic of eternity, had been bleached pure by the ocean before the tribes themselves had formed and had passed down through the generations as part of the ruling dowry. And borrowed, if the term could be used, by Michael for the occasion.

West, the last station, belonged to air. It lay marked by a single sprig of mistletoe resting on a small gold plate. The plate, rimmed with symbols so ancient as to be unknown to all of the coven except Michael, would not yet be missed from his mother's possessions. By the time it was noticed missing it would be rightfully his—as would everything his mother possessed in her life.

Outside the circle stood twelve young men, grouped into four sets. Each group of three held responsibility for a cardinal point and faced the element to which they paid homage. Those at earth were clad in a rough-hewn brown cloth, sacking for the wealth of the land. Those at fire stood in red satin, a glossy cloth reflecting the flickering candle flame. Those at water wore blue silk, a shimmery soft fabric that moved like a calm lake. Those at air wore white cotton, a wide and open weave that would not trap the wind. They chanted in a single voice, the sonorous tone rising and falling in perfect unison.

The golden circle itself was covered with thin, knotted strips of untanned doeskin, the north end left open to be tied closed after Michael stepped within—with the girl. The altar also faced north and held a ritual sword reputed to be made from the original trident of Paracelsus. A hickory wand, wrapped in red silk, lay across the sword's well-honed edge.

The ceremony prerequisites had been meticulously handled and the rite itself promised to surpass the planning. A girl of twelve, intact hymen verified, was being readied. Her older brother, knowing her first menstrual blood shed last month qualified her as a woman, felt his younger sister's virginity a small price to pay for Michael's favor—especially since he gave her only a few months before she lost the treasure on the streets, on her own, with no benefit to him.

Even the girl's name bode well for the ceremony: Stella for the stars, for the cosmos, for everything Michael wanted to reach and hold in the palm of his hands.

Stella—although frightened of her brother, the rumors of the coven seeped down like leaking sewage through the neighborhood and kept all but the most perverse at bay—accompanied him to the loft earlier that morning. She was promised a surprise, a treat, and she believed it to be true. Her brother had, on occasion, been kind to her. When she realized where she was, it was too late.

She struggled bitterly—scratching, biting, screaming, cursing in harsh gutter language. Stella's reaction had been anticipated and a Quaalude-laced Pepsi was ready, but without swallowing, she spit the sticky liquid in her brother's face. Laughing, she poured the rest at his feet. Michael was still prepared and her frantic struggles were countered with the pinprick of a hypodermic. Unfortunately, instead of the cached heroin, the only injectable drug available was a livestock sedative that caused hallucinations in humans:

PCP. A small oversight and Michael would find—and punish—whoever used the glassine bags of heroin for their own enjoyment.

Stella's slight form—slender and lithe, small breasts just beginning to bud—was carefully being washed and oiled, the preparatory ritual begun as soon as Stella could be safely neared. A young woman attended the girl. No female members were allowed in Michael's coven, but this sole attendant had served in a previous and successful ceremony. And no man could be allowed to touch the virgin, to taint her, before the moment of her sacrifice.

Stella stood immobile while her slim, almost boyish body was stripped and bathed. The gentle hands that massaged pungent balms onto her soft skin were soothing, inviting, and invested an intentionally erotic touch. Drugged, Stella felt the warmth the hands evoked spread through her body. Stirrings of an arousal with no comparison flowed through her veins. She swayed under the hands, moving into and against the strokes, her own subtle and unconscious gestures directing them to concentrate on her nipples. Then, by stretching, Stella found the hands would move down her body, would reach between her legs, would delicately brush the soft tuft of near blond hair, and would rub the small mound she had just herself discovered. The acolyte knew what fires she was setting and smiled behind her veil, secure in the role she was performing, a role of arousal she was most practiced in. Stella would be ready.

Panels of sheer white silk were knotted and draped from Stella's shoulders to form a tunic. The simple robe clung to the rich oils on the girl's skin, her erect nipples standing small and hard beneath the fabric. Her flat stomach and jutting hipbones were set off by a ribbon tied at her waist.

A single candle burned on the altar and greasy black smoke incongruously poured from the slight flame. Stella was led to the golden circle, where Michael waited impatiently. He bowed to the maiden as befitting her status and, on his knees, untied a strip of doeskin for her to enter. Stella swayed, the effects of the PCP most apparent in her mindless stumble, her half-closed lids, and her slack mouth. The fever dreams that burned behind her sleepy eyes were not visible. Only the heat emanating from her frail body gave any clue to the embers that burned in her slim loins.

Stella passed from the attendant's hands into Michael's. His heart swelled as his eyes drank her in. She was everything required, and more. A virgin who, having celebrated her twelfth birthday, was in her thirteenth year. A magic, perfect number.

Stella stood between Michael and the altar, facing the marble top. Michael moved closer to the woman-child, and as he lifted his hands, his saffron velvet robe fell open. He folded the girl in his arms and drew her to him, his bare skin rubbing against the oiled silk she wore. Her toes not touching the floor, held in place only by Michael's grip, Stella felt his hardness press against her and primal urges stirred in her drugged body.

He slipped his other arm behind her knees and, easily shifting the pliant figure, lifted her. She was weightless, a child in his arms, a priceless treasure to carry to the altar. Laying her down, gently ensuring the candle burned at her head, Michael reached for the small ceremonial sword with his left hand. He stepped back. All was in order.

The harmonious intonation of the chanters stopped abruptly. After a heartbeat's pause the sounds picked up again. Each group of three now began their own round. Discordance welled and filled the loft.

Black smoke from the single candle grew even thicker, massing instead of dissipating, and blanketed the high ceiling behind storm clouds. The room was suddenly cast in brilliant light as liquid fire poured from the black smoke, each flaming drop charged with sizzling energy. Molten lightning, a white-hot fire, flowed in an endless stream directed at Stella but

splashed apart inches before it reached the girl. The
fire force formed a crackling shield that covered, without touching, the still form. The girl's eyes went wide,
the effects of the powerful drug not adequate to counter
her absolute terror as this racing web of pulsing energy
surrounded her.

Michael's own eyes filled with grateful tears. His
choice was accepted. Stella would serve. The force
field dissolved and he moved forward to brush away
the tatters of energy that clung to the girl. His hand
stayed closed on the sword's hilt, ready.

Torn from her stupor, the girl was too terrified to
move and watched the point of the short sword move
nearer and nearer her unprotected body.

Slipping the finely honed edge between the sheer
silk and ribbon, Michael slashed her fragile belt away.
He moved the blade upward, its razor-sharp edge glistening in the candlelight, and cut the simple knots tied
at her shoulders. Spearing the fabric over her heart,
he purposefully drew a single drop of blood. He tossed
the tunic and sword aside. Stella's eyes stayed riveted
to her own nakedness, to the drop of blood that welled
between her slight breasts. She found her voice and
shrieked in terror and anguish.

Stepping between her legs, Michael grasped her
thighs and pulled her to him. His rock-hard member
sprang from between the velvet folds of his robe and
into the velvety warmth between Stella's legs.

Michael's face drew back tightly in a rapacious
smile, his even teeth bared, his dark eyes glinting with
obsidian hardness. He threw his head back and
matched her scream with one of his own, offering the
pairing of cries—one of pain, one of joy—as the only
coupling his masters would ever accept.

Her head fell back in the deeply cushioned chair.
Bree gasped as an electric shock ran through her. The
feeling passed so quickly she was unsure if she had
dreamed the moment, and realizing how tired she truly
was, she let herself drift into a much-needed sleep.

As she sank deeper into the cushions, the heaviness of her body surprised her. Even the knowledge that her exhaustion was more a result of the street encounter than from the full night's work did not stop the weariness from suffusing every inch of her being. And, of course, thinking about her mother . . .

Drifting, the air now tasted cool, sparked by a fresh mountain stream. The sounds of the street phased into the soft sighs of breezes whispered through treetops. Relaxing into the dream, Bree thought, I've never been here. What a wonderful place to rest.

"But, Bree, you have been here before," a melodic voice spoke to her.

Finding that she was able to turn her head, Bree remembered the soft-cushioned chair she rested on . . . somewhere else. "Mother, is that you? Where are you? I want—no, I need to see you so much."

"You shall, my darling, for we are truly one. But because you've taken a path outside our family, no one else recognized you. Look for me. Find me. Draw me down."

In the distance, Bree saw a richly embroidered wine-colored velvet robe, the robe her mother wore for only the most important occasions. The woman wearing the robe was too far away to clearly identify, but the dark, flowing hair—though no longer touched with gray—could only belong to her mother. A cool breeze touched Bree's feet, and looking down, she saw she was barefoot and there was no earth beneath her feet.

"Where are we, Mother? I know I've never been here before."

"I took you here when you were nine, my child. We held hands as you fell asleep, and I promised you then that you would travel to places known only to a few. We stayed until it was time for you to wake. How could you forget?"

"I do remember . . . but that was only a dream, Mother. No, I thought that was only a dream." With wonder, Bree looked about her. "It was real. We walked through the clouds and parted them, like this . . ."

Remembering the motion, Bree moved her hand in a graceful sweeping gesture.

The mist parted to reveal a white double door—a door twice her height and wider than her arms' breadth, made of the purest marble laid with precious stones and hinged with solid gold. Reaching out, Bree pushed gently at the door, her slight touch all that was needed to open it wide. Bree stepped through and immediately knew where she was: she was in her mother's bedroom. Acolytes surrounded the narrow bed where a very still figure lay closely covered, blankets tightly drawn to the woman's chin, scant protection against the chill emanating from the slight form.

A cold terror slashed through Bree. "No, you can't be dying." Bree heard her own voice crack.

"My body is already dead. They'll know in a moment, and they'll know to look outside this room for the chosen one. Be ready for them, Bree."

The thought burned on Bree's brow; the chill radiated through her body. Bree's eyes closed but still saw as her mother reached out with both arms to embrace her. Knowing only the love she felt, Bree opened her arms to capture the essence of the woman she treasured more than any other. They came together.

The cold disappeared as liquid fire coursed through Bree, reaching her heart, her center. Visible flames incinerated the dark-blue robe Bree wore and splashed red and gold on her flawless skin. The fire tenderly licked and caressed, circling her body in sinking spirals, reaching deep inside her, pulsing brighter and hotter.

Unbearable pleasure filled Bree. As her arms closed to embrace the warmth, Bree found herself clutching her mother's claret-colored robe. A final burst turned her vision white with heat, her mother's voice reaching her through the growing sound of waves crashing in a storm.

"It's your robe now, my darling. Wear it well."

"Don't leave me, Mother," Bree whispered, fighting to control the new power surging from her every cell. "Please don't leave me. I know it's time, but please stay with me awhile longer."

"Go now. Go and let the body rest so the spirit will be strong." Her mother's soft voice began to fade. "I'll be with you again."

Closing the gem-encrusted door to her mother's room, Bree locked in all that she had drawn down. What passed to her—the knowledge, the lore, the power—was as if it always had been a part of her consciousness, her being. Finding her weary way home through time and space was a simple task; rejoining her sleeping self was like slipping into a warm bath.

The heat Bree brought back to her dozing body quickened the settling sleep. She clutched tightly at the deep-red velvet robe she now wore and fell into a deep and dreamless slumber. Her mother's voice, far in the distance, called back to her.

"Rest. You must be strong for what you have to do. She will need you—very soon."

4

THE SCATTERED REMAINS OF THEIR MEXICAN DIN-
ner littered the table. Jeff refused to allow the hovering
waiter to clear away a single plate until they had finished every daub of mole sauce and folded every mor-
sel of fajita into the extra tortillas they ordered. The
guacamole now completely devoured, the last vestige
of yogurt scraped from the bowl, Jeff sat back and
watched Elise wipe a final crumb from her mouth.

"Another margarita, perhaps, one for the road?"
he asked, feigning the twirl of an imaginary mustache.

"Fortunately our road consists of walking four
blocks, though I think we might have difficulty maneuvering the park paths. If you're trying to soften me
up, you're sure doing a great job," Elise sighed. "Take
an exhausted girl to a spicy dinner, be sure she 'stuf-
focates' herself into a catatonic state, and ply her with
tequila. It works every time."

Looking surprised, Jeff responded with a straight
face. "I didn't know I still had to soften you up. I'd
always thought that once you married them, they're
yours for life, to do with as you please."

"Just try that, mister, and see how far you get. I'll
go for the bribe. Order the margarita."

Drinks ordered and table cleared, satisfied just to be
in each other's company, the couple sat back in con-
tented silence. Judging the peaceful moment as appropriate, Jeff leaned forward and took Elise's hand in
his.

"Darling," he began gently, "the other night you
mentioned your sister." Feeling her hand tense under

64

his, Jeff continued to stroke her palm and, pulling her hand to his face, kissed the fingertips. "I'm just curious. I love you, and as your husband, your lover, and especially as your friend, I want to know more about you."

A dense silence covered the table. Long moments passed while Elise searched Jeff's face. Satisfied, perhaps, with what she saw, or just resigned to confession, she answered.

"Jeff, it's not just my sister—my twin sister. There's a whole gray area of my life that sometimes—most of the time—I just don't want to think about. You are my friend, my very best friend, and I hope you always will be. Maybe that's why I don't want to talk about Talia, and well, I'm not even really sure what I don't want to talk about. Or why. It just seems as if my childhood, growing up, was something I read about and didn't really live."

Relaxing, Jeff smiled and reached for Elise's other hand. "I think I know what you mean. Sometimes I feel as if my life began when I met you. But you've met my family and sometimes I think you know more about me than I know about myself. I just want to know more about you. At least now I know your sister's name. Talia. Elise and Talia. They're both unusual, beautiful names. If your sister is as special as you are, I can understand why your mother gave you almost magical names."

A sharp intake of breath from Elise shattered the budding confidentiality. "Magic has nothing to do with it. They're family names. Our grandmother was Elise Margay and our great-grandmother Talia Dora."

"Sounds like a little matriarchy in the works, there," Jeff teased. "Do you have any brothers?"

"No." A shadow cast over Elise's face. "But I thought you were interested in my sister."

"I'm interested in you, darling, and because of that, I'm interested in everything that has to do with you. Having a twin is usually considered special. I'm just surprised I haven't been introduced."

"I don't know where Talia is. She could be any-where—from New Caledonia to Siberia to across town. Though I think I'd know if she were nearby." A trace of uncertainty crept into Elise's voice. "At least, I hope I would."

"Of course you'd know if she were nearby," Jeff prompted, still puzzled over the mystery in which he knew his wife was shrouding over the conversation. "I'm sure you'd be in touch. Twins, even when they argue, are almost always close."

"We were very close." The margaritas arrived, and using the opportunity to fuss with the table arrange-ment, Elise took a deep swallow of the icy whipped drink before continuing.

"Closer than most of the classic texts note about twins. We lived alone with Mother and had no outside friends. Before then, we only had each other. All those moments that a girl might normally experience with any number of friends, well, we only had the other to share with. Sometimes we couldn't stand being to-gether—not even in the same room. But what was worse, we couldn't bear to be apart."

To Jeff's confusion, Elise began to recite information as if lecturing. All warmth left her voice and a stiff, rehearsed quality took over.

"When you have two pubescent girls living in unu-sually close quarters, they begin to share similar man-ifestations. Darwin's cousin, Francis Galton, was the first to scientifically study twins, and he perceived that the lives of twins seem to lie under a sort of destiny or fatality, one that was wholly constitutional and in-born. He concluded that even with twins separated at an early age, between the balance of nature and nur-ture, nature was stronger. Talia and I shared both na-ture and nurture. We did everything together: played together, studied together, even shared the same dou-ble bed. I . . ." For a moment the normal warmth in Elise's voice returned. "I remember that closeness, at least before our high-school days." Catching herself, as if she'd strayed from a very specific outline, Elise continued.

"Talia menstruated first and I followed by a month. Yet"—Elise's voice again broke away from the singsong pattern—"it was always her cramps I felt. I felt her blood flowing before my own."

"Elise, what's the matter? You keep sounding like a textbook—not a person."

"Sometimes the only way I can deal with who I am is to be completely clinical about the subject."

"But we're not talking about a laboratory study. We're talking about you—and your sister."

Elise looked at her husband, unable—or unwilling—to break the tension.

Jeff saw this and kept pushing, determined to reach deeper, to pull this strangeness from his wife—with his bare hands if he could.

"It sounds like you and your sister shared a highly developed empathy for each other. As a doctor, Elise, you know that's very common among young girls, especially adolescent girls. Even with friends that aren't related. It's more than normal—I'd say it was expected, especially under the circumstances—for you and your twin sister to bond so closely."

Elise met his gaze with steady, clear eyes. "You're right. It's an area I specifically researched in med school. Which is why and how I sound like a textbook." A smile touched the corners of her mouth. "The twin relationship is the closest known tie between two individuals, but often good friends just entering their teens can have an almost psychic bond. It usually ends, or breaks, with dating, when one or both of the girls begin to transfer her feelings and thoughts to a boy."

"Is that what happened to you and Talia? You started dating and with the first kiss the bond was broken?"

A smile briefly touched Elise's mouth. "Almost on the button. We were finally allowed to go to school. The elders in our church tutored us at home and our work was good—as it turned out, our work was very good. The elders were good teachers and I guess being schooled without peer distraction can be very productive. There were no scholastic problems for entering high school. We were both tested and did very well.

"The only problem that developed was in our closeness. The first year at school we were inseparable. We walked to school together, had all the same classes, sat together, ate together, studied together, and of course, went home together. We almost never talked to anyone else.

"Then a boy talked to us. We were in the library, studying. Talia was especially good with words, she always had been. She was working on a short story for English class and I had my nose buried in a biology textbook. His name was Jason. I don't think he knew which of us he wanted to talk to, so he sat down facing us, directly in the middle. He was tall and gangly, but underneath his mop of blond hair you could see something special, especially in his eyes. They were deep blue, bright and clear, and when he looked at us, there was a sincerity, an honesty. His heart flooded into his face. I liked him right away. Talia took one look at him and I felt the shock wave she gave off. It was one of the last things I ever felt with her, or from her."

"Now, that sounds perfectly natural. In fact, I can't imagine anything sounding more normal. Your sister spotted a boy—it sounds like her first boy—and left you in the dust. Though why he didn't know enough to talk to you first I can't imagine. No matter what Talia looked like, she couldn't have shone like you do."

"It does sound pretty mundane, doesn't it? As far as looks, Talia and I were born identical—yet there was always a difference. We could spend the same amount of time outdoors and I would tan while her skin stayed creamy. My hair would get blond from the sun, hers would seem to darken. And I always weighed a few pounds more than she did. By the time we were in high school I don't think anyone took us for twins. We were just sisters."

"Why haven't you kept in touch? Did Talia marry her young man and have a house full of children? You said you didn't know where she was, but you must have some idea, at least through you aunt."

"She didn't marry Jason. She didn't want to, though he asked her at graduation. He pursued Talia relentlessly, following her everywhere, until she turned against him and . . . Well, none of this is important. Jason didn't marry anyone either. Our mother died in our last year of high school. I went to live with Aunt Phylis. I don't know where Talia went. We had a, an argument after Jason—I mean, Mother died. It was bitter." A shudder carried from Elise's shoulders through to her hands, still held in Jeff's.

"Darling, sisters do fight. All sisters have fights. You two must have been some exception to the rule not to have had any disagreements until high school." Jeff's soothing tone elicited a small smile on Elise's drawn face.

"I know all of this, intellectually. It's just . . . Well, a lot has to do with those 'gray areas' I mentioned. When Talia and I were in high school, I became, for the first time, my own person. Especially after she discovered Jason. They were as inseparable as we had been. The odd part is I didn't resent it at all, not when I discovered how free I really was. For the first time I could think clearly, by myself. I would walk home by myself and see the world around me. It was wonderful just watching, feeling, the change of seasons. Sometimes I'd stop and begin to wish I had someone to share it with. But then I realized, if Talia were there, I'd be seeing everything through her eyes—and that wasn't as pretty, as peaceful, as my way."

"You make it sound like Talia took over your life. I can't imagine that happening, not with you. You're too full a person, too whole, for anyone to affect you like that."

"I can't really explain it. Before then, before high school, when we were alone with Mom, it's just not clear. I can remember what the house looked like and

I can remember the woods around the house. I can even remember the places we would walk. One path led to a small stream and one to . . . well, to someplace we used to play.

"It's like watching your life in a mirror, but it's Talia I see in the mirror, not me. It's as if I wasn't always really there, as if I was a dream of hers. I have a picture, a photograph taken of Talia and me when we must have been eleven or so. I not only don't remember having the picture taken, but I don't remember the dresses we were wearing or anything else about that time or place."

The hovering waiter returned to clear the emptied coffeecups. The disappearing desert dish with traces of flan long ago eaten prompted Jeff. "Anything else before they insist we pay the bill for both the food and rental of the table?"

"We have been here awhile. Almost three hours—it's after eleven. If we quit now, while we're minimally ahead, we can roll ourselves home. It's been a long day and I'm ready for a warm tub and a soft bed."

"Damn. I forgot to turn on the hot water after the boiler was adjusted." Guilt shadowed Jeff's face, a face also showing signs of the long day. "Will you settle for a soft bed?"

"Only if you warm the bed for me. I've got to get some service around here." Elise's infectious laughter caused the only other couple left in the restaurant to look up and smile.

"Your wish is my command. A short walk home and a shorter hop into a warm bed." Moving quickly to behind Elise's chair, Jeff held it as she rose. "And if there's any other service I can provide, m'lady must be sure to let me know."

"M'lady will be sure to let you know."

Jeff smiled at his wife, loving her completely, feeling he now knew her better. He remembered how they would walk together on a beach, or sit by a fresh mountain stream with baited fishing poles hopelessly tangled. Their times together had been filled with peace and harmony, always of the here and now, and they had rarely talked about anything that didn't relate to them at that specific moment. They both knew, almost from the start, that their futures were together, with each other, and the need to plan their lives, in minute detail—or to review the past—never developed. Elise hadn't known he had any family wealth until they graduated college and she first visited his home on Long Island. She'd been overwhelmed by the house and its furnishings but soon relaxed and, knowing his father from the campus clinic, continued to charm the senior Dr. Vaughan.

Jeff often gave thanks to whatever gods may be for the lunch date his father made with him on that memorable day—the day he'd bumped into Elise when she was leaving the clinic.

Jeff and Elise gathered their coats and scarfs from the pegs along the back wall and murmured words of praise for the chef to the cashier, and they soon found themselves crossing the park. The silence between them was comfortable; yet, as they turned into their block, Elise stopped and put her hand on Jeff's arm.

"Jeff, something came up tonight while we were talking. You joked about it, and it's something I honestly hadn't given much thought to until you did. You called my family a matriarchy. It was. We were two sisters, no brothers. My father left us when we were born—at least that's what my mother told us. She said that he 'denied us,' but never explained what that meant. My grandmother died just after we were born and there were no other relatives. Aunt Phylis wasn't a blood relative, just a wealthy—at least by backwoods standards—church elder. Phylis told me that my mother and grandmother and great-grandmother, if not a few generations farther back, were each the only issue of their generation. Did you know—no, how could you?—that Crawford is my mother's name? I don't even know my father's name."

Jeff kissed Elise on her nose, a gesture he had begun, much to her amusement, to distract her whenever she worried excessively about anything. "Why don't you look on your birth certificate?"

"You know—no, you don't know—I don't have one." A sheepish look crept onto Elise's face. "Mountain folk sometimes were a bit lax in their record-keeping. Aunt Phylis has a bible listing all the congregations' births and deaths for generations, and she entered mine and Talia's when we were born. That's how you and I got our marriage license—Phylis had a certificate issued based on the bible records. It's not all that uncommon where I grew up."

"But," he asked, the question still nagging at his sense of order, "the bible must list your father's name."

"It doesn't, Jeff. It only traces the women in my family."

Jeff looked confused. "It's an odd coincidence, Elise, but as a doctor, you know it's impossible to have generations of predetermined and exclusive sex. There were, most likely boys born who . . . well, died early. Hunting accidents. Even you admit that the record-keeping in your Kentucky woods wasn't that accurate."

"I didn't say it wasn't accurate, Jeff; I said it wasn't official. We were miles from a hospital and, anyway, most women didn't birth in hospitals."

Holding Elise close, Jeff felt a trace of the confusion he knew she was experiencing. "Well, we'll just have to produce a house full of sons to balance out your family tree."

"I hope so, Jeff. I hope so. More than anything, I want that. And I want all our sons to have your eyes, and your nose and your mouth and your chin—"

"Enough!" Laughing, Jeff stopped at their steps. "Shall I carry you across the threshold?"

Cheered from her bleak mood, Elise shook her head. "No, I don't want to worry about your slipping a disc or something worse—especially for so young and virile a husband. That reminds me. With our different last names I'm thinking about a Mr. and Mrs. sign right under our doctors' shingle. Not only to stop the neighbors from talking, but I think it's time to begin breaking my family tradition—a bit.''

"First thing in the morning, I'll have the sign made. And let me tell you something else. You'd better like the sign, because it's going to be up a long, long time."

Focused spotlights shone hotly on the scattered papers and handwritten notes covering every inch of the corner desk. The rest of the cell-culture area was noticeably dimmer, allowing for an ultraviolet-light viewing at the autoradiograph.

"Your reputation precedes you, Dr. Blaiser," Frank Jordan said from directly behind the engrossed research associate.

Bill Blaiser was startled; his hand, holding a vial of DNA plasmid, jerked away from the gel screen. The glass vial crashed to the floor.

"Damn it, can't you knock like every one else?'' Bill Blaiser reached for a cardboard canister and efficiently began sprinkling a color-coded absorbent on the spill, marking the spot for the cleaning crew. "Or is sneaking up on people a product of your secret government training?''

"I was just checking the facility and was surprised to see the light," Jordan answered, taking a small step back from the accident, "until I remembered the work binges you seem to thrive on. I didn't mean to alarm you." He looked at his wet shoes, and a concerned look crossed Jordan's face. "That sample didn't contain anything harmful, did it?''

Blaiser pushed the glass fragments aside with his foot. "Well, it was the last of the HIV virus we had replicated. I guess I'll have to go back to the old centrifuge for more.''

"HIV? Oh, my God, not that!'' Jordan stood frozen to the spot, his eyes wide and glued to the stain on his shoes. "How you can even go near the AIDS virus is beyond me, mush less . . . Damn you! You're not wearing gloves or mask . . . That wasn't HIV, was it?'' Jordan nonetheless decided to play it safe and stepped back still farther. "What are you working on that couldn't wait until morning?"

Bill Blaiser pointed to the back-lit screen. Vertical bands of varying widths stood in rows, clearly spaced to indicate three sets of two rows each. The last set was incomplete.

"This is a fate map. Each of these sets compares a particular individual's DNA, specifically their nuclear DNA''—Blaiser pointed to the left-hand row—"with the same individual's mitochondrial DNA. As you can see in both these completed pairings, the similarities are unmistakable—with the exception of these bands in the southern region and the additional factor in each of the MtDNA maps. I was just about to complete the trio when you so rudely interrupted."

Jordan carefully studied the gel-based fragments. "It is interesting. I thought our DNA structure was constant, that is, within an individual."

"The nuclear DNA is," Blaiser answered, warming to his role, "but not the MtDNA, which is found only in the cytoplasm and inherited exclusively from the mother. This is the mother''—Blaiser pointed to the first grouping's right-hand column—"and this''—pointing to the corresponding column in the next set—"is the daughter. The two maps are so close that at first they appear identical, but the different factors are there. You know the MtDNA is our primary research area." Bill Blaiser looked steadily at Frank Jordan, the pleasure in playing instructor to a layman dissipated with the memory of their earlier meeting. "Our research and our findings, Mr. Jordan. Like the study you're stealing from us to deliver to some second-rate research team."

"That's a pretty heavy accusation, Dr. Blaiser. If you'd read your contract—"

"Save it. I heard you earlier. But that doesn't change the outcome."

Jordan pursed his lips, shaking his head in obvious

disbelief at the scientist's obtuseness. "You don't realize the practical aspects, Dr. Blaiser."

"Spare me. Right now the only practical aspect I have to deal with is washing up, changing this contaminated lab coat, and running a fresh sample in the ultracentrifuge. You did ruin the last remaining sample. Then, thanks to you, I have to wait another two hours for the MtDNA to isolate." Stripping his soiled jacket off, Blaiser pushed through the swinging doors, paused, and turned to look back. "I'd also appreciate it if you were gone when I return. This makes twice today you've thrown a monkey wrench into my plans. And you know what they say about a third strike."

Jordan nodded curtly and began to follow the scientist out. As his hand hit the door, catching it on the first swing back, his head snapped around to the row of centrifuge machines lining the far wall. The single ultracentrifuge, its small red power light attesting to its readiness, stood open. Calculating the time the scientist would need to complete his ablutions, Jordan strode across the floor to the large unit. Peering down into the single tub, lined with four inches of solid steel, he reached out to the delicately balanced titanium rotor blades.

"They also say the third time is the lucky charm, Dr. Blaiser."

Scrubbed clean, Bill Blaiser stood at the door to the cell-culture area, peering through wired glass. The room was empty—no Frank Jordan in sight to mar the procedure. Opening his assigned incubator, Blaiser took the covered petri dish he wanted from the tray, drew a small sample into a fresh vial, and returned the dish.

This particular sample had been replicated numerous times over the past months, more times than the facility was even aware of. The unknown woman it came from was alive, here in covered petri dishes in everyone's incubator. She was also alive, Blaiser knew, at home in his own small lab. She might also be alive in the real world. He hoped she was, as he had never seen or even imagined that such a wide disparity of the MtDNA fingerprint was possible; he was determined to find the secrets the factor held. Incubate and replicate, day after day. But now he had to move fast. Time was running out.

Crossing the room, he placed the single vial in the ultracentrifuge, checked the rotor's balance to within a tenth of a gram, and turned the setting to 80,000 RPMs. A small, boyish grin crossed his face; he'd lied about the processing taking two hours. He could stand here on one leg for the few minutes it actually took. Flicking the ON switch, Blaiser practiced standing on one leg, the same silly smile still stuck to his face as he projected what her bands would look like and how they would compare to his other chartings.

A soft beep caught his attention, and turning, he began to walk the short distance to the phone. From behind him, a deafening roar was accompanied by a shock wave that hurled him halfway across the laboratory. A mass of pressure pushed him back as the floor buckled under him. Instantaneously, a sharp pain wrenched his left shoulder—a direct hit of something shot at a high velocity. Hitting the ground face-first, Blaiser folded his arms over his head, a reflex action from his peace marching days which now saved him numerous cuts from the onslaught of metal and glass fragments that continued to shower around him.

After an eternity, moments later, all was quiet. Blaiser cautiously looked up and then around. Racks of equipment lay crushed on the floor, tangled and broken. The disabled ultracentrifuge—a deceptive piece of equipment looking like a simple top-loading washing machine but in reality the most well-armored piece of equipment in the entire facility—stood with its lid ripped open. The lid's thick rubber vacuum seals had torn off or disintegrated, a chunk of which rubber had solidly hit him beneath his shoulder blade. There was a warped, outward bulge in the four-inch-thick steel drum.

Moving nearer the unit, planning to pull the plug from the heavy-duty electrical outlet, Bill Blaiser gasped in amazement. The unit's lid, buckled and pitted, had a hole he could fit his hand through—a gaping rent that faced the spot he had been standing on just moments ago. He looked through the hole into the drum; the twisted mass of rotors resembled the spines of a wrecked umbrella with one rotor missing from the tangle. His eyes followed the trajectory anything shooting through the hole would have taken, and he sighted the missing titanium blade embedded in the far wall.

Backing out of the room, Blaiser rang for the biosafety coordinator. Let her try to explain this mess as an unbalanced axis or chipped rotor. This was no way to end a long day.

5

NED HARPER STOOD IN FRONT OF THE ANTIQUE BEV-
eled mirror, knotting his tie for the third time. The
tie's gray-and-blue abstract design finally hung to his
satisfaction, and knowing that all the details like
sharply creased slacks, perfectly laundered shirt, and
highly polished shoes were attended to, he stood back
for an overall inspection. Six foot, reasonably lean—
after all, he thought, a man of forty-five is entitled to
a few extra ounces, well, pounds maybe—and graying
at the temples. A soft grin picked up one corner of his
mouth as he brushed back his hair. It was, he reflected, as if he had specified "gray at the temples for
a distinguished touch but leave the rest of the hair full
and dark." He hadn't, but it had, to his advantage,
turned out that way.

Many things had turned to Ned Harper's advantage
in the last few years. After ten years in the state senate, representing his Long Island constituency—years
he had come to think of as his lean years—his name
had come to light in his party. As chairman of the
study Commission on Toxic Waste Disposal, a position his wife had urged him to assume, he'd issued a
scathing report that not only resulted in statewide public furor but became the basis for proposed legisla-
tion—since written and enacted. His name and face in
the limelight, the temptation to abandon his Long Island state seat came soon after, six years ago, when
an appointment to a vacant United States Senate seat
was seductively dangled before him. Accepting, in turn
leaving his own seat vacant, he'd taken his father-in-

law's advice to locate in a power city; he and his wife kept their island home but moved their primary residence to Manhattan. It had been uphill ever since. His speeches were noticed . . . and quoted; his appearance at any function was an assurance the event would always appear in print, and often on television. His star was clearly on the rise.

Tonight's dinner, a vital appearance in his just-announced quest for the gubernatorial race was, he was inexplicably sure, just the beginning of his path to the White House. He was the party's choice and there was nothing, and no one, in the way. Even the present governor—the man who backed his U.S. Senate seat—was retiring. By agreeing to stay out of the race the governor was, in effect, offering Ned his endorsement.

Then again, there was his wife, Holly. There was always his wife, Holly. Not being sure if she was a help—with her insatiable drive—or a hindrance—for the same reason—Ned saw no reason to dwell on what was, at best, a tedious situation. It hadn't always been that way. Holly had singled him out in law school and married him two weeks after he passed the bar and one week before he was hired by a prestigious Wall Street law firm as the youngest, highest-paid corporate-law associate ever to join the firm. A slew of rumors tied Holly's father's connections to Ned's fortuitous employment, but never one to look a gift horse in the mouth, Ned had done his best to ignore the subtle innuendos as well as the outright accusations.

Ned knew Holly's singling him out was too kind a turn of the phrase; it implied that he was the only one she ever had her eye on, or that she had shown an immediate and steadfast attraction and allegiance to him. Ned Harper was, in fact, one of a half-dozen budding attorneys Holly Varley had divided her time between, waiting and watching to see which direction they were headed. Half the flock was crossed off her hit list when they chose to develop their careers by starting off in Legal Aid or some other equally repugnant or altruistic way. Ned sometimes, and only sometimes, reflected that he, too, could have made that choice and been spared the years that followed. All in all, though, the trade was more than fair.

The first decade he spent with the firm of Varley, Thomas and Cummings had been easily tolerable, thanks to the regularly increasing salary and growing status that he brought home. The exhausting twelve-hour days spent earning it and the three-hour commute was also a benefit; he wasn't required to be at home, listening to his wife's eternal prattle or actively entertaining the endless list of friends and acquaintances. Holly took charge of all social details, exceptionally well Ned admitted, and all that was required was his occasional appearance at an event or two of her choosing. Their North Shore Long Island home was a showplace and Holly's vast social circle easily filled the void of marital intimacy.

The next decade had proved that professional life gets progressively easier the closer one nears the top. During that time Ned's office attendance was required but not always mandatory, and the occasional court appearance mere icing to his already polished image. All helpful criteria in developing his—or were they Holly's?—political aspirations.

Turning to the chaise longue on which Holly reclined, stretched as if waiting for the photographer to capture her meticulously cared-for being, Ned pulled back his shoulders and pulled in his slight paunch.

"Well, I'm ready. What do you think?"

"That tie simply does nothing with the suit," Holly noted, her slight eye movement barely requiring her to lift her mane of frosted blond hair from the position required to minutely examine the shape and color of each fingernail.

"Holly, my love, you've watched me struggling with this tie for the last thirty minutes. Why didn't you say something then? Did you think it would change and be 'right' after I finally got it tied?"

"Darling, I really didn't notice until you called my

attention to it. Here, let me choose.'' Rising with practiced grace to make the choice that was tantamount to a royal decree, Holly brushed off the skirt of one of her seemingly endless supply of designer gowns. She was careful not to mar the perfect manicure. Ned's closet reflected her meticulous supervision of the household, each article of clothing carefully hung with others of its like in an organized range of colors and tones. Reaching for the tie rack on the far wall, Holly's hand unerringly chose a discrete abstract, the one tie he probably owned that precisely picked up the smoky gray of the suit and highlighted the blue of Ned's eyes. "Try this, darling. I think it'll be a tad better.'' A self-sufficing smile played at the corners of her lips. "After all, appearances are everything, aren't they?''

Appearances, to Holly, were sacrosanct. Image was the inviolable symbol of status, and not to be taken lightly. The move to the city after finally achieving the suburban manor she considered her just due had not been borne without a trace of resentment. Their new home was a historic landmark on a tree-lined street, but the river view, in her opinion, was only accessible from the bedroom. The main salon looked out on the rooftops, and despite the fact that Ned considered the view charming—a touch of Paris, he noted—she found it terribly gauche; a few mimosa trees did not make up for acres of carefully tended grounds. She felt cramped in the crowded eight rooms on two floors despite the fact that they were, without exception, large rooms, and the unfinished third floor remained a thorn in Holly's side. When she showed the house to her friends, however, the third floor became "just so much room we didn't know what to do with it all.''

After discovering that her circle of friends considered the town house not only attractive but desirable, Holly's carefully controlled anger at the choice and location—she accepted the move but it wasn't the Fifth or Park Avenue co-op her heart was set on—subsided and her energy in restoring the brownstone's turn-of-the-century grandeur knew no bounds. Eventually the

third floor would be guest rooms, especially since she
had successfully navigated past the dangerous years of
required childbearing.

Holly was at her prime—physically, emotionally, and
socially. It was widely rumored, behind Ned's back,
that his appointment was to be credited not so much
to Ned's ability as to one bearing the imprint of Holly's
fine touch . . . and that of her father's. Her drive behind her husband's political career was well-known,
and respected.

Maintaining her looks—face and figure—was her
only other preoccupation, and maintaining her nail
lacquer was more important than assisting her carefully chosen and nurtured husband, who now struggled with the second tie.

Ned Harper has been a good choice, Holly thought
as she checked her evening purse for all the necessary
touch-up and emergency equipment. She knew she
might have been able to do better, but even Ned's
weaknesses were to her advantage. His overall lack of
direction was a perfectly designed match for her willful and goal-directed objective to place herself as first
lady. The Governor's Mansion, to Holly, was only the
first step. Yet, she admitted, Ned was a thoughtful and
thorough individual in any appointed task. His assign-
ments with her father's law firm had proved this to her
and had saved her from facing a messy divorce and
having to choose over.

Ned's reflection now showed a nattily attired individual who looked every inch the political aspirant he
was—inside and out. Knowing his wife's taste was, in
fact, impeccable did not prevent Ned from reprimand-
ing her, albeit under his breath, for not participating
earlier in creating the image she was determined he
present.

"Finished." Ned turned to his wife, his irritation
barely mollified. "Let's go. We're already running
late. If I haven't got this tie on right, T.D. will tell
me—and probably offer to fix it."

Holly bristled, but the momentary flash of anger was

covered quickly. "Yes," she smoothly countered, "T.D. is always most helpful, isn't she? Always Ms. Johnny-on-the-Spot with just the right phrase to drop to the press or just the right introduction. And always wearing just the right perfume." Holly paused, smiling wryly to herself. "Actually, darling, she is a gem. A bit of a bitch at times, but an absolute prize jewel. I almost wish I'd found her for you, then you'd have me to thank. She's been with us about four years now, hasn't she?"

Disarmed by his wife's acceptance of what he'd thrown as a intentional barb, Ned relaxed noticeably. Checking the freestanding, full-length dressing mirror—a heavily carved, ornate antique gift from Holly's parents—he smiled at his wife's perfect reflection.

"It's five years. But I didn't find her—she found me. I mean us."

Ned paused. He clearly remembered T.D. the day she first came into the old storefront campaign headquarters. It was after his near disastrous debate with Joe Collins, the summer before his first election in the city. He was ready to throw in the towel after the Collins' intraparty debate and could still recall the precinct meeting with absolute clarity: Collins' dusty storefront off Ocean Parkway in Brooklyn, the streaked windows and creaky folding chairs, the clouds of acrid cigar and cigarette smoke, and last but far from least, the debate topic—tenant-protection laws. Coming from Long Island, the last issue he had a good handle on was something as urban-focused as renters' rights. Collins decimated him in front of everyone—half the county committee members in the district.

The next day T.D. walked in carrying a newspaper. He looked up from his desk and all he could focus on was the headline HARPER FALTERS IN COLLINS' DEBATE. Finally, when he was able to see the stunning woman behind the newspaper, she asked if any volunteer campaign help was needed. He couldn't imagine needing any more staff—much less keeping the existing staff. Who would want to sign up with a 'fal-

tering' team? But she did, and she settled right in. If
Collins hadn't been caught in that illegal-alien work
scandal the next week, no matter how strongly it was
denied, he might not have needed any help for at least
the next four years.

"Now I remember," Holly commented, oddly on
the same train of thought. Her voice cut sharply
through his reverie. "That *was* strange, wasn't it?
After all, Joe Collins was known for his clean slate—
almost to the point of caricature. You know, the white-
knight crusader."

"I always worry when someone seems too perfect,"
Ned answered. "It's a sure sign they're hiding something."

"Oh. Like your T.D." Holly's retort was automatic, and before the few words were out she regretted
them. No need to choose sides—not now, she cautioned herself.

Holly's acid comment had exactly the effect she
wanted to avoid and stirred Ned to further the praise
he was lavishing. "T.D.'s different. She helped with
small things at first. Typing a speech my campaign
manager drafted, making subtle changes. So subtle at
first that my campaign manager—it was Howard Duncan at the time—was more than willing to accept the
entire speech as his own creation."

But Ned had noticed the slight shift of emphasis
T.D. inserted and he became even more impressed
when the newspaper coverage of the speech focused
on just the areas she had highlighted. Even Howard
had been excited, convinced it was Ned's presentation
of the speech. Ned joked about it at the time, telling
Howard that he was such a wiz manager he could just
draft out speeches in the future—T.D. was such a
crackerjack typist she would produce the finished copy.
Howard had been flattered, a state of being that lasted
about six months, until he noticed that the typed ver-
sions were varying further and further from his original submission. And then he made the fatal mistake
of complaining.

That was the beginning of the end for Howard and the point when T.D. came into her own. In a bitter argument the issue boiled down to Howard's ultimatum: "It's either her or me."

Made part of the salaried staff, T.D. was an able communications director. A new campaign manager was brought in from a successful Boston consulting firm and the professionalism of his new manager, and of course communication director, was unbeatable. Howard Duncan could never have done as well; T.D. was responsible for it coming together.

As far as Ned Harper was concerned, it also marked the turning point from his being just another senator mentioned in passing in the news to his being the one who was most often quoted, the one who made the headlines, the one who caught the public's pulse and imagination. It was more than her just being good at what she did—T.D. was his charm. If he was being superstitious, it didn't matter. She was his talisman; whenever T.D. had input into the situation, it went right.

"Is the car ready?" Holly inquired, so intensely involved in adjusting her pearls that she had entirely missed her husband's lapse of attention. The question itself was merely protocol. She knew that the car was standing at the curb, driver at the wheel, and that Ned would never again make her wait. The one time he had failed to tell the driver to be in the car, on alert, at least a half hour before any scheduled departure, she had refused to accompany Ned to a formal and very important dinner. He had looked foolish showing up alone and couldn't use the pat excuse of her not being well as she'd spent the afternoon in the public eye, fit and well, judging a local art show. Now, like a well-trained politician, Ned knew enough to keep his constituents happy, in particular, her.

"Yes, dear," Ned replied, checking his watch, fortunately as unaware of Holly's thought process as she was of his, "it's been ready for an hour now."

Scooping up her fox jacket—a coat, she reasoned,

would appear ostentatious, but the jacket was, well
almost a fun fur—Holly opened the bedroom door,
one of the few doors she encountered that she would
ever open or close for herself.

Following his wife down the carpeted stairs to the
foyer, Ned watched her slender figure move gracefully
beneath the clinging dress. Where, he wondered, had
his physical need for her gone? She was desired by
most of the men he knew, he saw it in their eyes and
heard them speak admiringly, sometimes almost reverently, about her. There was no question as to his
needing her, but now it was as a public partner. She
was right for him; she knew exactly how to present
herself and, he didn't hide the truth from himself, how
to shape his image. Even more important, she intuitively knew whom to nurture to their advantage and
with whom to avoid public connections or contact.
Holly focused her entire life on being the perfect politician's wife and achieved this multifaceted goal with
great aplomb.

She was true to him—in order to be true to herself.

I've been faithful to her, Ned thought. Yet this power
that's within my grasp is stirring a more primal need.
Holly may be too perfect—too cool and too collected—to touch, but I need to feel her under me, feel
her legs wrap around me, hear her moan with pleasure. Pulling his coat from the foyer closet, Ned
shrugged into the soft camel cashmere. Reaching out
to gently grasp his wife's bared shoulder, he pulled
Holly close. "For luck tonight," Ned hoarsely whispered, thinking not only of the formal announcement
of his candidacy but of later, in his freshly made double bed, and met her surprised lips with his.

"My God, man, I've spent an hour making up and
you plan to ruin it in seconds," Holly shrilled. "Are
you insane?"

Ned, stricken, fell back as if he'd been slapped in
the face. Long ago, he remembered, she'd used almost
the same words, but then, as a bride, she had touched
them with a warmth and humor that made her desire

for him crystal-clear. Pushing her husband away, Holly quickly reached for the front door, invoking the protection of the outside world to stop his advances.

It doesn't matter, Ned realized. Draping Holly's jacket around her shoulders, he thought of T.D.'s mouth on his—a mouth he'd never touched and had never before even considered, not until this very moment.

6

MICHAEL WAITED, ALONE. HE STOOD IMMOBILE IN the middle of the empty loft. To anyone who might have been watching, the early-morning light would have dawned on this tabloid—a scene frozen in place for all of the night—and most of the day before. Blackout shades, drawn to hide yesterday's ceremony from prying eyes, were torn down and now admitted the dawn.

He looked out the tall, multipaned window. His face was tight, drawn, the obvious effects of strain and sleeplessness etching deep furrows under his eyes and down his cheeks.

Michael had planned yesterday's ritual down to the grains of salt . . . and yet the rite had failed. He surveyed the room in the hope, perhaps, of discovering a flaw in last night's ceremony.

The thirteen present at the time were unquestionably needed. Himself, of course, and the twelve young men who guarded the four points of the circle. The gilt circle was still covered with knotted strips of doeskin, but the altar was now bare—except for stains of virginal blood from a deflowered maiden. The acolyte tending the girl had been dismissed before the rite began, and the girl Stella had been perfect . . . up to a point.

If there were one thing, just one, that was not according to plan, it was Stella . . . or what happened to Stella. By right she should have risen from the altar after the ritual rape—surely she couldn't have minded all that much—and fallen to her knees in gratitude for the honor bestowed on her. She should have looked at Michael with adoration and kissed the hem of his robe. Other women had. But Stella had even one more responsibility. She should have conceived—probably had—and borne the child made at one of the most sacred times possible.

The worthless bitch had gone out the window.

The PCP must have deranged her mind or the ceremony itself was too awesome for her to accept. Or both. *She could have ruled by my side*, Michael raged. *The conduit for my mother's powers reaching me, the mother of my child, a child conceived in my most powerful moment*. The symbolism was perfect and all the cunt had to do was relax and reap the benefits. Instead, she took a header.

Before anyone realized what she was doing, before anyone could stop her, the bitch had thrown herself off the altar. Michael's semen was still running down her legs, mixing with her own fresh blood, which was as it should be. She'd fallen to her knees, but it was a stumble, not a supplication. She was on her feet in a split second and at the window in less time than it took for Michael to turn toward her.

He'd moved one step and she'd torn the blinds from the window; he'd moved another step, opening his mouth to command that she stop, and she had the window open; he shouted for her to stop, to be stopped. And she was out the window, headfirst.

His attending coven retrieved the body, brutalized before the fall, crushed to a pulp afterward, and removed it to another neighborhood. Just another victim.

That had to be it! Her sacrifice had negated his! That selfish bitch cunt ruined the most important moment of his life. Too bad she was already dead. Killing her—bit by bit, piece by piece—would have been the ultimate pleasure.

Everything else had been perfect. Every preparation, every sign, every last movement, perfect down to the smallest detail. It should have worked, Michael's mind shrieked. *It should have worked!*

But it had failed. His mother's essence had not passed to him. And, he bitterly knew, the energy had to be drawn down by someone.

It had not been any of the acolytes waiting with his dying mother, as even he would expect to happen. He had his sources and this, too, was confirmed. No one in the room with his mother as she passed from life had felt the power return. The power had never been known to dissipate, it was always passed on.

Lifting a clenched fist, Michael raised it before his face. He opened his hand wide, looking closely at his palm. The power should be there, in his grasp. He swiftly folded his fingers back into his palm, grasping only the air. His tired eyes riveted on the empty space before him. It couldn't be, it shouldn't be, but it had to be. *Someone else had received the power.* He shuddered at the thought. There was only one possible person.

Weariness began to creep into Michael's body, slowly at first, then growing, enveloping, a leaden cloak laid heavily on his tired shoulders. He had not slept or eaten for a full day. In fact, he had not really eaten for a week. Since his mother had shown the first signs of approaching death, he had dined lightly and then only just before dawn, taking barely enough to sustain him, and had spoken to no one nor allowed any one to speak to him. He had kept himself ready, a perfect vessel for the power.

His usual sharp mind was feeling frayed and he hoped he could maintain the extraordinary alertness that he would need for the seventeenth hour of the second day—just a handful of hours away—when he must summon far more powerful help. Knowing that he would have to invoke a new ceremony—a far more dangerous one—did not discourage him. He was fueled with purpose.

So he waited. He'd sent Rafe, the first to join with

him and his most trusted aide, to retrieve the sacrifice for tonight.

Planning this contingency sacrifice had been Michael's first task when he formed his own coven. It had been commissioned from a crazed pathologist who, bored with the daily task of dissecting dead humans, preferred to work in his suburban basement on living animals. His private zoo was worthy of Dr. Moreau. Most of the man's mutilated creations held no interest for Michael: dogs with six legs, cats with heads sewn on backward, and even a venomous snake with a lizard's fast legs were of no use. The pathologist's finest achievement, simple yet elegant, was a surgically combined goat, two heads to one body. It belonged to Michael, paid for at enormous price, and waited to be used only if the first ceremony failed, as it had. Rafe had yet to return and the waiting only added to Michael's burden, a weight more and more visible as the minutes slowly passed.

Michael's youth was disguised by strong lines deeply etched into his face. Last year, when he decided to redirect his studies into the darker arts—knowing his mother's death was measurable distance of time away— physical age had fallen on him with a force. Within months, his raven hair turned grizzled and his youthful features sunk into the hollows of a man a dozen years older. Yet, while the energy needed to deal with powerful forces had quickly aged his body, his mind grew sharper, keener, quicker. His thoughts, now dulled by sleeplessness but still more directed than most, focused on his sister, Bree.

Earlier he had felt her near. His strong climax with the Stella-bitch had drained him, and at that moment, he had felt Bree's presence touch his. Then the cunt went out the window and his rage exploded into an uncontrollable blaze. It must have been Bree, Bree all along. Everything was Bree's fault! Bree had distracted him. She had—must have—drawn down their mother.

Bree. She couldn't use the force, wouldn't use it,

didn't know and would never know how to conquer power or gain untold wealths. She would never use the soul-searing energies for anything, any use other than a placid, docile extension of her healing knack—a minor trick she'd managed to nurture into a passable talent.

Bree! Tonight in the seventeenth hour he would drain her of what she had, what she couldn't or wouldn't use. And tonight he would succeed.

Now, though, he must prepare his bath and anointments. He would rest, though not sleep, leaving the pungent, drugged oils to seep through his skin and restore his energy. Tonight, with an offering that could not, would not, be ignored by his masters, he would regain the glory that was his by right. His sister's coincidental demise was a small price to pay, he thought, then smiled. Price? Hardly. It was willed all along.

Bree would cease to be.

Morning comes to the streets as gently as possible, afraid to waken sleeping tigers. Early light enters from the side before daring to widen its arc and take on the full responsibility of day. Debris, hidden by night's dark blanket, once again takes jumbled forms as long shadows are cast on the broken pavement.

Even with no one awake to see it, the small bundle was unremarkable. A rope tied tightly, but without apparent skill, was wrapped twice about a soiled canvas bundle the size of a large grocery bag. The bundle rested a good arm's length away from the alley wall yet was not immediately noticeable, if anyone would even look, as garbage cans toppled during a drunkard's blind stumbling spree spewed loose trash and hid the soiled canvas from any but the most diligent searcher.

First light reached the alley. The doorways within, still shadows in the darkness, stood out in sharp relief. The back door of the greengrocer's was easily identified by the high stacks of broken wooden crates, emptied of their produce and waiting for their next and last use as fuel for a trash-can fire. Farther down the alley, a rarely used back door to the adjoining tenement provided deeper shadows and shelter to any one resting there.

When he had a name it was Joseph, but it had been many years since anyone had used his name or called him anything but old man or bum or drunk or lump of shit. At first he had cared and it hurt but the names became easier to accept as time passed. If anyone had used his name, he wouldn't have, couldn't have, responded; it was last heard so long ago it was truly forgotten. The name belonged to another man, another life. Now it didn't matter what they called him as long as they left him alone in his alley. Alone to forage for food and to cadge dimes and quarters or even nickels or pennies until he had enough for the warming and life-sustaining no-brand whiskey or rotgut wine. This past fall and winter had been the best he'd spent in years, and the promise of spring in the air was, he thought, a sure harbinger of increased luck. Like finding this alley with the deep-set doorway for sleeping and a produce store providing wilted greens and rotted fruit for meals was a blessing. He easily managed the winter with trash-can fires and kept away from the shelters that forced him to spend his entire day trying to find a place to sleep the night.

The alley even led to a busy street, the main shopping street in the neighborhood no less, with harried women rushing from stores to home and willing to drop a coin in his hand just to avoid him. Or maybe, he thought, some of our superstitions have stayed with us. Take care of the beggar on your street and you'll stay well and fed. His own mother had dropped coins in the broken hands of a beggar, cautioning him that to give to them was to ensure you didn't become one. It may have worked for her, but it hadn't worked for him. It was now his dirty and broken hands reaching out for whatever anyone would drop in or near or even throw in his general direction.

Miraculously, a quarter of the pint of raw red wine was left in his unbroken bottle. That, and enough

change in his pocket to ensure the first pint of the day
bode, he was sure, for a successful day. He quickly
drank the potent, overly sweet liquor to fortify himself
for the most difficult task of his day: getting up. Raising the bottle to his parched lips was painful, but the
small, inner heat the wine generated eased his aching
bones; he uncurled from the doorway.

Grateful for the fortification, no matter how slight,
the old man hobbled to the greengrocer's doorway.
This morning he hoped for a pear or even an apple,
no matter how bruised. As if the success of his venture
had been ensured by fate, visible under a wilted cab-
bage leaf were both a battered pear and a half-eaten
apple.

Breakfast consumed, the old man brushed off his
tattered jacket and took a quick inventory. The night
had been chilly and searching for a new pair of socks
would go high on his list. Life was simple, the old
man knew, unless you tried to confuse it with things
like clean underwear. He had long ago learned that
looking in the immediate vicinity was the easiest first
step, and pocketing a blackened banana for lunch, he
walked back into the alley.

These garbage cans are always a mess, he thought,
not remembering that until he worked his way home
late last night they'd stood straight, in neat rows. Kicking the nearest can aside, the tied canvas bundle caught
his eye. Pushing the rubbish aside, he pulled the canvas package toward his doorway. Tied too neat to be
garbage, the package could contain all his needs.
Clothes and money and maybe even shoes or a coat.
In fact, a package not only wrapped this well but made
of sturdy canvas had to contain treasures enough for
his every need.

Crippled hands, whose only real function is to
pocket change and twist open bottles, makes slow
work of knotted cord, but the morning booster of red
wine had steadied him enough to manage the task.
Pulling the last knot away, the old man reached out to

open the canvas, and as the heavy fabric fell away, he jumped back from his seat on the step.

"Damn fools," the old man muttered aloud. "Who would wrap two bloody goat heads and then leave it on the street."

He kicked the package and loudly complained to no one, anyone, everyone, who might hear. The old man's alcohol fogged brain didn't notice that the two goat heads were joined at the neck.

7

Second-floor windows, especially those polished clean, attract the rising sun by calling out their
promise of acceptance. The light enters boldly, confident of its welcome, streaming through freshly laundered lace curtains, lace hung for the very first time
in bedroom windows. Such a morning promises a lifetime of equally brilliant mornings. Such a morning is
always like no other. Even the chill of an early-spring
breeze, resolutely slipping through the slightly opened
window, seems to pause to be warmed before circling
the room.

Elise felt the day before it began. Dark dreams had
stalked her throughout the night. She had found herself alone, very alone, in the woods of her youth.
Fighting her way through the brambles, struggling to
reach home in the deeping twilight, she had come upon
a clearing just as night closed in. Chilled, hoping for
a fire for light and warmth, welcome flames sprang
from the earth in front of her, but as she moved toward
it, the blaze raced around the perimeter of the clearing, and trapped her. Caught in the circle of fire, she
watched in amazement, then terror, as cats with emerald eyes walked through the flames. They paced her
every move, stalked her, and finally closed in on her.
They slashed at her with their razor claws until one
cat, larger and bolder than the others, sprang at her
and caught its talons in her throat. There was no way
to pull the cat free, not without tearing her burning
skin. Instead, Elise had held the cat, squeezing and
crushing until the cat's claws loosened, one by one,

from her torn skin. With the last claw pulled free, she woke, breathless with a pounding heart, but the panic lingered until she'd washed her face and changed her sweat-drenched gown. Back in bed, she rested with her eyes shut, but sleep did not return.

Eyes still closed, Elise breathed deep of the fresh morning, the cool air clearing away the dark clouds of night, and listened to her husband's deep breathing as it slowly turned to the shallower breaths of waking. She slipped close to him and curled herself around Jeff's warm body.

Elise finally allowed one eye to open, to confirm it was still early enough so she could, free of guilt, not yet having to face the chores lined up for the morning, close the single eye and drift back into a deep morning sleep. A dreamless sleep. A low groan escaped as the reality of the hour struck home: eight o'clock was, undoubtedly, time to get up.

Slipping the covers aside, Elise pointed her foot toward a waiting slipper, dismissing the nightmare and lost sleep, planning her movements for the next hour, beginning with a pot of fresh coffee. Amused, Elise thought of how, after almost five years of marriage— but only this last week regularly keeping the same hours, they had rarely drawn the same shift at the hospital—her husband could still be surprised by her habits. The occasional overlapping days off hadn't prepared either of them for the regular routine of living together.

Never an alert riser, Elise needed to prepare the coffee the night before, the pot ready to plug in when she stumbled into the kitchen. Jeff had probably never thought through the implications of her having the coffeepot filled, either because he was ready to tumble into bed or, more often than either of them cared to recall, because he was still working his shift. On the other hand, Elise had never realized that Jeff was so unbearably chipper in the morning. Any head start she could get was worth the effort—not only so he wouldn't see her at her worst but so she wouldn't have to face his bright, alert, and distressingly awake chatter.

Halfway out of bed, Elise found herself pulled back by strong arms, the back of her neck being the target for a well-placed kiss.

"You've got to be kidding, Elise. It's just past eight. I thought we promised ourselves just a little bit of leeway the next few days."

" 'Morning, darling. This is leeway—at least for me. I need the next hour to regroup."

"If you let me, I'll help." Jeff's suggestion, accompanied by a theatrical leer only someone fully awake could manage, was followed by pulling the lightly quilted cover over his wife. Elise slipped back into her husbands arms, grateful for the closeness, the protection, they provided.

Wondrous that despite her exhaustion her desire for her husband was so strong, her body spoke for her as she joined in their gentle morning lovemaking. Their bodies knew each other well and played a single symphony, moving fingers pulling notes and chords from the silky flesh of the other. He slipped into her, unerringly guided by instinct and by the warm wet trail she left for him. Each time was the same and each time so different, limbs wrapped about one another, sculpted in symmetrical balance. Their rhythms easily matched, a metered prelude, a joyous rhapsody, then a tempestuous crescendo. Her strong climax met his, as it so often did, their reluctance to part as strong as always.

Elise broke the comfortable silence. "One of these days I'm going to take up smoking."

A laugh shook Jeff's body and parted them. "Okay, why are you going to take up smoking?"

"Oh, it just seems so perfect to lie back after a great romp in bed and to light up a cigarette, artfully blowing billows of smoke about."

"You smoke during the great romp. How many people can say they do that?"

"Not many, I'd venture. But, then, they aren't married to you. Or were you just fishing for that?"

"Not a bit. But I'll gladly take it. Now, for that coffee I'm learning to be grateful is put together the night before. I think you're rubbing off on me." Jeff sat up and swung his bare legs over the side, flexing his shoulders to stretch out the night.

"You do that once more with your body and you're coming back to bed," Elise murmured hoarsely. "I think you're rubbing off on me."

"That is definitely my intention. Now, up, or we really won't get started. It's almost nine."

"Yes, sir, coffee on the double." Grabbing a clean pair of jeans on the way out, Elise called back, "If you plug the pot in. I'm taking the upstairs bathroom."

"Well, I guess it's only fair. But I need the bathroom, too. I, ah, didn't hook up the downstairs sink yesterday."

"That's okay. You didn't hook up the hot water either."

Groaning, Jeff slipped on his jeans. "That takes care of my morning. What about yours?"

Emerging from the bathroom with a mouthful of toothpaste, Elise looked puzzled. "I just remembered. Bree didn't stop by yesterday. She was going to come over in the afternoon."

"She may have had a rough shift—I'm sure you remember what they can be like—and slept in. We were out so late that if she came by on her way to work she would have missed us." Zipped into comfortably worn denim pants, Jeff rummaged for a clean work shirt. "Don't forget—you're the unpacking crew. I can never figure out where to put things. See you downstairs."

Rinsing out her mouth with the icy water, Elise made a mental note to call Bree and leave a message on her machine—right after the first cup of coffee.

The morning had fully arrived before it made any impression on the woman still sleeping in her deep

easy chair. First, street noises filtered through the
dreamy haze: mothers yelling out to children to be
home right after school, an occasional blast of a car
horn and the clanging of storefront gates being opened
for the day's business. Then, the full light of day finally permeated her closed eyelids, pulsing patterns of
white on white visible through the thin skin.

Familiar noises, yet somehow out of place, Bree realized as she opened her eyes and slowly focused on
the wine-colored robe she wore. A deep sob escaped
as the sharp pain of realization returned. Her mother
was gone.

From the corner of her eye the blinking message
light of the phone-answering machine demanded attention. Closing her eyes to ignore it, Bree suddenly
sat bolt upright. The time. It was early morning, the
time before she usually got home from night shift.
When she came in, the school bus had already left,
yet she just heard it again. What time is it? Could it
be late afternoon? That would make sense in her sleeping pattern but not in the street noises. All the clues
pointed to her having slept once around the clock.

Reaching out to the blinking message light, the
number six surprised her. JoJo had assured her that no
one would call, that right now everyone knew to hold
back. Who would be calling? Pushing the automatic
rewind and replay button, Bree watched the red glowing numbers decrease . . . five . . . four . . . three
. . . two . . . one . . . stop.

The first message was simple: it was JoJo calling
back thinking she might be still awake and wanting,
he said, just to let her know how much everyone cared.
He would call, his taped voice said, before she went
to work that evening to see how she was. The next
message was JoJo again: it was evening, he said, if
she was there would she please pick up the phone. He
would like to hear her voice. The third message increased the faint chill already in the air: it was her
supervisor from the hospital calling. Where was she?
the voice briskly demanded—the shift was already

short one person and her tardiness was not appreciated. The fourth and fifth messages were also from the hospital. Number four briskly informed her that if she thought that just because she had given notice she could leave them shorthanded whenever she felt like it, without having the courtesy, nor the responsibility, the scratchy voice amended, she would get her due. The fifth explained her due, which was not to bother working the remaining shifts. They could do without her. Not wishing to hear the sixth message from the hospital, Bree was about to turn off the machine when JoJo's voice came through.

"Your mother, Bree, has died. There wasn't time for me to see her, to tell her"—his voice broke but, after an audible intake of breath, continued—"what you asked. But I'm sure she knew. They said she was talking to someone in her last dream. They thought it was you."

It was me, JoJo, it was me, Bree thought, holding her mother's robe tight against her shaking body.

But what do I do now?

Rafe ran through the streets, his head pounding from the night before. For starters, he had drunk much too much wine, and drunk, after the failed ceremony, he had accepted the responsibility to retrieve the special sacrifice for tonight's ritual. Then, to give himself the extra boost, he stopped home to shoot the heroin he'd taken. He hadn't known it was being saved for the ceremony, and when Michael raged about its loss, he was too frightened to return it. The glassine packets all but burned a hole in his pocket—and his mind—during the charged ritual. Being sent out gave him the chance to destroy the evidence by doing it up proper. Quality shit, too.

Rafe had resolutely borne the long subway ride to the heart of Queens borough, his high a mellow blanket. He especially enjoyed the moments when the graffiti-scarred train bounded along the elevated trestles and teased him with the possibility of missing the track at any of a number of sharp curves. The last stop was within walking distance of the pathologist's home.

There, in the windowless basement, Rafe deftly wielded a gold knife, entrusted to him for the purpose, and swiftly cut the living animal open. The joy and power Rafe felt when he tore the still-beating heart from the two-headed goat grew into a mindless frenzy as he was first to taste the heart's blood, hot and still pulsing. Only the heads were needed, and Rafe was given the honor of retrieving the offering.

Michael had trusted Rafe and Rafe had betrayed this trust.

Again.

Rafe's lean body moved quickly through the same alleyways he remembered traveling the night before as well as through twisted passages he'd never seen before. On top of what was already in his system, he'd bought a pint of applejack to enjoy on the walk home. The cheap brandy was the final straw. He'd blacked out and lost the parcel.

Michael would rage, and Michael's rage was deadly. Rafe had to find the canvas bundle, had to ensure its secrecy, and had to deliver it for the next night's— tonight's!—dark and powerful ceremony. His life depended on it.

Rafe turned yet another corner, breathless from his nonstop search. Knowing that his route of the night before should have taken him from the subway entrance—no, from the liquor store—to the loft would normally have limited his hunt to a few specific streets. Unfortunately, the abusive amount of substances in his body and the resultant black-out left him confused as to where he'd wandered, and forced him to considerably widen the area.

The past hour had been spent at a level of high agitation and extreme anxiety. If he didn't find the package soon . . . well, he didn't know what he would do.

Turning into another alley, Rafe paused to let his eyes adjust to the shadows. At the far end of the alley a bundle of rags was piled high in a tenement doorway. Closer to him, the back door of a greengrocer was littered with broken crates of trash, and the smell of stale wine and urine soaked the air. Understanding the scene was automatic to Rafe. That pile of rags was another bum who'd picked over the trash and drank himself back to sleep before the sun reached midday.

Rafe started up the alley, walking at a steady pace, carefully scanning both sides. The end of a piece of rope caught his eye, and with a deep intake of breath, Rafe moved toward the trash can toppled over the ragged rope.

Walking around the garbage, not wanting to disturb the area should it contain what he hoped against hope it would, he fell to one knee at the end of the cord and gently pushed the trash can aside. He let out the breath he hadn't realized he was holding: four dead eyes stared back at him. The two heads lay undisturbed on the open canvas, the sight of them probably frightening off whoever had been curious enough to open the package. Gingerly rewrapping the prize, Rafe carefully tied the knots that would save his skin.

Standing with the canvas parcel held reverently under his arm, Rafe took a long, slow look about. Thoughts churned in his already throbbing head: if kids had opened the package the contents would have been spilled out on the cement, the package and heads destroyed in an act of token vandalism. He remembered enough about being a kid to know what he and his friends would have done. Probably hung the heads from the fire escape or put them in someone's window—someone who had recently offended them, and there was always someone to fit that bill. But to leave the heads resting on the canvas, apparently untouched, that wasn't the way kids would act. The bum sleeping it off, on the other hand, could have opened the bundle and, not seeing anything of use, alarmed at what he did see, backed off.

Instinct told Rafe that this was the answer. The old man had seen the heads. A twisted smile came to Rafe's face. He couldn't have wished for a better solution. Not only did he have his package back, in perfect condition—Michael would never know the difference—but he could easily resolve the fact that someone had seen it.

Slipping his hand into his deep jacket pocket, the balanced weight of the gravity knife as familiar to him as his comb, he closed his fist on the handle. A short, sharp flick of his wrist brought the razor-honed blade out; three short, sharp steps brought Rafe to the snoring old man.

"Thanks, old man, for making my morning," Rafe murmured to the old man just before he plunged the five-inch, stainless blade into the back of the derelict's head, matted hair easily parting to its sharp edge. Hearing the bone crack, he twisted the blade farther into the soft brain tissue; the steady pressure and twisting he gave the knife unconsciously mimicked the mechanical motions he used to penetrate a woman. The low growl of pleasure that came from Rafe was climactic, and as he held his position over the body for longer than it took to ensure a kill, a warmth spread through his groin. He dropped to his knees, twisting the blade again, thinking of his mother neatly sectioning a grapefruit, not wanting the moment to end. The pleasure subsided and Rafe pulled the knife clear. He carefully, meticulously wiped the stained blade on the old man's jacket.

Calm again, and very satisfied, Rafe whistled a popular love song as he swaggered back to the street, the canvas-wrapped bundle secure under his arm.

8

THE THREE RESEARCH ASSOCIATES HUDDLED, CON-
versing rapidly in hushed tones that increasingly over-
lapped as their discussion grew more and more heated;
each had privately carried the weight of the previous
day's revelations, weighing the disclosures against their
own personal goals. The day's grace period to decide
elapsed, each scientist had independently made a
choice. Summoned back to the large conference room,
they heatedly compared the rationales for their individual decisions. Frank Jordan had removed himself
to the end of the table and was in deep conversation
with the project chairman.

"I wouldn't have told them as much as we did, not
without your direction," Jordan said, his displeasure
apparent in the petulant way he pursed his mouth and
the nervousness of his hands tapping the files he again
held. "Sometimes I think the person holding the
chairman of the advisory board position should be
barred from any administrative decisions. If you hadn't
opened the subject, we wouldn't be here now."

"It was needed. These men stumbled upon a discovery that would normally make them famous and,
yes, possibly win them the Nobel. At least put them
in the running for the prize. We can't just take away
their proudest moment without telling them why."

"What if they don't agree?" Jordan asked, his tem-
per rising. "What if they insist on publishing, even
with the explanation and the agreement they signed?"

"I think we can keep them in line. What we're
promising isn't immediate fame but greater resources

than they'd ever otherwise have available. And money. If man is capable of using more than his five senses, we'll discover it here, at Spiral. I think we'll find they're truly research scientists, willing to expand their findings in the direction they now know we're heading. Not just glory-seekers.''

''Like separating the wheat from the chaff,'' Frank Jordan commented, his sarcasm readily apparent.

The other man smiled. ''Yes, like wheat from the chaff. And our golden grain will bear fruit for us. I feel it.''

A single voice at the table rose above the others.

''Damn! You weren't really listening yesterday, were you?'' It was Bill Blaiser. ''And you're completely ignoring what happened to me last night.

''We're working on a project so secret that we didn't even have, until yesterday, an idea what it was about.'' Blaiser was raging. ''Spiral my ass. We're not going to solve any problems here. Just create a few more. That's what they really have us doing. Only because we didn't have the so-called overall picture, because we didn't know the direction we were going, we made the natural mistake of finding a possible cure. The bottom line is they want us to create the illness.''

''Bill, you're overreacting.'' The calming voice of Judd Thacker broke through the tension. ''We're looking for existing abnormalities, not creating disorders. There's a difference.''

Ed Hawthorn pushed his horn-rimmed glasses back to the bridge of his nose. ''We *are* looking to improve the quality of life, but in a different way,'' he added. ''Just because this project, our project, isn't designed to produce high-profile discoveries, you pull out. We can't leave. Not now, not after we've seen what we can actually do.''

''That's exactly what I mean. What we can do. We found the probable—not just possible, but probable—genetic link for the suppression of killer viruses and we have to turn it over to some second-rate facility for them to develop.'' Bill Blaiser hesitated, his face heavily flushed. ''For them to credit as their own.''

''Damn it, Bill,'' Judd Thacker shot back. ''Haven't you seen enough work in labs to know that every possibility—and I use that word, not probability—doesn't pan out. If what we found can be developed and does evolve into a viable process for genetic-linked diseases, then we've done good work. Yes, it would be rewarding if the world, even just the scientific world, knew we were responsible. And maybe someday they will. But it's not the end product that's everything. We're scientists and we've made a commitment to this project, to Spiral, and we have to see it through.''

Bill Blaiser's face tightened, a hard glint flicked in his narrowed eyes. ''Mutants. That's what they want us to develop. How is that going to solve anything?''

''By furthering what we've already shown can be done,'' Judd calmly responded. ''We're studying natural genetic occurrences, not developing genetically altered mutations by recombination. Maybe, someday, by altering a single genetic code, by slightly shifting the protein balance of amino acids, we can produce that subtle change that routinely creates genius from average parents or prodigies born of mundane genetic lineage. But first, our goals are finding and identifying the natural factors. The insights we're gaining studying the MtDNA are invaluable.''

''It's still creating mutations, at least planning for it, and it's still a military project,'' Bill Blaiser said, his voice hard and flat. He stood, resigned to the immense chasm of opinion that existed. ''I prefer to follow our findings to whatever research facility they're going to, and continuing to work on them there. A safer facility,'' he added, staring at Frank Jordan. ''I don't accept Spiral any more than I accept the biosafety report that the titanium blade was accidentally contaminated with chlorine before it broke and unbalanced the ultracentrifuge.''

Hearing the finality in Bill Blaiser's statement, Frank

Jordan moved from the end of the table to the three scientists.

"And that's your choice, Dr. Blaiser, and certainly within your options. You'll be transferred within the week. Keep in mind, accidents do happen, even in the most secure facilities. All we ask—and I'm sure even you will agree it would be in everyone's best interests—is that you never repeat to anyone what was said in this room or about what's going on here."

Dr. Blaiser nodded in mute agreement. He would be leaving a large part of his work here for his associates to continue with, and leaving a small part of himself as well. Turning before he left, he paused and looked back.

"I wish you luck. But I can't work on a project where the goal is to change life as we know it into something . . . well, something else."

Ed Hawthorn lifted his eyes to the departing researcher. "Bill, even if that were the goal, if that something else could change life for the better for the entire human race, we should know what it is. We're on the threshold of entering a new realm of study. We need to have every resource we possess at our disposal."

"Even if it makes us monsters?" Bill Blaiser sighed. "No, I can't resign myself to that."

"Not monsters, supermen."

"The last person to use that term killed six million."

Dressed in slacks and a cardigan, his casual attire a sharp contrast to the finery of last night, Ned Harper quickly finished the last of his breakfast. Although already midmorning, Holly still slept soundly—Ned fervently hoped—and would remain in deep slumber until he was safely out of the house and on the way to his new campaign headquarters.

Last night was all he'd hoped it would be. The pillars of his political party rallied about him as their pride and joy. His welfare throughout the evening had been the prime concern of dozens of men that, just a few years ago, he had been in awe of. Of course, he still respected his fellow party members, but now they were just that. More important, they were now *his* supporters.

The rise of Ned's political star was not the only reason for this morning's hurried departure from his house, and his sleeping wife. Though Holly had been superb last night. Looking her loveliest, she had charmed and chatted with the best the city had to offer—the cream of society and the powerful movers and shakers. As usual, she would be well remembered for her beauty, her intelligence, and her wit. Holly was a definite political plus. But last night she smiled her way through the evening alone—not in her usual place of honor, by his side. That position had been commandeered by T.D. as soon as they walked into the room.

For the entire evening his attentions were held by his communications director: T.D. She had greeted them both at the door with her usual aplomb and aloofness and whispered a complete list of who was there, who would require a bit more attention and convincing, who his strongest supporters were and where they were in the room. T.D.'s briefing had taken a full five minutes and, Ned knew, even Holly was impressed with her thoroughness.

Score one for T.D.

Then T.D. took his arm, directed Holly to a group of senatorial wives, and steered Ned to a tight group of heavyweight Wall Street magnates—names he immediately recognized, even without knowing the stock market, as people on whose word the market rose or fell.

Score two, and three, for T.D.

Two years ago, when he began in earnest to garner his forces for this year's primary, T.D. had been invaluable in establishing the private coalitions and prime backers to target. The countless hours he'd spent in rooms full of aromatic Macanudo Lonsdale smoke, puffed from the handmade cigars he'd freely dispensed, were well worth the price. As proved last night by the quality names attached to his supporters. And, Ned realized, it was all T.D.'s work—every step of the way.

She had looked lovely, too. Not as striking as Holly, of course, but then, no other woman in the room could ever measure up to Holly in being so perfectly turned out for any occasion. T.D.'s approach had been, of necessity, more low-key. And, to his eyes, much more effective.

Wearing minimal cosmetics and jewelry in a room filled with woman wearing excesses of both, T.D. relied on her cool, lean looks to carry her through. And they had, remarkably so. She dressed in a simple floor-length, bottle-green silk shift, the green so closely matching her eyes he wondered how she could have found time to carefully shop to find it—especially with all the hours she put in at headquarters.

Her dark hair was swept up and loosely held in place by what seemed to be a single tortoiseshell pin. A pin, he thought of every time he looked at her, that needed just one small pull to free her long, full hair, letting it cascade over her bare shoulders. Her only noticeable cosmetic was lip gloss, her lips shiny soft and dusty pink, lips that he had first thought of pressing on his own just last night.

Catching himself holding a cup of coffee, now grown cold, Ned was annoyed he'd let himself lapse into the daydream. It was more important to leave the house, to go to his headquarters, organized by T.D., of course, in the Flatiron Building on 23rd Street. Not too far uptown yet far enough from the Village to avoid the stigma. A recap of last night was necessary, and besides, she'd be there. Leaving the remains of his breakfast, Ned quietly slipped into the foyer and, taking a jacket from the closet but not risking the extra minute it would take to put it on, left the house.

While not on the magnitude of a landslide election, last night's dinner was a landmark event, as his bus-

tling headquarters testified. The small handful of salaried employees had all arrived for work, on the same
day: that in and of itself a momentous occasion. The
growing cadre of volunteers had multiplied and unfamiliar faces cluttered the rooms, looking for any task
no matter how small.

Entering the busy offices, Ned smiled wryly, thinking that just last week activity like today's would have
been a pipe dream. It was, he was now sure, only the
beginning.

"We're on our way, Governor Harper," the husky
voice Ned had waited all morning to hear came from
behind.

Turning, a boyish grin touching his face, Ned Harper
saw the woman constantly in his thoughts, at least
since trying to kiss his wife before last night's dinner.
Finally last night, after five years, something special
had clicked between them.

"It's not governor yet. But I agree we really are on
our way—thanks to you, T.D."

Her husky laugh melted the tattered remnant of inner reserve he'd promised himself to use as a defense.
"I hardly think I deserve that much credit, Governor.
You do get a fair share of it, you know. And I'm just
practicing with the 'governor.' You know me, always
prepared."

"A fair share, then, T.D. No more. As for your
always being prepared, I think that's an understate-
ment." Her short laugh, an almost humorless bark,
puzzled him, but the activity in the room was too distracting to dwell on subtleties. Looking at the work
busily being consumed by compulsive camp-followers,
Ned realized that some of the faces looked familiar.
"Aren't those three in the corner from Alan Dale's
camp?"

"Were from, is more appropriate. They were first
on line this morning to sign up."

"Maybe I'm naïve, but I thought it was almost unheard of for volunteers to switch affiliations mid-
stream," Ned puzzled.

"Almost unheard of, but obviously not quite. They're here, aren't they?" T.D.'s logic seemed unrefutable, but unease still pursued Ned.

"But if they can switch their loyalty this easily, how can we be sure they'll continue to work with us?"

"Trust me. I know they'll be loyal. I'm sure of it." Her confidence in the captured volunteers was more than adequate to quiet Ned's fears. Whenever T.D. was this sure about anything, he knew she was right.

Turning from the crowded room to face his prize aide, Ned suddenly found himself fumbling for words. "T.D., you, ah, you looked lovely last night." Damn, he thought, I should have rehearsed this speech. Or at least had it written.

"Why, thank you. I hardly thought you had time to notice. The place was full of beautiful women. What chance did I have to compete?" Her intentional coyness escaped him as Ned rushed to answer.

"There was no one else in that room that even came close to you. You were a queen, they were all, well, costumed players. T.D., I wanted to tell you last night, but—"

As had happened the night before, Ned was stopped from saying anything further by the masses of people surrounding them.

"Later, Ned. It'll be soon enough, now. We've a busy day ahead." Her lips parted, T.D. touched her tongue quickly to her perfect teeth and, with a shrug, clapped her hands loudly over her head.

"Everyone," she announced, "our next governor is here."

Lighter patches of wall, where Bill Blaiser's collection of posters had brightly decorated the small office, were accented by the countless pockmarks of pushpin holes. The walls bore witness to his changing moods and current political, environmental, or musical stance; save the whales and sea-lion cubs had given way to save our wetlands and pine barrens; Rod Stewart and the Grateful Dead gave way to The Police, then

to Twisted Sister—mercifully for a very brief time—
then, in an entirely new direction featuring Yo-Yo-Ma,
Kiri Te Kanawa, and the few other classical music art-
ists who incongruously had poster sales of over a half-
dozen.

Still packing the last of his desk, Bill Blaiser was
lost either in his thoughts or in the Julian Bream cas-
sette playing on his portable music system. He fondly
referred to the tape deck as his ghetto blaster even
though the volume had never been turned up more
than a quarter, nor had it played anything raunchier
than Rimsky-Korsakov, unless one counted Phillip
Glass.

Whole-earth catalogs indiscriminately mixed with
volumes on cellular structure, *Rolling Stone* inter-
spersed with professional journals, and a vast collection of dog-eared paperbacks with jackets invariably
portraying rocketships, mythical beasts, or smoking
guns, were carefully being packed in cartons discarded
from the snack machine; some would say the contents
of said cartons had never made it as far as the coin-
operated device and that the peanut-butter-and-cheese
crackers were consumed directly from the cartons.

Dr. Blaiser had a well-earned reputation for eating
anything wrapped in plastic, that is, while the plastic
was still wrapping the anything edible.

A soft buzz from the security door announced a visitor. Pulled back from his chore, Bill pushed the intercom button.

"Which of you traitorous beings is knocking at my
door," he sneered, meaning every word.

"It's Julie, Dr. Blaiser, with some dinner."

"Shit, Julie, why didn't you say so?" he muttered
as he buzzed the door open. "You've got the combination."

"I did say so. I've also got my hands full. And last
but not least, I should never have had the combination.
These offices are designed to be private and secure,"
she said, looking over her shoulder to see if anyone
was in the corridor. "You forced it on me." Despite

her status as nutritionist and cook for the facility, Julie Murray had managed to keep what most considered an attractive girlish figure, one that denied both her approaching retirement age and her own secret passion for double chocolate-chip ice cream.

"If you didn't have the combination, I'd starve. How else would I get enough fuel to survive?" Sweeping the loose papers off his desk, Blaiser paused as he held the sheets covered with formulas and notes between his hands. "The hell with it," he said, and ceremoniously dumped the lot in the adjacent shredder. "It's all in my head, anyway."

"Dinner's light tonight. We're planning a large buffet—some visiting VIPs—and the kitchen's just about off limits." The small woman, still dressed in her kitchen whites, pushed aside a stack of paperbacks to slide the tray in front of the research scientist.

"If you want any," Blaiser said, gesturing at the books, "they're yours."

"No, thanks, romance is more my speed. I never could get into that farfetched stuff you read. It surprises me that you do, being a scientist and all."

"There's more truth in some of these books than within these walls." Pausing as he uncovered the tray—the double burger dripping cheese, the french fries hot and crisp—he looked back at the woman, a smile creasing the corners of his eyes. "Come to think of it, Julie, at least these books don't pretend to be something else, like what goes on here, and that includes the reality of dragon riders and the Self Gate."

Shaking her head at his nonsense—Dr. Blaiser was definitely one of her favorites, despite his oddities—the cook turned to leave but paused at the door.

"It looks like you're moving offices," she said, first acknowledging the piled cartons and bare walls.

"To another project, Julie, someplace else, though I'll sure miss you. You'd be one, if not the only, reason I'd be willing to stay," he added with a wink.

"I'll be sorry to lose you, Dr. Blaiser. I've never understood most of you scientists, walking about with your heads in the clouds, too preoccupied to eat a decent meal. You at least know enough to keep yourself healthy. I wish you luck.''

Chewing the large bite he'd just taken, Bill looked up. ''Thank you, Julie. And I don't know how you knew I was starving and needed an infusion just now, but you're right on target, as usual.''

''Oh, Dr. Blaiser, you're always needing food, there wouldn't be any wonder in my knowing that. But it was Mr. Jordan's suggestion that I bring you a tray.'' Julie smiled as she closed the door. ''He thought you might like a meal. So that you could finish up, he said.''

''Yeah, a last meal,'' muttered the scientist as he helped himself to a crisp fry.

9

THE TENEMENT'S PERENNIALLY RUSTY WATER WAS disguised by pink bubbles—meant to be white—as her kitchen tub filled invitingly with warm water. Bree looked down at the foamy surface as if it were a teacup she could read. What fortunes or omens would she find in the popping, scented bubbles. None, she realized with relief and gratefully slipped into the water. She lifted her head and arranged her long, ebony hair to fall outside the rim; she wanted only to soak and not concern herself with the washing of her hair much less the aesthetics of reading the future.

She pushed an escaped lock of hair away and again thought of her mother, the way the same obstinate tendril would fall into her mother's eyes. Just another in the endless series of remembrances that had been with her since waking. The warmth of the water seeped through, reaching even the cold spot deep in her heart, slowly relaxing her, slowly easing tightened muscles.

Too soon, the bubbles began to fall flat and the water grew cool. Bree pulled the tub's rubber plug open with an idle toe, willing her tension to drain out along with the water, and as her wish was being fulfilled, the phone's soft buzz called for her. At least my timing is back, Bree smiled to herself, the phone didn't ring until *after* my bath. She padded to the front room, wrapping a soft white towel around her, and reached for the phone just as her recorded message clicked on. Sinking into her easy chair, Bree again thought of her fortunate timing—leaving the machine on was an oversight but a welcome one; screening calls right now was a rather good idea.

Elise's concerned voice began to leave a detailed message—apologizing for missing her yesterday, asking if she was all right—but it was the sincerity behind the words that convinced Bree to answer the call. Interrupting the recording, Bree quickly picked up the phone, suddenly realizing she needed a reasonable story for her whereabouts during the last twenty-four hours.

"Hello, I'm here. I was just in the tub so I left the machine on."

"What a relief. When you didn't stop by yesterday, I was worried." A small laugh came through the phone. "Well, to be honest, I didn't worry until this morning. There was so much to do yesterday, by the time it was done I fell into bed—too tired to think."

A plausible excuse clicked into place for Bree. No complicated story about her absence would be necessary, just a simple twist on the truth.

"I was going to come over this morning and see how you're doing. To help, as a matter of fact. I'm finished at the hospital—they've, ah, agreed to let me leave earlier than planned."

"That's terrific, Bree." Elise's enthusiasm left no room for any questions as to why Bree was free earlier than scheduled. "Come over as soon as you can. I can't wait for you to see the front room—your office area and the waiting room. I've got the paper off and the walls all spackled. All it needs is a coat of semigloss and we can move the furniture in."

"That will be a momentous occasion. You must be tired of walking over everything that's stacked in the hallways and back rooms."

"I don't know. I think I'm sort of savoring these last moments of delicious confusion. It was wonderful waking up here this morning." Elise's voice took on a dreamlike quality and Bree could actually hear her smile.

"At least we can sleep," Elise paused, recalling her

disturbing dream, "eat, and bathe—if we use the upstairs bath, that is."

"Savor away. Elise, would it be all right if I came over late this afternoon? I want to help, but there's something I have to do first." Not wanting to tell her new employer and, more important, budding friend about her mother's death—it would open a flow of sympathy and condolences not included in her beliefs—Bree jumped to the purpose of her errand, rather than the cause. "I have to see my brother, Michael. It's family business and I know he's waiting to see me."

"We don't expect you to wield a paintbrush—a pen to schedule appointments is more than enough. Does your brother live nearby?"

"He's in the city," Bree cautiously replied, then felt compelled to add, "but I haven't seen him in more than a year. He moved downtown to be closer to his, ah, work. Then we had a, a falling-out over Mother's estate."

"I'm sorry, I didn't know your mother had died," Elise immediately responded, the sympathy in her voice just what Bree wanted to avoid.

"It was some time ago," Bree automatically responded, thinking that time was relative, "but there are still details that need attending to."

"Of course, but don't feel you have to rush over here to help. Take care of business and come when you can. Would you like to come for dinner? By tonight the paint should be dry and the downstairs water wet."

Hesitating, Bree thought of the emotional drain that meeting Michael this morning could involve. The last time they had seen each other a bitter battle had immediately erupted—and that time there had been no real reason for any argument. Only the fates knew what today's encounter would bring, but she could make a good guess. It would be exhausting. Then again, she could keep the visit with Michael as short as possible and use the rest of the day to recoup, maybe see JoJo and some others.

Deciding quickly, she answered within seconds of being asked. "I'd love to come for dinner. Just do me one favor."

"Of course, Bree. What?"

"Don't move one stick of furniture until I get there. I'll be there with bells on my sneakers. I'd love to share the moment of moving the first chair into the waiting room."

"You're as much of a sentimentalist as I am. I knew we had a lot in common. Consider it done. Not one stick of furniture will be moved one inch until you get here."

Setting a time for early evening, the women finished their phone conversation with a promise by Bree to bring a bottle of bubbling wine to toast the occasion. Her hand rested on the phone in its cradle as Bree looked out the windows to the sunlit day.

"I'll need more than wine after seeing Michael," she cautioned herself and, realizing she was still wrapped in a towel, rose to dress.

Stepping out her front door, Bree noticed that the day was warm and pleasant. The knot in her stomach, there thanks to the prospect of facing Michael, began to loosen as the early spring day and familiar sounds of the neighborhood reassured her.

"Bree," a voice called from a window across the street, "come and visit, have some coffee with me."

Smiling and waving hello, she shook her head and pointed to her watch. The neighbors were used to seeing her running to work at the hospital or, those that knew, seeing her start her home visits of clan members. When she said she didn't have time, they believed and took no offense, for, just as often, she would make time to visit with them.

The subway would, with one change at 14th Street, take her within walking distance of Michael's apartment on the Lower East Side. Why he would exchange one borderline neighborhood for one even closer to slum status was, at first, beyond Bree's comprehension. Soon, though, rumors of her brother's activities drifted back uptown. He'd acquired a tight-knit group of followers, young men who would do almost anything for him . . . and for the power he promised them.

Other stories reached her ears, but some she automatically discounted as having gotten garbled and twisted in the long trip uptown. Stories of a beautiful, dark-haired, green-eyed woman were whispered—a woman who was Michael's partner and who promised even more than he did. A woman of power. This was the easiest of all to ignore. If there were such a woman in the city, anyone on the same wavelength, she would know it, as she knew when Michael was active. Bree was confident there was no one else, but then again, her confidence ended where Michael himself was concerned. He'd always been erratic.

The subway ride passed in a blur, and forgetting to change trains, Bree climbed into the bright daylight at Union Square. She briefly considered returning underground to board the local but realized she was only a dozen blocks from Michael's East 5th Street apartment. Scanning 14th Street for the crosstown bus that could take her almost to his doorstep—all the buses turned downtown and cut through the alphabet city now called Loisada—Bree instead decided to take advantage of the fine weather, especially after sleeping through a winter of days, and use the time to clear her head.

Walking quickly, Bree soon found herself in Tompkins Square Park. She wished this encounter were already over, no matter what the outcome. The park's weekday inhabitants consisted of the area's actual residents, a congenial mix of ancient Ukranians, middle-aged Hispanics, and colorful youths of all heritages. Despite conflicting sound systems, Bree found a shaded bench beside the bandshell where, oddly, the broadcast polkas, salsa music, and heavy-metal rock music seemed to cancel one another out. She sat quietly, watching the people, looking at the first green buds on the trees, breathing deeply, regrouping. It was vital she be as together as possible for this encounter.

An hour passed in the blink of an eye and it was time to continue. Refreshed, the remaining few blocks disappeared in what seemed like just a few steps.

Reaching his building, Bree stopped and turned to look up at his windows. The shades were drawn, but knowing the night hours he preferred to keep, she was not surprised.

Bree put her foot on the cement stoop, and as soon as she shifted her weight to that foot, her ankle twisted. She reached out to the metal banister for support, and a coldness shot through her arm, freezing her hand to the railing. Daggers of ice sliced her body and an immobilizing terror suffused her entire being. The activity on the street faded away and Bree found herself surrounded by dense fog. The step she still felt under her twisted foot was her only contact with reality.

He knows, Bree thought. As if in answer to her unspoken words her brother's angry voice was thrown like a parcel of bricks, hitting her with the same impact the heavy package would have. She fell, crushed, to her knees, literally blind and deaf to all but his voice.

"I know," the voice grated inside her head. "I know Mother died, but no one with her was chosen. And I know it didn't come to me. I called on all my powers but I couldn't draw her down. She didn't come to me!"

The voice grew and reverberated inside Bree's head, repeating, screaming the last phrase, *"She didn't come to me,"* over and over and over. The intensity of the words thrust bolts of excruciating pain through her. She felt as if huge spikes were being pounded outward from within. The steady throbbing spread and grew as an all-encompassing pain threatened to tear through bone and flesh just to escape. Then the voice, his voice, grew even louder.

"I know because I tried to reach you and you weren't there. You were with her. Mother came to you. You, the bitch goddess of the ailing."

The bitter and angry words grated against her and echoed as the decibel level rose to an unbearable pitch. Her earlier, definable pain was almost wished for as a single, sustained, all-engulfing agony burst inside Bree's head and seared through her, preventing any thoughts of her own. Still on her knees, her hand still unwillingly clutching the banister, Bree could only hold on for dear life as his venom-drenched words rushed over her in a solid wave of torment, an anguish so rich it threatened to pull her loose from her forced mooring.

"She chose you, you stupid bitch. You don't even know who you are, what you hold." The voice reached an intensity that threatened to destroy Bree's last vestige of sanity. "Worse, you don't want it. You want to heal, dressed in a prissy starched white uniform. You feel safe dressed like all those other so-called healers, where you can lose yourself in the crowd. You're so much less than you could be. You can't use it, the power. You'll piss it away healing old ladies. You haven't the strength, even if you knew how, and you never will." The words hissed out at her and metamorphosed into a terrorizing wail, grating her flesh.

Then, with the same suddenness the horror had struck, it subsided. Catching her breath, Bree found she was again able to think.

The truth hit.

He was right.

Michael had practiced steadily for years to rule by his power. She only used hers to heal—in a hospital, no less. She'd hid from herself, from what she was destined to be, by telling herself and others that this was the right way, the safe way—the only way—to be in today's world. That by being a real nurse she would bring a learned knowledge backed by her natural healing powers. But she was really only hiding from herself.

Although the pain was gone, a torrent of words and unrelenting feelings continued to rain about her like physical blows. Michael was right. He should have the power, he should. She should give it to him, she must. He's right, he's right. I will pass it on. *He's right!*

Strong arms folded about her and pulled her back from the building, breaking her hold on the banister. With the release of her hand, the street slowly came into focus.

"JoJo. What are you doing here?"

"I thought I'd find you here. Don't you know you're not ready to face Michael? Bree, don't you even know what's going on?" JoJo looked at her as if she were a child he'd found wandering lost and alone. "Come with me, Bree," he gently urged. "Come with me and we'll explain."

Looking at her friend, her eyes still glazed from the intense trauma, Bree could only nod in agreement.

"Yes, JoJo. I think it's time."

"It is. I just hope it's not too late."

It's time, T.D. thought.

The evening rush hour streamed by the campaign office and, with this signal to the end of the workday, staff and volunteer workers, still charged with enthusiasm, grudgingly began to leave. T.D. sat motionless at the fifth-floor window and watched the street scene, amused by the crowds rushing to homes or restaurants or friends. She held a cup of coffee in her finely boned hands, enjoying this rare moment of relative quiet. Feeling meditative, she contemplated an abstract idea.

From her vantage point the people were currents in an ocean, flowing to and against the shores of sidewalk. The uptown corner of the building, a sharp angle that gave the Flatiron Building its name, was the bow of a ship breaking through the waves of humanity that ebbed past. How easy, T.D. mused, to be a captain of so many fates, a master of so many souls, especially when one keeps a firm hand on the helm. And now it's time to steer her ship toward home port.

Ned Harper crossed the deserted office to her desk and slipped into the chair facing her. Openly admiring her sleek profile, he noticed the faint tinges of dark under her eyes.

"You're tired. You've put in quite a day. On top of last night—and all that it took to make last night the success that it was—it's no wonder." Reaching across the desk, he touched her elbow.

As if awakened from a light sleep, T.D. started at the touch. "Ned, I'm sorry, I didn't realize you were still here. Did you say something?"

"Only that you look tired." Realizing that his words could be considered unkind, Ned amended them. "Beautiful, but tired. You've done an incredible job this last week, and on top of everything else, dealing with the hordes that descended on us today is above and beyond the call of duty."

Sipping the last of the coffee, T.D. smiled coyly over the top of her cup. "A few hours ago you were complaining that these hordes were all my fault. I thought you were blaming me."

"Blame you? Never. I've always prayed, often fervently, for supporters coming out of the woodwork. I just never thought it would happen to me. I'm afraid I don't quite know how to handle it yet."

"Just leave it to me, Ned. Just leave everything to me."

"I do. That's why I'm worried about you. You do look tired and I rely on you so much."

T.D. pushed her chair back, rose, and walked to the coffee area with her empty cup. Putting it down without refilling it, she clicked the automatic drip machine off.

"I didn't have a chance to ask you," T.D. said. "What did Holly think of last night?"

"She couldn't stop talking on the way home. To be honest, most of her chatter escaped me, but a lot had to do with how this senator's wife invited her out or that congressman told her how lovely she looked. I think it was mostly the champagne. Holly's usually more directed in her thinking than that kind of talk would indicate."

"Of course she is," T.D. encouraged. "Holly is the perfect wife for a gubernatorial candidate. Did she say anything else?"

Ned pondered the question for a moment. "I didn't wait for her to wake this morning and only spoke to her briefly when she called this afternoon—she told me that messages were also piling up at home."

A small smile played with a single corner of T.D.'s mouth. "Did Holly mind that I took charge of you for the evening?"

Ned shrugged his shoulders. "She didn't mention anything like that. After all, we had work to do—you and I. Holly was pretty busy herself at the party. But she did, by the way, ask about you."

"Oh . . ." T.D. turned back to face Ned. "What did she ask?"

"If you had made it in to the office after last night. When I told her you had, she said to give you her best and to tell you what a help you had been. I didn't tell you earlier because . . . well, it sounded a little patronizing. I've been trying to rephrase it, but I guess I'm just too tired to make it meaningful." Ned stood and held out his arms. "You're so much more important to me than I could ever put into words. No matter what I say, it'll sound trite. But"—awareness lit Ned's face—"you know that, don't you?"

"I know that Ned," T.D. said huskily. "I've made sure of that." And she deftly stepped into his waiting arms.

The taste of her mouth was as he knew it would be, soft and alive, with a compelling taste of exotic spices. Lost in the kiss, Ned realized that he needed T.D. more than ever. Right now the campaign was second, and not a very close second, to the growing heat he felt.

Slipping his arm tightly about her waist, Ned pulled T.D. closer. "Where do you live?" he asked, his voice almost breaking with suppressed hunger. It briefly crossed his mind that he was surprised he didn't know.

"Near. Very near."

10

Julie Murray's tears flowed profusely. She cried with both a heartfelt sorrow at Bill Blaiser's death and the confusion of her own guilt. Only an hour after she brought him his supper tray and just as she tossed the day's food-splattered apron into the laundry, alarms sounded throughout the facility. Rushing into the long corridor, she found the few others still on the premises equally confused as to the cause of the alert—the worst fear, of course, being that one of the deadly viruses had leaked from its sterile containment and was, somewhere, loose. This dreaded thought, a very real concern and one foremost on everyone's mind, kept each individual from moving away from the door to their office and from moving closer, perhaps, to a contaminated area.

It wasn't until the medics, their worn green scrubs closely matching the gray-green walls, nearly raced into her that she realized someone was ill. It wasn't until she followed the racing gurney, intravenous bottle clanking, down the corridor into the left wing, that she knew, two turns before reaching his office, something had happened to Dr. Blaiser.

Frank Jordan stood at the open door to Bill Blaiser's office, dispassionately directing the paramedics to the slumped figure behind a cleared desk. Packed cartons stood against one wall, ready to be carted to the four-wheel-drive Jeep Cherokee the scientist kept highly waxed, pinstriped, and named.

Stunned into silence, Julie stood rooted to the spot just outside the door. Breathless from her chase, she watched as the expert team thoroughly checked the still figure. They didn't even begin revival procedures. Looking at Frank Jordan, one medic slowly shook his head. The other lowered the gurney into position. Julie frantically searched for an answer, her tear-filled eyes focused on Jordan just in time to see him nervously nod. A slight twitch at the corner of his mouth was the only life in his composed face. The gurney, loaded with Blaiser's body, slowly started its travel on the reverse route, its lifeless passenger covered from curious eyes, its purpose no longer urgent.

"My God," she finally gasped, turning to Jordan, "what happened?"

Jordan looked directly at her, his eyes holding hers, his face a perfect mask.

"He choked on a chicken bone, Mrs. Murray. Dr. Blaiser was alone, but he did manage to hit his emergency button, the one that rings directly into my office and the security gate. By the time we got here it was too late."

"A chicken bone? Impossible! I brought him a food tray, hamburger and fries, an hour ago," Julie said, more confused than before.

"You know how he was always snacking, Mrs. Murray. There's a take-out carton on the floor next to his desk, and it's still half-full."

"But he didn't have time to eat, finish packing," Julie said as she gestured at the filled boxes, "go out for food, and return. I brought him dinner an *hour* ago. And where's the tray I brought?" Looking around, Julie Murray could find no trace of the earlier meal. Her head whirled with shock and something else, something she couldn't identify.

Jordan's atonal voice broke through the mists clouding her thoughts. "He must have dropped the tray in the cafeteria when he went out for more food. If you look, I'm sure you'll find it. Dr. Blaiser was under a great deal of stress lately, and as I'm sure you know, he ate more when he was upset."

Looking at Jordan, Julie could only nod her head.

"About the VIP luncheon, Mrs. Murray," Jordan continued, taking her arm and leading her away from the near-emptied office and back in the direction of her own territory, the cafeteria and its adjoining kitchen and office, "what do you have planned?"

"I have the menu all ready, Mr. Jordan, if you'd like to see it." Tears continued to trickle down her cheeks. "A hot buffet for twenty."

After checking and approving the meal, Jordan left Julie Murray alone in her cubicle, admonishing her to be sure that all preparations were complete and well-executed. The luncheon, he strongly impressed, was very important to the continued funding of the facility. These were the people who approved grants. She assured him all would be perfectly in order, then the tears returned in earnest.

"Why Dr. Blaiser?" Julie asked herself, again and again. The tears finally subsided and she glanced at her watch. She should have been home by now and, reaching for the phone, Julie—who had watched family and friends pass away over the years, and for whom she always asked the same question, why?—punched out her own number to ask her husband to pick her up tonight. She was too upset to drive.

Frank Jordan sat, silent and alone, his hands worrying a rack of paper napkins, in a corner of the deserted cafeteria. He listened to the sobs from Julie Murray's cubicle. Her deep sigh and the sound of her using the phone stopped his distracted activity. As quietly as possible he leaned forward to hear what would come next. Her shaking voice reached him across the darkened room.

"Bert, I need you to pick me up tonight. I don't think I'd better drive." Silence, the sound of listening, filled the room.

"I didn't know you kept count of how many times you picked me up," Julie gasped. "You know I only ask when it's important." Again, the pause.

"No, I do not make a habit of hysterics," Jordan

heard her snap into the phone, "and I'll be waiting out front. As usual."

With this unexpected conclusion to a long, hard day, Jordan allowed the first smile he'd been able to muster all week to break loose on his tight face. Someone with a reputation for hysteria, no matter what suspicions he'd seen in her eyes, would never get very far with her doubts. A small point would be to surreptitiously spread the rumor of Julie Murray's emotional instability.

Stretching back in the molded plastic chair, he clasped his hands behind his head and, still smiling to himself, watched the dietician leave her office to wait for her ride.

Standing on the freshly painted steps in front of Elise and Jeff's row house, a chilled bottle of wine tucked in her large tote, Bree suddenly found she was close to complete exhaustion. The day had been a long one. JoJo and their friends, their clan, had taken her by the hand and spent hours talking to her. Teaching her. Instilling in her, they said, the fundamentals of her new role as high priestess. Her responsibility, passed on from her mother. Bree listened, attentively and at great length, asking questions when unfamiliar territory was covered, but to her surprise—even she believed she'd ignored the clan's ways—she found that she was intimately familiar with most of the material. The one gray area, the one where she asked the most questions and the one where she received the fewest answers, was in trying to discern what Michael was doing. Her brother's move to another part of the city kept his activities from the watchful eyes of the clan; he remained a mystery to most, but even those who dared venture a guess were too frightened to commit to their theories.

All Bree wanted was to have a normal evening, with normal people, not listening to her supporters tell her what her responsibilities were and how to best fulfill them—or warn her about facing the wrath of her pow-

erful brother. An unexpected anger began to rise,
overcoming the exhaustion she felt. She'd never asked
for any power, never wanted anything more than to be
a healer.

The door started to open and brought Bree back to
the moment; she managed a passable smile.

"As promised, chilled wine, work clothes, and errands done. I'm all yours, as soon as you let me in."

"You have your own key, Bree. It's time you used
it."

"I forgot, believe it or not. Next time. Anyway, the
key is for office hours. You're not open for business
yet."

"Just a few more days and we will be. Not that long
at all." Elise's infectious cheer caught Bree and the
two women hugged warmly in the foyer.

"I'm so excited," they said in unison, throwing back
their heads to laugh at the shared moment.

"I'm so glad you're here." Elise held Bree's hand.
"You have to be the first to see what we've done."

Swinging around, Elise opened the foyer doors to
the freshly painted waiting-room and reception area.
"Here it is! What do you think?"

Looking at the spotless walls, Bree felt secure. "It's
wonderful. I can't believe you did everything yourself.
You even trimmed the windows and doors in enamel
base." Turning to Elise, Bree was truly amazed.
"You're supposed to be the resident doctor, not the
handyman."

"One of the resident doctors; the other has just finished the downstairs plumbing."

Laughing together, the women headed for the cozy
kitchen. "I'll never tell the patients, should they ask.
We'd have trouble justifying the fee schedule if they
knew their doctors moonlighted as renovators."

"Don't worry, Bree. Except for the two women Jeff's
father referred to us, and only because they've both
moved to the city and can't see him on the island anymore, no one we're going to see is even aware of a
concept like fee structures. Our office charges will be

low because . . . well, being in this house and in practice is everything we want. All we need concern ourselves with is meeting overhead.''

"Admirable, Elise," Bree sighed. "But that won't furnish the nursery or pay the mortgage when you're too pregnant to practice.''

"Let's wait until I get pregnant before we worry about furnishing the nursery. It might be a while, at least until we get the practice running well enough to hold its own.''

"You're the doctor. By the way, what is that Mr. and Mrs. Vaughan plaque doing on the door? I know it's traditional to hang a shingle out front, but you already have the Dr. Elise Crawford and Dr. Jeffrey Vaughan sign.''

Laughing, Elise took Bree's arm to guide her past two large cartons of books blocking the kitchen archway. "Private joke, Bree," she said, then added with alarm, "You don't think it looks odd, do you?''

"No," Bree warmly responded, "I think it looks just fine. It might even save me having to answer 'the' question that was bound to have been a number-one priority of patients.''

Jeff's amused voice reached them from the kitchen before they entered the room. "Why, do you think our patients would have been more concerned with our conjugal status than our fees?

"You were eavesdropping, honey," Elise countered with a soft kiss to her husband's unshaven cheek.

"I'd hardly call it eavesdropping. There's not a single eave between here and the foyer. Besides, you know I'm tuned in to everything about you.''

"How about shaving before dinner? I'll even let you use the upstairs bath.''

"Now that I've got sinks working in both baths on this floor? I'd rather use the newly installed product of my handiwork.''

"Suit yourself, but at least upstairs is clean. I've been working in the front room all day—take a quick look. We're going to have a grand ceremony after dinner to launch the reception room.''

"Oh, my," Bree gasped in mock horror, "and I thought you wanted to drink the wine, not use it to launch a room.''

"That *is* a much better idea, Bree," Jeff said over his shoulder as he disappeared with razor in hand. "We'll do it you way.''

"Can I help with dinner?" Bree offered, noting that the kitchen was clear of any food preparation and, as a matter of fact, clear of any food.

"Oh," Elise said, a bemused look lighting her face, "we're having dinner catered." With that, the door bell sounded. "That should be it now.''

The delivery man stood sullenly at the door, two bags of Chinese food at his feet. Wordlessly presenting Elise with the bill, he carefully counted out her change and, apparently approving the tip, walked down the steps in a slightly better mood.

Bags of food still in her arms, Elise turned sharply away from the front door. An urgency edged her words. "Bree, get away from the bathroom door.''

Jumping, and moving closer to the door in the process, Bree nudged against the doorjamb. Before she could ask why, a loud yell of frustration came from the bathroom, followed immediately by a flood of water from under the door. Standing in a large puddle, shoes soaked, Bree looked questioningly at Elise. The door to the bathroom opened and Jeff stood there, chest bare, razor in hand, and half his face still lathered. The drainage pipe from the sink was collapsed at his feet.

"If I call a real plumber to come first thing in the morning, we can still open on schedule," Jeff muttered.

"Finish shaving upstairs, the food is here." Elise brushed past her husband. Bree, still standing in the widening puddle, watched Elise's back as it disappeared into the kitchen.

"She knew what was going to happen," Bree said out loud.

"Bree"—Jeff put his hand on Bree's arm—"she always knows when things are going to happen. Or," he added, "at least she always seems to."

"If you two are going to stand there and chat all evening, the food will get cold," Elise called from the kitchen.

"Use those warming ovens you brag about," Jeff countered on his way up the stairs. "I have to finish shaving. Doctor's orders."

In the kitchen the two women recaptured their closeness of just moments before.

Her curiosity getting the best of her, Bree turned to ask, "How did you know something was going to happen?"

"I don't know. I mean, I didn't know anything was going to happen, at least not something specific. It's just that sometimes, well, sometimes I know when something is going to happen." Elise turned away from Bree. "Don't think I'm strange or anything, Bree."

"It happens to me, too, Elise. That's why I asked."

The women looked at each other. They knew each other from a year of working in the same hospital, yet it simultaneously occurred to both of them that they might not know each other that well at all.

"I knew we had more in common than our interest in health," Elise said with a strained smile. "But an occasional hunch doesn't count for much, does it?"

"Maybe it does. How occasional are these, uh, hunches, and how strong?" Bree pursued the line of questioning with vigor. Her afternoon with JoJo and the others still fresh in her mind, she wondered if one of the reasons she had been drawn so strongly to Elise was a deeper, more common bond.

"Oh, you know, occasionally," Elise hedged, her nervousness apparent in her clumsy unpacking of the food sacks. "They're not important and I don't usually remember them afterward. I would already have forgotten about the pipes if you weren't here, asking.''

"But, Elise, if you do have these premonitions, well, maybe you're psychic. I have some friends who—" But Bree's offer was cut off by the sudden change in Elise.

Elise's face became tight and drawn, the corners of her mouth pulled in tense white lines. "I don't have premonitions," Elise snapped. "I must have heard the pipe break, or something. I knew Jeff was working on the sinks and it was just a good guess.''

Animosity now hung heavy in the air, as real as a chill wind blowing in from outside. Bree eased off her pointed questions and decided to take another tack. "It's just that I spent the afternoon with some friends and we were talking about, well, hunches and things.''

"It sounds like you have an odd assortment of friends, Bree," Elise responded, cool and aloof. "I didn't realize you went in for all this hocus-pocus stuff.''

Realizing that this was unfamiliar territory, and for Elise uncharted, Bree chose to gracefully exit the conversation. "If I really did believe in hunches and stuff, I would be winning lotteries and having my household help heat up the food, wouldn't I?" Winking broadly to emphasize the fact that she was transferring the food, cartons and all, to the warming oven, Bree continued to banter lightly.

Jeff's tread on the stairs brought an immediate change to Elise's mood.

"What were you saying, Bree, about not launching the room but pouring some of the wine into ourselves? God, you're quick, I didn't see you move the food into the warming ovens. I'm surprised you figured out how they worked. It took me days.''

Bree looked sharply at Elise. Elise didn't recall lighting the oven, moving the cartons of food, nor did she seem to remember their conversation. Had she blanked out on everything since Jeff went upstairs?

Bree distracted herself by fumbling in her tote bag

for the handcrafted corkscrew she brought for the housewarming. Her mind still churning, Bree recalled how well she and Elise worked together in the hospital. There *was* a bond between them that went deeper than their shared interest in medicine or even of their growing friendship. Bree had felt it before, but it was always elusive. Now, for the first time, she realized what it was and why it was so vague. Elise also had a power, a gift. Bree wondered if Elise hid it from herself as well as she hid it from others.

Spending the afternoon with her people and finally acknowledging herself as leader of the clan had clarified many things for Bree. Most of all, it forced her to face what she herself had been avoiding: her power, a power that went far beyond being able to reduce a fever with the touch of a hand or of starting a broken bone to mend. If she hadn't been so busy hiding her own gift, she would have noticed Elise's. Now the question was, What was Elise hiding? Hiding even from herself?

Triumphant in her search for the ornate corkscrew, Bree carefully composed her thoughts. "The only problem with carrying all of your earthly possessions around is trying to find any particular one. For that reason, and also because it happens to be a momentous occasion, I would like to present you with this— and have one less possession to carry around."

Jeff reached out for the highly polished, wood-handled utensil. "This is terrific, Bree. What is it?"

"It's a corkscrew, of course, made from a petrified grape vine."

Jeff laughed. "It must have grown only fermented grapes to get this petrified."

"It's lovely, Bree." Elise said. "We can keep it out, in plain sight, as an objet d'art."

"Yes," added Jeff, "and no one need know that we're really just keeping it handy for the moment office hours are over."

"We've a few more days until we have office hours,"

chided Elise, "and I'd rather not wait that long. Let's open the wine and get some plates out."

"I'll get the plates," Bree offered, welcoming the opportunity to keep busy.

"And I'll get the glasses," Elise added.

"That leaves me to either put the food out or open the wine," Jeff said.

"Open the wine," both women chimed in unison and, laughing at the reestablished camaraderie, soon had the table set for three.

The wine bottle opened with ease and Jeff filled the three glasses.

"A toast is often the pourer's prerogative, and I choose to take it." Raising his glass, he faced the two women he knew he would be spending his days with. His nurse looked at him with trust and his wife with love. Jeff addressed the wine in his glass. "To all of us, for being here at the beginning, and to all of us for a long, long time."

As she raised her glass for the toast, Elise was startled by a gut-wrenching grip. She felt as if her heart had stopped after one frighteningly intense, final beat and had plunged into her bowels. For a moment as long as eternity she waited for the second heartbeat, convinced it would never follow. Forcing the smile to stay on her face, she quickly searched for a reason. It wasn't her time of the month, and she knew she was well. Her father-in-law had just insisted on another complete checkup, another of his tyrannical examinations forced upon her twice a year. Suddenly the frequency of Hal Vaughan's insistent physicals weighed heavily; maybe she was ill, maybe her father-in-law was tracking some deadly disease without telling her.

Moving the wineglass to her lips—a simple act, yet one she needed to will herself to complete—a heaviness entered her arms and began to drag them down. The glass slipped from her grasp and shattered.

"Oh, my dear God," Elise moaned as she crumbled to the floor, "I can't even toast my future."

11

AN ALL-ENCOMPASSING HUNGER ROSE IN NED HARper's loins as he followed T.D. along the busy sidewalk. The scores of people that hustled past him, sometimes jogging his arm or brushing his shoulder, might not have existed. His eyes stayed riveted on the dark hair undulating softly a few steps in front of him. That, and an occasional glimpse of her chiseled profile when she surreptitiously turned to see if he was still a discreet distance behind, kept him fully entranced.

T.D. had suggested that they leave the office separately and that he follow her home—just in case either, or both, should encounter a familiar face. His admiration for her attention to detail, on any and all levels, would have been commendable if his desire to possess her had not been all consuming. Her hips' rhythmic movement accented the slim skirt she wore, split in the back to upper thigh. Ned wondered how he could have spent the entire day in the same office as this creature and not have noticed such an open expanse of shapely leg. His eyes remained locked on the moving figure, his thoughts focused on closing a door behind them.

Turning into a less-crowded street, T.D. looked back to ensure her new direction was noticed. The small smile barely touching her lips continued to haunt Ned even after she turned her head away. Tasting her lips was the one fantasy of his life that, so far, had been fulfilled; her face stayed in his mind's eye, obscuring his vision. It was impossible not to think of his hand resting on the small piece of thigh that kept winking into sight, and he knew, was absolutely certain, that the moments to come would live up to his wildest expectations. The image of flesh on flesh burned in his vision. Each blind step brought him closer to fulfillment. Ned heard his name softly called. Looking up, he realized he had gone past her building.

T.D. was on the top step of her brownstone's stoop, her key poised at the door. Knowing full well why Ned had missed seeing her turn into the building, she waited for him to return. Opening the heavy wooden door, she slipped into the dim hallway and stood in the small foyer, holding the door ajar to prevent the automatic lock from engaging.

Cautiously slipping into the vestibule, Ned couldn't wait any longer. He brusquely pulled T.D. to him and buried his mouth on hers.

"Wait, just a few more minutes," she whispered, leaning close to his ear, lightly licking the lobe. "It's just upstairs." Gently pulling away, T.D. opened the inner door and led him to the stairwell.

"I'm ready to take you here and now. I can't believe I feel like this. I haven't acted this way since high school. I've seen you every day and until, well, until last night never really thought of you as more than the most competent communications director a candidate could have."

T.D.'s sensual laughter did not diminish his need. "Well, Governor, I know why you didn't notice until then. It just wasn't the right time."

"The right time is now, right now. Which is your apartment?"

She pulled away and nodded toward the staircase, motioning for him to follow. As if anything could have prevented that from happening . . .

Reaching the second-floor landing, T.D. turned back and blocked him from climbing the last step. "I'm on this floor. Do you think you can wait about thirty seconds more?"

Looking up at her from his step, Ned smiled. "I'm not sure." He found he was at just the right height to reach around and clutch the buttocks he'd lustily admired for the last half hour. Pulling her hips to his face, he pressed his mouth to the thin skirt fabric. Feeling her heat rise, inhaling her musk, his senses reeled and he found he could not pull away.

She let her head fall back, her body raging with joy. He's here, she thought. He's mine. I've done it!

T.D. moved his hands from her hips and stepped backward, running her fingers lightly down his arms. They found themselves holding hands. "You'll have to." Laughing, almost to herself but deciding to share the thought, she leaned toward him. "Next time I'll be more careful projecting. It's a spell, you know."

"If this is a spell, you can cast one on me anytime," Ned answered, his voice hoarse, his thoughts no further than the bed he fervently prayed waited for them on the other side of the door.

Unlocking the simple latch, T.D. let them both in. "I guess I didn't realize you were halfway there," she said softly as she stroked Ned's cheek.

"Let me take you all the way there," Ned said, and swept her toward the glass doors closing off the bedroom.

Her large satin-covered bed, gleaming in the soft light subtly left on in the corner, took up most of the small room. Dozens of throw pillows filled half the bed, the profusion so great they fell invitingly to the floor. An almost cloying scent rose from the dim light—floral essence rubbed on the bulb filled the room with the odor of seductive, smoldering flowers.

"Is this for me?" Ned teased, further stimulated by the erotic chamber. He began to undo her skirt. "Or do you just have it ready and waiting?"

"It's for you, Ned, it's definitely all for you."

The lushness of the room, heavily draped in tapestry, set it far away from the streets they had just walked. Any windows the room contained were hidden behind folds of heavy fabric, cutting off not only light and sound but the presence of the city. Lost in the intimacy of the room, clothing easily fell away.

"Oh, Ned, you've no idea how much this means to me. No idea at all."

As Ned stroked her silky skin, his thoughts went no further than the hardness he wore between his legs. Still standing, he found himself entering her. While it wasn't what she had planned, her ready wetness held him tightly in place. Unable to move inside her, Ned moaned softly and tightly gripped her buttocks. He greedily pulled at her, pushing himself farther in, not letting her make any movement.

Impaled—but not about to let this man choreograph her seduction—she clenched her vaginal muscles, milking the shaft inside her. Ned groaned, his body shuddering with each of her contractions. They were as still as a sculpture, their only movements hidden inside. Ned's breathing intensified and he pushed her up and away, then pulled back, his arms finding the strength to move her in the smooth fluid motions of coitus.

T.D. balked. It was too soon to fulfill him; there needed to be more intimacy for him to remember her by.

Lifting herself from him, she pulled away. "I guess I forgot I was halfway there with you," she said softly, leading him to the perfumed bed. "I'll just have to be more careful, won't I?"

Beyond words or their meanings Ned moved to the edge of the satin cover, pulling her with him.

"Oh, dear fates, she's fainted," Bree gasped. "Jeff, do something, you're a doctor."

"Loosen her waistband," Jeff calmly instructed, not allowing his fear to show. Elise had fainted before—too often, he felt. But scores of tests and examinations had shown nothing, except, perhaps, a propensity for fainting. At times he suspected a pattern but, as yet, had failed to discern its nature. If only, he thought, I could remove myself emotionally, I'm sure I would be able to diagnose.

Reassured by Jeff's control of the situation, Bree relaxed. Elise was, she saw, breathing regularly and, having been made as comfortable as possible, would soon come out of the swoon. "Has this ever happened before?"

"Yes," Jeff tersely replied, wondering how much he should share with this woman, whom, while he instinctively trusted, he did not know all that well. Admonishing himself for overreacting, Jeff reminded himself that he was a doctor and Bree a nurse—and consulting with her would be a natural thing to do.

"That is," he continued, "she has a history of fainting, or sometimes just swooning, spells. There seems to be a pattern, but I can't quite pinpoint it. Help me move her to the couch."

Together they gently lifted Elise's limp body and carried her to the room planned as Jeff's office—the only room other than the kitchen reasonably organized. A large red leather couch, bought used but in good condition, stood against one wall under a framed Chagall reproduction, a gift from Elise on their first anniversary. The print, an expensive silk screening, was of Marc Chagall's *Homage to Apollinaire*. After seeing Elise's fascination with the work, Jeff had researched the subject and found that, aside from being a tribute to four of the artist's closest friends, the central subject was the image of Eve, springing from Adam's rib but still a part of him. He'd romantically asked Elise if she thought they were like Adam and Eve, building a new world, and she'd shaken her head.

"No," she'd said, and he remembered how her eyes dulled and her face paled. "I'm not part of that picture." And having said that, she fainted.

"Take tonight," Jeff continued after they had arranged Elise in a comfortable position. "You were here. We were just sitting down to eat. We'd been talking about nothing really important or horrifying or otherwise emotionally debilitating. Opening the office in two days is an important event but one we've been gradually working up to, not a sudden shocking event."

"That's true," Bree responded, carefully sifting

through the evening's events. "There was the flooded bathroom, though."

"Come on, Bree, a flooded bathroom is hardly cause for a fainting spell. Especially long after it happened. It was already mopped up." Jeff's tone distinctly conveyed his annoyance of Bree's suggestion.

"Jeff, I don't mean the water itself, I mean what happened before."

"What happened before? I was shaving and the pipe came loose. Hardly anything to faint over."

"No, I mean that Elise knew it was going to happen."

"You said that at the time."

"Yes, and you said she always knows when things are going to happen, or"—Bree looked thoughtful—"if I can remember your exact words: 'at least she always seems to.' What did you mean?"

"Elise does seem to know things; she's always been very sensitive. But being intuitive around me isn't that difficult. I mean, with my being the plumber it doesn't take all that much imagination to figure out that a pipe is going to come loose."

"Jeff, I think it's more than that. Elise is sensitive and intuitive, that's very true. Perhaps more than you realize, perhaps even more than she's willing to admit to herself."

Jeff's back stiffened. "Perhaps you think there's something wrong with my wife's mind?"

"No. Not wrong. Just, perhaps, different." Sensing the animosity she was causing, Bree pulled her next comment back, realizing that if anyone should know how difficult the stress of denial was, it was herself. There was something here, but finding out exactly what it was needed to be handled far more discreetly.

"After all," Bree switched tactics, "I agree sensitive people are usually intuitive, and while they seem to rely on feelings rather than facts, the feelings are almost always based on a myriad of information. Something is going to happen because a series of subtle events have pointed in that direction. Like Freud's conclusion that 'there are no accidents.' The pipes are a good example. Elise knew you'd just put them in and knew"—here Bree allowed herself a sly smile as the truth of the statement she was about to make could not be overlooked—"your, ah, expertise as a plumber. Last, but not least, she knew that the sink was being used for the first time. It's only logical that she felt something was going to happen."

"Of course, Bree," Jeff relaxed. "That's exactly what I've been saying all along."

Elise's eyes began to flutter and a soft moan escaped from her dry lips.

"Get her some water," Jeff said to Bree. Bree hurried to comply. "Darling, are you all right?" he asked, his entire attention returning to his wife, her pale face raised to his.

"Of course. I fainted again. I better have my iron levels checked. I can't believe I fainted again," she repeated, still dazed. Elise's embarrassment was a regular occurrence when she woke from a swoon.

"You're in perfect health, and you know it, though we will check your iron. You're not anemic, though, probably more likely just exhausted from painting and plastering."

Bree smiled as she saw Elise sitting up, her color returning. "Here's some water, drink it all. I'll be right back."

Gratefully accepting the tall glass of cool water, Elise sipped it silently.

"Are you feeling better?" Jeff asked, the concern in his voice masked but unquestionably there.

"Much, much better. I think you're right about overworking. I think, in fact, I fainted just to have an excuse to lie down."

"Dr. Crawford, when you start making diagnoses like that, I know you need a rest."

Bree entered the room carrying the opened wine and three filled glasses. She'd swept away the shards of Elise's broken glass and found a matching goblet.

"I just thought that since brandy is often used to

bring someone out of a swoon—and I'm speaking authoritatively as an avid reader of gothic romance and not merely as a nurse—we could finish our toast in here.''

"Excellent idea, Bree.'' Jeff smiled as he reached for two glasses. "As a voracious viewer of forties' melodramas on late-night television, and the medicine practiced therein, I agree.''

Handing Elise her glass, which she took with a steady hand, Jeff raised his. "To all of us, for being here at the beginning,'' he repeated his earlier toast, "for a long, long time.''

'Make that forever, Jeff,'' Elise softly said as she raised the glass to her lips and sipped the wine. "Our forever, whatever it may hold.''

Bree stood quietly, not intruding on the tender moment she saw unfolding before her eyes. Yet, she feared, forever may hold more than they expected.

Basking in the warm afterglow of climactic relaxation, Ned reached over to stroke T.D.'s sleeping body. To him, the touch of her skin matched the satin sheets for smoothness, and the perfume that permeated the room was no match for her own wondrous scent.

Her dark hair splayed out on the pillow, and hesitant to wake this wonderful woman, Ned amused himself by combing her dark chestnut locks into long curlicues on the peach pillow. T.D. lay silent, amused, as her hair was formed into swirls to the accompaniment of Ned's soft, tuneful humming. Keeping her eyes closed, she slowly stretched her arms above her, arching her back, knowing the graceful lines of her body would hold his interest. Feeling the shift of his hands from her hair to the curve of her back, she rolled over and smiled sleepily at her new lover.

"T.D., you're so beautiful. Sleeping, waking, walking, talking—''

"Ned . . .'' She stopped his litany by gently touching his lips with her finger. "As my lover, you'll have to stop calling me by my initials, especially here in bed.''

"I don't even know your name—or names, I guess, one for each initial."

"It's Talia Dora," she whispered as she dropped her arms around him and, again, pulled him close. "In private, of course."

The take-out food, kept warm and moist in the holding ovens, provided welcome and needed sustenance. Dinner conversation stayed light, and by the end of the meal hearty laughter from all three filled the kitchen. Soon, too soon, they all agreed, the evening came to an end.

Walking Bree to the door, Elise appeared more vibrant than at the onset of the evening. Bree's own exhaustion had dissipated with the earlier emergency but was again rapidly closing in on her and she began to make good-byes. "Thanks for feeding me. I'll work it off tomorrow, if I may. Not having to go back to the hospital has left me feeling freer than I thought possible, but also a bit at loose ends."

"There are no loose ends, Bree," Elise said with an odd smile. "I know, now I know, that it's important for you to be here."

"Of course it is! I've been looking forward to working with you and Jeff—the Doctors Crawford and Vaughan—for months now. It's about time it's really happening."

"It's more than working here, Bree. I think you know that. I don't fully understand it myself, but there's something else—for both of us—that's going to happen. No, it is happening, and will be here with us soon."

Taken aback, Bree thought of her own crisis: her mother's death and her new position in the coven. Her mother's last words to her—that "she" would need her soon. Was "she" Elise? It had to be. There was also Michael, though how could Elise be involved? Yet, looking into Elise's clear hazel eyes, Bree knew Elise was right. There was something else, something that involved Elise very deeply and that intertwined with her own life.

"Bree, I need to talk to you," Elise whispered. "There are things I can't talk about with Jeff—not yet anyway. Things I know but don't understand. Somehow I think you'll understand them." Elise continued to look directly at Bree, her gaze unwavering, and raised her voice while switching the subject. "I'd very much appreciate your help tomorrow. We can set up the reception area to be completely functional and finish the examining room."

"And talk," said Bree, softly but firmly, now knowing that her fate was bound with Elise's. This was the woman her mother warned she must be prepared to help. They would find out how.

"No," Elise again lowered her voice to a whisper, "I need to talk to you tonight. It can't wait any longer. I've kept things inside for too long and it's time to let them out. I don't know why—not exactly anyway—but you're the only person I believe I can trust. Can I call you later, after Jeff is asleep?"

"Of course," Bree gently answered. "I'm going right home now and I'll even turn off the answering machine. In case I doze off your call will wake me."

"Bree, thank you." Elise smiled her relief. Starting to close the door, she paused and, taking a trembling breath, added, "When I fainted tonight, it wasn't because I was drained or tired. It was just the opposite. All of a sudden I felt as if I were so full of life I was going to burst. There was more to me—not less. I only felt like that once before, during a terrible argument with my sister. Tonight was the same feeling: a surge of fullness, of being, I'm not sure what it is but I need to talk to you."

Bree reached out to touch Elise's fingers, curved around the sturdy door. "I'll be there," she answered. "Just call."

12

"JORDAN'S A SHIT," ED HAWTHORN RAGED "AS ADministrator of this facility his competence is equal to that of an aardvark monitoring giraffe feeding habits."

"I could better argue for or against your position, Dr. Hawthorn," Judd Thacker calmly responded, "if I understood your rather obtuse analogy. Are you by chance suggesting that he has his head in the clouds?"

Hawthorn cracked a small smile. "That wasn't what I had in mind—though, now that you mention it, there is some truth to the theory. I was thinking more of Jordan being a pigish creature with his snout buried in the earth, sucking up insect life. Admittedly a foolish picture but one that sprang to mind."

Judd Thacker continued to refill his pipe; the pipe, he'd often expounded, despite the stereotype—or because of it—was as vital to his image as the diplomas that hung, laminated onto mahogany, behind his desk. The bottom edges of the certificates were carefully aligned to the top of his seated head—he'd even taken Polaroid shots during their hanging to ensure the effect was complete. Once the pipe was fully stoked, Thacker nodded to his still-flushed associate, thereby announcing his intention to again speak.

"Despite Frank Jordan's questionable personality traits, he has, nonetheless, proved an adequate administrator. Funding has flowed, new equipment requisitions filled with an amazing alacrity, not to mention with barely any inquisition of the requester. Considering we've been given a minimum of direction, we've been afforded a maximum of latitude in what we do and how we're able to do it. If I'd had a Frank Jordan at my previous facilities, we might have gotten somewhere. This is, of course, despite the gentleman's rather obnoxious attitude toward us as individuals, wherein he seems to imagine us as pieces of equipment. His lab, make no bones about it, is well-outfitted, down to the humanoid types working within his hallowed walls.''

"But, Dr. Thacker," Ed Hawthorn responded, using his associate's title as formally as his associate had used his, "that shit withheld vital information from us. And look at what happened. We have to turn over the work to another facility and Bill Blaiser is dead.''

"Vital information? I hardly consider the source of our funding vital to our research. As a true scientist, we must—''

"Forget about the funding. What about our direction?''

"Ah, well, yes, that would have been helpful. On the other hand, look where we got without it.'' Judd Thacker cheerfully tapped his pipe into a large marble ashtray. "We were told to carefully research the cytoplasm, to ignore the nucleus, and we found a completely new factor in viral interventions.''

Hawthorn was running his hands through his thinning blond hair, his increasing agitation causing him to forget his own cardinal rule of not touching the receding and thinning crown one stroke more than absolutely necessary for grooming.

"Yes,'' Ed Hawthorn continued, by now vigorously massaging his scalp with both hands, "but we were given no idea of the scope. We had two choices: to go with the viral DNA or that in the organelles. We headed in the wrong direction for the project. They wanted the organelles containing MtDNA, and if Blaiser was right about the ultimate goal . . .''

"Again, my young friend, look at what we achieved.'' Judd Thacker waved his pipe stem toward the younger scientist. "We're not being paid these high salaries to feel guilt about discovering a replicable factor *and* developing a new vaccine. On the other hand, now that we've accomplished something rather significant, we've assured our funding's continuance. All we do is shift our research.''

''In what direction?'' Hawthorn asked, his agitation exhausting him. ''Fingerprinting mitochondria DNAs? Larger facilities than ours have been doing that for years. Emory University has exhaustively traced this female legacy, producing a biological history of mankind. Which direction are we supposed to go?''

''Let's call it a hunch,'' Thacker replied, leaning forward, catching and holding Hawthorn's eyes, ''but I think we're looking for a specific genetic history— from the donor of that unique sample we were given. The one sample where the subject was not identified. The one where we found the MtDNA structure went beyond the point that accounted for all genetic history already known. You know as well as I that the genetic code is universal, that the same codes are used in part by every organism—from bacteria to man. The 'primeval soup' is Biology 101. But that sample continued beyond any mapping ever made. I, for one, would like to know what that factor means.''

''You seem to think our entire project was designed to break down that specific sample,'' Hawthorn retorted. ''To find what that factor is—and what it does.''

Judd Thacker nodded. ''I don't think it started out that way—based on our chairman's explanation of the project's beginning—but, yes, right now I'm quite sure that's our direction. Perhaps even the reason for Jordan being added to the staff. He did point out that it was the unique MtDNA factor that allowed him to access federal funds.''

''We don't even know who the sample is from,'' Hawthorn protested.

''We don't have to know. All we have to do is work with the samples.''

''I can't believe you said that,'' Hawthorn exclaimed. ''You can map MtDNA fingerprints until kingdom come, but unless you've a live organism to match them against, all you have is a collection of autoradiographs.''

''I suppose that's true,'' Judd Thacker admitted. ''But right now we're not being given any live bodies. Just fresh tissue samples, twice a year. And until the day a body is produced to match the samples, I'm perfectly content to analyze the structures.''

''Spoken like a dedicated research scientist,'' Hawthorn sneered. ''I, for one, like to accomplish something, and spending my life mapping a single individual's MtDNA structure—no matter how unique—is not what I had in mind.''

''Patience. I'm quite sure that all this funding isn't designed to produce a series of autoradiographs. There's enough DNA and MtDNA photos in existence without adding another stack. We'll be given the subject herself to work with.''

''A woman, that's right. Sometimes I forget the tangibility of the subject. Mitochondria DNA is inherited exclusively from the mother,'' Hawthorn noted. ''The old Children of Eve legacy. What was that tribe that contained the greatest variation of MtDNA?''

''The !Kung of the Kalahari in Africa,'' Thacker absently responded, still engrossed with his pipe, ''are considered to hold all possible variations of the structure and, as a result, be the oldest known group of humans.''

''You had that answer ready for me. Why?''

''Because it's something I've already thought about. I've even compared our sample to the !Kung variations.'' Judd Thacker calmly looked at Ed Hawthorn. ''And there's no match. Our sample goes beyond—far beyond.''

''That's impossible. Your match must have been flawed.''

''It wasn't. I reran the analyses every which way from Sunday.''

''But if the Children of Eve theory is solid, what's the lineage here?''

''I don't know. How about Daughters of Lilith, for

the time being.'' Thacker grinned, finding his own rare attempt at humor amusing.

''We're working with the Lilith Factor.''

Pulling himself back to his usual state of pomposity, Thacker looked directly at his associate. ''In reality, though, we'll have to wait for our subject to be made known to us before we expound on these theories.''

''I just hope it's sooner than later. I'm losing patience.''

Thacker's laughter filled the office, in and of itself a rarity. ''You're amazing. It's just one day since we were given a specific goal and you're already chomping at the bit. But,'' he continued, ''I think you're right. I also have a hunch we're on a 'push' now and something concrete will happen soon.''

''For starters, we need this so-called subject, live and on the premises,'' Hawthorn said, all apprehensions about Bill Blaiser's death erased in the excitement.''

''For starters you're half-right. We need the subject on the premises.''

Wearily unlatching the fourth and last lock, Bree entered her darkened kitchen. The absence of light was welcome to her tired body and drained mind; nothing to be seen meant nothing to be done and invited one to ignore all else, to slip into bed and much-needed sleep. She couldn't tell Elise not to call, knowing that Elise's need was real and intertwined with her own, yet the thought of a dreamless sleep was infinitely more appealing than a long phone conversation. Sleep was calling to her as a lover would—beckoning her into the bedroom, enticing her between smooth sheets, promising her a wondrous pleasure.

Lighting the stove under the ever-present kettle of water, Bree further used the match to light four candles. The candles, a prayer to her mother, provided all the light she needed or wanted. Opening the kitchen cabinet, Bree rummaged through orderly rows of boxes and tins, looking for a caffeine-based tea. Practice

what you preach, she scolded; herbals are fine for relaxing but I need the real thing. If there was coffee in
the house, I would drink it.

Once the cup of hot, strong tea was in her hands,
Bree walked to her chair by the phone. It was only
hours ago she had woken in this chair, her mother's
presence still lingering in the room. Closing her eyes,
Bree let herself drift. No, there was nothing there now.

The beverage loosened the knots in her neck and
gently prodded her awake. Slipping gratefully into the
overstuffed chair, she was barely settled in before the
electronic buzz of the phone demanded her attention.

"It's me, Bree," a warm masculine voice reached
her.

"JoJo, I can't talk now, I'm expecting a call. An
important call."

"This is important, Bree. Something is happening.
Michael held a ritual tonight. It wasn't one of ours. In
fact, it was Grand Grimoire."

"That's impossible, JoJo. Michael's coven doesn't
hold high-risk ceremonies. None of the covens do."

"This wasn't an official coven, Bree, they're all accounted for. You know Michael has set himself up with
a group of outcasts, renegades like himself, and there's
no way of tracking what they're doing. Early this evening, after you left us, Alice and some other sensitives
began to feel the echoes of his ceremony. They said it
was very, very strong. Mama Alice was shaking when
she told me about it. I tried to call you but there was
no answer."

"JoJo, I can't talk now, but if you come over early—
come for breakfast—there'll be more than this to dis-
cuss. I'll know more then, but something is happening
and we're all involved. Michael will not get Mother's
powers. Trust me."

An audible sigh—of relief or disbelief, Bree wasn't
sure which—was heard. "I'll be there Bree, about
eight."

"Good night, JoJo."

"Bree, one more thing: be careful tonight."

Smiling at the phone, Bree agreed and gently broke the connection. Before she had a chance to remove her hand, the phone again rang.

"Bree, thank goodness, I kept getting a busy signal."

"It was just my boyfriend, Elise, wanting to see me."

"Tonight?"

"In the morning, for breakfast. I wanted to be alone, tonight, to talk to you."

"Bree, I know you're tired and I know this may seem strange, but somehow, with you and on the phone, I think I can finally talk about things that have been haunting me."

"I know what you mean, Elise. The phone takes away the intimacy, the pressure of having the other person right there."

"I knew you'd understand."

"I feel that way myself, sometimes. Elise, I must ask you about what happened when the pipes broke. You knew. It wasn't just a feeling or a hunch based on Jeff's ineptness, was it?"

"No, Bree. I knew. To be honest, I thought Jeff was perfect, that he could do anything. I closed my eyes for a moment and, in that instant, saw the pipe burst."

"You said it happened before. When?"

"Often. More often than I care to admit. I just know things. In college I always knew who passed or who failed. I even knew when someone close to me was ill, or going to be. My roommate came down with influenza so often I gave up telling her days before, when she could have rested to avoid the worst of the virus. One time I saw Jeff hurt and bleeding. The vision was so real it frightened me for hours, until I could get him on the phone. Jeff had gotten badly scraped when the newsboy ran into him with his bicycle—just minutes before I finally got through to him."

Barely pausing for breath, Elise continued in a rush with the need to unburden herself after a lifetime of silence. "But it's even more than that. When I was a child I lived alone, on a Kentucky mountain, with my mother and sister. A twin sister, Bree. I remember almost nothing about her, not really remember, anyway. Where I would know things, she could do things. Once or twice I did something, but she did things all the time."

"Elise . . ." A chill ran through Bree. "What are you talking about?"

"My sister could make things happen. She would just think about them, I guess, and a cow would fall dead, or a dog, or a barn would go up in flames. One time I found that I was able to, well, reverse what she did. It was with a small dog that had followed us. She, she hurt it and I made it well."

"Elise, I'm beginning to realize what we have in common. Besides our both being healers. I have a brother . . ." Bree paused, unsure of her own ground, then reversed direction, "But tell me more about your sister."

"There isn't too much more, not that I remember. There was another time, one other time, in high school. A boy, his name was Jason, looked at us and she decided, well, that he was hers. He stayed hers for all of high school, then, at graduation, asked her to marry him. She laughed at him, told him no, that she was finished with him. She didn't need him anymore. He was heart broken and turned to me. For comfort, for friendship . . . I guess like any teenage boy, to prove to himself that he was still attractive. My sister was outraged. She got me alone and told me she hated me, she never wanted to see me again. Then we fought, really fought, scratching and tearing hair and kicking. I felt her anger like I'd never felt it before. It pressed on me and filled me and tried to take me from inside." Elise's disembodied voice wavered, her shaky breath was ragged even over the phone line. "It felt, like . . . It felt like what happened tonight. When I fainted. Why I fainted."

"Was it her, tonight?"

"I don't know, Bree, I don't know. I do know that I had to tell you, but I don't know why. It doesn't sound like I know much of anything, does it?"

"It sounds like you know a great deal. If anything, it sounds like you're afraid of what you know." Bree paused, then asked a question that suddenly came to mind: "What happened to the boy, Jason?"

"He died. An autopsy was done, which was unusual for the area, but it was a growing town and he was from an affluent family and had been in perfect health. They said it was a heart attack, that a valve burst. No one could explain it any further."

"When did he die?" Bree felt she knew the answer but had to ask.

"While my sister and I were fighting," Elise wearily answered. "I think it was—"

"I know what you think," Bree cut in. "And you're probably right. You, your sister, I've heard of—even seen—strong bondings that could, well, kill."

"You do understand, Bree. But understand this, too. It wasn't me. I tried to bring him back, but it was too late, much too late."

Elise paused, the horror of the long-ago moment once again as vivid as the day it happened.

"Jason was laid out in the mortuary. His eyelids were sewn shut—I didn't know they did that—and I stood over him and cried and cried. My tears fell and streaked the makeup they'd put on him. He, it, struggled to open his eyes, but the thin lids couldn't pull the threads apart. The smell—his body fighting to come to life when it was already decayed—was overwhelming. I'll never forget, yet I've spent my life trying to forget. My sister left town in a fury directed against me and everyone else. I haven't seen her since."

"Why have you ignored this power?"

"Bree, until tonight, talking to you, I'd managed to forget about Jason. I'd managed to forget a lot. But something is happening now to bring everything back."

"From just talking to me?"

"Yes, in part, but I think Talia's back. I feel her nearby. She's always been strong and directed, but I think, well, I think she's with someone else. Someone like her."

Bree broke the silence that followed. "If she is nearby, there's one person I can think of that she might be with."

"Who?"

"My brother Michael."

Michael's rage reverberated off the draped walls. Rafe cringed in terror behind the altar, ready to drop to his knees for the protection the marble slab could provide.

"The heads had been touched, that's why the ceremony didn't work. Do you realize what you've done?" Michael's voice rose to a level Rafe had not thought was humanly possible. "You've let someone handle them. Who?"

"He's dead now," Rafe said shakily. "It doesn't matter if he's dead, does it?"

"It obviously mattered. All the time of planning this sacrifice, ruined, because I trusted you." Michael spun on his heels and paced the circle still marked on the floor.

Rafe felt the anger abating and began to relax, coming out from his hiding place behind the altar. Maybe, he thought, Michael would . . . His thoughts stopped when a blow to his head, wielded by Michael, knocked him to the floor.

"You fool," Michael sneered. "You incredible fool."

An absolute sureness filled Michael. His eyes narrowed, his skin tightened. A greater vision was revealed to him, its complete truth as basic and infinitely sustaining as the very air he breathed, and the events of the past few days fell neatly into place. It wasn't all Bree's fault, though she was the root of every one of his problems. It wasn't even that cunt Stella's fault:

she was only the conduit for his god's disapproval, the victim she was meant to be.

It was Rafe, Rafe all along. Rafe had betrayed him and lessened his power. Rafe had soiled the sanctity, the purity, of the first ceremony by stealing the uncut heroin, a natural product approved—no, demanded— by his master for the insidious destruction it brought. Rafe had forced him to use some chemical compound unacceptable to his dark lord and master, and Stella's death was the result. His master would not let Stella live, for her life and her bearing of the child would seal the pact.

Rafe had ruined the second ceremony, the Grand Grimoire, a ritual that brought the powers of the underworld to the surface. The ceremony was designed to open a channel between their world and this one— the risks of unleashing such a power assumed for the successes it could bring. It too had failed to let Michael reach his mother's power, a power now unquestionably held by Bree.

But Michael was feeling stronger, more powerful than ever before. Something had entered him during the ceremony, and it wasn't of his mother, of that he was sure.

This was something else, a dark strength, an energy he knew he didn't truly control, but it filled him and satisfied him; it was unyielding and mighty, and even though it wasn't his, not to keep, having it was intoxicating, which was better than the nothing he had before.

Michael reached out and grabbed Rafe by the nape of his neck. He shook the youth, using one hand to easily flip the limp body from side to side. At first the movements were slow and almost graceful, like an animal shaking her young. "This creature betrayed me," Michael heard himself say. He felt his vitality increase, his anger grow, the fervor of his actions become more and more intense, until Rafe was being flung about like a rat in the jaws of a rabid dog.

Rafe mewed like the trapped animal he was, a whine that finally broke into sobs.

"No, my lord," Rafe begged. That he was over his head, in deep-shit trouble, did not escape him.

"Please forgive me. I will be loyal forever. Just forgive me this once."

Michael seemed almost to swell in size, his strength growing with each passing moment. "It wasn't once. It was twice. But I've no doubt you will be loyal forever, forever until you die. Unfortunately in your case, there's only one way to ensure this."

Still holding the youth by one hand on the nape of his neck, the hand closed tight. Rafe's eyes bulged as the pressure on his throat tightened. He kicked wildly but his feet were nowhere near the ground, nor could his legs reach the man holding him.

Michael's own neck corded, though there was no effort being used to hold the youth. He was separate and apart from the action, no more involved, no more exerted than if he were shaking out a dust rag.

His hand opened and Rafe fell. The youth held his bruised neck and gasped for breath. Tears rolled from Rafe's eyes as he scrambled back to hide—the altar had protected him before, if he could only reach its cover now.

In one stride Michael was standing over him, his foot pressing down on the small of Rafe's back. Rafe was pinned to the floor, completely immobile, and he briefly thought that the weight on him was more than any one man could exert. The thought was brief, for in the next moment he felt Michael lean over and grab his arm, then the gut-wrenching, blinding pain of his arm being torn from its socket and his blood pulsing out and hearing the arm thrown casually aside to hit the far wall before his other arm was torn and tossed and then his leg and other leg and how could this be happening in seconds . . . ? But it had, and in those seconds Rafe's body pumped its last drop of blood.

Michael stood back, covered in blood. He was holding a foot, Rafe's foot. Confusion clouded Michael's eyes. Before him was the dismembered torso of what had been his first and most loyal supporter. So the guy fucked up. He was a junkie and that happened with junkies. But he liked Rafe and would have given him another chance.

Again a surge filled Michael. His resolve returned, he was sure again. Of course Rafe had to die. He would have only ruined something else. What was important was *who* he served—what *they* wanted. That was the only thing that mattered.

And, of course, getting back at Bree.

Michael smiled. When he had her power—on top of what possessed him now—he would be omnipotent.

BOOK TWO

13

ELISE ROLLED TO HER LEFT SIDE, WHICH, WHILE IT faced her away from Jeff, usually succeeded in inducing sleep. Even though there was a long tiring day behind her, even though she was surrounded by everything that should bring security, and thus peace and rest, sleep still eluded her. Elise knew the old wounds and memories she'd successfully locked away were regurgitating, trespassing on her carefully constructed new life. The torments churning inside were warnings . . . but for what? Beginning to confide in someone else had, at least, opened her own eyes, but her talk with Bree just three nights ago had barely touched the surface.

Turning back to her sleeping husband, Elise looked at his broad shoulders and strong back outlined in the moonlight. The tightness in her chest began to loosen and she reached out to pull the blanket around him against the slight chill.

It was his love that protected her. No, that wasn't right; the reality was he allowed her to hide. Alone, she used to wake screaming, cold sweat soaking through her nightgowns. A benefit of falling in love was not having to wake up alone. Jeff would be there. A shadow crossed Elise's thoughts—or was it the other way around? Did the fears push her into his arms? How stupid—she shook her head—of course I love him.

Yet it was time to face who she really was or, smiling bitterly to herself, what she really was.

When daylight finally stole into the room, Elise was still awake. Eyes dry, she moved from the bed to the bath with new resolve. Whatever the day held, she was ready to face it. Splashing cool water on her puffed face, she reached for the eye drops to hide her red-rimmed eyes.

"This is no way," Elise murmured, "to start the first day of private practice."

Woken by the unfamiliar clash of pots and pans, Jeff rubbed his sleep-filled eyes. The enticing smell of coffee reached the second floor.

"If you're making breakfast, " he called out, "better wait until I get there to show you how to crack an egg."

Sitting across from Jeff in the cozy kitchen, the oven still warm from baking muffins, Elise found herself more relaxed than she would have believed. To her surprise, she was even wide awake and eager to tackle the day ahead. She pulled their appointment book close to her, pushing aside dishes to make room.

"How's our schedule for today?" Jeff asked, sitting back, content.

"Bree called Mrs. Sandoz and Mrs. Harper, our two referrals from your father, and booked three other patients from the neighborhood," Elise answered, checking the day's page. "We're in good shape. All we've got to do is—"

"Clear the breakfast dishes so anyone peeking in the kitchen won't compare our housekeeping to our professional practice," Jeff completed the thought.

"A hearty breakfast was a good idea," Elise groaned, "but do I really have to move?"

"It would have been a better idea if you knew how to cook." Jeff said, already at the sink. "But your coffee was great. As usual," he added after seeing Elise's pained look.

"Thanks, it's the least I can do after you turned out flawless homemade muffins, an omelet that was almost a soufflé, and somehow managed to turn those overripe peaches into a terrific sauce." Elise smiled. "I've got to earn my way, somehow."

''Come here and kiss me, you fool, '' Jeff imitated a leer. ''I'll show you how to earn your way.''

Kissing her husband lovingly on his forehead, Elise continued with the kitchen chores.

''Talking about earning our way, though,'' Jeff continued, ''what did we finally decide to do about billing procedures?''

''Oh, we'll ask for payment at the end of the visit. Billing will only increase our overhead.'' Elise said, concentrating on scrubbing a dried bit of egg. ''Keep in mind, though, that most of the people in this neighborhood are used to waiting hours because the doctor has drastically overbooked, or doesn't schedule at all, and then they get five minutes in front of the doctor, usually with all their clothes on. The fees have been low but so has their care.''

''In that case we might have to wait some time before we can pick up a steady practice,'' Jeff said. ''At least our overhead is low.''

Laughing, Elise pushed her husband to the doorway. ''Go put your whites on. I'll wash and iron them myself to keep costs down.''

Pulling her to him, Jeff covered her mouth with his. The front door interrupted, and breaking away, Jeff tenderly smiled at his wife. ''Those muffins and jam were good, weren't they? I can still taste them on you. Are there any left?''

''Just enough for Bree,'' called Elise as she returned to the sink.

Jeff was still smiling as he opened the front door. ''Oh, we were just talking about you. You get to take the food from the mouths of starving husbands.''

Moving past Jeff into the foyer, Bree removed her cape and headed toward the kitchen. ''What is he talking about?''

''Nothing, Bree. I saved you a home-baked muffin and jam. He's just feeling the strain of our first day in practice.''

''Oh,'' said Bree, her mouth full, ''he meant these muffins, didn't he?''

"How could he? He's already eaten three. What time is our first appointment?"

"Nine." Wiping the crumbs from the side of her mouth, Bree sipped her coffee. "Mrs. Harper. She was Dr. Vaughan's—old Dr. Vaughan, I mean, Jeff's father's—patient on Long Island."

"Just call him Hal, Bree, like we do. If he ever heard you calling him old Dr. Vaughan, he'd turn blue." Elise put the last plate away and turned to face Bree, a puzzled look in her eyes.

"She's been in the city for a few years now, though. Hasn't she been seeing someone during that time?"

"Yes, she has. She had her patient records transferred to a doctor downtown, near where she lives. I guess she hasn't been happy with the doctor she's been seeing. She called your father-in-law for another referral."

The door bell rang for a second time that morning, startling Elise. Glancing at her watch, she motioned to Bree, "And it's nine o'clock on the dot. At least we know she's prompt. Let her in, and leave the front door open while I slip into a jacket."

"Are you sure you want to leave the door unlocked?" Bree questioned. "This really isn't the best neighborhood, and you're a doctor, with medical supplies, and—"

"Yes, I know," Elise continued, "with drugs. And there are junkies in this area. I think we can deal with them. You and I can, anyway. We've never picked up on the talk we started on the phone, but somehow I know that you and I can handle just about anything. The door stays open during office hours." Moving into the corridor, a shortcut to her office, Elise turned back and stage-whispered instructions to Bree. "Bring Mrs. Harper right into my office. I'll meet her there."

Slipping on her white jacket, Elise stood on the other side of the closed office door waiting for the sounds of Bree showing Mrs. Harper to her seat.

Why had she said that to Bree? How would they handle a robbery? They could, of this she was sure

. . . Yet, how? Shaking her head to clear the confusion, Elise entered her office.

Holly Harper sat there, her mouth open and eyes wide at the sight of Elise.

This woman can't be the doctor that Hal Vaughan recommended so highly. Not this woman.

Elise moved to her desk, smiling reassuringly at the woman sitting in front. Elise saw—no, felt—the disbelief.

Effecting her most professional manner, Elise walked to the back of her desk and leaned over to offer her hand. "How do you do, Mrs. Harper. I'm Dr. Crawford—Elise Crawford." The handshake was silently reciprocated. Worried that her first impression was not going at all well, Elise slipped into her chair and picked up Mrs. Harper's file.

"I would imagine, Mrs. Harper, that you would like to wait to ask your present doctor to transfer your records, but I'll need some information in the meantime."

Holly Harper's silence was overwhelming, her only activity a steady stare that followed Elise's every movement.

"Yes, of course," Mrs. Harper finally broke her own silence. "But please call me Holly."

"Thank you, Holly. If you're comfortable calling me Elise, you have a deal. It might not be professional to some, but I've found that it helps with establishing a rapport. That, sometimes, can be more helpful in medical diagnosis than a battery of tests."

Holly Harper broke her stare and smiled at the young woman doctor. "I like the idea a lot, Elise. I haven't heard such sensible and basic advice since I moved away from Hal Vaughan. You're his daughter-in-law, aren't you?"

"Yes, I am," replied Elise, pleased that the initial barrier was down and they were talking. "You might have noticed the Mr. and Mrs. sign just under our medical shingle. Jeff put it up so people wouldn't think we were friends practicing together. Or, more likely, living together without lawful sanction."

"I approve of your using your maiden name—it is your maiden name, I take it? Why did you chose not to use your husband's name?"

"I'm not sure my answer will appeal to any ERA suppporters, Holly. It's traditional in my family for the women to use their mother's name."

"I'm glad—no, relieved—to hear that," Holly said, and sat back in her chair, perceptibly relaxing. "In fact, I owe you an apology."

"Why?"

"When I first walked in here, I was speechless, by your resemblance to, well, someone I know. I would have almost sworn it *was* her, except your hair is lighter. And your eyes are different, now that I look closely. Yours are hazel, or are they brown? And you have more color, more life to your complexion. Unless that's all cosmetic blush, of course."

The air in the room seemed to stop moving, motes hung motionless in front of Elise's eyes. Street sounds, a moment ago barely noticeable but present, stopped.

"I'm afraid I overreacted, but it was purely on an emotional level. There's already enough of this woman in my life. Anyway, if all the women in your family use their mother's name, she couldn't be your sister."

"Who, Mrs. Harper?" Elise asked, knowing that the answer would identify the person responsible for the renewed sense of dread she'd been experiencing. The person causing the dreams and the guilt and the doubts. The only person who could reach inside her and twist her soul. "Who are you talking about?"

"I thought you were going to call me Holly. Oh, the woman I'm talking about. No one you'd know, most likely. She's been working with my husband as his communications director for the last few years. A clever young woman." The lines in Holly Harper's face grew taut. "A very clever young woman."

"What's her name?" Elise asked, trying to appear

casual as fear rose like a living creature inside her, contracting her breating and stilling her heartbeat.

"T. D. Harrah. Everyone calls her T.D., and believe it or not, I never thought of asking her what the initials stand for."

Fighting to gain control over herself, Elise put down the file she was clutching tightly. Picking up a pen, she carefully arranged a smile on her face. There was a good reason why Holly Harper had never asked what the T.D. stood for. Talia Dora had willed it that way.

"Let me ask you about childhood diseases," Elise began the consultation, "and then you can tell me if there's anything specific bothering you."

Looking in the mirror, Talia's neon-green eyes shone with a surreal light. "You know. At last you know." She spoke to the reflection as it clouded and merged in silver mists with a likeness almost identical to her own.

"I've waited a very long time, more than ten years now . . . since high school," she crooned at the reflections, the two like faces pulsing against each other, into each other, a glowing hologram in the dimly lit room. "Now that you know who I am, where I am, I can reach out and really touch you."

Talia's own dark-chestnut hair faded to a sun-streaked brown, then darkened again to match her own reflection. Her brilliant green eyes softened to hazel, amber flecks glowing warmly, then shone neon green again. Her milky white porcelain skin turned golden, then paled again. Pulsing, pulsing, pulsing—the reflections merged and cleared in time to her heartbeat, each portrait fighting for its moment of dominance.

"We were one. We would have stayed one, but you choose to ignore what—who—you are. You took part of me with you, and I want it back. Elise, I'm going to have it back. I will be whole. I'll be as strong alone as we were meant to be together."

The throbbing image increased in intensity, the rhythms of the strobes lighting the room.

Now that the first seeds were planted, Talia knew they would grow and begin to erode the false serenity her sister thought she could surround herself with. Flourishing like malevolent weeds, they would soon choke out all else; they would become so strong they would crack through protective brick walls and bind so tightly they would squeeze the last beliefs from Elise's trusting soul.

Her eyes half-closed, a humorless smile set firmly on her finely boned face, Talia reached out to touch the mirror. Her hand reached the reflection as it merged into the softened features of Elise. Talia's eyes snappped open to see the resolution of her sister's face.

"No," she screamed. "It will be me, and only me. You can't live, you can't win. You won't! You don't know how. You haven't time to learn."

Shuddering, she stepped back from the mirror, her own reflection firmly back in place.

Talia breathed deeply, clearing her mind from the reeling shock she had felt when Elise's reflection had coalesced over hers and for just a moment held the image for an instant longer than Talia had willed.

Her composure regained, she knew she was right, that the time was right. Elise would never realize what was happening to her, and even if she did, there was nothing she could do about it. There was no one to help her, nowhere for her to go, no one to show her how to use her strengths, her powers.

Talia had trained too long to needlessly concern herself with Elise's impossible victory. Smiling to herself, Talia knew that even if Elise should unleash her untrained strength, as she had as a child, she herself would still win. She had taken care of all possible contingencies, and then some.

There would be no Elise, no possible threat ever. Only her own victory. She would stand alone, holding political strength through her complete control of Ned Harper, and when Michael reclaimed the power that was due him, she would have that as well. No one would be able to touch her.

Strange, she smiled, drawing the velvet cover over the gilt mirror, how her and Michael's paths had crossed. The instant she'd laid eyes on him, walking in the East Village, she knew she had found the missing piece to her puzzle. The puzzle of how to ensure complete control over her destiny. The seduction was easy, the capture easier still; she'd revealed just enough to whet his interest and she promised more than enough to unquestionably bind him to her.

After all, they had something in common: he with some foolish sister—she with the same.

Perhaps, someday, she and Michael could be more than occasional lovers. When all was in place and any and all stumbling blocks were removed from their path, perhaps they would become partners in a far greater power than either could achieve alone.

Perhaps it was meant to be, their fates wound together by their similarities and their strengths.

Perhaps, Talia shrugged, she would have to rid herself of Michael if he became bothersome.

Just as she would rid herself of Elise.

14

"TODAY WENT A LOT BETTER THAN I THOUGHT IT would," Jeff said as he poured freshly brewed coffee into three waiting mugs.

Elise kicked off her shoes and tucked one leg under the other, resting both elbows on the kitchen table. She held her face in the palms of her hands. "How did you think it would go?"

"I didn't expect a steady flow of patients." He smiled. "At least not the first day."

"Wait until tomorrow. Let's hope we didn't satisfy the curiosity of the entire neighborhood in one short day," Elise said, a wry twist to her smile. "On the other hand, I'm almost ready for a day off."

"You two are incredible," said Bree, leaning back in her chair. "Either it's going to be not busy enough, or too busy. What would satisfy you?"

Eyes twinkling at the seated women, Jeff turned to put the coffeepot back on the stove. "Now that you ask . . ." he began, only to be met by a loud groan from Elise.

"You had to give him a straight line, didn't you, Bree? Or, before you comment further, dear husband, a not-so-straight line. But back to the subject at hand, today went very well. If most days go nearly as well, we won't have to worry about my washing and ironing our uniforms."

."I think I'd better tell you both, " Bree hesitated, "that all the patients today weren't paying patients." Both Jeff and Elise turned to her, a silent question simultaneously forming on their lips. Seeing their apprehensive looks, Bree hastened to add, "At least they can't pay right away. I'm sure most of them will pay, in time. Most paid something, anyway."

"What do you consider something, Bree?" Jeff cautiously asked.

Pulling the office ledger closer and flipping it open, Bree skimmed through the day's entries. "Well, both Mrs. Harper and Mrs. Sandoz wrote out checks for fifty dollars, which includes the lab work we do right here." Pausing, she saw that both doctors were waiting for her to continue. "And, umm, Mrs. Johnson—her daughter had the inner ear infection—paid twenty-five, which includes the medication you gave her."

"What else, Bree?" Jeff sighed.

"Four patients gave ten or fifteen dollars each, and the other three promised to pay something by the end of the month, and—"

"Bree, do these patients know our fee?" Elise asked, almost afraid of the answer she knew might be coming.

"I do tell everyone that the initial examination is fifty dollars, which includes some routine tests, but most say they'll skip the tests."

"What you're telling us is that the three of us, working from nine A.M. to seven P.M., made a net total of less than two hundred dollars," Jeff sagely noted.

Scanning her column and appearing deeply involved in the mental arithmetic it detailed, Bree finally looked up. "That's right, Dr. Vaughan. It's absolutely amazing how you figured that out so quickly while I had to carefully add up all these separate numbers."

After a moment of stunned silence, the room burst into activity.

"Spaghetti for dinner, everyone, " Elise said as she jumped up and pullled down the large pasta pot hanging from a cast-iron hook.

"Where's the laundry detergent?" asked Jeff. "I'd better get these whites into the washing machine if they're going to dry by morning."

Sensing the good humor underneath the sudden task-oriented activity, Bree stood, stretched, and began walking to the front door. "I, on the other hand, will go home to my luxury apartment, lavishly tip the door-man for accepting today's deliveries from Saks and Bloomingdale's, run a bubble bath, and defrost the small but perfect steak I'm having for dinner. Good night, all." Bree slipped on her coat and twirled around and through the door she held open, gracefully closing it behind her. "Oh, by the way"—she popped her head back into the foyer—"it's after dark. Lock up." And she was gone.

"Alone at last," Elise said.

"Spaghetti sounds pretty good to me," Jeff answered.

"I think so, too. We can use the carbohydrate boost. A nice salad, and there might even be some strawberry ice cream in the freezer, if we're lucky." Elise moved to fill the large pot with water.

"What do you mean, if we're lucky? We're very lucky." Jeff smiled at his wife. "We have each other, and that's just the beginning."

"It might be nice to have a chicken for the pot."

"And a car for every garage," Jeff quipped. "In the meantime, we've got enough." Pausing, Jeff continued. "I had an interesting patient today. I wanted to call you in but you were treating the boy with the burns on his arm and hands—you were soothing him so effectively I didn't want to disturb you."

"He was crying hysterically when his mother brought him in, more from fear than pain. There was a fairly bad second-degree burn on his forearm. His hands, fortunately, were barely scalded. I don't think his mother will continue to keep pot handles facing out where her children can reach them. At least I hope not. It's so simple to prevent most accidents if people would only take a minute to think."

"Like that sharp knife you just put in the soapy water, dear," Jeff pointed out. "You, conversely, seem to leave yourself wide open for accidents."

"But they never happen to me, do they?" Elise

paused. "No, they don't. I've never really had an accident. Not even tripping over a piece of broken sidewalk or catching my finger in a door. That's odd, isn't it?"

"You lead a charmed life, darling."

Alarmed by the direction the conversation was taking, Elise suddenly remembered what her husband had started to tell her. "What was your interesting patient all about?"

"A boy, twelve years old. He was dazed, could barely talk. His responses were so slow he answered questions minutes after they were asked."

"Was he being sullen? A lot of kids nowadays affect that kind of attitude. They think it makes them tough."

"No, not specifically. I mean, no, he wasn't being sullen in not responding. His eyes were dilated and he was even having trouble walking. Uncoordinated. But I think you're right about him being one of the toughs. He had quite a few battle scars for a kid his age."

"How did he get here?" Elise asked.

"His mother brought him in. She said that he'd stayed out all night last week—from the way she said it, I took it that it was something he did quite often—and he'd been that way ever since. At first she thought he was tired and let him collapse in bed. When she came home from work that night, he was still there, and hadn't moved since. She's had to feed him, lead him to the bathroom, even clean him after his toilet."

"Drugs?" Elise questioned.

"None in his system, at least not that I could determine. I ran a quick blood scan while he was still here. I think anything stronger than marijuana would have showed up. But don't forget it's been a week. His blood work looked normal."

"Concussion?" Elise asked, barely pausing in her food preparations, dropped pasta in the boiling water.

"I feel like I'm back in school with these one-word questions." Jeff grinned. "No, I checked his scalp for bumps, cuts, or any abrasions. Not a scratch."

"This is odd," agreed Elise. "What next?"

"I suggested a complete workup at the hospital but

his mother refused. She said their medical insurance had lapsed and they couldn't afford it.''

"That I can well believe, based on Bree's ledger."

"Yes. About Bree. She came into the room at that moment and the boy looked at her. His pupils contracted and his eyes responded to movement for the first time since he'd been in my office. Bree asked what the matter was and looked at him. I hate to admit being second-guessed by a nurse, but she said she thought it was a virus that's been going around the neighborhood. Bree said some of her neighbors had gone through almost exactly the same symptoms and were fine in a few days.''

"It certainly is an odd grouping of symptoms. Was there any fever?''

"Not while he was in my office. His mother hadn't taken his temperature; she said he'd felt cool to her touch. But after Bree looked at him, he started coming around.''

"I've heard of stranger things than influenza causing stupor. In fact, his coming around in the office isn't so strange, not when you take into consideration the fact that he'd already been lethargic for almost a week,'' Elise added.

"I guess. But there was one other thing that just didn't add up. He first appeared alert and then, oddly enough, afraid. The fear itself was directed at Bree. He literally cringed when he saw her. He put his hands up, as if to keep her away, and started making little mewing sounds. I would swear he recognized her, then he wouldn't even look at her. Just kept looking away, at his mother or me, or down at his feet.''

"Perhaps he was just surprised to find himself in a doctor's office and she happened to be the first person he focused on.''

Jeff considered the possibility. "I thought of that and that's probably what it was. But it was, well, unnerving to watch his reaction.''

"Private practice is sure to be a b. unnerving at times, but it's all ours. And now . . . ,'' Elise brightened as the food timer rang, dismissing all further thoughts of work or work-related topics from the conversation. "Dinner is served."

The evening walk home was a pleasure for Bree. To be out at the hours other people were out, to be coming home to make dinner at the same time most people ate their main meal, and to look forward to sleeping at night, in real darkness rather than light dimmed by lined curtains, was, Bree felt, being part of the real world.

Frightened by the recognition in the boy's eyes when he saw her in the examining room, Bree had to quickly overcome her own fear with the knowledge that there was nothing the youth could say, or do, that would prove anything other than she had witnessed an attack by neighborhood ruffians—and had tried to prevent it. While her own rationalization sounded plausible, even to her, she also realized that the boy would say nothing. If he did, he would only further incriminate himself.

Sighing to herself, Bree knew that this was just another reason to be grateful for keeping normal hours. Not wandering around at odd hours, encountering the dregs of the neighborhood finding their way home in the early morning. Waving at neighbors across the street, Bree turned at the stairs to her building.

Reaching out with the downstairs key, she noticed the lock was broken, again. Thinking that if she didn't find a drunk sleeping it off under the stairs—and be forced to argue with her own conscience as to whether or not to evict him or leave him be—she'd be lucky, she pushed the door open and started for the stairs.

A pleasant, sweet odor reached her. Wrinkling her nose, she tried to place the smell. It was too floral, too fragrant, to be anyone cooking, and it definitely wasn't the fetid stench of a passed-out drunk. The scent was lightly perfumed with an unusual spice. There was a touch of cinnamon and cloves—those smells she recognized—but there was a subtle undertone that was unknown to her. The word "incense" popped into her head.

She stopped short on the first stair and a chill ran through her. No one in this building burned incense. Once, years ago, there had been some pot heads who used incense, but that had been an ordinary sandalwood variety, the kind you can buy at almost every cigarette stand in the neighborhood.

This was more than an inexpensive stick or cone, burning to disguise other smokes. This was a true incense. Someone, nearby, could be praying, but that would mean they knew the ways well enough to make a proper offering—and no clan lived in this building.

Bree's instincts told her differently. There was no positive vibration associated. And this was not from someone in the building.

The cloying scent grew stronger, heavier, more intense, filling her lungs and muddling her thoughts. Dizzy, she reached for the banister, first noticing a hazy blue light illuminating the dim hallway. The odor grew thicker, more tangible, and with each step Bree found it harder and harder to breathe. An overpowering rush of the scent—now that of dead and dying flowers—filled her lungs, and sent her into a coughing spell.

The racking coughing cut off more precious air. Fighting her way up the steps to her landing, Bree found the haze turned into dense smog. Unable to draw a breath free of the noxious odor, unable to see her hand before her despite the cold, blue light, she felt a presence even more frightening that the reality of smothering. Eyes watering, gasping from the efforts to breathe, she staggered the last few steps and reached her apartment door. The space around her door was clear, an oasis in the miasma.

Michael. It had to do with Michael. As she let herself into her sanctuary, her legs trembled as she carefully made her way to the easy chair. The phone-answering machine indicated messages, and seeing this, Bree felt drained, empty. *How can I keep helping others when I don't know how to heal my own flesh and blood?*

She closed her eyes, a single tear escaping, then reached out to rewind for the first message.

Frank Jordan sat in front of the desk, comfortable in the deep leather chair. Behind the desk the tall, rugged chairman, still dressed in a conservative three-piece suit and rep tie, tapped a pencil's eraser end on a lined yellow pad, the pad covered with notes from Jordan's recital of the evening's events.

"Not only that, it seems we're slowing down. The reseach itself hasn't produced one single breakthrough from our test subjects, including this subject you're keeping secret from even me," Jordan concluded.

"Frank, I don't see anything that really has gone wrong," the chairman said. "First, Blaiser's death will be easily forgotten. He'd become a thorn in our collective sides but his voluntary withdrawal from Spiral removes him from our jurisdiction, and you fortunately had the foresight to obtain his signed request for a transfer. There'll be no major investigation and the concerns of his associates will quickly dissipate. By the way, I think the, ah, manner of his death quite inspired."

Jordan literally snorted, the sound a mixture of disbelief and derision. "You must be joking. It was stupid and risky, not to mention incredibly unsophisticated—especially considering when and where it occccurred."

"That's exactly what I mean, but your perspective is off." The older man pointed his finger at Jordan. "It was a simple, ordinary accident, with no one around to apply the Heimlich maneuver. What else could be more acceptable? In fact, anything else would have been immediately suspect. The ultracentrifuge misfire fortunatley didn't harm him, or there'd have been a tedious investigation by the manufacturer . . . and the police. A lab accident? We don't use volatile chemicals or poisons or anything else that could be accidentally mishandled. And any exposure to the viruses we've on hand could take years to effect damage. Whoever heard of an immediate genetic misfire?''

Jordan's face brightened and he chortled softly. "Well, there was *The Fly*.''

"I'm only surprised you know of it.''

"Actually, I was told the film was a documentary. I'd seen Jeff Goldblum in *The Race for the Double Helix* and that was a docudrama. It was days before I realized *The Fly* wasn't one also.''

"To continue," the chairman said, smiling despite his intention to quell any levity; the gullibility of his administrator was legend. "Any other type of accident would have been even more risky. If there had been a car accident, it would have involved getting Blaiser out of the facility. And the what-if factor there was too great. What if he stoppped at a local watering hole and had a few too many before the accident? And what if he'd developed loose lips while drinking? Or what if the brakes didn't fail? And so on.

"Everyone's already accepted the chicken bone, and as unimaginative and simplistic as it might seem, for the same reasons it's thoroughly believable. Efficient, clean, and nonsuspect.''

"Maybe I'm still upset at being the one to stuff the bone down his throat," Jordan mumbled. "My career of late hasn't been very satisfactory. I've been behind a desk, not back in the field, although, '' he brightened, "that was my favorite territory.''

The chairman paused, analyzing the conflicting emotions—part pain, part longing—on Frank Jordan's face. "We all do things we find distasteful," he said softly, putting his hand on the younger man's shoulder. "Blaiser had to go, for the life of Spiral. And thanks to Blaiser's find with Jordan and Thacker—replicating the new factor—we'll get funding for extended research, even though we haven't yet, and I stress the word *yet,* come up with anything concrete toward our structured goal.

"If anything, I'm concerned about this VIP visit tomorrow.''

"It's today," Frank Jordan noted, checking his watch. "In less than six hours. But it's only a glorified tour. No real decision-makers are included, just a handful of federal people including a gubernatorial hopeful who might, or might not, be influencing us after Election Day."

"That's who and what I'm concerned about. That hopeful is Ned Harper, a former patient of mine," the older man stood, stretching.

"Ah, yes, your private practice." Jordan smiled. "An odd eccentricity, even among such a decidedly eccentric bunch as you scientists. It doesn't afford the low profile we insist upon, you know."

"You're getting more arrogant than even I thought you could manage. Your royal use of we, for example. The only royal here is the type of pain you've become in that nether part of the anatomy. Remember whose funding started this project. I'm not one of the scientists and, yes, I maintain a private practice. My practice, as I like to point out in reports, has provided us with the major share of the subjects for this study."

"Including our mysterious source," Jordan dryly pointed out, "whose blood and tissue samples you deliver on a regular basis. But never the body to go with them."

"I'm sure about her, surer than I've ever been about anything. When I first tested her, it was routine. Then I went further for, well, personal reasons. Let's just say I wanted to know more about her genetic balance because of something important to me. Her mitochondria DNA fingerprint was totally unexpected, and that's when I realized I had to keep her isolated. She doesn't realize there's anything out of the ordinary involved in her semiannual examinations."

"Assuming you're even on the right track with this patient, how can you be sure of keeping track of her?" Jordan's question was barbed, as he intended, with malice. "Not knowing she's a subject, she can walk, run, fly away—at any time."

The older man smiled, his face breaking into the

warmth that endeared him to his private patients. "Not this little bird. I've got her under a better hold than anything you could ever, even given free reign of your bureaucratic imagination, devise. She won't go anywhere."

"Then what are you worried about?" Jordan asked.

"That low profile you insist upon. You're in charge of the tour, and remember, don't use my name."

"You're the chairman, Dr. Vaughan. Where will you be?"

"I've got to pay a visit to my little bird," the older man said. "Just to make sure the gilding of her cage is holding up."

"You seem more enthusiastic than usual," Jordan commented. "May I ask why?"

"Ah, yes, I meant to mention it. I've also just learned our little star subject has a sister, a twin no less. And that could be the best news ever. Perhaps our subject will be allowed to live a normal life, after all, now that we have what should be an exact genetic duplicate available to run tests on—directly on, that is."

"I still don't understand what the problem is in using the subject herself," Jordan asked. "We've had dozens of other subjects through this facility for tests and there's been no problem."

"Yes, but we'd most likely want to keep this one for some time. The testing on her will have to go far beyond the simple genetic scans and fate maps we've been doing. We already know her MtDNA is different, only a 99 percent match to normal. What we need to find out is how this manifests itself in her."

"Maybe it's not 99 percent," Jordan quietly noted. "Maybe it's 101 percent."

"I know," Hal Vaughan readily agreed. "That's exactly what I believe!"

15

"YOUR FATHER SAID HE'D STOP BY LATER," ELISE told Jeff over double scoops of strawberry ice cream dripping with warm, extra-thick chocolate sauce.

"Good. I'd like to hear what Dad has to say over our cash proceeds from the first day."

Giggling, licking the ice-cream spoon, Elise found herself thoroughly relaxed, enjoying the moment. It wasn't until now, with the anxiety finally dissipated, that she realized she had spent the better part of the day hiding a buried knot of tension.

"Jeff, I know we once said we wouldn't talk about work while we're alone like this, that our time together would be just ours, but . . ." Elise began but found she wasn't quite sure what she wanted to tell her husband.

Not noticing her confusion, Jeff began to clear the last of the dishes. "That's all right, dear, I'm quite used to your contradictions by now."

"What do you mean?" Elise felt an unfamiliar rage begin to grow. "I hardly think you're one to talk about contradictions. You can't even put plumbing in correctly much less make an effective diagnosis without your nurse."

Elise felt her skin tighten. Her fury was directed at her husband, who had nothing better to do than end a day with contradictions and criticisms. The anger grew, perceptibly clouding the air around her.

"Elise, what are you talking about? What on earth does my ineptitude as a plumber have to do with the admittedly stupid comment I just made?"

"It's just one stupid comment too many and one more than I care to hear," Elise heard herself saying. Her anger was mounting; yet, beneath it, she felt a different panic, a panic borne of unfamiliar, hateful words she knew had no real meaning. Yet the bitter words continued to tumble from her lips without forming in her mind.

"I've never once contradicted myself. But when I finally want to talk to you about something important to me, you can't stand to hear about anyone other than yourself."

Tired himself, Jeff shot back. "You do change your mind, you know. You painted one whole wall pale yellow before you decided that it wasn't the color you wanted, and that was after you had the store mix at least eleven different swatches. I was there, I counted. Then, you sent back the reception furniture after you took two weeks to pick it out. Not to mention the countless purchases you make and return, and—"

"Shut up," Elise screamed. "What gives you the right to criticize me? Who the hell do you think you are? Just because your family is well-off and your daddy could buy you everything you ever wanted, you think I'm dirt."

"Oh, my God, Elise." Jeff paled, lowering his voice. "Why are you saying these things? What's the matter?"

"Matter? Nothing's the matter! In fact, I've just seen you for what you really are. A selfish, spoiled child who has never grown up. Who never had to grow up and who never will."

"Elise, stop this, I love you," Jeff pleaded.

"Oh. Because you love me everything is all right?" Elise's eyes narrowed as she looked at him slyly, a twisted smile touching the corners of her mouth. "Your love sucks, do you know that? I didn't get through medical school on your love and I didn't complete my residency on your money. Remember that. I did it by myself, for myself."

Turning away, Elise raced for the stairs. "I'm not

sure why I even went out with you." Stopping on the first tread, her venom continued to pour. "For a rich kid you sure didn't show me a good time. I could have gone camping by myself. In fact, boyo, I don't think you would have managed without me."

Stunned, Jeff watched his wife disappear up the stairs. Rooted to the spot, he stood and replayed her words over and over in his mind. Not able to find any reason, any trigger, for the explosive and surprising behavior, he turned back to the table, surprised to find his father standing there.

"Dad, how long have you been here?"

"Long enough, I'm afraid. The front door was unlocked—I went to knock and it pushed open."

"We must have forgot to lock it after Bree left. Dad, I'm sorry, but"—Jeff looked tired and beaten—"but it's been a long day."

"Jeff, you don't have to apologize to me. More important, what's the matter with Elise?"

"I don't know. It has been a long day, though."

"Not that long a day, son. I know that girl. Watched her work her way through school, watched her put in twenty-hour days and six-day weeks at the hospital. What else is bothering her?" Hal Vaughan asked, looking suspiciously at his son, as if some dire secret were being held back from him. "Is she well?"

"She's fine, dad, really. I don't know what's the matter. I know—this isn't like her. But some of the things she said just now were so ugly they seemed real. Like she really was holding those feelings back until now."

"No. Not Elise," Jeff's father quickly said. "Not Elise. Ah, Jeff, could she be pregnant?"

"I don't think so. If she is, it's not more than a few weeks, not long enough to warrant any hormonal imbalance." Jeff managed to smile at his father. "Besides, Dad, most doctors today don't accept prenatal depression as a clinical diagnosis."

"They haven't had as many pregnant patients as I have, that's why," Hal Vaughan answered. "It's something, that's for sure, not just Elise being off her feed. Don't forget, I'm her physician and I know the gal. What happened to start her off?''

"She wanted to tell me something and I made an inane remark about her not being able to make up her mind, or something equally stupid. I know I was wrong''—Jeff looked sheepishly at his father—''but this wasn't, isn't, the first time I've said something thoughtless. Elise always manages to put me back on the right track when I'm wrong—tactfully, gently. This time she tore through me.''

"What did she want to tell you?''

"I don't have the slightest idea. I opened my big mouth before she had a chance to tell me.''

Hal Vaughan's professionalism was eroding, his paternal instincts winning out. "How about PMS as a diagnosis, then. Would you accept that?''

"I've got to accept something, though Elise has never acted quite this way. I'll see PMS and raise you a long day,'' Jeff countered.

"That about covers it.'' Hal grinned. "And not a bad idea, either. Where are the cards? We can both unwind a bit. Maybe Elise will come down and join us.''

Looking at the stairway, Jeff thought of the probability. "I don't think so, Dad. But I'll get the cards if you get the beer.''

"You know, Jeff . . .'' The senior Dr. Vaughan paused while opening the refrigerator. "I wonder if this ties into her confusion about her family. She started telling you about her sister last week and those memories seemed pretty difficult for her to handle. On top of that, starting your own practice . . . By the way, did you show at least $150 on the books today?''

"Almost $200,'' Jeff grinned as he rummaged for a deck of playing cards. "Why?''

"I was just remembering my first weeks in practice. The whole first week I grossed less than you did today. It takes months to really get going. I didn't want to scare you off with tall tales of who catches the smallest fish, but it's always this way when you start out on your own.''

"Elise will appreciate hearing that"—Jeff looked up from counting loose cards—''if I can get to tell her about it. I think she was expecting to start out at full steam.''

"If Elise has a flaw,'' Hal noted, ''and mind you I said *if*, it's that she tends towards the naïve. Worldly sophistication is not her strong suit.''

"Talking about suits, all the cards are here. You deal.'' Jeff tossed the deck and placed icy steins filled with frothy dark beer on the table. As he sat across from this father, the worry creases in his forehead deepened. ''But how can you say *if* she has any flaws. Especially after what you heard tonight?''

Pausing middeal, Hal looked at his son. ''Jeff, you've a way to grow yourself. Tonight just proves she's human.''

Reminded of the bitterness that his wife had spewed at him, Jeff picked up his cards, forgetting to pursue the idea that Elise could be upset over something specific, something to do with her family. ''Sometimes I think you love her more than I do, Dad.''

"Perhaps I just try to understand her more, Jeff. But I do know I'm very glad you married her, son,'' Hal Vaughan responded, also distracted by the cards in his hand. ''Very glad indeed.''

The elderly man left Bree's apartment, limping somewhat less than he had when he arrived. Only JoJo and a mother with her adolescent son remained from the earlier crowd. The mother, a hefty woman who'd spent the last hour chewing her lower lip, had insisted on waiting to be taken last, even though her son was obviously in pain.

Looking in the woman's frightened eyes, Bree asked how she could help.

Tears welling, the woman almost whispered. ''I didn't want anyone else to know why he was hurt. I wouldn't have even come to you, but he's still spitting blood.''

Looking at the boy, who was holding one arm across his abdomen, Bree recognized the youth as the victim from the assault of last week; she was immediately reminded of his equally young assailant, seen that afternoon in the office. Aware of the coincidence and irony of the situation, Bree tried to appear casual.

"Why are you afraid to let anyone know your son is hurt? Boys can fall down. They hurt themselves playing all the time.''

"He wasn't playing when he was hurt,'' the woman responded bitterly, hissing the words and keeping her head down to hide her shame.

Running her hands over the boy's chest, Bree found a cracked rib she had missed setting in that early morning's rushed healing; afraid he'd wake before she'd finished, anxious to get away before the other boys saw who she was or what she was doing, she had been careless. Not that she succeeded in going unrecognized today, but at least now she knew they wouldn't talk.

Holding her hand over the rib, imagining the clean white bone ends melting together, willing them to knit into a whole, Bree didn't comment on the mother's words. The lung was scraped, not punctured, and she concentrated on the ripped tissue, on staunching the bleeding. Focusing, directing her energy to the internal wound, she gave fully of herself. As the raw edges knit together, as the blood ebbed and finally stopped, Bree breathed a deep sigh of relief. Finished, drained, she sat back and reached for the cup of tea always nearby.

"It's all that madman Michael's fault,'' Bree heard the woman saying. "If he hadn't gotten the young boys involved in running his dirty errands, downtown to here, this wouldn't have happened.''

Startled, Bree put down her cup of tea and leaned forward. She reached out and pulled the woman around, forcing her to meet her eyes. "What about

Michael,'' she asked, holding her breath while the woman returned the even gaze.

"You should know," the woman spit out each word. "He's your brother." Easing her son into his jacket, the boy apparently more comfortable but sleepy, the woman continued. "Don't expect payment for healing what you're responsible for. Everyone knows that he's furious with you and is taking it out on everyone else."

The door closed behind them and minutes passed before Bree could bring herself to turn to JoJo.

"What's happening? How can she say I'm responsible for anything Michael might do?"

"People are talking, Bree. Michael has some very loyal followers, young men who, well, who wouldn't be allowed in other clans. Two of his boys were once asked to leave Mama Alice's group, but no one in the coven would say why."

Shock showed on Bree's face. To be accepted took years of proving yourself. To be asked to leave was almost unheard of. Yet the privacy of the clan came above all else and secrets were always kept. Except, it seemed, in Michael's group. The renegades were beyond control.

"But, JoJo, what does this have to do with me?"

"Michael has told his followers that you have something he wants, something that's his by right, and that he's going to take it from you. That boy was attacked by two of Michael's hopefuls. They're too young to be part of his coven but they'll run his errands, stay nearby, hoping that when they're of age he'll choose them as alternates. The boy you just healed had spoken out against Michael. He was almost killed, but you knew that, Bree, didn't you?"

"I knew he was attacked. I was passing by, on my way home that morning. It was the last night shift I worked and I saw two other boys attacking this one."

JoJo turned away from her. "Don't you think it's strange that you should just be passing by? Michael is testing you."

Taken aback by this thought, Bree paused before answering. "No, not then, JoJo. That was before. Before Mother died. He wouldn't have had a reason then."

"Michael's been known to plan ahead," JoJo said, his face set with lines of concern. "He knew it might happen. But now he really has a reason, Bree, and if this is any indication of how he could reach out to you, then—"

"Don't say any more," Bree gasped, remembering her near suffocation in the hallway. "I know you're right."

16

HER CLOTHING LAY CARELESSLY STREWN ACROSS the bedroom. Elise stood in front of the long window, the chill night air raising bumps on her smooth skin. Her irritation, the feeling of being stifled, only increased when she left Jeff standing in the kitchen and stormed upstairs. By the time she reached the bedroom she was already tearing at her clothes. Tossing her skirt and blouse to the floor, she topped the pile with her lacy bra and panties—frilly underwear, she claimed, gave her feminine confidence even while wearing prim outerwear.

Night had fallen swiftly and the cloudless sky was clear. The streetlamp nearest the house was out, thanks, Elise thought angrily, to some street vandals who found it amusing to throw rocks at any target in their path. Above the rooftops a waxing moon loomed large, its edges softened by a halo of the city's carbon-monoxide-laden air.

The double framed windows, each panel further divided into nine panes by neat white wooden strips, reflected back Elise's nude body. Glimpsing herself, she realized it had been a long time since she had last looked, really looked, at herself. Stepping back from the window for a clearer image—not to remove herself from being seen from the street—she lifted her arms above her head and watched her full breasts jut forward; stretching her arms back, she twisted her torso into poses sometimes glimpsed in men's magazines. Lowering her arms, she began to caress herself, starting slowly and gently, letting each hand travel leisurely, intimately, over her body. She was pleased.

As she backed farther away from the window, into the center of the room, the bed bumped the backs of her knees, and welcoming the thought, Elise lowered herself onto the cover. Grasping her breasts, she lightly played with her nipples and felt them harden under her touch. Smoothly, she ran her hands down her abdomen, enjoying the warm and silky feel of her own skin. She spread her legs and reached between them to continue her explorations. She moved back to her breasts and worked over each nipple until it peaked in sweet pain. Over and over she caressed her velvet skin, each time completing the cycle by returning her long fingers to the heat rising between her legs.

"Oh, God, Jeff, you never touch me like this," she murmured to herself. Rapidly stroking the soft vulva crease her fingers led her to, quickening the intensity as her excitement grew, she let gentle waves of pleasure encompass her as she brought herself to climax. She lay spent, and a cool breeze ran across her damp skin, chilling her.

Images flooded her mind. Familiar places with tall pine trees and rock formations covered with spongy, green moss flashed before her. She drifted further into the comfortable twilight of dreamy peace. She found herself wanting to walk into her vision, anticipating where the forest path would take her. The sounds were the same as those she remembered: birds trilling, the rustle of small animals hidden behind leaves, the soft whisper of a gentle breeze. Light poured through the high branches and showered, speckled and broken, to the carpeted forest floor, soft under her feet.

The trees thinned, as she knew they would, the path curved slowly to the left and ahead—just where it always was—rose the hill. The hill with the cave. Only she was grown now and it wasn't a cave, not really, just an overhanging ledge of rock shadowing a soft indentation, room size, in the hill. The smell of moss and damp earth, familiar to this place, filled her senses.

"Welcome home," a melodious voice called.

Shading her eyes, Elise sought to define the figure standing ahead of her, hidden in the dim of the stone shelf overhang. A light laugh sounded and silenced the birds; the stillness—at first peaceful—grew oppressive.

Neither moved. The shaded figure stood as still as the surrounding rock. Elise, feeling exposed and vulnerable even in sunshine, found that she could not walk forward, that she could no longer hold her hand up to her eyes to shade the sun, that she could only stand there in the unnatural quiet, listening to her own shallow breathing.

There was no sense of time, only of the two of them, standing so near, yet so far, from each other. In the passage of hours or in the space of a heartbeat, the shadows lengthened; the sun was no longer in Elise's eyes but rather moved away from her and onto the hair, the forehead and now the eyes of the woman standing but a few feet away. A soft voice broke the silence.

"We cannot stand in the sun at the same time. It's as it always was. There isn't room enough for both of us."

The sound of the voice was at once alien and familiar to Elise. The shadows shifted again as the woman raised her hand, holding it palm out to reflect the light back to Elise.

"Look at your own hand," she said, and Elise did, and saw her own hand diffused by shadow. Looking around and finding nothing that could cast the shadow, Elise turned and looked into the brilliant green eyes moving closer to where she stood, frozen.

"You see, dear Elise, there really isn't sun enough, or room enough, for both of us," the woman said. "Only one of us can be." A small smile played at the corner of the woman's lips.

"But you know this, my darling sister," the woman continued, "of course you know this. It's why you've run all these years. Run away from the knowledge, run away from me. Hoping, I'm sure, that it couldn't be true. Who's to blame you''—Talia shrugged her slim shoulder—''for wanting not to believe? It made your miserable life that much more acceptable. And it made my life that much easier.''

Trapped in silence, the air that sparked before Elise had a color, a life, a fire all of its own. Struggling to free herself from her prison, Elise swallowed and found she could make a noise, a small sound like the breath of a bird. She concentrated, and the hypnotic motes began to dim. She found she could will her throat to move, but her voice sounded dusty and unused.

''Talia, I knew it was you.''

''My dearest Elise, there are so many things you know. Yet you hesitated before you really knew. Why do you think that was?''

''Why did you bring me here?'' Elise countered, and found that her voice was wavering, her rising fear again threatened to choke off her words.

''I didn't bring you here, I merely asked you to come. It's strange, don't you think, that you find yourself compelled to answer even the most polite bidding of mine,'' Talia mocked.

''I don't want to play with words, not now. Why did you bring me here?''

''It's simple, I wanted us to be with each other again.'' Talia swept her arm into the sunlight, gesturing to the rolling hills and nearby glades of trees. ''Here, where some of our best memories are. Here, where we were together, where we were one, for the last time.''

Confusion glinted amber in her hazel eyes. Elise's gaze followed the outswept arm and took in the rich countryside. ''Yes, of course, it's beautiful,'' she agreed.

The laugh that had stopped all sound came again.

''Beautiful. You really are looking at the scenery.'' A sadness came into Talia's voice. ''Fool, oh, you're such a fool. And we could have been so strong together. That's what I regret the most—it's the only thing I've ever regreted. We could have been one but for your fears. Now I have to be alone.''

Confused, Elise reached out to her sister. "You don't have to be alone. We can still be together.''

A bitter laugh erupted. "When, on birthdays and holidays? Your world of reality is a fantasy. We can't be together—not the way you've chosen to live. You've run from what we could be, from what we are. The odd part is I don't blame you for what you've done. Sometimes, looking at others, I almost wish I could have run and hid and never had to face who or what I am.'' Talia's mouth twisted. "But it's too strong in me.''

"I don't understand,'' Elise pleaded.

"You do, but your fear hides the truth from you. I don't know where the fear came from. If I'd have known you would turn out so weak, I would have taken your hand and given you the strength to overcome the fear. But I didn't know. Not until you tried to save Jason. When I took his life—and I had to for us to survive—you tried to bring him back. I think I knew before then—you'd often be twenty steps behind me as if cleaning up a mess I'd made, like spilled jam—but I never really isolated what you were doing, or trying to do, until Jason. Even as children I feared that you and I could never be one, as we had to be. But when you almost succeeded in saving Jason, animating a body dead for days, I knew it was true. I also realized, for the first time, that you had power.''

Again, remembering the incident was more frightening than the realization that she had failed to save Jason. Elise moved back, farther into the shade.

"And that was the last thing you ever did of any worth.'' Talia green eye's glinted cruelly as the sunlight washed over her. "For which I should be grateful. I watched you through others. You were determined to do well in the world, in their schools, in their ways. I was also determined to do well, Elise, but I was working with what we had been given. Our gifts, our special gifts.''

Hidden memories stirring, Elise became aware of a dim hum coming from the small cave. The smell of long-dead flowers rushed to her, taking her aback.

''You do remember my trademark''—Talia smiled—''the scent of dying flowers. Sometimes I wish you didn't, that you had succeeded in your goal of normalcy. I wouldn't have to destroy you.''

''You can't,'' gasped Elise, the stench now closing off her air. ''You said we were one. How can you destroy me if we are the same?''

''We were the same,'' Talia said sadly. ''Now I have to take what you still hold and make it my own. The only way I can do that is to end the sham you call life.''

''I'll fight you,'' Elise said through clenched teeth, her eyes tearing from the now visible fumes.

''Would that you could. I would welcome the sport.'' A flicker of amusement danced in Talia's bright-green eyes. ''Would that you could. You can, you know. In fact''—Talia paced toward her sister—''you *will*. For all you hold dear, you will. Consider this a warning, then.

''I was going to take you here, to let you rest where we grew up together.'' Talia again gestured to the hills and trees. ''But this way will be better. A warning, then. You have time, a short time, to prepare for me. Three days to find your strengths. They're there, you know. I could always feel your will. Your will against mine. Three days from now I will come for you and take all that you possess as my own.''

Moving into the shade, Talia turned back. ''One clue, my dear sister, a helpful hint I never thought I'd share with you. I had to cultivate my ability. It took me years to grow strong, to learn to use what we both have. You only have a short time, so use it well.''

Reaching out her hand to a nearby boulder, Talia closed her eyes and drew the light and darkness together. She shone in the shadow, seeming to cause the effect rather than be part of it. Her movement was slight, a push forward in the direction of the solid rock, and it crumbled to dust at her feet. Opening her eyes, she looked at her sister.

"This is what I can do with my body. My mind is even stronger. What I want you to know is that you, too, have this in you." A bitter laugh rang from her soft throat. "Perhaps even more than I do. I can tell you this, a painful admission, because I know, beyond any question or doubt, that you'll never learn to use it. You probably won't even try."

Stunned, Elise looked at the pyramid of dust dissipating in the gusty wind. Raising her eyes, she saw there was no one near. Alone, she shivered in the sudden chill.

And pulled the cover over her.

Lying on the bed, her hands still between her legs, Elise heard her husband's slow footsteps on the stairs as he tentatively made his way to their room.

17

HOLLY SCANNED THE TRIPLE TIER OF SHOES stretching over one long wall of her walk-in closet. The shelves above were stacked high with matching purses, coordinated belts, and carefully folded scarfs. She made her choices for the Friday-morning press conference—alternates ready, depending on the unpredictable spring weather—but couldn't shake the feeling that something was going to happen; more specifically, something was about to go wrong. The strong political upswing she—no, they—had been on lately was reaching an apex, and once this peak was claimed, she was sure they would have to fight to remain on top.

The strange resemblance of her new doctor, and yes, she would conditionally accept Elise Crawford as her doctor—there was something she trusted in the younger woman, a caring coupled with competency—to her husband's communication director was, for starters, unnerving.

Holly knew her instincts were almost always right and, in fact, couldn't pinpoint any one time they'd let her down. On one hand, Elise Crawford would soon be an excellent practitioner and even now possessed the skill, ability, and elusive talent to be a fine doctor, better than many far more experienced. On the other hand, something was about to go disastrously awry.

The unease Holly felt, a growing anxiousness she could not shake, came in part from the scheduled press conference. It was unlike T.D. to go wrong on important contingencies, and scheduling a conference for a Friday morning was careless. Media coverage would miss all the weekday dailies, being relegated to Saturday morning's lesser-read edition. Holly had once researched the weekly papers and kept the closing-dates list current. Of the seven weekly papers of any importance, all but one closed its news desk on Wednesday—the last on Thursday—and all were on the streets by Friday noon to reach the readers who used their weekend to catch up on, and shop in, their neighborhoods.

Yet, T.D. had insisted on holding this important conference on a Friday morning. The party last Sunday night was in and of itself an event that had all but assured Ned's acceptance as the party's choice for gubernatorial candidate. Last Monday or Tuesday, or even next Monday, riding on the current supportive swing, would have been far, far better, but it would seem T.D.'s hold over the Ned Harper campaign was all but complete. Smiling bitterly to herself, Holly entertained the passing thought that if T.D. shared Ned's bed, her control would be complete.

Closing the door to her closet, Holly walked to the full-length, ornately carved antique mirror standing in the corner. She looked carefully for any signs of gray that her hairdresser could repair, and her immaculate reflection glimmered back at her. Just for a moment, a long-enough moment to raise the hair at the nape of her neck, the eyes reflected back seemed brilliant, neon green. A flicker of a second, no longer, and her own pale-blue eyes were again clearly defined in the silvered glass.

Enamored of her own reflection under any circumstances, Holly now found herself not unwilling to move away from the mirror—she was unable. Watching her chest rise and fall in measured beats, knowing she should force herself to turn aside and go on to other tasks, Holly could not pull herself away from the mirror. Her breasts rose with each long breath and flattened each time the air was drawn from her. Stifling a growing fear, Holly again tried to pull herself

away from the reflection; other than to open her mouth
to gasp for air, to fight for breath, she could not
move. Each frightened gasp took in less, far less, of
the precious air than was forcibly expelled—was being
squeezed—from her constricted lungs. The reflected
alarm in her blue eyes wavered into the brilliant green
she had seen moments ago, a green she now recognized, as the walls of the room began to fade from
around her.

They were T.D.'s eyes. A surge of jealousy rushed
through Holly's veins. It wasn't enough that bitch had
her husband suckered into a dependent relationship,
but now the slut was invading her own bedroom. The
neon-green eyes stared back, cold and hateful, as
T.D.'s familiar face began to form around them. The
head in the mirror was thrown back in sensuous enjoyment, a mocking smile on moist lips wordlessly
formed Ned's name, silently pleading with him to fuck
her, begging for more; yet the green eyes never moved
from Holly.

Holly stood, drained, exhausted, watching as Ned's
face and bare shoulders appeared, coalescing behind
the woman in the reflection. She watched as his mouth
found its way to the woman's long neck and as his
hands moved from behind to cup the full breasts; the
hard nipples touched, flattened on the glass separating
the figures from Holly. The hand, Ned's hand, was
still wearing the wedding band she had placed there;
his hands stroked and caressed and moved down the
bitch's supple body, both figures fading back, as if a
hidden camera were panning to allow Holly a complete view. His hand, the same hand again, her wedding band glinting brightly in the reflection, moved
past that bitch's flat stomach, and as the cunt threw
back her head and melted against his body, the hand,
the ring, disappeared into the curly bush between her
legs, the bitch cunt's juices wetting her wedding gold.

A cramp doubled Holly over as the woman in the
mirror laughed, sending the bitter sound of her mirth
into Holly's once private bedroom. The glass dark-

ened, the appalling images faded, and Holly again saw herself as she was. Then, within the blink of an eye, the laugh lines around her eyes grew deeper and deeper still, fanning out in spiderwebs on dry and brittle skin. She watched as the gentle creases framing her mouth turned into deep furrows, her healthy glow turned pallid and spotted, her coiffed hair became gray and frazzled, her clear blue eyes turned milky and clouded. She watched as the vibrant woman she was, had been, aged, decayed and rotted before her own eyes.

The glass again darkened and Holly—as a younger woman, younger than she was now—stood facing her. Puzzled, Holly reached out to touch her youthful self even as the image in the mirror also reached out. But the image was lifting a bloody hand, holding a shapeless mass. Holly saw it was an embryo, a human fetus less than two months old, a boy-child. Clutching her womb, mimicking the blinding cramp that Holly had just felt, the mirror image threw the amorphous gore against the mirror, the barely formed face splattering on the glass—but not before Holly saw its soft blue eyes open and look directly into her own, perfectly matching blue eyes. A boy, she'd aborted a boy, and never knew. So long ago.

The green eyes quickly flashed back into the mirror, wicked in their merriment.

An unfamiliar emotion born of terror and loathing threw Holly's adrenaline into high gear, and with a single burst of energy, she pushed herself away from the mirror. Falling away from the ominous reflection, Holly fell to the softly carpeted floor, gasping for each breath as if she were a marathon runner whose final burst had just put her over the finish. Her vision cleared and the room slowly came back into focus.

As she pulled herself up on her bed, Holly's mind raced. This was, she unfailingly knew, the trumpets of war. T.D. was sharing her husband's bed, somewhere, somehow. And T.D. wanted more than she would ever let her have. Firmly grasping the edge of the bedspread, Holly pulled it free and, in one long, fluid motion, flung it over the offending mirror. Standing in front of the neutralized weapon, she appeared as calm, cool, and collected as she had been long—painfully long—moments ago.

I've always been good in a fight, Holly thought, and this looks like a hell of a battle. But it wouldn't hurt to have an ally. Reaching for the phone, Holly efficiently sorted through her choices. In control, though shaken, the word "doctor" came to mind, and right now only Hal Vaughan would do. Though the young woman doctor would eventually prove herself, her uncanny resemblance to T.D. was not to her credit. Besides, in any event, it wouldn't hurt to have her long-time doctor, an attractive, older male, escort her to tomorrow's press conference. Just in case.

"It's time," Michael announced. He had changed from his saffron robes into soft corduroy slacks and a silk knit sweater.

"Almost," Talia replied. She moved away from the window; the play of the streetlamp turned her chestnut hair to ebony, red to black and back again.

No lights had been turned on and the room remained, hours after sunset, deeply shadowed. The gibbous moon, a sliver away from fullness, hung low in the evening sky; the warm amber reflection it cast was the only light in the high-ceilinged room. Bare floors, waxed to a high gloss, shone back the image: two people standing regally in front of a floor-to-ceiling window, both engulfed by a suspended golden disk, one that seemed much too close to possibly exist in space.

"When, then?" Michael, turning to look out over the rooftops, calmly asked. His growing need for fulfillment was carefully hidden from the one person he dared not antagonize.

"Very soon," Talia whispered. Sensing the raging energy all but radiating from the man next to her, she smiled and nodded. His training, she knew, had been excellent. So good that he could almost keep his excitement—no, his frustrations—from her. Almost. He would never be able to hide anything from her. No one could.

She turned to face Michael. Her eyes were level with his sensuous mouth—a full upper lip curving deeply over a pouting lower—a mouth never fully closed, always sipping air. Raising her head to meet his dark stare, Talia reached out her milk-white hand and touched his powerful shoulder.

"Two more nights, two more days, no more," she promised. Catching the sharp glint in his eyes, the only betrayal of his otherwise calm face, Talia added, "but, also, no less. Then, within hours, Michael, it will all be ours. Not one moment sooner." Talia shuddered, not sure if it came from within her or was brought on by the urgency of Michael's need. "I gave, I mean give, my word.

"Besides, " she continued, "there are mundane matters to attend to. It would be fanciful of us to think that just by achieving great cosmic power—satanic in your case, Michael—we could rule the world. It doesn't work that way, not in this age of iron and steel buildings, bridges than span continents, and media communications to all but the smallest villages.

"No, Michael. Perhaps in your clan world of covens you can grasp the so-called throne whenever you're able to seize it or when the stars permit—whichever comes first—but outside your minuscule universe the rest of the world will go on as before. And you'll not have one whit more authority in it, or control over it, than you had before." Talia paused, weighing whether to tell Michael more. Realizing this was an opportune time, she continued. "What I'm planning, what we're doing, is by far grander."

His agitation growing, Michael found he was no longer able to contain his anger. Talia would soon sense his emanations and there was no reason to hide it from her any longer.

"You're wrong, Talia," Michael cut hotly into her monologue. "Your continuing saga of 'how we will

rule the world' is getting on my nerves, and I'm tired
of hearing about how you have it all figured out.

"Power is absolute," he continued, "and when I
have it, I'll rule with the respect of my people—a large
number of people—who are important and who will
fully understand the extent of my control. What you're
planning is all show, a grandstand effort to make headlines. It's not going to bring you any more control,
only press coverage from people who have no idea
what you truly are, to be read by others who care less.
You want your picture in the paper, to be involved in
the politics of the time, not the history of the time-
less."

Seeming amused, Talia gave no sign of the growing
anger she was ready to unleash at the man standing
next to her. "Michael, where will your so-called power
take you to live when I condemn the buildings you and
your followers live it? And what will your absolute
control get you when you're arrested and put in jail?
How will you rule your prison empire?"

His shock glared brilliantly in the darkened room,
his fear crackled audibly. "You wouldn't."

"It's not really what I have in mind, Michael." Talia
turned back to the window, waiting as his panic ebbed
back into control.

When he calmed, she continued. "It's just a question of what cards you're holding. You can't see further
than your little world and yet it could be so easy for
someone in a stronger, politically powerful position to
easily change your universe. You're living now at the
whims of others, others who don't know you, don't
care if you exist or not. Not yet. No one has any reason to interfere with you. But they could. And they
would, if *we* weren't in that dominant position."

"But that's not what *I* want. Our agreement was that
I'd draw down my mother's force, that I would be high
priest. Now you have me running for political office."

"You can have everything we agreed you should
have. You don't have to run for office. I've got Ned
Harper to use for that." A smile played on Talia's

composed face. "But you have to support me, fully, and really look at the long-range plans." Talia spoke softly, knowing that to raise her voice at Michael would only incite him further.

"You sound like a damn marketing executive instead of a witch." Michael all but spit the words out on the floor.

"I never said I was a witch. That's your name for me, again based on your little world—a world, incidentally, you rejected for the blacker arts."

"Then what are you?" Michael challenged.

"Something else entirely. The one, the only, the original something else. Do you want the unabridged version? I'm the product of generations of breeding, one family, one line. Where I was born there are those who worship my family—my grandmothers, great- and great-great-great-grandmothers . . .

"Or do you want just the hard facts. I don't know how I evolved, but there are no others like us—I mean, like me."

"I don't understand." Michael had become petulant. "You told me you and I were alike, that we could be together and powerful. Now you tell me you're different and want to be apart. Which is it?"

"Both. Can't you take yourself out of the narrow rut you've lived in all your life and for once see beyond this room?" Talia gestured at the walls surrounding them. "I'm not asking the impossible, I don't need you to understand. How can I ask that when I don't know myself? But it would be helpful if you understood the simple rules of power here on earth."

"Then tell me what you are, at least what you do know," Michael pleaded. "I don't understand."

"Before my mother died, she told me I was descended from women who were special. She wouldn't, or couldn't, define it further. She told me I'd find out how, how I was different, by myself. She was distraught because she knew she was ill and wouldn't be there for me—and my sister. That's what really alarmed her, that there were two of us. It had happened only once before that she knew of, that twins had been born in our family. She said they fought bitterly with each other from birth and only one reached puberty. The one who survived was still greater than the others before her, and more powerful than any since. She said that we had this same greatness. And she was right. Why, I could bring this building down with sustained thought!'' Talia, striding the length of the room reached a fevered pitch, then pulled herself back and continued.

''My mother said her grandmother died after seeing us, that the old woman's last words were testimony to our power. She was cautioned to keep the wood fires that sedated us burning. That smoke was like a shot of Thorazine—it kept my sister and me totally in check. Only when I was far enough away from our cabin did my mind clear, did I come fully alive. One day, away from the smoke, I realized that my sister would never be one with me. That's when I knew it had to be me. Alone.''

Michael began to wander aimlessly about the room, his attention and interest obviously waning. ''Terrific stuff, Talia, you even sound like a politician. You haven't told me anything new. If fact, it sounds like a rehash of my story with Bree.'' An amused light gleamed in his eyes. ''Can you really bring this building down with sustained thought?''

''No, not really. I'm afraid I exaggerated there. I got carried away. My control is really over people, not things. Though I could make you think I devastated the building.'' A small smile played at Talia's mouth. ''Sometimes I'd like to snap my fingers and crumble a boulder, but I can only do that in minds. On the other hand, I could control a crowd and have them tear the building down, brick by brick. And that, Michael, I can do. Make no mistake about it.''

''Then why haven't you used this control?'' Michael asked, genuinely puzzled. ''You could have anything you wanted. Jewelry, furs, incredible cars, just by telling someone, a sales person, to give them to you.''

"Without a teacher to guide me I've had to find my own way. While I was still in my teens I saw a sapphire pendant in our town's jewelry store and wanted it more than anything else. I walked in and the owner just handed it to me, not even remembering the incident five minutes later. When he noticed it missing, he reported it stolen. I couldn't wear it, so it wasn't worth having.

"What good is a sapphire necklace—or a dozen, for that matter—if you can't wear it, can't sell it, can't own it. What I learned was that the next time I wanted something, I had to let everyone see me gain it. The jewelry-store owner was a widower, not that old, and I made him lust after me. People saw, and talked, but when, a month later, I wore the sapphire, everyone thought he had willingly given it to me. When he saw me wearing it—and I made sure he was the first—even he was confused.

"I learned to manipulate the situation to fit the need." Talia paused, moving closer to Michael. "Now do you understand?"

"Are you using me?" Michael asked.

"A little, Michael, just a little. But, then, you're using me as well, aren't you?"

"A little, Talia, just a little." He smiled down at her.

"Just remember, Michael, when the time comes, I may have to go on without you. But we'll both have what we want."

"That's a long time away, Talia, and we still have right now." His desire burned hot, his hardness straining against his clothes.

"It's soon, very soon."

"Now," Michael repeated, on a different wave length than Talia. He wanted her now. He was sure that by taking Talia physically he would be possessing what she was. The combination fueled him to an uncontrollable pitch. Reaching out, he circled her slim waist and pulled her to him.

Talia let herself go to him. This was unimportant—

but he wanted her and she did need him. And tomorrow she would give Michael something he really wanted—a gift he desired even more than he lusted for her—though she doubted he could tell the difference at this moment.

Talia had found she could reach Bree, testing her with the scent of dead flowers, with the cold blue light. Now that she knew she could reach the woman, she would do more. She would give Michael his sister.

18

JEFF, ALONE IN BED, FLOPPED DRAMATICALLY TO HIS other side. A wide-awake restlessness—peculiar in someone so recently able to nap in hospital linen closets during long shifts—agitated him further and was turning his skin to sandpaper. He analytically listened to the sounds echoing up the narrow stairway from the kitchen below: a lid being pried from a jar, its sharp contact with the tile counter sounding like a thunderclap in the night; the tearing of wilted lettuce leaves was the storm, renting the sky; the soft gurgle of salad dressing being poured was the deluge that threatened to drown him.

Damn her, he thought as he punched his pillow into a senseless shape. It sounds as if there's a microphone on the kitchen counter and she's broadcasting her salad making. She should be lying here next to me, as she always does after making love, whispering wonderful things about us so we can slip off to sleep in each other's arms.

But even making love had been different tonight. Tonight an unfulfilled need had continued to rage in Elise, and even before Jeff had finished climaxing, his semen still pulsing, his senses reeling, she was out of bed and into the bathroom, running water to wash herself. She'd emerged, scant moments later, dressed in her jeans and his shirt—all the clothes the bathroom contained—and, with barely a glimpse at her husband, headed down the stairs.

There was no together tonight, Jeff realized. Wounded, he recalled his excitement at the subtle difference in Elise. He hadn't expected her to be awake, much less receptive, when he'd come upstairs. Not after the fit she'd thrown earlier. He'd come upstairs quietly after his father left, as not to waken her, but instead of a sleeping wife found Elise sprawled, naked on the bed. Elise, who slept summer and winter in knee-length shirts. He was surprised, but it hadn't taken him more than a second to move into the arms she held out to welcome him.

Elise had been stronger, smelled muskier, had emanated a sensuality that was unlike her usual softness and acceptance when he approached her, when he entered her. Tonight she had controlled him, teased him, excited him, guided him into her, and met his every movement with force—driving him farther and deeper than ever before. Then, finally, she rejected him.

A draft from the partially open window chilled him and swept any thought of sleep from his eyes. Jeff swung his legs from under the quilt and sat up, head in hands. The feeling of being closed off, of not knowing the person to whom he has just made love—no, had shared passion with—grew, and as he slipped into his oversized robe, a deeper chill than that from the draft reached inside him. It just wasn't the same person. His Elise.

Shaking his head to clear the thought, Jeff walked to the bedroom door, listening for her sounds. The idea was foolish, he knew—no, cruel. Just because his wife was reacting from an undefined anger and had taken it out on him, his hurt pride was shifting the blame back to her, trying to read her as unbalanced. Stop! This is the same woman he married and lived with in a cramped two-room apartment for five years— without once getting in each other's way. This is the woman he shared his residency with, while she completed her own, and even when they worked opposite shifts, they were together. Very much together. It was the same woman he had loved a thousand times before, down to the small scar in the hollow of her neck.

Yet, the sprawling house now felt cramped, as if he

were intruding on her privacy. Though they spent their waking hours together, working side by side, she was pulling away to create her own sense of time and place. No, the woman he had made love to tonight was not the same woman he had fallen in love with.

Jeff started down the stairs, wanting more than anything else to shake the unfamiliar feeling of aloneness. He tried to remember when Elise had started to build this wall between them, when the first brick had been set. The wall had been under construction for some time, he knew, but tonight the mortar had finally dried.

The soft carpeting on the staircase muffled his footsteps, and reaching the bottom, Jeff paused, tightly gripping the banister. Had it been less than two weeks ago that Elise first closed him out? Yes, the Monday before they opened their practice when, at dinner, she wouldn't share with him. The night she had been talking about her family . . . and her sister.

Ned Harper returned, weary, from the VIP laboratory tour. He'd seen everything, heard even more, and understood very little, but the facility was of obvious importance to the federal types and he'd been grateful for the invitation. Genetic research on animals was for left-wing anarchists or right-wing power-mongers, neither the sort of person much less politician that he prided himself of being. He could understand genetics in vegetables, crossing strains of tomatoes to create a firmer, seedless variety. Or the like. But working with animals was tampering with . . . well, going too far. Nonetheless he'd been a courteous, admiring observer. As long as it was funded with federal monies, he didn't have to concern himself with the aesthetics of the situation. If state funds became involved, he would, unfortunately, have to learn more. Perhaps T.D. could draft a briefing for him on the subject.

His foot reached the first-floor landing before he heard his wife weeping. He was momentarily stunned at the sound; the last—no, only—time he heard her cry was when, more than ten years ago, she'd returned from a doctor's appointment mysteriously distraught, refusing to share the reason for her distress yet denying any life-threatening illness. Rapidly covering the few steps leading to their bedroom suite, Ned burst into the room.

Holly sat, huddled in her favorite chair, her feet tucked under her long robe, her head pressed into the crook of her arm. In between sobs, her short ragged breaths rippled shudders down her back.

Quietly approaching his wife, Ned reached out and gently touched her shoulder.

Holly's head flew back. Her red-rimmed eyes glared accusingly at the offending hand. "Get away from me," she hissed. "It's all your fault."

Taken aback, Ned obeyed and moved away to a facing chair. Searching for any clue as to what could be disturbing Holly to this extent—and not finding any answer—he silently waited until her sobs subsided before speaking.

"What's my fault? What happened?"

"You and that woman, that's what happened." Holly ran her hand through her tangled hair. Reaching toward a box of tissues, she turned to face her husband, her eyes streaked with ruined mascara, cheeks glistening wetly.

Ned was leaden, unable to move for fear that even the slightest gesture would give him away.

"What woman, darling?" he gently asked, risking a movement to pass Holly the tissues.

"Your trusted communications director, of course." Holly spoke clearly, her voice no longer trembling. "That quiet, competent, not to mention beautiful and bitchy woman with the brilliant green eyes who has taken over your life and is now trying to get into mine."

Sinking into his chair, Ned started to answer but paused, looking around the room. The spacious room held, at the far end, a king-size bed, abutted by a pair of low antique dressers. The far wall was a series of louvered doors: his dressing room, his wife's, and closest to the sitting area they were in, the door to their master bath. In between the dressing rooms they shared was a free-standing mirror—a mirror now draped with their bedspread.

"What happened, Holly?" Ned gently prodded. "Tell me." His thoughts raced, the most frightening depicting a scene where T.D. confronted Holly. He knew that such an event would be highly unlikely. He trusted T.D.; she'd been with him for years and had long ago proved her discretion and tact. Yet, he also knew, when emotions enter a relationship, many things change.

Holly looked steadily at her husband, beginning to wonder if her intuitions were correct, her visions real. Glancing toward the shrouded mirror, she shivered, remembering not only her own altered reflection and the carnal scenes she had been forced to watch but the malicious emanations that had palpably surged from the glass. The malignant force that had all but gripped her and thrown her to the floor was real. No, she knew, she was right. It was T.D. The why was only a suspicion. It was senseless to provoke confirmation from her husband at this time, if he knew at all. The how was completely beyond the realm of any reason, and that, more than anything else, tormented her.

"Never mind," Holly finally answered, still pale but composed. "I think it actually had very little to do with you, after all."

Ned wisely chose not to pursue the issue. He leaned forward and kissed his wife on the forehead. Moving to his closet to change, he felt his wife's eyes on him; reaching to remove the cover draping the mirror, he turned to look back at her. The terror in her eyes was unmistakable, and as he pulled off the spread, she swooned.

Rushing back to his wife's side, Ned did not notice the spider's web of cracks in the mirror's now cloudy surface.

Bree's eyes flew open, any trace of sleep erased by the sudden drop in temperature in her bedroom. This

was a dream, she reasoned as she watched spreading
frost etch patterns on the outside of the window panes.
The outside of the panes, she realized, not the inside
as would happen if the cold were real and outside.

Pulling her cover closer, Bree tried to close her eyes,
convinced that if not a dream, the cold was just a
momentary hallucination.

Ever since her mother had appeared to her, she had
found herself having moments of confusion, disori-
entation. Her senses had betrayed her time and time
again. She had been frozen to Michael's banister, obviously in fear of confronting him; the smell of incense in the hallway had to have been an olfactory
hallucination, the eerie, blue fog a visual one. Yet, the
most disturbing occurrence had been tonight. Before
falling asleep she had experienced soft caresses,
ghostly hands making gentle love to her, and her own
suppressed needs surfaced and betrayed her. Bree
shuddered as she remembered her body responding to
the unseen hands, and her denial grew even stronger.

Just as the smell of dead flowers had faded when she
reached the top of the stairs, and just as the hands
stroking her thighs had lifted as soon as she opened
her legs to admit the phantom lover, this cold would
leave the room when she rose to open the window,
admitting the pleasant spring night.

Bree moved to leave the bed and found she could
not.

She smiled to herself. This inability to move was
proof positive that this was only a dream—motor responses locked during REM sleep—and she let her
body relax and sink deeper into the soft bed.

But the cold continued and went beyond the empir-
ical senses; it reached its icy tentacles deep, probing
her primal fears.

Unable to close her eyes, wide awake in her nightmare, Bree frantically looked about the room. The
windows were now completely covered with frost,
barring any view to outside. An icy white mist was

forming, even as she watched, on all the surfaces in the room. She reached for the bedside phone to call for help, but it was frozen to the cradle; Bree's mind raced for a reason.

The only salvation to the bitter cold came from a growing spot of warmth between her legs, a warmth that radiated outward and kept the surface of the bed above freezing. The frost, now visibly coating her hands and arms with delicate crystalline patterns, was being fought from within. This warmth was the deciding factor; this wasn't a dream—it was really happening. Her instincts fought back, warming her, warning her. Bree's denials shattered like sheets of thin ice as she concentrated on keeping the warmth flowing from her body. The slow, liquid heat seeped from her pores and enveloped her in a comforting wrap.

Bree's breath frosted before her own eyes as the room's temperature plunged even lower; the frigid cold continued to hold her prisoner in bed. She was using every dram of willpower she could muster to stay awake, to keep from freezing.

The moving yet gentle refrains of a piano sonata flowed around her, music filling the room. A classical piece, familiar but not immediately identifiable. Her own meager tape collection contained only a few classical pieces—mostly Mozart, some Beethoven, and a variety of chamber music; this was not anything she owned.

Lulled by the masterly rendition, concentrating on the sonorous chords, Bree closed her eyes to the sweeping majesty of the perfectly executed music. Still, a fraction of her consciousness kept her awake, urged her to move; she might now be able. To throw her feet over the edge of the warm and enveloping bed into her cold slippers now solidly covered with ice and to grab her robe—the claret-colored robe—carelessly draped over a nearby chair, and run, run for the door. It would be warm outside; the cold was only here. But the cocoon of her own warmth lulled her, along with the strains of the ethereal yet almost childlike music playing close, closer still, blotting out all else, invisible earphones concentrating the sound and draining any will to move.

The music. It was Chopin, a piano sonata. A piece she now recalled but still couldn't name. The gentle and slow meter battled with her urges to flee; the building musical movement closed out all else.

A chilled porcelain lamp cracked from freezing. The intrusive sound of its breaking reached her awareness just as the music named itself. Chopin's piano sonata number two, his funeral march, slipped into the familiar and obvious refrain for which it was well-known, a refrain hidden deep within its complex score.

The slight warmth she had generated suddenly vanished and Bree plunged into the same subfreezing atmosphere as the rest of the room. No longer comforted, Bree pushed the cover away and again tried to rise; her body was incapable of any movement.

She fell back, now uncovered, hearing the closing refrain of the sonata, the lone and forlorn piano march. Her mother's sad face hovered before her, outstretched arms unable to reach Bree, to hold her, to provide warmth. There is no warmth in the grave, Bree thought as she slipped into a stupor. The final piano chord echoed in the still room as she closed her eyes.

Closing the refrigerator door, Elise shuddered from the chill. She'd been gazing blankly into the refrigerator for so long, the butter was softening. She knew she had behaved reprehensibly toward Jeff, but he was no comfort. For the first time since she'd known him, she saw him for what he really was: shallow and selfish. He made love to her tonight with a renewed vigor and passion that she instinctively knew was not directed toward her.

Confused, Elise struggled to clear her thoughts. She knew it was foolish to condemn her husband for making love to her like she was someone else; yet, at the same time, she was a different person—someone more enriched than the silly creature she had been before.

She'd never thought of herself in the third person before, yet now she was filled with images of her own life, a seemingly shallow series of episodes.

Forcing herself away from these churning concepts, Elise moved toward the stairs. Torn between wanting to reach out and embrace the man she had married, and wanting to reach out and angrily push him away, she began to climb the stairway. Conflicting emotions continued to rage within her, changing back and forth and back again. She slowly mounted the stairs. Each step she took, each tread her foot touched, reversed the thought process. Again. And again. As her foot reached the topmost landing, the conflict resolved. She needed help to understand, and right now, only one person could provide the answers.

If she were to survive—Elise shook her head—she meant resolve herself, she'd have to talk to Bree and tell Bree everything. Everything she knew, everything she could remember.

Which, Elise thought, isn't much.

19

"**F**OR A FRIDAY-MORNING PRESS CONFERENCE, I'M impressed with the turnout," Holly said to T.D., barely suppressing the smoldering need to comment on the absurdity of holding a conference after the dailies published their last weekday edition.

T.D. smiled archly, intentionally delaying any response to the candidate's wife in the hope the woman would dig herself deeper into the unintended but extremely welcome trap she was walking into. The two women faced each other, each with their formal, public mask firmly in place. Realizing Holly's aplomb would not permit the woman to comment further, T.D. surveyed the room. "Yes, it seems to be coming along. Our celebrity guests have all arrived—those 'loyal supporters' who use any appropriate opportunity to get their picture in the media. Of course, the television crews aren't all here yet, but they're always the last to arrive. What with the manpower involved for each shot, it's amazing they make it in time to set up for the wrap-up." Spotting a flurry of activity near the door, T.D. loooked toward the commotion.

"Fox broadcasting and cable news are already here," she said over her shoulder as she moved away, "so that must be one of the networks arriving. Must see if I can help—or at least offer some suggestions as to which is Ned's good side. The one thing I've found"—T.D. now smiled almost sweetly—"is a Friday press conference always, and I mean always, gets more air play than any other event at any other time— short of national or international disasters, of course.

The dearth of news coverage on weekends insures the extra play.'' Pausing, unable to resist the final shot, T.D. continued to smile at the surprised woman who had obviously not expected the broadcast media to be in such obvious attendance. ''Any news, even Ned Harper, is better than the latest bag-lady count.''

The conference was being held in a private room reserved at the reopened El Morocco; the club was not only a city landmark but, to the world of movie fans, Art Deco devotees, and the general wave of kitsch buffs and nostalgia fans, a cultural one. The location, T.D. assured Ned, would be influential. His reputation as a ''typical'' Greenwich Village politician, erroneously based on his home address rather than his conservative politics, would be detrimental not only in the upper East Side's silk-stocking district—where potential, monied contributors lived—and in the intellectually oriented upper West Side, but more important, statewide. Village politicians never fared well outside of New York City, a precedent they would, T.D. assured, break.

Mock-zebra-skin banquettes lined the room, but it was the walls of autographed and framed photos of all-the-celebrities-that-ever-were that had caught the interest of those in attendance. Watching the crowd watch each other, while at the same time surreptitiously stealing glances at her husband at T.D.'s side, Holly nonetheless managed to keep her eye on the arched entrance, anxiously waiting for the reassuring sight of Hal Vaughan. The adage about a shoulder to lean on was never more appropriate, Holly knew; despite her ramrod stance and smiling face, she needed physical as well as emotional support—now more than ever.

In this room full of people Holly stood quite alone, apart from the decision-making process, including even simple choices such as this buffet menu, and as always, away from the public-policy shaping. Now she was cut off from the man himself.

Hal Vaughan stepped into the room and Holly let

out a deep sigh, first realizing she'd been holding her breath.

Ned Harper's overall political stance had been carefully balanced to appeal to the widest possible margin of voters; his liberal and services-oriented statements were given the broadest local coverage and the more conservative-directed activities were fed to the statewide press services. While all political announcements should result in a balanced portrait of the ideal politician, only the most dedicated investigative reporter would be able to put together the true picture: that of an individual with almost no real position or conviction.

T.D. had such a reporter in mind. Today's conference would establish, for the record, a seemingly liberal position on prison reform, a statement designed and worded to provide the final contradictory proverbial straw. Today's coverage of Ned's protests of current city- and statewide court procedures—from arrest and arraignment through the trial and eventual incarceration—would receive very little actual attention. Print coverage would be light, as designed, and the brief taped spots were unlikely to pick up on the real nuance. It wouldn't be until the days just before the election, when the people were weighing the important factors prior to casting their votes, that the picture of an insecure, wavering, and contradictory candidate would be revealed.

When this day came—and it would, using the details she herself provided—T.D. would pull her coup. Not only would she successfully integrate all components of Ned's campaign into a brilliant master strategy but she would lash out at the opposition for not having the scope to understand the plan. Ned would heroically assume office, her precisely weighed and balanced platform finally apparent to all. A double-double cross.

Such final-hour grandstanding was also, T.D. knew, the only way to ensure the election and continued support for Ned Harper. Ned was a weak individual who, at this moment, most likely firmly believed in each and every segmented opinion he gave—opinions that she carefully researched, wrote, and convinced him were his own. Without a carefully timed climax it was possible—no, probable—he would appear the vague, hesitant candidate he really was. It was too soon, though, to set the final stage and too important to keep statements, like today's, which was in conflict with earlier positions, unnoticed.

The conference started and Ned's charismatic voice recited the precisely structured words he'd painstakingly rehearsed. An occasional falter, and the resultant glance at his notes, was always accompanied by a boyish grin that disarmed all but the most cynical reporters. T.D. stood apart, keeping discreet count of the slips. She knew that too many flubs during any presentation would destroy the carefully calculated effect of natural spontaneity and begin to irritate the audience—and an audience of press, once annoyed, was dangerous. They could begin to pick apart the pieces, and it was much too early in this campaign for that to happen.

She would have liked to work with Ned late into the night before, perfecting his delivery, ensuring his level of comfort with the speech, but it was more important to spend the time with Michael. Michael was pulling away from her, and cementing their bond, especially at this point in time, was a priority.

Besides, T.D. smiled to herself as the well-modulated rise and fall of Ned's amplified voice reached out to the dozens of accredited press gathered, she had at least ensured that Ned met with no warm, and thus distracting, welcome from his wife. Holly, headstrong and independent, should have had nothing to do with Ned the night before if, as planned, she held him responsible for the vision sent to her.

"Any questions, ladies and gentlemen?" Ned's rich baritone flowed into the large room.

Again fully attentive, T.D. listened carefully to the questions and anticipated-as-rehearsed answers. The

energetic press, pumped full of coffee and highly sug-
ared cakes, shot back question after question, yet not
one dealt with the overall picture nor questioned any
of the few loose threads only T.D. was aware hung
frayed from the campaign tapestry she had carefully
woven. Breathing a sigh of relief, T.D. smiled broadly
at Ned and rose to take her position beside him at the
podium.

"If that's all, a prepared text of Governor Harper's
position is available at the door." she said—with carefully omitted phrases to be inserted at a later date, she
silently concluded. "Thank you for coming." Flicking off the microphone, T.D. leaned toward Ned, intentionally excluding Holly. "Terrific, Ned. Just
consider this one more victory on your road to the
state capital."

Holly watched T.D. lean toward her husband, her
irritation building. Here, in this bright and crowded
room, the irrational fear she'd carried over from the
night before was being replaced by a more tangible
series of emotions — jealousy, resentment, and the
budding of pure, unadulterated hate. It no longer mattered by what means the younger woman had reached
into her home and violated her personal territory, what
mattered now was the quiet words they were exchanging, the intimacy with which they looked into each
other's eyes.

At Holly's side, Hal Vaughan stood stunned. The
young woman who stepped up to the podium was his
daughter-in-law. Almost. Seeing her there, her facial
expressions impossibly like those he was intimately
familiar with, he was doubly amazed that he had overlooked her earlier when he arrived. But then, of course,
Holly's distress had involved his entire attention on
both a professional and personal level. Now, focused
on the candidate and his aide, Hal was speechless. The
differences in coloring could be cosmetic. If this wasn't
Elise's twin, it was her exact double. But if it was her
twin, why hadn't Elise said anything to Jeff about her
sister being in New York? On the other hand, consid-

ering it had taken Elise so many years just to mention a sister, it shouldn't come as a surprise.

His anticipation growing, Hal turned back to Holly Harper. First, ensure Holly is returned safely to her home; the harrowing tale she'd told him of last night needed to be analyzed in the light of day. Second, find out more about this T.D. Harrah. What, he wondered, did Elise say her sister's name was?

Clutching her purse tightly, Holly rose to join the pair leaving the podium. In two long strides she was next to her husband, proprietarily slipping her arm through Ned's, covering his hand with hers—which, she realized with a start, was in turn covering his aide's hand.

T.D.'s slightly arched eyebrow was the only clue that she found this moment unusual, more so amazing in light of the effort she had expended the night before to shatter Holly's assurance and self-esteem. A slight smile barely twisted the young woman's face, a smile born of the immensely pleasurable ways she was devising to further distress the wife of the candidate.

Pulling her husband's hand away, Holly continued the polite banter normally following a successful conference. Leading her triumphant husband to the door, she turned back to T.D. while she continued her aimless pleasantries.

"Oh, and I'm sure you won't mind my taking Ned away for the weekend. He's had enough politics for the week, don't you think? It's time for a change. Maybe out to the Island for some air, or just a quiet weekend in the city. Don't worry, I'll have him back to you Monday morning, fresh and recharged for the week."

Another time for you, Mrs. Harper, thought T.D., I've plans for the weekend myself.

Hal Vaughan, his plans to tend to Holly changed by her abrupt departure, turned to the woman now by his side.

"Miss Harrah," he formally addressed her, offering her his hand, "we haven't been introduced. I'm Hal

Vaughan, Mrs. Harper's doctor. You're to be congrat-
ulated for this conference.''

Distracted, T.D. shook the hand offered her while
not letting herself lose sight of the departing candidate
and wife, seething as they smiled and chatted with
camp-followers and well-wishers on their way out. She
barely felt the scrape of his nail on her wrist, dismissing it as an act of clumsiness.

''Miss Harrah, you look very familiar. I'm sure I've
seen you somewhere before. Do you, by any chance,
have a sister in this city?''

T.D.'s attention snapped back to the man addressing
her.

JoJo felt the chill as he neared the apartment, the
warmth of the hallway ended abruptly an arm's distance from Bree's door. He had woken from a fitful
night's sleep, filled with disturbing dreams he could
not remember—that in and of itself unnerving. Dreams
always stayed with JoJo until he could sort them out
and identify not only the components but determine
any prophecy they held.

This morning he woke, bathed in sweat, with no
recall of any part of any dream, just a hollow feeling
coupled with physical exhaustion. He'd stayed in bed
far longer than usual trying to sort out his confusion,
waiting for a fragment of the night's musings to return
to him. There had been nothing but a vacuum, an
emotional emptiness that extended to his physical well-
being, and drained him further.

By the time he rose, a solid dread filled that emptiness.

Cup of coffee in hand, JoJo thought of Bree. Slam-
ming the cup on the already cracked counter, he cursed
himself as he rushed to dress. *Why hadn't he immediately thought of her!* Leaving the unfinished coffee,
JoJo rushed through the morning crowds, covering the
few blocks between the apartments in record time.

Standing before her door, experiencing the preter-
natural cold that surrounded it, he knocked firmly and

waited. And knocked again. And again. His initial panic dissolved, replaced by unwavering determination. He had to get in. Reaching for the doorknob, JoJo's fingers touched iced metal—the cold so devastating it shot through his arm like an electric shock. This, he immediately knew, was more than he could handle alone, but there was no time to call for help. If something were wrong inside—and JoJo knew beyond any shadow of a doubt that whatever waited beyond the door was trouble—he needed to get in now.

The icy knob turned easily in his hands, and with no further effort, the door swung open on its own volition. Looking beyond the door, not yet ready to enter, he saw a thin white crust of frost covering every surface in the kitchen. An immobilizing emptiness washed over JoJo, and stilled his intense desire to rush into the front room to search for Bree.

As he took his first cautious step, the air warmed noticeably, the frost melting in a growing radius around him. Drops of condensed moisture began to run down the hard kitchen surfaces, soaking through the curtains and towels. Feeling as if he was walking through water, the density of the air awkward and slowing, he moved on. Each small step he took warmed the air, his body pushing back the cold, his presence bringing life back to the room.

He entered the small living room through which Bree's bedroom lay, his mind refusing to project what he would find there. Turning to enter the bedchamber, he felt the cold reach out in one final and malevolent icy blast before it dissipated.

Bree was lying pale and still on the bed. What was left of the cold emanated from her moribund body.

Backing into the living room, JoJo reached for the phone and quickly punched in the number he'd memorized to reach Bree at work. He waited patiently while the connection was made. The phone was picked up on the first ring.

"Dr. Crawford, you don't know me. My name is JoJo. I'm a friend, a good friend, of Bree's. Please

come to her apartment now. Right now." Listening to
the readily agreed response, he murmured confirmation of the address and gently replaced the phone in it
cradle. Without moving his eyes from the figure lying
in the adjoining room, he lowered himself into Bree's
overstuffed chair to wait.

"I don't know what I can do, JoJo." Elise stood
distraught at the foot of Bree's bed. "She's dead."

"I don't think so, Dr. Crawford. I know she's still
alive. I can feel her presence."

"That's superstitious nonsense. I'm a doctor, a
medical doctor, and I'm not about to listen to your
mumbo-jumbo. We should call the police."

"Not yet, Dr. Crawford. Bree told me a little about
you. About how you can sense what's about to happen.
She had a feeling about you, a very strong feeling,
that you're hiding a far greater ability than she could
even guess at."

Elise paled and spun around to face the slender,
swarthy man standing near the head of the bed. He
was taller than she, and his classic features—the cliché "tall, dark, and handsome" jumped to mind—
were drawn tight in concern. His deep-set eyes bored
into her own with unmistakable intensity. Lowering
his eyes first, JoJo shook his head.

"I know, Dr. Crawford. I know she was right. Even
I can feel it. Your strength. And I don't have a fraction
of what Bree has."

"That's nonsense," Elise shot back, forgetting the
promise she'd made to herself: to open her heart and
her mind, to accept and to use. "Bree was prone to
superstition and fantasy, the result of being fed this
claptrap by you and your kind."

"No, Dr. Crawford, Bree was more than a believer.
She was a doer. A healer. Like yourself." His eyes
filling with burning tears, JoJo turned to Elise, who
was now gripping the bedspread tightly. The tension
in her face was reflected in her clenched and whitened
knuckles. "Heal her," he said, simply and directly.

"She's dead, you fool. Can't you see that?" Elise hissed back, her suppressed memories stirring uncomfortably. Forgotten episodes and buried emotions surfaced against her will: helpless animals, burnt and bloodied beyond recognition, moving again under her hands; a roommate's asthma attacks, chronic since childhood, vanishing; her tears again falling on Jason's decomposing body . . .

Elise turned away, ready to leave the room. *Anything but face the past!*

JoJo saw and moved to block her way.

"No. Help her. You need her, Dr. Crawford, more than you know. You have to bring her back. Without Bree . . . It's not for me, Dr. Crawford. You need her. I don't know exactly why or how, but without her you'll be crushed and it's going to be soon. That's *why* she's been hurt. Bring her back." JoJo's voice broke, and he moved back away from the bed.

A flicker of green passed behind Elise's hazel eyes, masking the amber light, and a sense of strength and purpose grew within her. Doubt still showed in her awkward movements as she inched toward the woman who had been her nurse, who had promised to be her friend, but a calm sureness and growing awareness crept into each step. A glance at the man silently sobbing brought her and her resolve to the last step.

To Bree's still form.

Reaching out, Elise lifted one cold and lifeless hand between both of her own. There was nothing there, nothing at all. As before, when she first examined her.

Out of the corner of her eye Elise saw JoJo's head raise up to watch her. Hope and something else, belief, shone on his face. Knowing she must try, that although nothing could possibly come of it she would additionally be burdened with this man's sorrow and loss if she didn't, Elise leaned down to Bree's bloodless lips and brushed them with her own.

The lifeless hand she held trembled. A nerve reaction Elise knew, perhaps rigor mortis was already setting in. Brushing the dark hair from Bree's forehead, smooth in the perfect repose of death, Elise once again leaned to the dead woman, a distasteful shudder rippling down her own back.

Pressing her lips to the dead woman's forehead, she softly blew a deep and warm breath onto the cold skin—colder than death, colder than the vast emptiness of nothing—and whispered into the luxurious hair of the dead woman, wishing—no, willing—Bree to be alive.

The cold fingers she still held gently closed around her own. Pulling back, Elise looked in wonderment as Bree's dark eyes fluttered open.

20

SIPPING SOUR, UNHEATED COFFEE LEFT OVER FROM the morning's pot, Jeff paced between the kitchen and his office. Barely tasting the bitter grind, he again tried to repress his growing fury; only the busy patient load today had kept him from allowing his anger to explode into the rage he felt justified in nurturing.

Elise's disappearance in the middle of their busy morning had gone unexplained. Bree had not arrived for work, but Elise had been adroitly maneuvering the patient flow, handling the phones, and consulting with those patients who wished to specifically see her instead of Jeff when, immediately after one of the many phone calls, she had shrugged off her jacket and rushed out, leaving Jeff to cope with the day's load as best he could. The crisis resolved itself when Jeff recruited a young woman—who preferred anyway to wait to see Dr. Crawford—to cover the phones and maintain order in the waiting room. The neighborhood girl, who turned out to be a surprisingly able assistant, managed the day's traffic single-handed and, while not able to see the woman doctor, did pocket a day's wages for her efforts. Elise, though, had not called in at all that day.

The front door's familiar groan, despite numerous sandings and oilings, reached Jeff midstride between kitchen and office. Discarding the coffee cup that had become a prop rather than a vesssel, he strode into the foyer in time to strike a posed stance at the foot of the stairway—legs firmly planted and apart, arms crossed over his chest.

229

"Where the hell have you been all day?" he shot at Elise even before the door closed behind her.

Her face was tired, lips bloodless. Worry lines he never noticed before were vertically drawn between her eyebrows, in stark relief against her pale skin. A flicker of concern crossed Jeff's thoughts, but the option of finding a vent for the anger he'd carried all day won any contest of which role to play.

"I've been with Bree. She was taken . . ." Elise paused, her eyes vacant while she had to search for words, ". . . ill. Very ill actually." Her defenses down, her total exhaustion apparent to any but the most calloused observer, Elise started for the stairway and, foremost in her mind, to sanctuary from the events of the day—alien scenes that played and replayed over and over until she wanted to tear them out and bury them deep in the ground, far, far away.

"You could have called from the hospital," Jeff demanded, moving to block Elise's ascent.

"We didn't take her to the hospital," Elise murmured, her head pounding with greater and greater intensity as she reached for the banister. "We brought her back—I mean, treated her—at home."

Latching on to her phrasing as more fuel for his raging anger, Jeff threw his arm across the stairway to prevent Elise from taking the first step up.

"Who were you with? Who did you meet?" Jeff demanded as an ugly current of jealousy swept across his already unstable emotions. "It was a man who called, wasn't it?" His face, now inches from his wife's, was heavily flushed, spittle pooling in the corners of his snarled mouth.

Thrown back by the sheer force of his words, Elise leaned against the wall as much for support as for the fact she had nowhere else to move.

"JoJo, Bree's friend. He was the one who called me this morning." A flicker of empathy for her husband pulled Elise back from the deep, dark places she had been forced to reopen, and things she still couldn't fully accept yet now knew it was impossible to deny.

"Jeff, I'm sorry. I just realized I didn't even tell you where I was going when I ran out of here. And then I didn't even call. You must have been worried sick."

"Worried? You left me all alone to handle a full booking of patients and all you can say is you're sorry. Let me tell you something, Dr. Crawford, I didn't have time to worry about you. I was too busy seeing my appointments and yours. If I hadn't gotten lucky with some fast thinking, I would have had to close the doors for the day and that would have really looked good, don't you think, the new doctors in the neighborhood closing up in the middle of the day for no reason with appointments made and confirmed . . ."

Jeff's tirade showed no signs of abating as Elise stood and listened, openmouthed. His words droned on, enumerating the patients he saw and how he dealt with each one. Her mind raced to understand the point he was trying to make. He was angry at her for leaving him alone. There'd been no concern, no worry, just frustration at having to cope with a busy office. Closing her eyes, Elise let Jeff continue his monologue, hoping he would wind down and take her into his arms. His dispassionate bitter words, set in an atonal delivery, were merely background music to the jangling memories of the day.

After Bree recovered, the three of them had sat, the entire afternoon, and talked. Incalculable cups of tea later, drained and exhausted, Elise had begun to understand what—and maybe even who—she was, or at least a good part of it. While she intuitively knew they weren't entirely correct in their assumptions, at least they tried to understand. Her lifelong feelings of loneness coalesced into a clearer understanding of how to be whole, for the first time—with a great price to pay for the privilege: the price of no longer hiding from the truth. If she could manage to unravel the tangled web she hid within, it would only be with the help of Bree and JoJo. They had spent the long day talking, explaining how Elise needed to draw on her own reserves, her energy, and her strength.

She would have to take control, for the first time in her life, and even more awesome, to prepare to defend herself. The dream where Talia had threatened her was not a figment of her imagination. It was real.

Frightened and feeling more alone than she ever had, Elise trudged her weary way back here, to her home. But now she saw it wasn't really her home—not any more than any of the other buildings she had once lived in, any more than the rooms she had lovingly decorated with her favorite colors and possessions. Her home had been in the cave in Kentucky, and that because she shared it with Talia Dora. They *were* one; she hadn't escaped. Yet.

What Bree knew, she patiently explained; she saw the patterns that made Elise's aura were strong and powerful but unfulfilled. In her healing, Bree had even seen it before but never as vital and directed. Siblings, most often twins, would actually share their deepest thoughts, feeling the pain of the other, even across continents. With Elise and Talia Dora, there was something more: a symbiotic bond far beyond the norm. There was an immortal strength bred into them—both as one. For, Bree had explained, Talia was right: there should have been only one.

And, Bree and JoJo concurred, eventually there would be only one. They knew it to be so, knew it with absolute certainty. They cautioned her that now, in her burgeoning awareness, Elise was unlikely to have the ability to be the one to succeed.

They coached Elise into the evening, forgetting the outside world, concentrating on the inner world of her mind and being. Suddenly, Elise realized Jeff's voice had stopped some time ago, at least it must have, to judge by the intense scrutiny she was receiving.

"I asked you what you've been doing," he said, "and how you could manage to spend a whole day and most of the night taking care of one patient, outside a hospital."

"It was more than that, Jeff," Elise wearily responded.

"I just bet it was," he snarled, "and since you obviously have no intention of telling me what else it was, I'm going out."

His anger exhausted, Jeff grabbed his jacket and was out the door before Elise could begin to conjure up words that he would listen to, much less believe. If it had taken her almost twelve hours to listen and finally accept, how could she expect him to absorb even a fraction of the fantastic story she had to tell? Her quandary was solved, for the time being. Jeff had no intention of listening and it appeared he would rather have an audience for his histrionics than an explanation.

Bone-tired from the day's events, Elise slipped the problem of Jeff into a small corner of her mind and replaced the concern with a fantasy, soon to become a reality, of a steaming, scented bath.

"I believe you've failed." Michael glared at Talia, his eyes buring with malice.

"Perhaps it wasn't my failure, dear one, so much as your underestimation of your dear sister's strength." Talia stood rigid, appearing calm and regal but with knuckles whitened from tension.

"I never estimated Bree's strength to you," Michael retorted, "and you knew she had garnered Mother's force. If this is an example of your planning and ability, I think I cut a deal with the wrong partner."

"If that's what you think, you should go running back with your tail between your legs to your loving sister right this very minute. Fall on your knees and beg her forgiveness for ever doubting her and ask her, with the most heartfelt sincerity you can muster, to accept you and take you into her inner circle." Talia's cool reply leaked venom.

"If Bree had an inner circle," Michael said, equally bitter, as he spun to face the pacing woman, "I might."

Standing stock-still, facing each other, Talia and Michael glared at each other, each refusing to look away. Two sets of eyes—bottomless brown and neon green—glinted with bitter viciousness, sparking visibly at their proximity. A charged atmosphere began to fill the loft; the air grew still and heavy, laden with ions ready to burst into life at a single word, the slightest gesture. There was no movement as they continued to stare at each other, the hate growing and building and forming into an irrevocable reality.

From the darkest corner of the room a tangible shock wave of electrical static roared forth, blinding in its brightness, birthing a lightning ball whose fire-hardened core could be felt as it hovered. Talia's eyes glowed even brighter as the force flew into Michael, dissolving into his skin, doubling him over, immobilizing him.

Long moments passed before Michael's head slowly lifted, so slowly Talia's own sense of time slowed to match his rhythm. He knelt there, breathing. Just breathing.

For each extraordinary deep breath he took, inhaling until she wondered how his lungs could hold so much, his shoulders would roll under his shirt, muscles rippling through the thin fabric. Each long breath he released tainted the air with a foul stench, a fetid mixture of organic decay and sulfur.

Watching the sensuous movement of the muscles tensing then relaxing, Talia found herself rocking on her heels, wanting to reach out to help him rise. He was calling to her and, for the first time, reaching her.

Her hand moved unwillingly toward him.

Snatching back her outstretched hand, Talia concentrated on stepping back, away from the huddled figure. He took another deep breath, and another, the room itself now pulsing to Michael's breaths. Each inhalation perceptibly increased his size, each exhalation filled the air with more noxious odors. She was hypnotized by the slow, steady rhythm.

A quarter of an hour passed and the fouled air was thick enough to see. Talia was still frozen in place. Finally, the walls stopped moving and the harsh sounds of Michael's breathing stopped.

He rose gracefully, unwinding from his crouched position. As Talia stepped farther back, her eyes widened and her mouth opened in a silent gasp. What was standing before her was not the man who'd fallen to his knees.

With a shock she realized Michael's own beliefs were strong, his satanic worship more than merely the veneer she'd taken it for.

It was far taller and incalculably broader. She knew Michael's size well. She had held him close, coiled her long legs around his muscular body, wrapped her thighs about his hips, and curled her ankles at his buttocks to pull him deeper into her—all to seal their covenant. Her legs could not open wide enough to reach around this figure now before her. The shirt Michael had worn was torn and shredded across this being's shoulders, and as the arms lifted toward her, the last remnant of fabric fell away. There was no question of sex as the tatters of his pants lay in ruins on the floor; the erection was larger than Michael's forearm.

Its eyes slowly opened to meet hers.

The sound of Talia's scream cut through the silent loft.

The eyes were red, totally red, no definition of pupil to iris to sclera was visible. They glowed as fiery embers, their heat searing into the back of her head.

"You have toyed with my pawn too long." A deep and powerful voice filled the large room.

"I've watched," it continued, "and have been amused by your wiles and ways. I wondered how far you would try to take him. Thank you for giving me an opening to come out. A small loss of control, your anger carries very well, was all I needed."

"Who are you," Talia whispered, her throat constricted. "What are you?"

"I'm Michael, of course, you know that. Perhaps there's just more to me than you thought. What I need to know is how much there is to you."

A hand double the size of that which had once caressed her reached for Talia.

The room crackled with electricity and filled with foul odors, heated and burning like incense from hell.

A foot almost the size of a diver's fin slammed down in front of Talia. The weighty impact shook the floor. Her eyes level with the bare, hairless, and smooth of nipple chest, she suddenly realized the creature was devoid of any truly human touches. Even the caricature of a penis that stood erect, throbbing, between its legs was impossibly constructed. It was a smooth shaft jutting out from the groin, no protective hood or sperm-producing testicles attached. It was not a human organ—it was a weapon.

The golemlike creature gripped her shoulders and pulled her close, forcing her face against its damp, sour skin, pushing the ramrod member against her thin linen slacks. Talia felt the heat from the pulsing shaft burn through the cloth, and the horrific image of this monster trying to penetrate her, of herself being literally ripped apart, threatened her sanity. Bile rose in her throat.

She struggled to free a leg, and with every ounce of physical strength she had, she rammed her knee into its groin. There was no effect, not even an indication that her blow had been felt. She continued to fight to free herself, but it held her pinned tight. She screamed, but it gave no indication it heard. She sobbed, her tears bouncing onto its malodorous skin.

It howled as the first tear ran down its chest, scaring the skin like acid. It moved back, pushing Talia aside. She crumbled to the floor, near spent, how to escape was the only near rational thought she could muster. Her eyes were already dry and the few tears she'd shed—the only ones she'd formed in countless years—were not a defense she could count on.

Twisting herself around, avoiding the clutching fingers by a split second, Talia scurried to the nearest wall. There would be only moments until it closed in on her—barely enough time to call forth even the barest trace of her energy. Fear diminished her strength, she'd learned that long ago. Her first priority was to get a grip on herself.

She breathed deeply, and the room began to steady in her mind. Less than a minute had passed since she'd avoided Michael's grasp, or whoever or whatever that really was; and realizing this, she also suddenly knew that the creature was a body that took orders by remote control.

The delay in its response was her only advantage. Each of its movements lumbered and seemed to split the air, leaving only a vacuum in its cumbersome wake.

Feeling her way along the smooth wall, her back flush against the flat surface, Talia knew she was too shaken to use the defenses she'd taken years to hone. Her shoulder hit a metal canister and sent a sharp pain down her arm. Barely glancing at the fire extinguisher, Talia's eyes moved to the accompanying ax, securely bracketed next to the alarm box. As her hand reached for the smooth wooden handle of the weapon, a soft groan sounded from where it stood. Turning back to face the creature, her hand curled on the ax handle, Talia let out a sigh of relief. Kneeling on the floor was the comparatively slight form of Michael, naked but clearly himself.

Moving his arms to cover his body, Michael fought for breath. He raised his head, eyes clouded in pain, his look an accusation.

"Since you've the only game in town, Talia, what do we do next?" he gasped.

Turning to the tall window, hiding her face from him, Talia let out a deep sigh of relief. Long moments passed as she continued to gaze out at the tops of buildings. Michael thought she had brought the change on him. She wished she had, but it was small-enough compensation to know that he was not able to call forth that amazing being on his own.

"Try again," she barely whispered. Turning back to Michael, she watched him unbend and flex himself, loosening his clenched and spastic muscles. Talia reached out to help him rise. "This time," she amended, lifting his face to hers, "we'll both try."

Helping Michael to one of the two tall chairs by the window, Talia sat facing him. Reaching forward, she took his hands in hers.

"One of the reasons we partnered, dear one, lest we forget, was to join our energies. This function has somehow gotten lost with our displays of individual strength. We know we're strong, but we both know there are limits to our abilities. What we didn't know, and are just beginning to learn, is the strength of the people we are trying to maneuver. No, to destroy." Talia paused, letting Michael's hands fall limply to his lap. She slumped back against the carved chair and gripped her thighs, shifting from a graceful position to one of willful arrogance.

"What you don't know," she continued, "is that I wasn't all that successful with Ned's wife either. Holly isn't quite as vacuous as she seems. The images I sent, coupled with her own torments, should have crumpled her. Instead, she came back stronger than I would have imagined."

Michael, now alarmed, sat up, his animation and attention returning. "I didn't know about Holly. What did you try—and fail," he maliciously added, "to do?"

"I'm glad to see you're back, love." Talia smirked, sincerely relieved that Michael was himself. "Holly was a minimal effort. A basic guilt intensification coupled with some rather ugly visions. It seems, though, that Mrs. Harper has very little real guilt and either a rather large capacity for horror or an almost total disregard for anything not tangibly part of her life. I think that if I sent her a gift wrapped box from Bonwit's with her husband's head inside, she'd probably take it back for exchange. I think we can eventually wear her down, but she's not a priority. Her presence right now isn't hampering us in the least. I can't move any faster with Ned than I am already. Perhaps we can arrange for him to be widowed right after election.''

"Right now we have Bree to contend with," Michael cut in. "Your plans to be Mrs. Governor can wait.''

"I don't want to be Mrs. Governor, " Talia snapped, "but will be, if only to accomplish what we want. After all, neither of us has quite the credentials for election. We can only control the elected." Talia paused. "But you're right. Bree is the next step—an important one. She should be weakened from her near demise, though I'm still not exactly sure how she escaped, and I promise not to go for such high drama next time. Bree can interfere right now, and the pairing of Bree with Elise is more than coincidence, I fear.'' A worried look crossed Talia's face. "Though what it is, I can't say. If you and I are fated, what are they?''

Michael shrugged, unwilling to give the subject much thought. His only concern was Bree's absorption of what should be rightfully his. "You knew they were together. That was no secret. But once my sister senses what we're doing, I don't think she'll back off. She's always managed to get in the way, especially when I wanted something. She . . .'' Michael paused as childhood memories returned, of his sister snatching away a neighborhood girl just as he had the young woman ready to submit—his first sexual experience rudely interrupted by his sister's interference.

"Spare me your memories,'' Talia cut in before he could reminisce. "It's enough to know she's potentially a danger and must be dealt with. Just as Elise must be. Besides, our goal can't be reached unless they are both completely nullified. Unless we accomplish that, you and I will never hold enough power—even between us—to be successful.''

"What about Elise?'' Michael asked. "What have you done to reach her?''

Talia raised her hand to ward Michael away. "Nothing, yet. But she's all mine to deal with. Don't touch her. If I don't handle her myself, the transfer to wholeness will be damaged. Besides, she's nothing.'' Talia smiled. ''She knows nothing, has no idea what she holds, and has spent her entire life denying who she is. She will be our willing guest of honor here at our loft, a veritable piece of cake.''

Michael shook his head. ''The last woman credited with public reference to a piece of cake lost her head. I think we should take precautions.''

''No,'' Talia shot back. ''She's all mine. Although,'' she continued after a sobering pause, ''you can help by getting her here. Perhaps we can kill two birds with one stone—Bree and Elise, that is. Even though they've known each other for some time, they've only recently bonded. Right now they've not worked together as we have, and don't have the combined resources we have. Use Bree to get Elise here and we'll succeed.''

Elated by the thought, Michael rose and leaned forward to kiss Talia's forehead. ''That's good—very good. Of course it will work.'' Realizing for the first time he was naked, Michael sat back down. ''If you get me some clothes, I'll handle it.''

21

Hal Vaughan rushed into the overheated office, dressed in topcoat and gloves, bustling with energy. Frank Jordan sat primly behind his desk, the IN and OUT trays stacked to overflowing; he looked starched and deceptively priggish, as usual. Eyeing the mass of jumbled papers, Vaughan let out a spontaneous hoot.

"I never would have suspected you of harboring a cluttered desk." Hal Vaughan grinned. "I expected you to have, at most, one sheet of paper in the OUT box, with the rest of the desk being as orderly as the image you've successfully, up until now, projected."

"Stupid bureaucratic nonsense," Jordan mumbled, tapping his ballpoint pen on the typed pages in front of him. "Editing report after report to ensure the correct impression gets through to the powers-that-be. When"—he grinned—"all that should be necessary is for me to check a 'yes, no, maybe' box and for them to trust the people in charge."

"Like you, Frank?" Hal Vaughan asked, his own grin still firmly in place.

"Like me. I'm project administrator and handpicked for the position. My experience speaks for itself. My background is obviously not in question here, only my future. Despite the number of administrative successes I've had, I still have to spend Saturday's dotting every 'i' and crossing every 't.' "

"What would you rather be doing?"

"What I was originally trained for: fieldwork."

Hal Vaughan turned his back to hide his surprise.

241

He hung his coat on the brass clothes tree just inside the door, stuffing pigskin gloves into the pocket. "Somehow, Frank, I don't see you working outside the pristine environment of a lab facility. You don't look the type for hands-on work—not with your wardrobe. On the other hand, I should have guessed from the way you dispatched Blaiser."

Glancing at the inch of starched, immaculate shirt sleeve showing from beneath his pin-striped, dark-blue suit jacket, Frank Jordan grinned. "In the old days I was known to work in whatever attire was appropriate for the job, but in a way, you're right." Looking up at Hal Vaughan, he met the older man's bemused gaze with his own, steel-gray, ice-cold eyes. "Nowadays, I worry about my hangnails. Anyway," Jordan said as he clipped the finished report together, dropped it in the Out box, and leaned back, "you came in all fired up and ready to go. What's happening?"

"I've been thinking, Frank," Vaughan began, "it's time to give ourselves a push. We've been moving along all right, but even with the viral breakthrough, we haven't made enough progress. Not in the right direction."

"You're right. But we didn't have the team specifically directed until now."

"You and I know that, but we also know it isn't enough of a reason—not for those who approve the funds. We have to look at where our research can go from here."

Jordan nodded his agreement. "And that's not going to be very far. We haven't given them anything to work with except a few blood samples, some tissue cultures, and a few possible borderline subjects. You're right on target. After I conducted the VIP tour, it suddenly hit home: if we want to ensure our funding, it's time to do more."

"What are the powers-that-be, those with the almighty buck, looking for?" Hal Vaughan asked.

"Mutations. But true mutations are rare. The one in a million that does occur is usually so insignificant it's not worth the time or effort, much less the funds, to decipher. For example, a one-generation, nontransmittable tendency to hard fingernails. Or soft ones.''

"One in a million is pretty good odds," Vaughan commented. "We should easily be able to come up with enough mutations to keep the funding flowing."

Frank Jordan's excitement was tangible. "It's not what they want; it's not what they originally funded us for. You know what we've latched on to—and they want to see results!"

"The 'powerhouse' of the cell, the mitochondria, is responsible for all energy-conducting activities," Hal Vaughan cautioned. "Our prime subject not only exhibits an incredibly high Mt count, but has an additional genetic code, this Lilith Factor our researchers have named. I believe, strongly, it did not mutate within the individual—that it's inherited—and have more than just intuition on which to base that assumption. But you're right, we have to know more, even if it finally means exposing the woman. First, though, I would have to remove her from her present, um, circumstances. And that's not as simple as it sounds."

"Why this sudden change of heart, Hal?" Frank Jordan looked curiously at the older doctor, searching his lined face for a clue. "You've been the primary force in preventing us from reaching the subject."

"I know, but I'm afraid if we don't move now, we might lose the momentum, the funding, and possibly the subject. Her gilded cage is beginning to show signs of tarnish." Hal Vaughan's weariness was growing obvious by the minute. "But before we get to her, I told you I learned of a twin. Now I've found her and, believe it or not, obtained a skin scraping—unfortunately under less than clinical circumstances. The tissue sample, which should be considered contaminated and therefore not valid, still shows a marked similarity to our prime subject. The same factor is there, which is why I'm convinced the genetic balance is inherited. It could even be mutable. But first we need a clinical sample from the twin. Frank, your wish to get back into fieldwork might be attainable. Do you think you can get this woman?''

"Get her to what? Visit the lab and participate in the study? Why didn't you just ask her when you met her?''

"Frank, you've been part of the administration too long. There's a time for stealth—and this is the time. You know I've been keeping my name and face out of sight. And the connection here, between this other twin and everything else, is too convoluted to begin to explain. Take my word for it. We have to, what's the word, snatch her.''

"Snatch is the word, but before I risk facing a field maneuver, I have to know why you're not just inviting her to participate. If anything goes wrong, it's my neck.''

Hal Vaughan looked long and hard at the project administrator. His lips were drawn in tight lines and his eyes blinked rapidly as he sorted out how much he had to tell Jordan before he would get his cooperation.

"Okay, Frank, you have a need to know. The woman, the twin, is connected with the Harper campaign, and you heard his negative noises about genetic research. On top of it, Harper's wife is convinced that this woman is harassing her through some sort of psychic projection. Knowing what we know, where our research is directed, do you think you're actually going to get that person into our facility with an invitation?''

"No. But a snatch is heavy-duty shit. How do we explain her disappearance?''

"Use your imagination! Sedate her—a shot, chloroform, whatever it takes. We'll get her into a facility—not here, somewhere closer—and then let her loose. Muggings happen every day. But you've got to catch her, find her, off guard.''

"I could find Adam and Eve's grandmother,'' said the wiry administrator. "What's her name?''

"T. D. Harrah. And, of course, she's with the Ned Harper gubernatorial campaign.''

"What do you think this has to do with Harper?''

"Nothing. Life is complicated enough without searching for questions where there are no answers. It's just a coincidence."

"I wonder," Jordan mused.

"Frank, you're looking for acorns in a peanut patch."

"No," Jordan continued, "I've learned that there are very few real coincidences about. The only saving grace is that the answer is probably not vital at the moment. So we, ah, invite Ms. Harrah to visit us?"

"Yes. And the sooner the better."

What about the other one? Her twin," Frank Jordan quietly asked. "We'll need her as well."

"No!" Hal Vaughan shot up in the chair, his voice overly firm. "We're not ready for her yet. I've got to, well, arrange things so she won't be missed too much. Besides, we've been working on her MtDNA and the logical step is to see if there really is the complete match I've initially substantiated. Ms. Harrah will do very well for now."

"Someday we'll have to have both of them."

"Yes," Hal Vaughan agreed readily. "Someday we will."

Frank Jordan reached for a clean sheet of lined paper and the telephone. Punching out the area code and directory-assistance number, he asked one simple question. "Information, I need the number of Ned Harper's campaign headquarters."

Jordan looked up at Hal Vaughan, the pupils of his icy eyes dilating as if from drug-induced excitement. "We'll start with the basics, then a credit check to find out where she lives. From there I can trace what she does in her spare time, and where she goes is where I'll go."

"I could use a breath of fresh air."

A day spent in his wife's clutches invariably left Ned physically and emotionally drained. It had taken his most skillful political maneuvering to dissuade her from a visit to their Island home for the entire weekend. Despite Holly's bright and cheerful demeanor, and her promise of fresh air, Ned knew that there was a stronger reason for her desire to get away. The mirror in their bedroom had been removed, ostensibly for reglazing.

He managed, instead, to convince Holly that a day at the museums, perhaps a brief gallery tour, would suffice to renew his physical and intellectual vigor, and by doing so, he skillfully played on her conceit in being seen at all the right exhibits, with all the right people. Holly made a quick series of phone calls before they set out on their Saturday day trip, ensuring that they received a proper audience at each of their stops. Politically, Ned admitted, her planning had been impeccable; seeing the right people ensured support and important votes. Still, Ned would have preferred a day at the Bronx Zoo.

But, he told himself, with the primary election only six months away, it was vital that he be near his campaign headquarters, in touch with his staff, and available for any policy statements. Ned reached for the phone. *Maybe T.D. will be willing to plan some strategy tonight.* After the sophomoric ideas this phrase evoked subsided, concern set in. He'd never asked her to work on a weekend before, but then there had never been a before, before. He would bring a bottle of good Chardonnay—or maybe the Sauvignon Blanc that Holly liked so much—to the office to sip while they reviewed the thrust of the next few weeks' speeches, stances, and activities.

This, Ned knew, was the real reason he was loath to leave the small island of Manhattan. T.D. was on it.

The sweet cinnamon smell of her perfume returned to haunt him. *How could he have overlooked such perfection, there, right at the tip of his fingers, within his reach, for so long.* Smiling to himself, Ned thought about the past five years they had worked together, side by side. They weren't all wasted, he knew. The years had given him the background to really know her, to know that she was sweet and pure, talented and able.

During the whole of that time she had been at his side almost every day, no matter how early the day started or how late it ran. Boyfriends, of which he couldn't really recall any, had never interfered with her work. Searching further for any occasion he might have seen her with another man, he dimly remembered a young aide in his office, oh, about three years ago. There had been some hand-holding and evenings when the two of them left together, waving good-bye to him.

What had happened? The boy—Charlie something, Parker—no—Charlie Palmer—had disappeared. Completely. He'd not only not shown up at the campaign headquarters but had left his apartment untouched and was never heard from again. His family had finally come to collect his belongings and vacate the apartment. A nice young man, Ned remembered, who probably just met with an unfortunate accident. Fortunately before anything serious, like romance, developed.

The ringing phone cradled to his ear, Ned thought of stroking T.D.'s smooth skin, of how she would feel as she melted in his arms. Had it only been this week that he had first tasted her mouth, experienced the quick touch of her probing tongue? He felt he knew her every curve, the soft hidden folds her body took as it surrounded his, yet he also knew he just wanted to know. A soft click on the fourth ring started the recorded message. Damn it, she was out. Probably just running errands; it was late Saturday afternoon and she could be at the grocer's or doing laundry. A good time actually, Ned rationalized as the announcement wound to a close. I'll leave a message and go to the office and wait for her to call me there, or better yet, to meet me there.

The midtown streets were indeed bustling with shoppers and strollers as Ned walked to the Flatiron Building. Holly was easily convinced that his evening best be devoted to catching up on paperwork at the office; she was weary from the day's touring and welcomed a nap and the prospect of reviewing her videotape library. There were, Ned realized, a number of letters that could be drafted for T.D.'s fine hand to finish—or was it usually the other way around? No matter, he was sure he could find papers to shuffle and maybe even read.

Turning the last corner, Ned sighted a familiar jacket topping snug slacks, cladding an achingly familiar figure, crossing from Madison Park to the Flatiron. Elated, Ned broke into a jog; she had gotten his message and come right away. His key ready, Ned entered the lobby just as the elevator door slid closed. Punching the call button, he shifted from one foot to the other, eyes glued to the floor indicator. It stopped on his floor, their floor. It had been her! A wide smile broke out on Ned's face; no force on earth could have, at that instant, removed his ear-to-ear grin. The one self-service elevator operating on weekend schedule returned to the lobby and he boarded before the door was fully open.

Reaching his floor, Ned bounded down the corridor to his office door. A strip of light glimmered from beneath the door. The first thing he would do would be turn out the foyer light. No need to be interrupted by well-wishers or overzealous volunteer workers, not this evening.

The deserted office was silent; only the sounds seeping in from the street below broke the eerie stillness a workplace can evoke on a weekend evening. He stood still, listening for her sounds, and a warmth rose in his groin. No, he cautioned himself, one time in bed doesn't mean she's a possession. She was not a woman to be rushed. Their single evening together was more than a beautiful memory, the silky touch of her warm thighs wrapped around him more than an erotic fantasy. Yet, she might be harboring regrets; she might have even come today, at his bidding, to tell him that she'd made a mistake and couldn't see him anymore. She might even leave his campaign.

A gut-wrenching fear gripped Ned, dispelling the rising passion. He would, he cautioned himself, handle today as gently as possible. As a schoolboy courting for the first time. If only he'd thought to bring flowers or chocolates, or some other gift—pearls. No, an emerald. T.D. evoked the brilliant cold light of emeralds; she emitted the presence of a gem—finely cut, priceless, and eternal.

Faint creaks in the rear office signaled her presence and placed T.D. in his office. Ned breathed a sigh of relief; she was there, waiting for him. His earlier passing thought about flowers returned and took hold of his imagination. Of course, there was a flower stand right across the street. He'd noticed giant peonies, their explosion of pink softness, layer upon layer of silken, tissue-thin petals. They would be a perfect symbol of his endearing feelings.

His keys still in his hand, Ned turned back to complete his brief errand.

The stillness of the room was perfect; no one would interrupt. Ned's actual candidacy wouldn't be official for weeks, the fall primary not even news yet. Everything else was in place; all Ned's scheduled public appearances were tightly confirmed, press strategy ready down to the last handshake. All that remained was the fulfillment of the schedule.

Her schedule.

And she had to work it here. This was the closest she could get to Holly.

Despite the sarcastic excuses she'd given to Michael, she urgently needed to reach Holly and would try anything. Not to be dismissed lightly, that lady. A surprising resilience wrapped around a core of tensile steel. Years of watching Holly's fashion parade and noting her constantly filled dance card had not prepared her for the take-charge, about-face that Holly pulled. Talia had expected, at the least, a nervous and pale Mrs. Harper at the press conference, a woman who had been thoroughly shaken and bearing all signs of a sleepless night; but the Holly who had arrived, with flawlessly applied cosmetics, not a wisp of hair out of place, and as stylishly dressed as always, was as jarring to T.D. as she expected she had been to Holly the night before.

Perhaps the horrors visited had not been as well-planned as they could have been; the twisted embryo could slowly have dissolved into putrid flesh accompanied by nauseating odors, and the aging of Holly's own flesh should have been more dramatic. Perhaps maggots streaming from her withering eye sockets and rolling off a rapidly decaying tongue. It just hadn't been enough to really frighten the woman.

And of course, the vision had not been sent from where Holly really left her presence; a single possession—that of a barely used husband—was not enough. That, more than anything, was likely to be the cause of the failure. Here and now, that would be rectified.

Sweeping the clutter from a desk often used by Mrs. Harper to schedule her varied social appointments, Talia shook out a saffron-colored, velvet altar cloth and carefully spread the finely embroidered material flat. A nuisance, to be sure, but Michael forced her to promise to carefully follow at least the appearances of his belief. It was a simple concession to make for his support, and she now knew he was skilled enough to know if she reneged on the promise. Her own way was much simpler—just sit quietly and concentrate—but after the monstrous change he'd exhibited, she was more than willing to try his techniques.

Spreading her fingertips, lightly brushing Michael's altar cloth, Talia closed her eyes and softly began to hum—a tuneless sound, a wordless mantra. The dissonant tone came from the back of her throat and she let herself drift, using the sound to travel on, slowing her breathing to encourage the trance. Through half-closed eyes Talia saw the room around her fade, as if a heavy fog seeped through the floorboards, until she was alone in the mist.

The desk remained—it was her touchstone—and the presence of Holly grew stronger as she called out to the other woman. All extraneous sounds ceased, all irrelevant sights left—only the touch of velvet and soft gray mist, only her own monotone song.

Closing the door gently behind him, Ned stood with the single wrapped flower, a very costly token, and briefly wondered what had made roses go out of fashion. Again confident that the front door was secure, the foyer light out, he made his way to the back, casually holding the peony to place before T.D.—no, she said I should call her Talia. Hopefully he could slip in unnoticed, while her beautiful nose was buried in paperwork, and place the flower on the speech or letter she was, most likely, carefully reworking to his best advantage.

Ned heard the monotonous hum as he reached his closed office door. Oh, well, he thought, so she can't carry a tune—that flaw just proves she's all that much more perfect. Surprised at the dimness of the room, street light straining to reach through dusty windows, Ned stood quietly while his vision adjusted. There, standing tautly on legs planted firmly apart, her head thrown back and arms held stiffly out to either side, stood Talia.

What is she doing? Why are the lights out? Why is she making that noise?

Stepping awkwardly forward, Ned loudly cleared his throat.

"Talia, I'm glad you got my message . . ." he began, waiting for a response. Realizing he hadn't penetrated her reverie, Ned stepped even closer.

"Talia, what are you doing," he pleaded.

She had not moved from her rigid position, and looking at her, Ned saw a statue delicately cut from fine marble. Nothing about her looked alive; the atonal sound could have been coming from anywhere in the

room, and seemed as if it were. The room itself was
unreal: shifting shadows where no light registered, an
impossible silence except for that damned hum. He
moved forward again, one slow step at a time, and the
taste of fear was sour in his mouth. This wasn't Talia,
it couldn't be. Reaching out to assure himself that this
was flesh and blood, his trembling hand stopped before he could touch her.

Damn, touch her, she's real, he commanded himself, and with a grim determination Ned grabbed the
cold, stiff arm.

Her eyes shot open. Cut off mid-note, the guttural
hum stopped abruptly. She turned her head slowly to
him, as a life-size mechanical doll might. There was
no trace of any emotion present in her unblinking eyes.
How could I have thought of her eyes as emeralds?
Ned wondered as he stepped back, fear overriding awe;
they're more the surreal polymer of neon—they're not
part of nature.

Entranced, Talia saw Ned from a distance; her
struggling consciousness realized the danger in his
presence, her ethereal self knew any danger could be
dealt with effectively. Especially if it had to do with
Ned. Irritated at the disturbance but amused at the
vantage point she now held, Talia saw not only the
shell of Ned Harper, soon-to-be gubernatorial candidate par excellence, but also the man within, all two
dimensions of him.

Joy—all engulfing, all fulfilling—replaced her irritation; for the first time she knew that this was the
right man. And the right time. Primed to reach out,
she would recast through him to reach his wife. He
would direct the poison to drain his wife of her will,
her beauty. And maybe, Talia hoped, he would draw
back some of his Holly's essence to solidify himself.
He could certainly use some fortification.

Turning to Ned, Talia allowed the warmth he craved
to return to her eyes. Reaching for the flower, now
bent in half, she gently removed it from his clenched
fist and moved closer to him.

"Is that for me? Thank you."

Dazed, Ned shyly held up the peony, not noticing the stem he'd crushed in his fear, not seeing the altar cloth she folded with her free hand, not caring that Talia had been standing alone in a darkened room, not remembering the fear he'd felt—only how her warm flesh now felt pressed to his.

"It's always for you, Talia," he said.

"I know, Ned, I know."

Slipping into his arms, she let her lips meet his. Her mind was a blur of activity. She was worried about her promise to Michael—to use his methods. Alone, she had not succeeded with Holly, but it would be more effective with Ned carrying the psychic hold, magnifying it through his devotion to her and his inability to deal with loving two women at once; right now Holly was not the favorite in this race and that would work strongly in her own favor. Her way, then.

Reaching out, Talia let herself flow into Ned, reaching the depth of his id and, finding nothing suspicious—no hidden dreams, no secret ambitions, no unknown aspirations—coiled her own will about his, gently, firmly, securely. Closing in, tightening, snuffing out the small flame that dimly burned with his feeble energy, she lighted her own in its place; a stronger, steadier glow, brightening even as she willed it into life. His mere physical presence would be enough to work with; now her cause would burn within him.

Ned pushed her away and his eyes went wildly wide and unfocused. A surge of energy, the likes of which was completely unknown to him, never before experienced on any level, filled him. It seemed to start at the base of his skull, burning white-hot, then burst forth to course through his body in almost unbearable waves of pain and ecstasy. A band of ice ringed his forehead. His breath was taken away from him, his lungs compressed and held deflated, no amount of effort could bring the air back into his body. A sharp pain crushed his chest, radiating down his left arm as his heart fought a losing battle to maintain control.

Without regaining a single breath, his eyes still wide with the shock and terrifying beauty of the moment, Ned Harper slumped forward in Talia's arms.

His body, heavier for the absence of life, pushed against her and crushed her against the desk. Talia, weakened from the surge of power she'd loosened into him, buckled under and slid to the floor, pinned under the deadweight. Lying there, under her former lover cum source of all plans and expectations, Talia felt a single, frustrated tear trickle from the corner of her eye, along the ridge of her finely chiseled cheekbone, past her ear, and heard—as a sound louder than the crashing of a magnificent thunderclap—the remaining tear fall to the floor.

Pushing his weight off her, she rolled to her side. A cramp doubled her and she lay in a fetal position. Silent sobs racked her body; her grief was deeper than she could have imagined. It was of dreams crushed, plans turned to dust. There was nowhere to turn. Nowhere. Except to Michael. And Elise.

Michael . . . his plans would have to be hers, but she would do it oh-so-much better.

Elise . . . who would still be destroyed, now for the sheer joy of the moment.

Talia's cramps subsided as the new dream, building the fallen sand castle back into a even greater ivory tower, began to grow.

22

"WHAT SHOW ARE YOU TWO SEEING TONIGHT?" Hal Vaughan asked as he entered the brownstone's cozy kitchen. "It's six o'clock and you should be dressed and on your way out—that is, if you want to grab a bite to eat first. Or are you planning an after-theater supper?"

"Oh, hello, Dad. How did you get in?" Jeff looked up from the patient records he was reviewing, his distraction at his father's appearance genuine but not, in fact, attributable to the case histories in front of him.

"The door was open, and it's good to see you too," the senior Dr. Vaughan answered, and met his son's lackluster gaze with a searching one of his own. His flesh-and-blood's apparent physical well-being and, more important, his son's depression filled the older doctor with relief; further manipulation, twisting the knife in a still raw wound, would be easier than anticipated.

"What did you say about a show?" Jeff asked as he tapped the patient cards into a neat stack. His father's unexpected arrival was not to his liking, but then again, not much had pleased him of late.

"I just wondered if you and Elise were going out tonight. It's Saturday night, remember. No office hours tomorrow—you can sleep late. I know it's been years since you kids had anything close to a normal schedule to live by so I thought I'd drop by and remind you."

Jeff pushed the cards to the far corner of the table; the distance he kept the records away from himself, neat and tidy, was a small step in controlling the distance he could keep the world at bay. An orderly world, a directed life, suddenly gone awry.

"Remind us of what?" Jeff asked, turning to his father with a small smile, carefully arranged—lift the left side of your mouth, he thought—on his otherwise composed features, and hope the gut-wrenching pain . . . No, there's no pain, I'm just empty, it's all hollow, it doesn't show, it doesn't matter, he'll never know how I really feel, just show him a nice face.

"That it's Saturday night."

"Oh. Yes."

Looking at his son, Hal Vaughan felt a surge of caring, the first twinge of honest emotion he knew he'd had in a long time—years even. Since Louise died eight years ago. Since he tried to cover the loss, the emptiness, with work—work that would be a monument to the woman he loved, dearly loved, completely, passionately, without reservation. His son's mother. He owed it to Louise to protect her legacy and her son, but he also owed Louise the research he had wholeheartedly embraced in her name: finding the genetic code that drained her of life, took her energy, left her a shell of the vibrant woman he'd married. And Elise was the solution, the single bearer of that factor, the only person that had passed his way with the same mutated cell—a simple divergence from the norm that, in Elise's case, seemed to be growing and strengthening. Not fading, not killing, like Louise's.

When he first tested Elise, only one of scores of students looking to earn extra money by participating in lab experiments, he couldn't believe his luck. Louise barely cold in her grave, and before he'd even fully outfitted a laboratory, the same genetic code appeared before him. Elise had been the first, then the only one, out of dozens, then hundreds, now tens of thousands. She had been the only one.

Encouraging Jeff to pursue the girl had been easy; having him appear at the laboratory when Elise was scheduled posed no problem. Jeff was malleable and the young woman bright and attractive. That they were both planning medical careers was just another bond between them and that they fell in love and married additional insurance that Elise would be there, available, when other subjects were found to be compared.

But Elise remained the only one whose mitochondria DNA showed that unique factor. To find she had a twin was a godsend for the project—and for Jeff; he could keep Elise awhile longer. But, one thing was for sure, it was time to start pushing them apart. There was another problem, one he had not taken into consideration. Until all the causes and effects were known, Elise could not be the mother of his grandchildren; every precaution to prevent a pregnancy must be taken. The only positive method of birth control was abstinence; separate the husband and wife, first emotionally and then physically.

"Where's Elise?" Hal Vaughan asked, reminded to ask for her and noting her absence from the room. "Resting after a long day?"

Jeff's look darkened, his face became even more sullen. "She's out," he answered, not moving his eyes from his father's.

"Will she be back soon?"

"I've no idea when she'll be back, and before you ask, I don't know where she is."

"This isn't like her," Hal Vaughan commented, more curious than concerned, "or like you, not to know where she's gone."

"Listen, Dad, I'd appreciate it if you'd keep your comments to yourself." Jeff turned his head away but the bitterness in his words hung in the air between them. "Elise is out and it's all right with me—in fact, it's just fine with me. So what gives you the right to come in here, asking where she is, and berating me for not knowing? Who the hell put you in charge of investigation?"

Taken aback, Hal Vaughan physically moved away from his son. Jeff was seated but twitching nervously, a sign of his readiness to bolt from the table and even physically lash out at his father.

"Jeff"—Hal Vaughan took the gentlest tone he could muster, calm and soothing—"talk to me."

Jeff expelled a chest full of air. His head dropped forward to cradle in his crossed arms; his shoulders shook with silent sobs. Long minutes went by without a sound, then Jeff lifted his head, red-rimmed eyes searching his father's face.

"Dad, I don't know what's happening to us. Everything was perfect until last week. Now Elise doesn't talk to me—she doesn't share. She gets up in the morning and comes downstairs to practice but there's no 'us' anymore. We were closer when we worked apart." Jeff paused, trying to calm himself. "Maybe we just thought we were close because we were apart. This seems to be the first time we're really together—and we're not."

"Sometimes new things take time to get used to," Hal Vaughan consoled while his own thoughts raced. The timing was perfect to separate them, yet this was his own son who was suffering. It would be so easy to say the few words that Jeff needed to hear, to encourage his son during this trying time, and to even explain what he himself knew about Elise. In a moment of crystal-cold clarity, Hal Vaughan decided.

"Jeff, I had my doubts about this marriage from the start. Elise is a nice girl, but what do you really know about her? She is, after all, an orphan, and while her aunt seems nice enough, the sketchy background she's given us, you, is suspect, to say the least. I think that some deep-seated neurosis has finally become evident, as witnessed by her current erratic behavior."

"Dad, I love her," Jeff pleaded, his resolve building as he faced the accusation of his wife's emotional imbalance. "Elise isn't neurotic. There's something else going on, something I don't understand, and I won't listen to your outrageous, offhanded, and completely unprofessional diagnosis."

Jeff paused, digesting his own words, sorting his feelings. When he spoke again, his voice was firm, steady, sure. "You know Elise as well as I do, you've always been the first to support her. What's gotten into you? Hell, I half-expected you to tear into me for behaving like a wimp, but I'm glad you didn't. It forced me to realize I *am* behaving like one. I don't know what's the matter but I'm going to find out and help her—if she needs my help.''

Hal Vaughan leaned heavily against a sturdy wooden chair for support; his face was ashen, his shoulders slumped, but his eyes were still clear. ''There's a lot you don't know about your wife, Jeff, and I think it's time I told you.''

''If you know anything that can help me help her, then by all means tell me,'' Jeff countered, gesturing his father to sit. ''I'll put on the coffee.''

Hal began to explain how he had found Elise, how and why he had brought them together, and finally, told Jeff about Spiral.

The pot of coffee gone, Jeff sat staring, disbelief clearly written on his face, at his father. ''I can't believe you've kept this from me all these years. What the hell did you think you were doing, keeping Elise on a short leash like a pet animal? I'm at a complete loss to understand . . . No, I take that back; maybe I can understand. But I'll never accept what you've done.''

''What I've done!'' Hal Vaughan exploded. ''Your little wife is the one who's done it. She's the mutant. I didn't make her that way. You're just damned lucky I'm around to tell you about her.''

''Dad, your mistake was not telling me years ago. To be honest, maybe I wouldn't have fallen in love with her. I don't think I would have had the courage to pursue a woman I knew wasn't completely normal, no matter how obscure her abnormality was. And it *is* obscure. You've no idea what this genetic trait causes or effects. Or if it's natural or a mutation. You said Mother had a related genetic factor, and died. If that factor was the cause of Mother's death and Elise shows the same factor, then maybe Mother was—maybe I am—the mutant. Not Elise.''

"Jeff, I just want to save you the loss I went through."

"If you did, you went about it in the worst possible way. But it doesn't matter. I love Elise and you've given me another reason to stick by her. Now I know she needs me. Or at least could need me."

On cue, the front door scraped open, admitting Elise.

She looked at the father and son, their weariness covering them like a shroud, and her own exhaustion was replaced by a surge of maternal instincts; she was ready to tuck them both into soft, clean beds.

"I'm sorry I'm late," she said, crossing the hallway to stand beside her husband, kissing the back of his neck. "I was with Bree. She's much better now."

"Honey, you promised to let me know where you went," Jeff cautioned, tenderness replacing the anger he would have lashed out with earlier.

"I left you a note"—Elise gestured to the stove—"right where you'd see it."

They both turned to the bare stove. Looking at his wife, Jeff raised a quizzical eyebrow. "Yes?"

Pointing to a corner of paper peeking out of the space between the stove and the wall, Elise grimaced. "It slipped."

Grabbing his wife, Jeff spun her onto his lap. "Mrs. Vaughan, I am installing a large blackboard first thing in the morning."

"Tomorrow's Sunday." Elise laughed, her words lost in the curve of his neck.

"And I think I'd better be going." Hal Vaughan stood. He seemed years older than he had been when he arrived.

"Dad, why don't you stay here?" Elise asked, concerned about his haggard appearance. "The guest room isn't ready yet, but we've a comfortable convertible couch in Jeff's office. Private bath and all."

Jeff quickly stood, almost dumping Elise to the floor. "No, honey, Dad said he had an early-morning round of golf he couldn't miss and has to get back to the Island tonight. Right, Dad?''

Nodding in mute agreement, Hal Vaughan turned to leave. Stopping at the front door, he looked back at the couple, who, in a close embrace, considered him already gone.

Putting down the replica antique French boudoir phone, Holly Harper continued to stare at the metal-and-plastic object; it could have had a life of its own. A spark of her own awareness was present, no more; she could think of nothing, do nothing. It was over. Ned, found dead of a heart attack in his office. Just moments ago. Each short, swift thought a separate concept. Ned, lying there, found only by chance when his campaign manager stopped in to retrieve some work for an at-home Sunday.

No, there was no pain, the doctor said. No, she wouldn't have to come to the hospital. No, she shouldn't be alone. Yes, they'd call her mother for her. Was there anyone else? No, I don't need a doctor. Yes, there are sedatives in the house. No. I won't take anything until my mother gets here. No. No. No. Noooooooo. Numb.

Sitting there. Hand still resting on the phone. In case it rang. Just in case. If I lie down, I'll never pick it up again. It won't ring. Who would call? The restaurant to check on why we missed our reservation? Hardly.

Seconds later—or was it hours?—the doorbell rang. Holly went to the door. She knew she wasn't really moving, but somehow each step brought the door frame closer, the doorknob nearer, the latches to within reach. The groomed woman standing there wore an ankle-length fur and held a crumbled linen handkerchief, its monogram artfully peeking from her petit, gloved hand. A leather overnight bag, with matching monogram, was next to her left shoe, which, while not personally monogrammed, carried crossed the Gs designer initials.

Mother, perfectly turned out for a dramatic entrance, even on the spur of the moment, no matter what the occasion, correct for any and all occasions. Mother, if I ever wondered where I learned it all from, you've just put that question forever to rest. Yet, seeing the pain—or was it pity?—reflected in her mother's eyes, Holly shed her first tear and rushed into her arms. The dam of water broke and flowed from her eyes, down her cheeks, onto Mother's furred shoulders.

"Wait just a moment, dear, let me dismiss Harold." Eunice Varley turned away to wave off the chauffeur waiting curbside in the silver-gray sedan. "Now, dear . . . Oh, Holly, I'm so sorry. A widow, at your age. It's so awful. And before the election, no less. Not even a governor's widow. Here, help me with my coat and let's get my bag inside. Can I get you anything? I've my tranquilizers right here in my purse. Everything will be all right."

Holly's tears stopped halfway down her cheek, rapidly evaporating in the arid, factual atmosphere that blew in with her mother.

"Just like your father," Eunice Varley continued, barely pausing for breath as she watched her coat carefully hung on a padded hanger. "Cut down in his prime, and you barely settled in your marriage. Be thankful you have no children. It's always worse for them. We women, wives, cope."

Eunice turned to Holly, gently tugging off the close-fitting leather gloves, carefully placing them on a side table near her matching purse. Her blue eyes matched the cornflower color of Holly's own, and glinted with the sparkle of diamonds . . . or ice.

"Have you made arrangements, dear?" Eunice asked, turning her back to her daughter, walking toward the concealed liquor cabinet. "Let me get you a brandy—if you haven't had one yet, that is. We must be careful now. It's so easy to slip into bad habits, you know. Have you had one? A brandy?"

"No, Mother, I didn't have, do, anything before you got here. I was, I guess, stunned."

Nodding her approval, Eunice opened the cabinet and generously filled a large brandy snifter, dutifully turning it over to be carefully sipped. "You can have a sedative before you're ready for sleep. I'll make up the guest room for myself, or would you rather use it tonight?"

"No, I'll sleep in my own bed," Holly said after a brief pause to sip at the brandy. "The memories there aren't all that strong. Arrangements? It's rather late now, isn't it? I'll call in the morning."

"Don't be silly. It's only ten P.M. and tomorrow's Sunday. I'll just make one call and everything, absolutely everything, will be taken care of." Eunice picked up the antique-style phone and began to dial, checking the number against a small white card she'd plucked from her purse. As she turned back to Holly, a shadow crossed her features. "I am sorry, darling. Really. I know how much he meant to you. We'll talk."

How much he meant to me? How much he meant . . . how much he meant to me . . . The words rang through Holly's head as she half-listened to her mother's clipped conversation, precisely directing the listener as to the facilities to be used, the flowers to obtain, the directions to be given callers, promising a list of the approved people to be admitted to the services, which cemetery plot should be opened, the voice droning on and on and on as Holly demurely—see, Mother, I'm always the lady, even in my grief I can play the part oh so well—sipped the potent brandy from the large balloon glass.

How much he meant to me . . . He *was* me. He was the part of me that I carefully picked, nurtured, planned, put in the public's eye, wanted elected. He was everything I couldn't be, that I needed a husband to be. Twenty years. Twenty years wasted. There's not enough time to do it all again. Holly's hands shook as she lifted the brandy glass to her lips, draining the remaining half in one gulp. Tears again stung her eyes. Oh, God, Mother's so right. I'm too young to be a widow. To spend the rest of my life chairing committees, sitting on boards, fulfilling myself with charity work. What a joke.

Eunice Varley, finished with her complex series of instructions, notes jotted in an appointment calendar now opened before her, watched her daughter's silent tears, noticed the drained brandy glass. "One more brandy before bed, dear?"

Silently but gratefully nodding her agreement, the lump in her throat effectively prohibiting any attempt at speech, Holly held the snifter out for a most welcome refill.

"What are you going to do now?" Eunice asked, extracting her price—conversation—for the second and probably last, Holly realized, drink.

"Go on. Stay here. I like this house now. In fact, the thought of living in the city, alone, is more tolerable than being out on our old estate, rambling about twenty-odd rooms."

"That's a small-enough decision for the time being." Eunice nodded her approval. "You've quite a bit more to decide and I had an idea during the ride over I'd like to present. I'm quite sure you'll think it extravagant right now, so please don't comment, just sleep on it."

Holly looked at her carefully coiffed mother, artfully applied cosmetics giving her the eternal look of a fiftyish matron. Bewildered, Holly nodded her agreement to listen. Here we go with the trip-to-Europe suggestion or perhaps a long cruise. What do newly bereaved widows do these days, anyway?

"I think, my daughter, your time has come. You should take over Ned's campaign."

Holly's dry eyes shot wide open; her constricted throat caught fire with the sip of brandy and she issued a sharp cough to expel the burning fumes.

"Run for office? Me? Mother, it just isn't done."

"Look around you. Ned's last opponent was a woman, on her own. She was ready, able, and qualified for the senate. And who was she? A nobody. Some rabble-rousing, left-wing bohemian. You, on the other hand, have breeding, education, are quite experienced in politics—you haven't fooled any of us for one minute. We all know you've been much more than the perfect politician's wife—and I'm quite sure we could garner up more than a modicum of support. That is, if you should decide to take over Ned's campaign.''

Holly fell back, laughing, on the deeply cushioned couch. ''I hardly think I can step into the gubernatorial race, just like that''—Holly snapped her fingers for effect—''but, Mother, you have a gem of an idea there. I don't have to sleep on it. You're brilliant. I think, though, the senate—the U.S. Senate, of course—would be a far more practical starting point. And more effective in the long run.'' Sipping the brandy, Holly grimaced at its harsh taste and pushed the snifter aside. She looked at her mother with admiration. ''How ever did you get so inspired?''

Smiling smugly, Eunice put her own, almost untouched brandy down. ''It's simple, dear. In my mother's day, one joined the ladies' auxiliary and garden clubs. In my day, one was allowed to go as far as the actually, dare I say it, coed administered charities. I was even considered for a planning board or two. You, my dear, are part of the new regime and I want everything for you that you want for yourself. Personally, I'd always thought you should have gone after it on your own instead of pushing your husband into the spotlight.

''Now let's wash your face, take a sleeping pill, and rest. We'll have a long talk in the morning.''

Crossing the room to kiss her mother's cheek, Holly moved to the elegant stairway, stopped, and returned to embrace the older woman. ''Tomorrow, then. Thank you.''

''Don't thank me, darling.'' Eunice rose to link arms with her daughter. ''Now I can come to visit and play your old role. I was getting so bored with the clubs and charities.''

23

"**Y**OU DID WHAT!" MICHAEL ROARED INTO TALIA'S face.

"I killed Ned Harper." Talia spoke softly, her voice dull. Her initial panic had subsided into a grim acceptance of the circumstance.

Leaving the campaign offices after sliding the leaden weight of the dead candidate off her, Talia rushed through the streets in a panic, brushing people aside, blindly crossing thoroughfares. She had barely avoided being hit by a delivery van but, in turn, made up for the affront against her own safety by broadsiding a stroller and knocking a frightened toddler to the sidewalk. When she arrived at her building, a scant half-dozen blocks away, she locked herself securely in. Hours later, her panic subsided, Talia set out for the downtown loft ready, almost, to tell Michael what happened.

"I knew something like this would happen," Michael raved, shaking Talia by the shoulders as he spat each venomous word directly into her face. "The biggest mistake I ever made was teaming up with you."

Talia's vented frustration let loose. She grabbed Michael's hands and tore them from her shoulders; holding his wrists, she shoved him away from her, back one step and then another. Barely disguising her fury, Talia thought of a myriad of accusations to throw back at him: his own inability to deal with his sister; the ragamuffin band of followers he called his own; this so-called power he made claims to. The last thought froze her and she closed her mouth, not one bitter complaint voiced.

Turning, she stalked away. Her skin still crawled with the desire to lash out and slap his face, to dig her nails into his soft skin and rake bloody furrows down his cheeks. Only the memory of the strong presence that had dominated him the night before stopped her from any overt action.

Her fluctuating emotions—fear balanced against the potent need to dominate—were impossible to subjugate.

"Ned was important, but I'll still find a way to the governor's office." A small flicker of delight lit Talia's face. "After all, I'm now an experienced and valuable communications director, a welcome addition to any campaign. Next time I'll avoid the personal complications. Right now it's more important to get Bree and Elise here, where we can deal with them, together."

"It's not the right time, Talia. You yourself convinced me of that," Michael responded bitterly.

"You're so fucking dense," Talia spit back, all control gone, her emotions completely unleashed. "You spend months telling me about planetary conjunctions, which shit can be done on which day of the week and at what time, what fucking colors you have to wear and how the stupid altar has to be aligned. The intensity of the belief you invest in the greatness of all this cosmic-power crap is monumental—and now you tell me it's not the right time. It is the right time, shithead, according to your calculations. I changed your schedule to fit my needs. Think, use your thick skull. This is the time you planned months ago. Damn, I don't know why I bother. It won't affect what we do, not one whit, one way or another."

Her frustrations spent, Talia found herself at a loss for words. Her outburst was risky and the potential loss great. Alienating Michael at this point was the wrong move. It was far wiser to continue to encourage, to nurture, him and his beliefs. To continue her usual, patronizing approach. He did have a power, a burning energy, that could, with careful molding, be used. The direction he chose was the worship of darker gods—not that it matter what it was he believed in. It was his strong belief that fueled his otherwise dormant source of psychic energy.

Michael stood there, his amazement replaced by a leaden look. This woman had just crossed the boundary of partnership and emerged his enemy. Swallowing hard, fighting back the acrid taste that rose in his throat, Michael felt his world crumbling. He needed Talia to destroy Bree. He couldn't do it on his own, he hadn't been able to. But then she too had failed with Ned, with Holly, and with Bree. If bringing Elise and Bree here was so fucking important, why couldn't she do it by herself? Why did she need him to execute such a simple plan?

Perhaps, he realized as a smile began to twitch at the corner of his mouth, it was because she needed him. Even more than he needed her. In fact, the spark of the idea kindled into a slow, steady flame: he didn't need her at all.

Watching Michael closely for any effect her bitter outburst would cause, Talia noticed the twitch of his lips. She continued to watch his face, ready to step forward and continue her tirade should he show any sign that her verbal whipping was effective, ready to physically move back should he make a move toward her or—the thought was more than frightening, it repulsed her to her core—should he show any sign of transmuting.

Intellectually, Talia knew that the monstrous being was no more than a psychosomatic transformation, that Michael, with his mostly latent psychic power, could turn himself in the horrendous creature she'd faced last night. She was sure—*positive,* she reassured herself— that there was no more to the otherwise inexplicable event than than: simply a self-generated manifestation, like a case of nervous hives or a religious zealot's stigmata.

The small flicker in Michael's eyes, deeply set in his otherwise stony, perfectly composed face, did not escape her attention. Nor did his slight movement to shift his shoulders back. He would not bend to her will. His body turned to her, and surprising herself, she felt ice form in her gut. No matter how he managed the manifestations, it was physically dangerous to her. Standing firm, Talia let her energy garner, collecting it into a solid force, and without waiting for him to move even a fraction of an inch in her direction, she expelled it. A fireball burst from her and flew to Michael—a man once her partner, once her lover, never her friend. It hung suspended—it was not meant to do that!—and fell to harmless tatters before it reached him.

Michael threw back his head, his laughter ringing in the empty loft. The timbre of the laugh changed even as it rolled from his throat.

"Not again, Michael," Talia said. The begging tone in her voice surprised her; she'd never pleaded for anything. This change in herself was more frightening than the shape beginning to form in front of her and Talia decided on the only possible course of action. She moved quickly to the far wall, the ax in her hands, before Michael turned. His eyes glinted amusement as his body pulsed and stretched. Adrenaline pumped through Talia and she used the surge, lifted the ax, and drove the well-honed edge into Michael's neck— a neck bulging with newly forming muscles even as she swung—nearly separating the head from the mutating body.

He lifted his arms to either side of his head, shock and bewilderment flickering across the face that was still mostly Michael. His mouth opened but no words emerged past the ravaged larynx. As he gasped for breath, his severed trachea responded to his lung's cry for air and pulsed, ignoring the fact it was ripped open, that there were no longer throat muscles to contract, and greedily sucked air through the torn opening.

Blood, rich red and pumping strongly, fled the body in a steady, throbbing stream from the multilated neck. Michael's mouth contorted in a silent scream, his insane eyes burned with hate for the woman he still struggled to reach. Talia watched, drained, immobilized by terror as he, as it, reached out for her. One

more step, then another, then his leg flew out from
under him as he slipped in his own spilled blood.

He fell and the head separated completely from the
body. The body still struggled to move—up, forward,
to reach a shocked and, for the first time in her
life, thoroughly frightened woman. Talia stood huddled
against the wall. A spasm shook the headless body—he
should be dead, she silently screamed—as he, it,
reached out and gathered close the bloodless head, its
eyes still glaring at her. The teeth were bared, a silent
mouth animated beyond the most nightmarish dream.

Time was frozen. They faced each other: a cowering
woman and a failing being. It, Michael, fell forward
into a crouch, supported by one arm, holding the de-
capitated prize in the other. Rearing back, it held the
head above. A spasm, a final shudder, gave it the momentum to throw the horrific head at Talia, hitting her
full in the chest.

Snapping jaws caught the thin fabric of her blouse
and clamped down; she screamed mindlessly as her fear
snapped into something worse. Talia maniacally fought
to disengage the staring head, its eyes now inches from
hers. Her fists rained down on the matted and bloody
hair she had, once, stroked with lust. Its teeth held
firm; its eyes still held hers. Her body shook as her
screams turned to sobs, the sobs to whimpers, as her
knees buckled under her, and she slid down the wall
supporting her, as unconsciousness took hold.

Frank Jordan stood in the deep doorway, a shadow
himself. An industrial building faced him across the
street. He was dressed in black—what he used to call
his uniform: knit cap, thick turtleneck sweater, dura-
ble slacks, and heavy but flexible boots. From his vantage point he could see the two entrances, both
fronting the narrow street, of the six-story building.
Large windows, twice again the height of those in a
residential structure, lined each floor.

He noted, and appreciated, the subtle architectural
touches of the building, from the Doric columns with

Corinthian caps bracketing the entrance and windows to the continuance of theme in the rows of miniature columns delineating the floors. The windows were narrowly separated from one another by iron support beams, ornately worked into decorative fluted pillars.

Seeing no lights or activity, yet knowing that his prey was inside, Jordan let his thoughts wander, imagining the building fifty years ago—no, a hundred years ago—when it was new: windows open to admit air and light, sewing machines operated by men and women who didn't yet speak their adopted land's language, spewing out garment after garment on the treadle machines they were paid abysmally low wages to operate. He pleasantly wondered if, by some fortunate chance, this could be the same building where fire trapped and killed hundreds, burning them alive as their screams filled the narrow street, and forcing them to hurl to their deaths on the stone pavement below. Letting his eyes trace a path from the uppermost window to the street, he smiled as he envisioned the cobblestones peeking from beneath the chuckholed asphalt, the stones running with blood, sticky with burnt flesh.

No, he sadly realized, that was farther uptown. But what a nice thought.

Keeping his eyes trained on the six rows of windows, Frank Jordan continued to search for movement. Finding none, he turned away from the street and lighted a cigarette, carefully keeping the short burst of flame cupped in his hands, hidden from any casual look, equally careful to keep the burning tip hidden in the pocket of his hand. Smoking was a small risk, and the wait could be long. The alcove stood equidistant from two streetlamps, neither lamp having quite enough light to reach the single doorway, each pooling at least three feet away on either side of where he silently stood. Surreptitiously exhaling the smoke, Jordan watched as the wispy tendrils diffused and melted into the faint mist of the predawn hours. Finishing the cigarette, Jordan crushed the burning tip between his thumb and forefinger. He spit on the ash not so much to cool his own burning flesh as to ensure that the slender tube was truly out, that its red eye would not betray his presence.

A noise turned his attention to the off-center doorway, the freight entrance; he was sure he'd heard a muffled thud from behind the double door. A brief moment passed and the thud came again. The sound—he intuitively knew not only from experience but from his uncanny ability to project exactly what should be going on in any given place, at any given time, if it was part of his assignment—was that of a bolt being thrown back. Sure enough, the massive door slowly pulled back, rusty hinges screeching their protest. Stepping around the partially opened door—no, he amended—squeezing through the opening as if she didn't want anyone else to get past, was his assignment. Ms. T. D. Harrah, looking tired and forlorn on this deserted city street. Frank Jordan calmly waited for her to close the door behind her, waited as she pulled a small ring of keys from her slacks pocket and, after repeated efforts at finding the right key, she secured the door.

She furtively looked around her and then up. Following her gaze to the third floor, Jordan watched with her—clearly sensing the nervous anticipation she was projecting—and, seeing nothing untoward, returned his gaze to the trembling woman. Noticing her torn blouse, Jordan smiled. A little rough-and-tumble with that boyfriend of hers, no doubt, which would explain the lost look back, no doubt hoping he'd be waving a fond farewell to her.

Frank Jordan stepped from the protective doorway and walked toward her, a woman alone on a deserted street, a woman spent from love making—a slender, delicate, and attractive woman.

His last lucid thought was how easy this would be.

Spinning at the sound of approaching footsteps, Talia hissed a primal warning, surprised that she had any fight left in her drained body, anything left to project. Barely conscious, prying clenched teeth from her blouse, and finding a clear set of teeth marks on her breast, she had almost lost herself to spasms of uncontrollable sobbing. Recovering her wits, she'd crawled away from the head and body, still unable to stand. The lifeless torso, heaving itself in her direction—though unable to lift itself from the floor—renewed the terror. Her heartbeat rapid, Talia had inched along the wall to the stairwell. Clutching the railing for support, she'd made the three flights to the street in record time—intact except for the useless shoes lost somewhere along the way—unbolted the door, and even managed to lock it again, only to find a predatory male stalking her.

After what she'd left on the third floor, no mugger or rapist was about to get in her way. The mere thought that anyone would dare try to impede her escape sent fresh waves of furious, blinding energy coursing through her veins, into her dulled mind now roiling and ready to burst at the slightest provocation.

Smiling and flicking the dead cigarette into the street, Frank Jordan moved closer to the bedraggled woman. Her hand raised as if to ward him off. He could understand her fright—alone, no one near by to call for help—and though his slight form wasn't usually foreboding, he realized her impression of him was as a potential threat. Opening his hands, palms up and out, he approached her as if she were a frightened animal, lost and wary of strangers.

Her eyes glowed, even in the dim light, neon green, and burned into his own, flashing a warning like a light emiting diode announcing the time. Still smiling, he moved closer, careful to keep his arms open.

The first, short burst of heat seared away his eyelids. He stopped but, already in shock and unbelievably unaware of his injury, he opened his mouth to call out, to demand that she wait for him. His parched and burning throat was unable to issue any sound louder than a bare croak. The furnace hot-heat again surged, now one long wave, erasing the street around him, locking him in the center of a massive fire storm.

The storm swirled around him, threatening to suck

him into its burning vortex. Somehow he could still see. His eyes began to ooze, not tears but a thick gelatinous substance he knew were his own eyes melting. Still, he watched the woman standing with her arm pointed directly at him.

Reaching behind, his blistered hands sought the .32-caliber semi-automatic strapped to the small of his back. His pistol, never closer than the wall safe inside the lab facility, was always with him on the streets. His hand—scorched flesh beyond pain—found the burnt pistol butt separated from the metal. The barrel was melting, dripping down the crevice of his buttocks and pooling under his shriveled and singed testicles, burning its way through his shorts.

Gasping at the incredible pain of his balls turning to ashes, he drew a deep breath, a final breath, searing his lungs from the inside. His mind was stubbornly active for moments more as the fire turned his gut into ashes, rendered his intestines into liquid fat, and finding nothing left in the hollow shell that once was a living man, left the shell of the man folded in on itself, pooling what had been Frank Jordan into a puddle of slime on the deserted city street.

Talia watched until the man doubled over and fell. The street was calm and cool, his fire neither seen nor felt by anyone but himself, and she walked over to inspect what she'd done. Smiling at the incinerated wooden pistol handle still clutched in the charred hand, she realized that no matter what the cost to her inner reserves, she had been justified; the man meant her harm, whoever he was, whatever he was after.

Tired beyond anything in her memory, thinking only of the nearest bed, only once did Talia think to look over her shoulder to see if anyone had been watching.

24

SUFFUSED WITH TACTILE MEMORIES OF ELISE AND the intimacy they'd shared the night before, a closeness not just of flesh but of spirit, Jeff reached over to stroke his wife's bare back. He drifted in the cloistered world of sleep, and the early-morning light and her nearness fueled his body. Yes, it's early but it's Sunday and I want this woman. I came so close to losing her— no, to giving her up—and I never again want her farther away from me than this. Ever.

Jeff moved closer, molding his body to hers, and felt her stir. Even from sleep Elise responded and stretched herself against him, joining her flesh with his. A low moan escaped her lips and her eyes fluttered open; he was already inside of her, his hardness filling her, a part of her own body. The biblical word cleaving came to mind—two as one, a completeness. Hoping the word had been in her wedding vows, she moved to meet his gentle strokes. The moment did not go unnoticed for Jeff either; this was worth having, and worth keeping, at any price.

Climaxing as one, spent, they stayed in each other's arms, legs twined, unwilling or unable to break apart, letting the moment drift and last, wishing it would go on forever—forever entwined, no reason to ever leave the protective confines of bed, no need to ever move.

"Breakfast?" Elise whispered. Jeff looked at his wife through half-open lids.

"Come to think of it, that's as good a reason to get up as I can think of. Plus," he shyly added, "nature calls."

The bedside phone peeled its electronic ring. "That's not the only thing calling." Elise laughed. "I'll get this call, you take care of yours."

Lifting the handset, Elise barely had the phone to her ear before the torrent of words poured from the receiver.

"It's Bree," JoJo spoke urgently, his voice low, not wanting to be overheard but conveying unmistakable intensity. "She woke a few minutes ago, hysterical, calling for Michael, crying for him. At first I thought she was still dreaming, but she's awake—at least I think she is. Her eyes are open, she's trying to get dressed, but the shot you gave her last night really knocked her out. She's still groggy, stumbling around, pulling on clothes. What should I do?"

"I'm not sure. I don't think it could be a reaction to the sedative," Elise puzzled. "What do you mean she's calling for Michael?"

"Listen for yourself," JoJo said as he moved his mouth from the phone and held it in Bree's general direction.

The single word, "Michael," screamed, sobbed, caterwauled, and echoed through the wires, reaching Elise, raising the downy hairs on the back of her neck.

"Keep her there, JoJo. I'll be right over." Elise was ready to hang up the phone and dash to the closet, but JoJo's rushed words kept her.

"I'll try, but I have a feeling that's going to be a more difficult task than you think. Unless I knock her out, I think she's headed out this door and down to Michael's place."

"Where does Michael live?" Elise asked, pulling the pad and pencil, requisite accoutrements for a doctor's bedside phone, close. Jotting down an East Village address, Elise grimaced.

The last place she wanted to go this morning, any morning, was the heart of alphabet city, and the address on East 5th Street was as close to its physical, and probably metaphysical, center as anyone could get. As an intern, she had often requested home health care for some of the elderly patients after their hospital discharge. The Visiting Nurse Service was, for many of the elderly, all the medical attention required; the brief hospital stay from which they were being discharged more a result of the patients' fears than any pressing medical need. Yet, even the Visiting Nurse Service, probably one of the most compassionate and efficient organizations in existence, refused to make house calls on certain inner-city blocks. This address was on one of those streets.

Jeff's cheerful humming sounded over the running water; he was shaving and grooming for breakfast. Smiling to herself—the crooning was new, even given Jeff's usual appalling good nature in the morning—she called into the bathroom. "Darling, I have to run out. To Bree's. That was her friend JoJo. It seems she's, ah, having a reaction to the medication I gave her last night."

Jeff poked his head around the doorway, his puzzled glance meeting her own frantic look. "I'll come with you. Two doctors are better than one, right? Then we can breakfast out."

"Tell you what," Elise countered, rushing to pull on wide-wale corduroy slacks while reaching for a bulky sweater at the same time. "I'll run over alone, and if there's anything unusual, I'll call you. No need in both of us dashing off this early."

Jeff's face tightened. "What is going on with Bree that you're keeping from me?" Watching her closely, he saw a shadow cross her eyes and cut her off even as she opened her mouth to protest. "No, there is something. You've got to tell me. I'm not just the guy next door, Elise. I'm your husband. And there's more to marriage than practicing and sleeping together." Putting down his razor and wiping his face of the last vestiges of shaving cream, Jeff crossed the room to face his wife. "There *is* something more, isn't there?"

Her frantic activity to dress and leave was halted by the question. Elise turned, vainly trying to formulate an acceptable response. Nothing came to her, nothing

but the truth. He does want to know. He will share
this with me. Maybe he can even help. It's time to
trust him, she realized, but there's only moments right
now and a promise will have to do.

"Yes, there is something more, but right now is not
the time to explain. Let me go to Bree's, alone. Then
I'll meet you back here—and I promise to tell you
everything."

Sensing the truth as well as the urgency in her voice,
Jeff nodded his agreement. "All right," he finally
said, "but this is the last time you go off without me.
I'll walk over to Broadway and get us a feast for breakfast—down to fresh kona beans for coffee. When you
get back, we'll have a magnificent breakfast, talk,
drink coffee, and talk . . . in that order."

Smiling her relief, Elise moved forward and kissed
his smooth cheek, swiftly continuing on and out the
bedroom door. "That'll be terrific. I'll be back soon.
I promise."

Thirty minutes later Elise found herself speeding
downtown, the gypsy taxi traversing the deserted city
streets in record time, wondering whether bringing Jeff
along might not have been a good idea, after all.

She should have called home after finding Bree and
JoJo gone—JoJo obviously unable to keep Bree in tow
until she herself arrived—knowing that the next stop
would be the lower East Side. It would have been easy
to call, there'd been a phone right on the corner. The
phone might even have been operable, though it probably wasn't, but should the subject arise, her excuse
could be that it wasn't. Still, Elise thought as her apprehension grew, it would have been a good idea to
try. The explanations she owed Jeff went far beyond
the norm, and even the time afforded in this taxi would
have helped make a dent in the myriad details she had
yet to confess. Plus his presence could be helpful, especially on East 5th Street.

The guilt for not including her husband became a
foreboding and grew into firm conviction. She had to

call. It wasn't too late. Elise reached forward to tap the driver's shoulder, told him to pull over at the next phone, and finding a small handful of loose change at the bottom of her purse, fed the phone. The phone rang twelve times, she counted, two more than the phone company recommends you let a phone ring. He was out, getting breakfast most likely. Just like him. A man of his word. Why couldn't he have gone back to bed? She could still turn the cab around and be at their front door by the time he returned, losing only minutes but gaining an ally. Wishing she'd called earlier or never thought of calling at all—Jeff's absence was now strongly felt—Elise returned to the waiting cab and reconfirmed her original destination.

Possibly the best, if not only, time to visit this street, or even contemplate the neighborhood, Elise realized as the taxi drew in front of the building best guessed at being the correct one—no complete set of house numbers existed anywhere on the block—is now. It's far too early for the street people to begin their day, they've probably just ended it, and the unbroken quiet promised relative safety. Not only were no people around, the only other vehicle she'd seen in blocks was the medallion taxi now turning the corner, escaping down Avenue B.

The significance of the empty taxi registered; Bree and JoJo must have arrived just minutes ago. Rushing to pay her fare, she found herself halfway up the stairs even before she heard Bree's cry from the stairwell.

"Michael, open up. It's me, Bree. Open up, Michael. Please," Bree sobbed, her voice choking, her pounding increasing, even as Elise rounded the landing.

Supported by JoJo, Bree had fallen against the door. Tears streamed down her ashen face. Visible relief spread over JoJo as he saw Elise standing just a few feet away.

Talia shifted on the mattress, her body racked with aches and pains. The toll of the night before, ending just a few hours ago, had taken its toll. By the time she'd walked a few blocks, crossing Houston Street, she realized she wouldn't find a taxi—the streets were as deserted as New York City streets can get—and even if she did find one, it might not stop for her. She looked like a drunken derelict: disheveled, shoeless, blouse torn, slacks stained with dark splotches that would not stand up to daylight examination, staggering from exhaustion and probably not able to talk coherently. Any taxi that picked her up would probably try to take her to either a hospital or the police station, neither of which would be tolerated.

Only sleep was needed. Her apartment was at least twenty blocks away, while Michael's just a few blocks. His keys were on her ring, as he had hers. Had had hers. The thought of a bed, any bed, gave Talia the boost she needed to face the short distance to sanctuary.

The five blocks to his apartment were managed with few looks at her disarray. If anything, she must have appealed to the small group of men congregated on the corner of 5th Street and Avenue B; as she turned into the block, a low wolf whistle followed her, along with offers of an escort to her door and beyond. Too wasted to even respond, politely or otherwise, Talia made it to the tenement. Her unprotected feet were torn and bleeding, her legs leaden, barely responding to the need to move forward. The final flight of stairs proved almost too much and she fell halfway up, hitting her head and opening a small gash on her forehead. Stunned, bleeding, she finally made it to Michael's door and, fumbling for the right key, let herself in, retaining her awareness only long enough to lock the door and throw the dead bolt before she fell, fully clothed, onto the unmade bed.

Incessant knocking slowly entered her awareness.

Breakfast was ready, surprisingly fussed at: platters of fresh Danish sat on a clean tablecloth; a bowl of cracked eggs, ready to be whipped into fluffy omelets, waited on the stove. This was the only time Jeff could remember setting a table, from the china and silverware to cloth accessories, in his life. There's a first time for everything—he smiled to himself—and resorting to platitudes, today feels like the first day of the rest of my life. Admiring the spread, he felt a satisfaction that completed the moment; everything was in place and ready.

The ticking of the kitchen clock, a decorative relic that not only worked but required winding on a daily basis, grew louder; the steady clicking of the second hand entered and soon consumed his awareness, forcing him to acknowledge its presence by noting the time. A little over an hour since Elise left; she should be on her way home. A phone call to Bree's would be more than appropriate, he realized, not only to check on Elise's schedule but to find out how Bree was. He flushed, embarrassed at not having thought to call earlier. If Bree needed help, he was also responsible.

Reaching for the kitchen wall phone, Jeff quickly punched in Bree's number and listened to the first three rings; the fourth signaled an electronic click and a taped message echoed hollowly through the open line. Leaving a brief message, hoping that someone was actually there who would pick up the receiver on hearing his voice, Jeff looked at the phone he still held, puzzled, feeling the first twinges of alarm.

It could have been more serious than Elise had thought and maybe they went to the hospital. The scenario wouldn't play right; Elise had been with Bree the night before and today's visit was ostensibly to counteract the sedative. That there was "more"—the more Elise had promised to confide to him—kept his mind whirling. There *was* more, and whatever it was, it was affecting the here and now. Right now.

A picture of Elise sitting on the edge of their bed taking the summoning call came to mind; she had pulled over a pad and pencil and jotted something down. Another phone number? An address? Taking the steps to the bedroom two at a time, Jeff quickly reached the nightstand and pad.

The blank page was still indented with the pressure used on the page above. Picking up the same pencil Elise had used, Jeff rested the side of the graphite on the pad and slowly began to rub, raising the numbers, one by one. It was clearly an address and, as the last number emerged, not a very good one. But whose was it?

25

Bree slumped against the door—its chipped paint flaking with the movement—and stood only with JoJo's help. Elise had her arms around the trembling woman before Bree found the strength or wherewithal to lift her head.

"You know you shouldn't be out of bed," Elise cautioned.

Bree shook her head. "Michael. He needs me. I felt him calling for me."

"It might have been a sedative-induced dream," Elise said, and tried to move Bree away from the door, back to the stairway, out of the decaying building.

With an unexpected surge of strength Bree pushed Elise back against the wall. The sudden movement jolted Elise, her body whiplashed, and an audible crack sounded when her head met the crumbling plaster.

"No! I know what I heard. Michael's in trouble," Bree turned to Elise, the timber of her voice now strong and the tone accusing. "I heard him cry out, in great pain. He called my name. Then, well, then there was nothing. Nothing, not even the feeling he was there. And there's always that." Bree's eyes opened wide as the realization of what she had just said sunk into her own awareness. Dropping her head to JoJo's shoulder, Bree began to weep.

The slight sounds of movement from inside the apartment were barely audible, but Bree heard them first. Eyes suddenly dry, Bree moved to the door as Elise rushed to intercept her. A shuffling moved closer to the door from inside and both women paused, inches away, listening. The sounds of bolts being undone reverberated in the shabby hallway, each thud echoing; the third metallic clunk followed by silence. Both women stared at the door, then at each other, waiting. There was no further sound. No further movement.

Bree reached for the knob only to find Elise's hand gripping her wrist.

"Wait," Elise cautioned.

Opening her mouth to protest but deciding any words would be futile, her eyes grew hard, and Bree forcibly shrugged off the offending hand. She turned to the door. Before she was able to complete her singular task, opening the door, the knob turned and the door began to slowly inch inward.

Bree, startled at the movement, stepped back, and collided with JoJo. She turned to him to apologize, and in the confusion Elise moved away to avoid being stepped on. By the time the three had settled themselves into new positions, the door was wide open. The woman standing there, disheveled but alert, neon-green eyes flashing, calmly took in the tabloid before her.

"I don't believe this," Talia said, nodding at each in turn. "My greatest wish come true. You must be Bree and, of course, Elise. I'd know you anywhere, Bree. You and Michael had a strong family resemblance. I'm sorry I don't know your friend"—Talia smiled at JoJo—"but any friend of yours is more than welcome." Talia's smile, on anyone else, would have been warm and inviting. Instead, each of the three in the hall leaned away, an offensive radiance emanating from the woman inside the room.

Stepping farther back into the room, Talia held the door wide and gestured for the trio to enter. In the light of day, the squalor of the room was singular: empty, unwashed cans of beef stew and macaroni littered the alcove that served as a kitchen; dirty dishes filled the single-basin sink, which also seemed to be the only sink in the apartment and which was the focal point of activity for teams of cockroaches; a partition, the planks of wood making up what passed for a wall mostly rotted or missing, afforded a view of a toilet commode. The allowance to indoor plumbing oozed filth, and more roach activity, from the cracks that ran down its porcelain base. Following their gaze around the room, Talia smiled.

"I'm sorry I didn't get a chance to straighten up, but I wasn't expecting you." She graciously gestured a universal welcome. "Please, do come in."

Bree didn't—or couldn't—move and held her arms out, barring the way to Elise and JoJo. "Where's Michael?" Bree demanded. Her face went slack. "What do you mean 'had' a strong resemblance?"

Still standing with her arm open to the room, Talia turned to Bree. "Don't you know? I would, if it were my sibling. If something had happened to Elise, anything at all, I would know." Talia turned to face her sister, and her face lit up with what, on someone else, could be construed as sisterly love. On Talia, here and now, the look bore only malice. Elise, stung, moved back.

Calmed, despite or because of the building grief, evading her worst fear, Bree looked quickly from one woman to the other. "My fates, it's your twin," she gasped, turning to Elise. "I thought you said you were identical? You're barely alike."

"Look closer, Bree," Elise said, not moving her eyes from Talia's. "We are identical. Our features, our bone structure, our size. The difference, as I'm finally realizing, is that Talia Dora has drawn her strength from somewhere else, and it isn't your fates. She's night to my day—the dark hair, the pale skin. And she's slimmer—not an extra ounce of flesh on those ethereal bones. Though I wish I could figure out the green eyes." Elise smiled at being able to manage even a touch of humor in what she realized was a critical moment. "We both had hazel eyes as children, but mine changed first. I lost the green, she lost the amber."

"I guess I just see things more clearly than you," Talia remarked, her chilly smile hardening.

"Somehow I don't think that's the answer," Elise said, pausing to take a deep breath. "If anything, they're the color of your soul, the color of decay."

Talia let out a hoot of laughter. Shaking her head, she looked at Elise and laughed again. Peals of laughter shook her until she doubled over, tears pouring down her face. The laughter stopped as suddenly as it had begun, but Talia remained folded at the waist, gasping for breath, reaching out for the floor. Alarmed, her healing instincts strong, Elise moved to Talia's side and knelt next to her, putting an arm around the shaking shoulders.

"I'm all right, dear sister," Talia sputtered. "It's just been a very long night and I'm more tired than I thought. Though," Talia continued, looking up at Elise and over to Bree, "I'm sure that I have enough energy left to be as gracious a hostess as possible, under the circumstances." Unfolding herself, Talia stood, still shaky. "Please come in," she continued, "and I'll tell you what happened to Michael. Your friend," she said, glancing at JoJo, "can wait here."

Bree pushed forward, past Elise and Talia, her eyes racing around the single room. She spun back to face Talia, her training noting that the woman's color was poor. The long night Talia mentioned had been extremely debilitating to her. "This is Michael's place," Bree demanded as the door was closing. "What are you doing here?"

JoJo found himself alone in the hallway, unable to move to join the three women. Puzzled at his inability to speak much less move, he could still hear Talia's answer as the door closed in his face.

"It's my place now. You might say Michael left it to me—in his last will and testament."

With those words the door clicked firmly shut.

Talia stood with her back to the room while she secured the locks. Elise looked at Bree. Confused and more than a bit concerned by this unwelcome but not entirely unexpected confrontation with Talia, Elise sought her friend's support. Instead, she was met with Bree's all too apparent grief. The confirmation of Michael's death was fully registering. Bree's face was dramatically pale and the fine laugh lines around her eyes and mouth were chiseled in stark relief. Her dark hair, usually vibrant, hung limp and lifeless—a lank, pathetic frame for ashen and drawn skin.

Turning to Elise, Bree opened her mouth to speak, but no sound emerged. She pressed her lips together and slowly shook her head, beyond words. Elise moved to Bree and embraced her, gently urging her toward the only chair the room contained, a pitted and bent metal frame with torn plastic on both the seat and back.

"How sweet," Talia sneered, her voice dripping with mock sympathy. "My darling sister is tending to those in need, as usual. How touching that this is the way I'll always remember you."

"Bitch!" Elise exploded, the last remnant of her composure shredding in blind anger. "Haven't you done enough harm for one day? Or do you have a quota to meet?"

Talia threw her head back and laughed heartily, sincerely. "That's quite good, sister mine. If I didn't know you better, I'd actually think you had some spunk."

"You want spunk?" Elise threw open her arms and closed her eyes, willing, feeling, pushing, reaching out with every last fiber of her being. She would encompass all the spite and malice she knew her sister bred; she would envelop the hate with love, smother the evil with good, snuff out the bitterness with her own hope. She would cure Talia of herself, of the decay and rot that festered within, and Talia would emerge new and pure, again the sister she could share with, the sister she'd always wanted. She would do this with the strength she knew she had—the strength she'd been told she had. *Been told . . . been told,* Elise heard herself think, even above the white noise she was

charging the air with. *But do I know?* And at that moment, Elise hesitated.

Opening her eyes, Elise saw Talia standing against
a misty sky, gray streaked blue surrounding them. The
walls were gone, the room was gone. They were elsewhere, a nowhere with only the growing sound of the
wind for company. From far away she felt Bree's pain,
felt Bree trying to reach her, but saw only wispy smoke
tendrils form and curl around Talia's bare leg.

"You had me worried there. For a moment, anyway.
I don't think you've ever been that upset before, dear
sister," Talia said, her voice betraying her nervousness. "I should probably be glad you've led a shel-
tered life. Your pains have been small, your joys only
slightly more relevant. You certainly show a talent in
cutting loose, but a very unpracticed and unschooled
one. And, then again, your sniveling empathy will always get in your way."

Talia stretched, flexing herself from her neck down
her supple spine. "But you've spent your fury. We're
as we should be," Talia continued, growing sure and
strong again. "Just us, alone with the elements. No
one and nothing to stand between us or in our way."

With a start Elise realized that they were both naked, the only cover the fog that brushed their skin,
clinging, dissipating, and coalescing again, like foam
on a stormy sea.

"Yes," Elise answered, surprised at her own calm-
ness, "this is the way we should be. Together."

"Almost right, dear sister," Talia bit back. "A
more accurate phrasing is that we shouldn't be separate."

"I don't understand. That's what I said."

"No, it isn't." Talia waved her index finger at Elise,
a teacher chiding a pupil. "Let me be more precise.
There's not enough room for both of us. I can't be
while you are. I used to worry that someday you might
discover what you have inside you. Now you do know.
You've touched it, held it—worse, you've just used it
and even managed to bring us here." Talia swept her

arms open into the fog. "You'll want more. I know you will. And there's only room for one of us to have more."

"You're wrong," Elise cried out. "All I want is my life, the way it is, with Jeff."

"You will want more. There's no way I can ever let you have more. Do you understand?"

"I'm afraid I do," Elise answered, despondent with the realization of what her sister meant: Talia would not stop, ever, until she was the sole surviving twin. The hollowness inside Elise defied her own analysis. She knew she was afraid—the danger she faced had been fully impressed on her by Bree and JoJo—but there was more. A loss. A great loss. Not only of her sister, of having a sister, but of what she herself was, what she herself had been.

She *was* different now.

"Good. That will make it so much easier," Talia cooed, picking up only Elise's crushed hope and depression.

"I don't think so," Elise sadly responded. "I've too much to live for."

Both women reached out to the other, a simultaneous movement that brought their fingertips together. Electricity exploded at the contact, a brilliant burst in the darkness that stained the thin air around them. A wind picked up and circled them, the breezy sound growing to a deafening roar, and tore at their hair. Long locks of golden brown and chestnut black blew about, twisting every which way, braiding strand into strand, creating a single halo of light and dark, one tiara worn by two women.

They were pulled closer and closer by the whirlpool wind, a tornado that bound and drew as if with an invisible rope, bringing them together. The wind continued to increase steadily, drawing them nearer, inch by inch. Their outstretched arms folded from the pressure, and elbows bent, they struggled to push away from each other. Only their hands, palm to palm, kept them from an unwilling embrace, from being crushed in the vortex that was surrounding them. The wind blew even harder.

Elise knew she couldn't sustain the strength, that she was already beyond her endurance. She felt a lessening of pressure. She was weakening.

Talia threw back her head and let loose with a piercing cry—one single, sustained note. The pitch was perfect, the sound beyond the range of human.

Then it was still and dark and they were elsewhere.

They were still facing each other, toe to toe, nipples pressed against each other's breasts, their lips almost meeting. There was only quiet and blackness and pinpoints of light, stars in the cold vacuum of space. Their auras surrounded them as a life-sustaining bubble of heat and air, a silver globe pulsing brighter on one side, then the other. They stared at each other, eyes locked, need against need, being against being. Their souls were joined and torn apart only to be rejoined and torn again, each rent dimming the globe, each destructive pulse further lacerating the life force surrounding them.

Each time their forces met, their wills collided and one side would dim. Half the sphere dimmed, then the other, then both sides would burst into brilliant light only to fade again. The battle wore on, and on, equal and debilitating.

Their hands, still palm to palm, were slowly lowering, the exhaustion of both apparent as they swayed to and fro, leaning toward then away from each other. Each desperately searched for the fatal chink in the other's armor.

It appeared as a dark line on her smooth torso, a simple scar that traced downward from the cleft of her breasts—a single drop of black ink dripping on alabaster skin—and opened a path to her core.

In a final nova the globe burst and, with the change, one woman crumbled, the other falling to her knees in exhaustion.

* * *

Rooted to the spot, JoJo stood silent guard, unable to hear anything from inside. Not a word, not a whisper, reached him. He stood, not even thinking of moving; not only because he couldn't move, he wouldn't. Bree was inside.

From nowhere and everywhere a sound arose, the only sound in the hallway. Concentrating on the facing door, JoJo knew the sound came from within the room. Long moments passed and then a change in tempo, a breaking in the subtle rhythm, followed by a rushing sound that he felt from the soles of his feet to the ends of his hair. With the vibrations coursing through the thin walls JoJo was startled back to an awareness of where he was and what he was doing there.

Anxiety was building; a cold fear gripped him, but still he was only able to move his eyes and then just enough to glance at his watch. Ten minutes had already passed. He exerted himself even more, trying to move, trying to reach the door, straining against invisible bonds; the bindings holding him were stronger than anything he had ever experienced. Anyone watching JoJo would think that he was merely standing there, calmly waiting for someone inside the door he was facing. Unless they looked closely. If they did, they would see the sweat pouring down his face from the exertion he was using in an effort to free his body from that spot.

Fifteen minutes had passed, and exhausted from his efforts, JoJo was near collapse. Yet to all eyes he continued to stand facing the door: the perfect picture of the patient escort.

The sounds from within continued to grow: a frantic rushing changing to a torrent of wind, a howling, a screeching—the noise of a ferocious storm at its peak—then a shrill cry for release reaching above the shattering noise. A cry that could have been of the wind or from one of the women, a cry heard only by him. Impotent, JoJo still stood, tears of frustration running freely down his cheeks.

All was suddenly, finally quiet. JoJo collapsed, in

spirit as well as in body, folding to the floor as an almost welcome unconsciousness overtook him.

Hearing the dull thump, Jeff took the steps two at a time. The slumped form of a man lay halfway down the narrow corridor, the man's arm reaching out to the closed door in front of him. Three more quick steps brought Jeff to the man, just as a low moan escaped from beyond the closed door. Jeff wavered, torn between wanting to examine the unconscious man and the frantic need to break the door down. The decision was taken from him as the man's eyes opened just as the door's lock snapped free.

JoJo, unable to speak, nodded wildly at Jeff, his eyes blinking rapidly at the opened door. One more quick step, over the man, and Jeff was in the room.

The room was chaos. Yet, even in his first, wild glance around the room, Jeff realized all the damage was not caused by whatever had just happened. The single room's broken furnishings were toppled, trashed against pitted walls. Heavy curtains, once designed to keep out sunlight, were torn from the windows and lay in tatters on the floor. A filth-encrusted kitchen alcove was covered with broken dishes and shattered glass.

Seeing no one in the room, Jeff turned back to the man in the hallway, who was now up on his elbows, rubbing his throat.

"They're in there," JoJo said, his voice raspy and breaking. The painful act of speaking was followed by a coughing spell. "They've got to be in there."

Jeff moved into the room, bewildered at the destruction, desperately seeking a clue. A lump of curtains stirred and Jeff rushed to it, tearing the shreds aside. Bree's eyes flickered half-open. Her face was pale and drawn, her lips parched, cracked, and bleeding.

"Elise, find Elise," she sobbed, her words echoing the single thought that had consumed Jeff since he left 122nd Street and raced to this lower East Side address.

The confirmation that his wife was actually here revitalized him. He leapt to his feet, literally turning in midair, and began tearing at the first object he could reach, a filty and torn mattress shoved against the wall. He pulled it down to the bare floor and the profile that peeked from between shredded sheets caused a sob of relief to escape from his lips.

"Elise, darling," Jeff shouted, and lunged to the still woman. He tried to reach out to her face, but the cold hit his hand before he could touch her. She was radiating such intense cold that there was no doubt as to the absence of life within. Stunned and speechless, Jeff found the strength to pull the sheet remnant away from the dead woman. He fell to his knees, staring, grief-ridden, a hollow shell with only his blood rushing through his veins and roaring to his head to remind him of his own life.

Long, anguished moments went by before Jeff's head began to clear, his heart beat to return to normal. It wasn't Elise. The woman's hair was dark, and even in the stillness of death, harsh lines marked her thin face. Turning wildly around, Jeff spotted another place, the only other place, in the jumbled room where Elise could be. A pair of leather running shoes, Elise's, peeked from under a toppled table, the table propped against the wall to shelter the body pinned underneath.

Crawling on his knees, unable to stand on his shaking legs, Jeff reached out for the table's leg and yanked it with every ounce of strength he possessed. The table almost flew across the room, lifting completely off the floor and landing, top down, on the broken china and glass.

The sudden movement startled Elise to consciousness and she bolted upright, eyes wild, ready to scream.

Her scream was one long, piercing, gut-wrenching, bone-chilling sound. Seeing Jeff effected no pause. Her shriek went on and on—one tone, one sound filling the room—until all the air was gone from her lungs, the pain from her mind, and as Jeff held her close, stroked her hair, and willed his love to her, Elise collapsed in the arms wrapped tightly about her.

Standing in the doorway, JoJo shakily moved to Bree, who was pulling herself up from the littered floor. As he leaned over to help her, his eyes met hers and he froze; the whites of her eyes were red with broken capillaries, her tears were blood. Waving him away, Bree stood and nodded at him, simply nodded.

''Call an ambulance,'' Bree whispered, the few words causing even more blood to well in the cracks of her parched lips.

JoJo hesitated. He wanted to hold Bree, just as Jeff was holding Elise, but the bloody stare that Bree fixed on him defied him to make so much as even a move in her direction.

Dropping his head, JoJo backed out the door to find a phone.

Epilogue

Elise felt the sting of the intravenous tube taped to her arm even before she opened her eyes. It was a familiar device—though not to *her* body—alarming but nonetheless comforting. The last week had proved totally disorienting to her, taking her from a steady, regulated, and organized life to a nightmare world where every reality was twisted, every fear exposed. Let me be in a hospital room, she silently pleaded, and not some insane doctor's laboratory.

Opening her eyes, she found the room unquestionably one in a hospital—and unusually bright. Strip lighting ran along the juncture of wall to ceiling and allowed a dim light to reach even the farthest corners.

The next anxiety—why are all these lights on?—was quickly followed by relief. There was no place where anything could hide.

Looking around, Elise realized she was in an intensive-care cubicle, thus the reason for the full lighting. She recognized the ICU equipment: a monitor hanging above her head showed five separate signals, clear yellow currents on a sepia background. The steady electronic chartings attested to her stable cardiovascular and neurological rhythms, her pulse and blood pressure were constant, and her breathing regular. Even at a glance, she analyzed the readings as very good. *If I were my own patient, I'd be out of this room in hours*. The IV was attached and its monitor operating, but the nearby respirator thankfully was not.

A video camera focused on her bed, and with a touch of whimsy, Elise stuck her tongue out at the silent, staring eye. Struggling to move the bed into a

semiupright position, hoping her activity would be noticed and a nurse called to her side, she felt a stab of
apprehension. The initial comfort of waking in a hospital was replaced with confusion. Why was she here?
The last thing she remembered was getting out of a
taxi on East 5th Street. All else was a blank. Wait,
another piece was coming back . . .

Jeff burst into the cubicle, his grin so wide it ran the
traditional ear to ear. Another piece fell in place, Jeff
holding her while she was . . . was screaming? Was
that right?

"Thank God, Elise. You're awake!"

"How long," she began, her lips dry and painful,
"have I been out?"

Seeing her discomfort, Jeff poured fresh water into
a glass, and held the angled glass straw to her parched
mouth.

"Two days. Two very, *very* long days."

"Have you been here all that time?"

"Just about. You've forgotten you saw me yesterday,
though I did get a smile out of you then. They threw
me out last night, but I came back and conned an
intern into letting me catch some sleep on his cot."

A laugh rose in Elise's chest. The wide smile
cracked her lips and transformed her grin into a gri-
mace. Reaching for the petroleum jelly, Jeff carefully
spread a layer on her mouth. He smiled warmly into
her eyes as he let his finger delicately trace the outline
of her lips, leaning down to kiss the tip of her nose
when he was done.

"Much better." Elise pursed her shiny lips. "Have
you ever thought of going into the medical profession?
You'd make a terrific doctor."

"Don't tell me you've forgotten that as well." Jeff
laughed. Content in each other's company, the couple
sat quietly, their eyes speaking volumes.

"It seems I don't remember much," Elise broke the
silence. "Jeff, what happened?"

Jeff sat back, still holding Elise's hands tightly in
his, ready to supply the few details he could.

"Both you and Bree were severely dehydrated. No one has been able to come up with a plausible explanation as to why, but then again, no one seems to be able to formulate much of a theory about anything that happened in that room. Bree's eyes were completely bloodshot. The admissions doctor said he'd only seen such badly damaged capillaries once before—in a deepwater diver who underwent traumatic pressure changes."

"Bree!" The alarm in Elise's voice sounded loudly over the electronic circuitry of the monitoring equipment. "How is she? Where is she?"

"Bree was kept overnight for examination and released yesterday. She'll be fine and her eyes will heal. She's off for a week with her friend JoJo to a family farm in Pennsylvania."

Jeff paused. The question he'd been wanting to ask weighed heavily on his mind, alleviated only by the relief of Elise's waking.

"Elise, what did happen in that room?"

"I . . . I don't really remember." Unexpected tears sprang to her eyes. "Bits and pieces are starting to come back: Bree in a hallway, a door opening . . . but . . . but what did Bree say?"

"Not much. She said she tried to reach you but you were too far away. She wouldn't say any more. No one understands what she means. Do you?"

"I'm not sure . . . there's something else . . . someone there . . . another woman in the doorway, but I can't make her out." Tears began to flow freely down Elise's pale cheeks.

"There was another woman in the room," Jeff ventured, afraid to open a raw wound but realizing that if it's to be done, the hospital was the best place to precipitate any hysteria.

Elise leaned forward, her eyes suddenly dry. The face of the woman in the doorway came into sharp focus.

"I thought it was you, Elise," Jeff began, reliving the terrifying moment. "My heart stopped. God, I was so frightened. I thought it was you. At first all I saw was a part of her profile, she was almost completely covered with a torn sheet. It was your profile, your nose, your chin, your mouth.''

''Talia,'' Elise whispered. She nodded to herself, more pieces falling into place. She sat up, straighter, surer. ''It was Talia. My twin.''

Relieved that Elise had made the conclusion herself, Jeff tightened his hand on hers. ''We've made positive identification. It was Talia.''

''How did she die? She is dead, isn't she?''

''Yes, quite dead,'' Jeff answered, surprised at the phrasing of the question. ''As to how she died . . . Well, there was an autopsy that resulted in inconclusive and inadmissible findings. The verdict is that she froze to death in Michael's apartment.''

''It's spring, nights are still cold. Perhaps the apartment wasn't heated. If her resistance was down, she could have hypothermiated,'' Elise rapidly overrationalized. ''It's odd, but why is there any doubt?''

''She was freeze-dried, as from an immeasurably cold vacuum. Her organs crumbled to dust when they opened her for the autopsy.''

''I need to see her,'' Elise said, determined to confirm the end of her nightmares. She pushed the cover off and dropped her bare legs to the floor. The aches and pains from her bruised body hit her full force, shooting from the soles of her feet to the top of her head.

''Whoa. You can't get anywhere with this IV attached,''Jeff said, and gently pushed his wife back into bed. ''Anyway, she's already been cremated. Her attorney claimed the body after he saw the newspaper headlines, even though she wasn't identified in the articles. It seems Talia had left very specific instruction as to her remains. And while it might be time to remove the IV, it's too soon for you to be out of bed.''

Buzzing for the nurse, Jeff pulled Elise's patient chart from the foot of her bed. He stood back reading while the nurse checked the monitors and rang for the attending physician. The doctor arrived within minutes and plucked the chart from Jeff's hands, giving Jeff a tired look that clearly implied there was nothing worse than having a doctor for a patient unless it was a doctor and her doctor husband.

Blocked from the activity, Jeff backed into the adjacent cubicle, catercorner to and visible from Elise's. A middle-aged woman lay motionless, her skin covered with a pasty sheen. He watched the erratic registering of her vital signs on the monitor and noted, in particular, the dead line of the EEG brain scan. Jeff caught his breath, thinking for a moment of how this could have been Elise and how lucky he was.

The activity in Elise's cubicle was winding down, but Jeff took a moment to pull the woman's chart. She'd been brain-dead for weeks, ever since she was brought to the hospital—a severe trauma to the head caused in a car accident. The chart clearly indicated a NO CODE, the "do not resuscitate" that her family had officially requested. No extraordinary measures were to be taken to save her life—yet the woman lingered on. There was an IV hookup—the woman was being nourished—and a respirator aided the breathing function. She was scheduled for transfer to an intermediate facility the next day where her body could continue to function for years, and years, to come.

Jeff looked up from the chart just as the doctor attending Elise motioned him over. Her IV tubing was disconnected and the news was good: Elise was to be discharged from ICU to a regular bed and probably would ready to go home in a day or so.

A discreet cough from behind Jeff brought the next news, which wasn't good. Hal Vaughan stood, hat in hand, looking past Jeff to Elise.

"She looks well, considering what she's been through, " Hal noted.

"I didn't think you'd have the nerve to show up here," Jeff fumed, keeping his voice low, hoping Elise wouldn't hear. "Besides, what could you know about what she's been through?"

Hal Vaughan stood silent, thinking of Frank Jordan. Jordan had been on his errand, tracking Talia Harrah, née Crawford, and what remained of the project administrator was grisly enough to send shudders down the strongest man's back. He'd been called to identify the body and could still smell the burnt flesh, malodorous even in the chilled morgue. There was no doubt in his mind that Talia had effected the cremation. The "how" of what she had done was the reason for the Spiral project in the first place.

What concerned Hal Vaughan even more—and the reason he was standing in front of his daughter-in-law's bed—was that if Talia was dead—freeze-dried—there was only one person who could have done that. And he was looking at her.

The awesomeness of this woman's potential was everything he'd hoped it would be.

But that's not what he said because that was no longer what he was prepared to face.

"I know that her sister died and that she herself has been through a severe trauma," Hal finally answered. "That's enough reason for me to show some concern and want to visit my daughter-in-law—and my son."

Jeff looked long and hard at his father and finally granted the older man a small nod.

They moved closer to the bed and Elise's eyes lighted up at the sight.

"Dad, I should have guessed you'd be here minutes after Jeff." Elise's voice was warm, but her lips were tight, her eyes narrowed.

Hal Vaughan forced himself to smile down at the pale woman. She was drawn from her terrible experience, but there was something else different about her, something he couldn't put his finger on. He continued to say words he hoped sounded sincere.

"I've been thinking about taking you up on that offer to move in—just to keep an eye on you. If you keep this up, one physician in residence won't be enough."

Elise laughed, the sound rich and full. Jeff stared at his wife, he'd never heard her laugh like that before.

"I can assure you, Dad, that I've no intention of landing in a hospital again, unless it's on my feet, attending one of my patients."

"Well, it could be a maternity room, you know," Hal automatically responded, surprised at himself for the comment. The words had come from nowhere and unleashed a chilling thought. "By the way, Jeff, there's something else I want to tell you, but let's walk out together."

"Dad, are you keeping secrets from me?" Elise asked, her curiosity seemingly piqued.

"No," Hal stumbled, "it's just that you didn't know about . . . Well, I mean, I didn't think you'd be interested . . ."

"She's interested, Dad. Anything you have to tell me you can say in front of my wife." Jeff looked at his father with a clear, direct gaze.

Hal continued to twirl his hat in his hands. "It's just that this project I've been working on is being disbanded, at my request. I, uh, finally identified the subject to the source of our funding when I told them she was dead. There didn't seem much reason in going on with the project, so for all intents and purposes they're closing us down. There is the HIV study to continue, of course, but nothing else."

Elise looked at her father-in-law, a distinct glint in her eyes. "Yes, it wouldn't be practical to have a secret project without a secret subject, would it?"

Both Jeff and Hal turned to her, amazed that she hadn't asked what project or any of the other questions that would normally be indicated from someone who had no prior knowledge of any project or testing. Or was supposed to have no knowledge.

"Let's say," Elise continued, "that my sister were named by you as the subject . . ."

Hal nodded in mute agreement.

". . . and that with her death and that of your administrator . . . Am I right so far?"

Hal nodded again, his throat constricted beyond words; the near phobic fear of Elise he'd developed when he heard about Jordan's death—and his immediate decision to cancel the research any way he could, to get out of the line of fire, to remove himself from any position of danger—rushed back to engulf him.

"You finally realized that there are things you can't tamper with. That the people—no, the person—involved will never let you."

Hal nodded. It was exactly what he thought. He took a step back. He knew he was as pale as Elise . . . That was it! She was paler, but it was a healthy, creamy glow. Not her usual vibrant flush. Her hair seemed darker, a shade or two. And her eyes were different. The hazel glinted green, more green than amber.

Elise pushed herself up on one elbow and pointed to the cubicle catercorner from hers.

"That poor woman's family. There's no hope for her, is there? Yet they have to go on, visiting the shell of the person they once loved, they think they still love—but it's not her, is it? Forced to have hope because it's the only decent way they can see her. It's just not fair."

Hal Vaughan kept nodding his head. There were no words.

Elise smiled and curled the finger she was pointing back to herself. The IV in the woman's arm wiggled and sprang free. Elise looked at Hal, his eyes wide, and she repeated the motion. The respirator plug popped softly from the wall.

"Don't," Elise cautioned, "call anyone. It won't be long for her now—and it *is* better this way."

Hal Vaughan backed farther away, still nodding.

Jeff looked at his wife, stunned. His father had been right all along—but this was his wife!

"Dad's right about something else, darling," Elise radiated joy up at her husband. "The next time I'll be in a hospital might very well be as a patient in the maternity wing."

Jeff's mouth dropped open, his pleasure at the news immediate. *This is my wife!* He repeated the thought. And he did love her.

"Jeff, you won't leave me, will you?" Elise continued. "Like my father left my mother and my grandfather left my grandmother."

"Of course not! I couldn't be happier at the prospect," Jeff answered immediately, without pause, without hesitation, his sincerity as apparent as his pride.

"Not even when you see our little girl for the first time?"

Jeff's mouth dropped open, the full realization hitting him, the loose ends of the past weeks lining up in a perfectly organized pattern.

"No," he answered, bending over his wife to kiss her forehead. "As long as I'm alive I'll be with you."

Elise smiled and took Jeff's hand. Her eyes met Hal Vaughan's and signaled her dismissal. Hal understood, clearly and completely, and backed out of the room.

"Then I'll keep you, too. I've always wanted to break family tradition: I'll be the first to keep my husband."